POKÉMON™

ADVENTURES

RUBY & SAPPHIRE

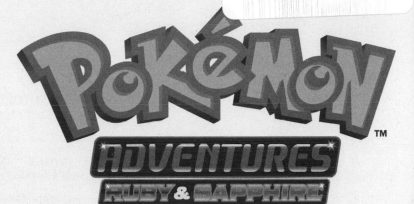

Pokémon ADVENTURES
Ruby and Sapphire
Volume 22
Perfect Square Edition

Story by HIDENORI KUSAKA
Art by SATOSHI YAMAMOTO

© 2014 Pokémon.
© 1995–2014 Nintendo/Creatures Inc./GAME FREAK inc.
TM, ®, and character names are trademarks of Nintendo.
POCKET MONSTERS SPECIAL Vol. 22
by Hidenori KUSAKA, Satoshi YAMAMOTO
© 1997 Hidenori KUSAKA, Satoshi YAMAMOTO
All rights reserved.
Original Japanese edition published by SHOGAKUKAN.
English translation rights in the United States of America, Canada,
United Kingdom, Ireland, Australia and New Zealand arranged with SHOGAKUKAN.

English Adaptation/Bryant Turnage
Translation/Tetsuichiro Miyaki
Touch-up & Lettering/Annaliese Christman
Design/Shawn Carrico
Editor/Annette Roman

Printed in the U.S.A.

Published by VIZ Media, LLC
P.O. Box 77010
San Francisco, CA 94107

10 9 8 7 6 5 4 3 2 1
First printing, May 2014

www.perfectsquare.com   www.viz.com

POKÉMON™ ADVENTURES
RUBY & SAPPHIRE

22
VOLUME TWENTY-TWO

Story by
Hidenori Kusaka

Art by
Satoshi Yamamoto

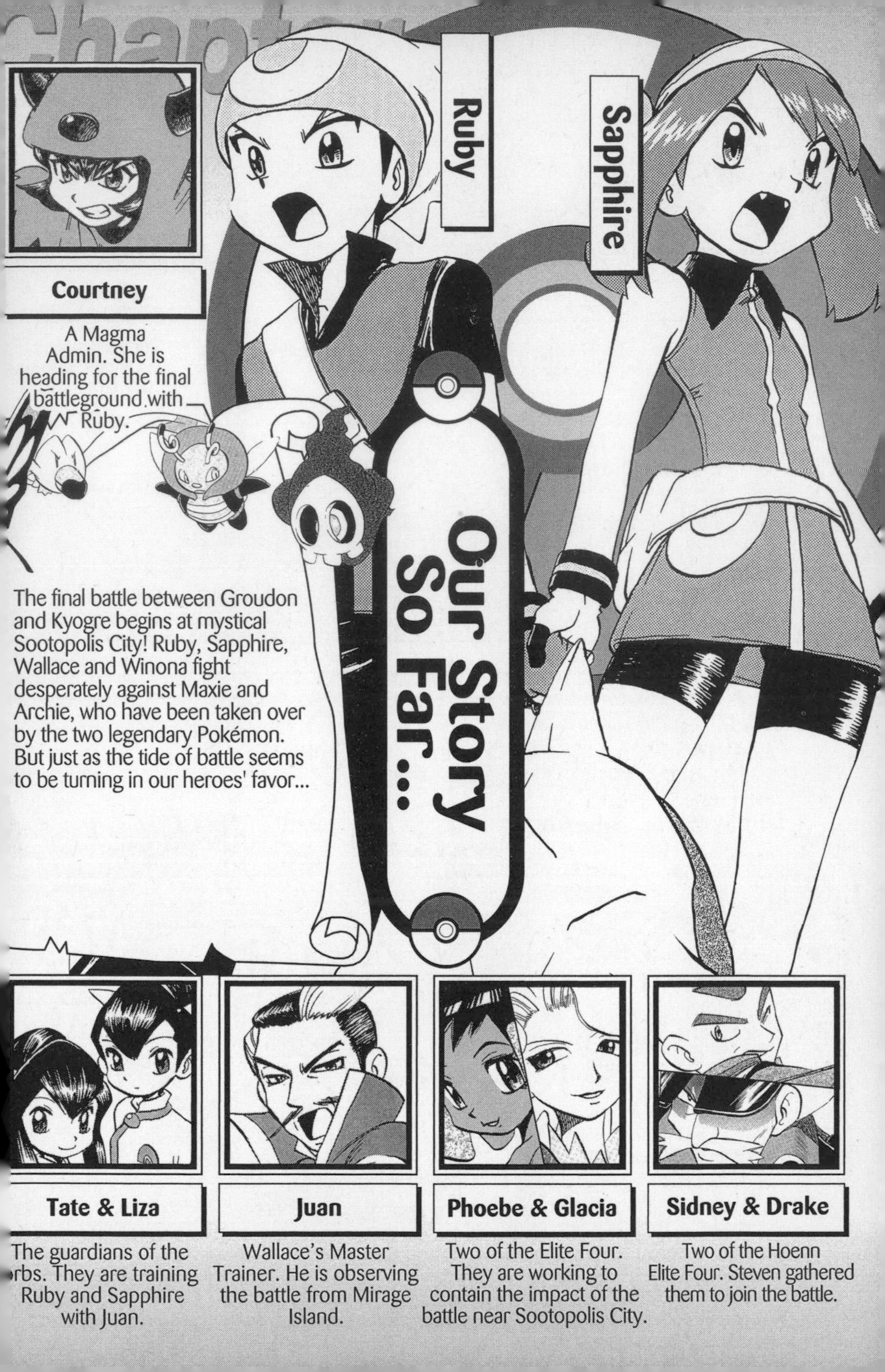
Our Story So Far...
Ruby
Sapphire
Courtney
A Magma Admin. She is heading for the final battleground with Ruby.
The final battle between Groudon and Kyogre begins at mystical Sootopolis City! Ruby, Sapphire, Wallace and Winona fight desperately against Maxie and Archie, who have been taken over by the two legendary Pokémon. But just as the tide of battle seems to be turning in our heroes' favor...
Tate & Liza
The guardians of the orbs. They are training Ruby and Sapphire with Juan.
Juan
Wallace's Master Trainer. He is observing the battle from Mirage Island.
Phoebe & Glacia
Two of the Elite Four. They are working to contain the impact of the battle near Sootopolis City.
Sidney & Drake
Two of the Hoenn Elite Four. Steven gathered them to join the battle.

Story of The Four

Winona

A Gym Leader who is also Sapphire's teacher.

Wallace

Ruby's Master Trainer. He accepted the Champion Cape from Steven.

Steven

Former Pokémon Champion. He solved the mystery of the Stone Plate.

Norman

Ruby's father. He awakened Rayquaza!

Just then a huge explosion occurs but Ruby and Sapphire are saved by Wallace's master, Juan, who trains them at Mirage Island. Meanwhile, Steven and the Elite Four are using Registeel, Regirock and Regice to hold back the destructive energy of Kyogre and Groudon.

But Ruby and Sapphire need to master the Red and Blue Orbs to truly stop the battle. Once the training is over, Sapphire tells Ruby her true feelings and Ruby, for some unknown reason, locks Sapphire inside the Air Car...!

Archie

The leader of Team Aqua. Also missing.

Maxie

The leader of Team Magma. Missing since a great explosion during the battle.

Gabby and Ty

Two journalists in search of the truth.

Pokémon Association President

The Executive Leader of the Hoenn Disaster Countermeasure Team.

TRAINERS OF THE FOURTH CHAPTER

SAPPHIRE ● AGE 10

A wild Trainer whose dream is to challenge and defeat every single Gym Leader in the Hoenn region!!

CHIC (BLAZIKEN ♀)
Introverted. Uses fire-type moves.

RONO (AGGRON ♂)
Mischievous. Proud of his toughness. Its favorite move is Take Down.

LORRY (WAILORD ♂)
Bold. Sapphire rides the waves on Lorry's back.

PHADO (DONPHAN ♂)
Befriended by Sapphire at Mauville City. Hasty nature.

TROPPY (TROPIUS ♂)
Sapphire flies through the air on Troppy's back. This calm Pokémon usually stays outside its Poké Ball.

RELLY (RELICANTH ♂)
Has the power to take people with it to the very depths of the ocean. Hardy natured.

RUBY ● AGE 11

A Trainer who wants to be the champion of all the Pokémon Contests. Visual beauty is a priority for Ruby. He has zero interest in Pokémon Battling. But does he secretly have a talent for it...?

MUMU (SWAMPERT ♂)
A Pokémon given to Ruby by Professor Birch. Easygoing. Represents Toughness.

NANA (MIGHTYENA ♀)
Intense. Represents Coolness.

KIKI (DELCATTY ♀)
Naive. Represents Cuteness.

FOFO (CASTFORM ♀)
Changes form in response to weather changes. Cautious.

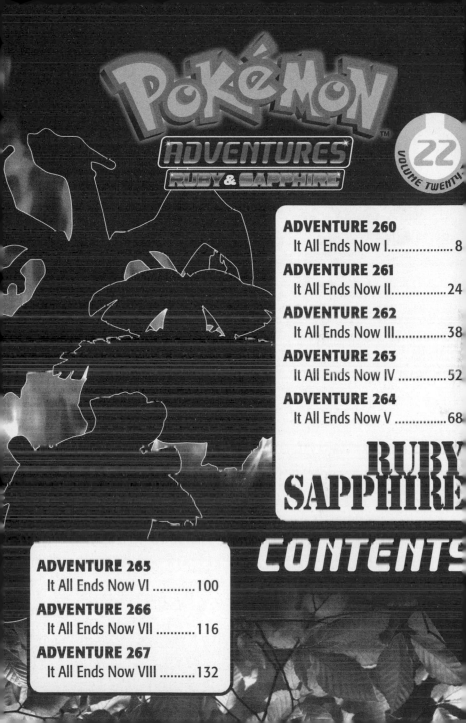

POKÉMON ADVENTURES RUBY & SAPPHIRE

VOLUME TWENTY-TWO

22

RUBY SAPPHIRE

CONTENTS

● Chapter 260 ●

It All Ends Now I

Pokémon Adventures Ruby & Sapphire

The Fourth Chapter

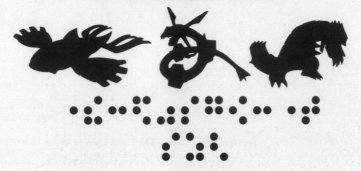

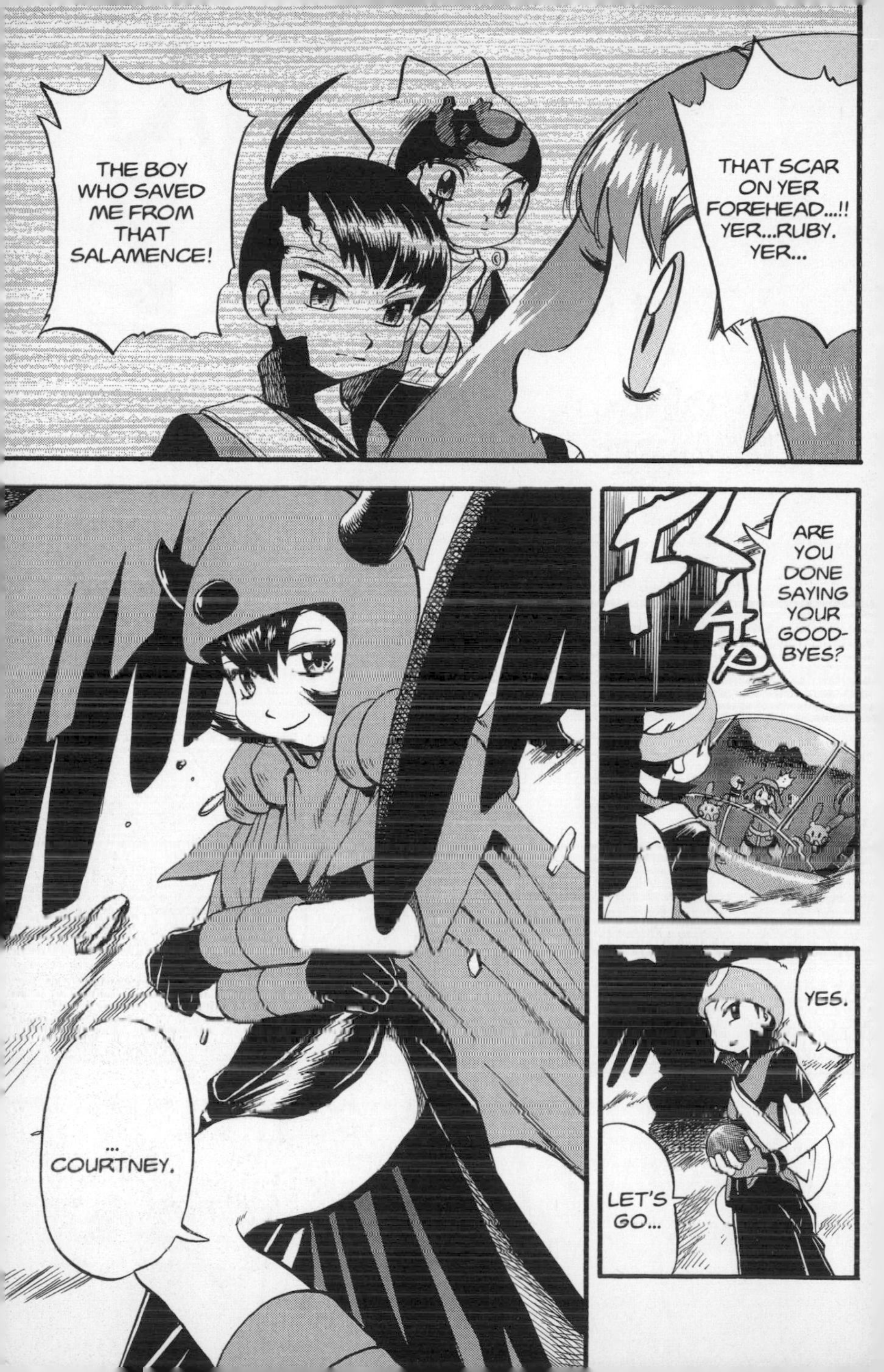
THAT SCAR ON YER FOREHEAD...!! YER...RUBY. YER...
THE BOY WHO SAVED ME FROM THAT SALAMENCE!
FLAP
ARE YOU DONE SAYING YOUR GOOD-BYES?
YES.
LET'S GO...
... COURTNEY.

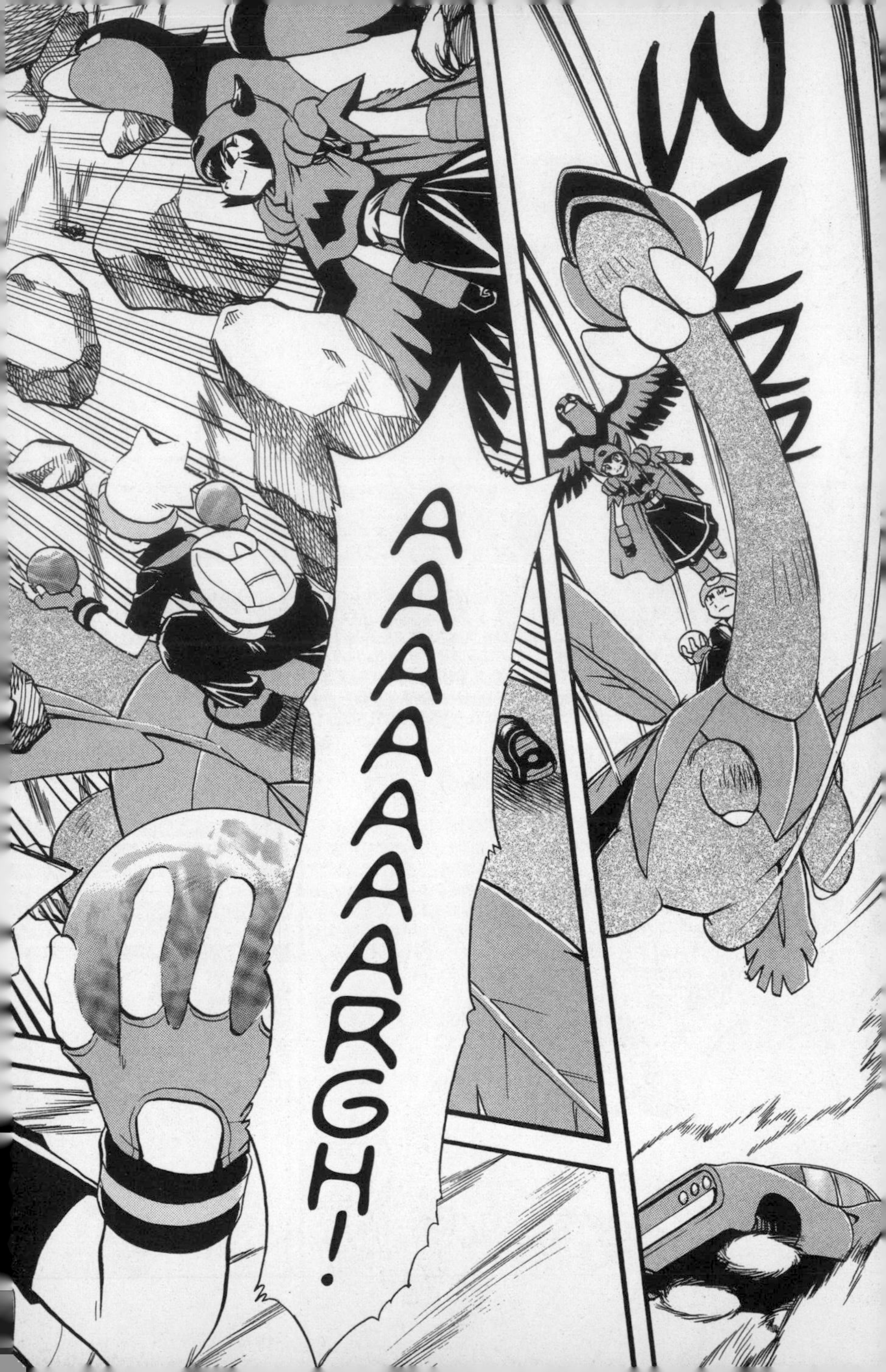
WAAAAARGH!
AAAAAAAAARGH!

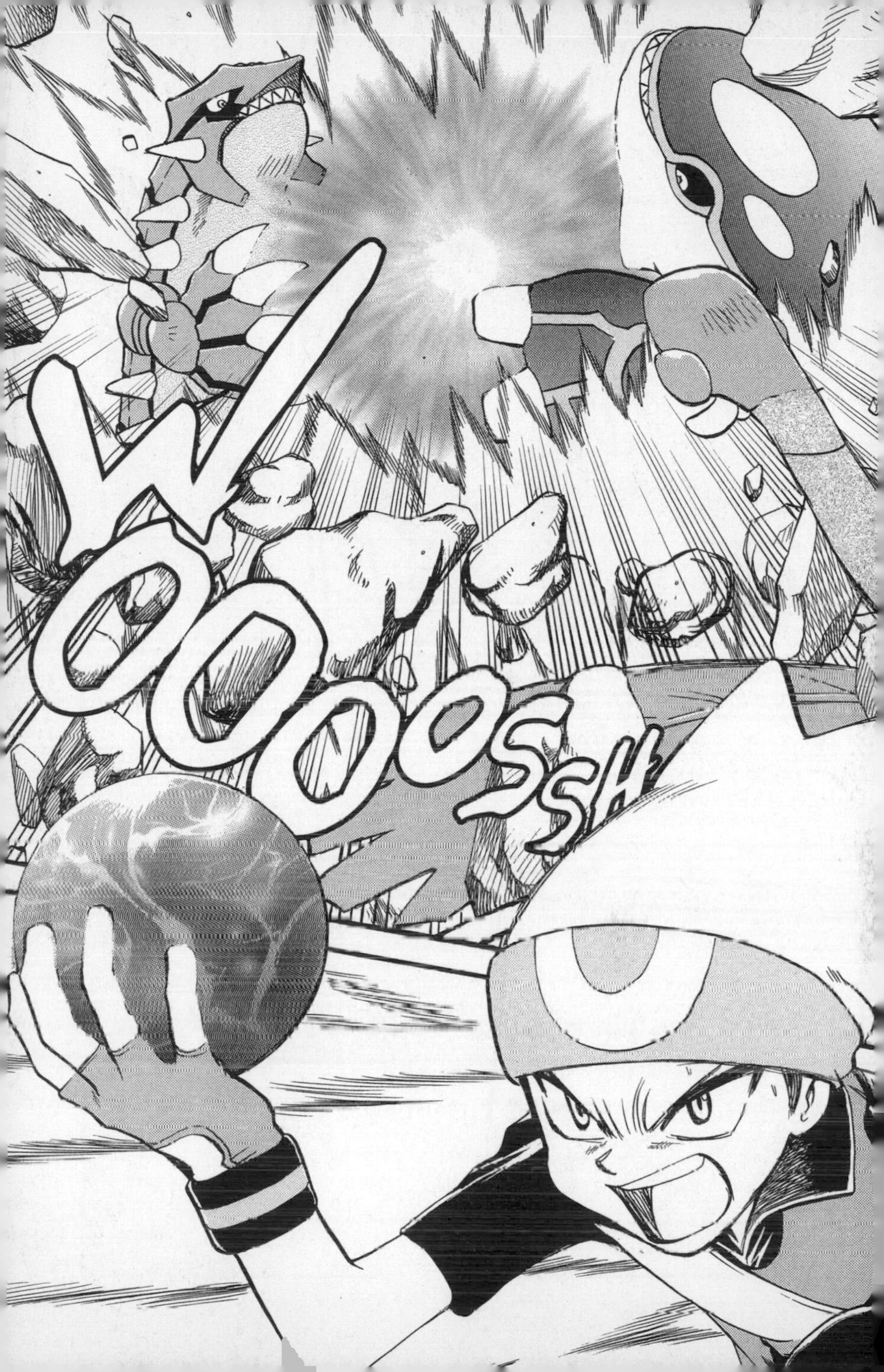
WOOOOSSH

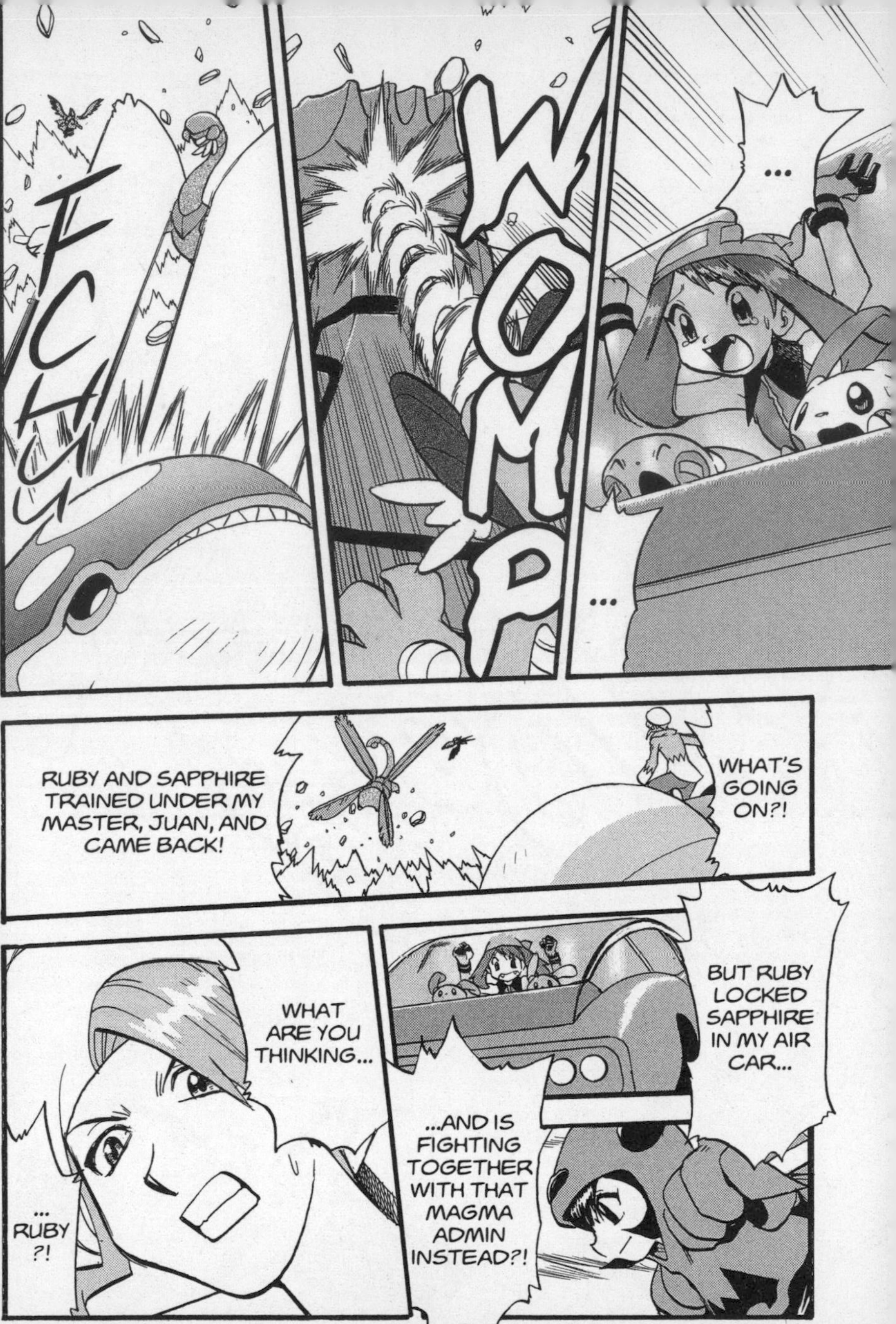
...
...
WOMP
FCHUUU
WHAT'S GOING ON?!
RUBY AND SAPPHIRE TRAINED UNDER MY MASTER, JUAN, AND CAME BACK!
BUT RUBY LOCKED SAPPHIRE IN MY AIR CAR...
...AND IS FIGHTING TOGETHER WITH THAT MAGMA ADMIN INSTEAD?!
WHAT ARE YOU THINKING...
... RUBY ?!

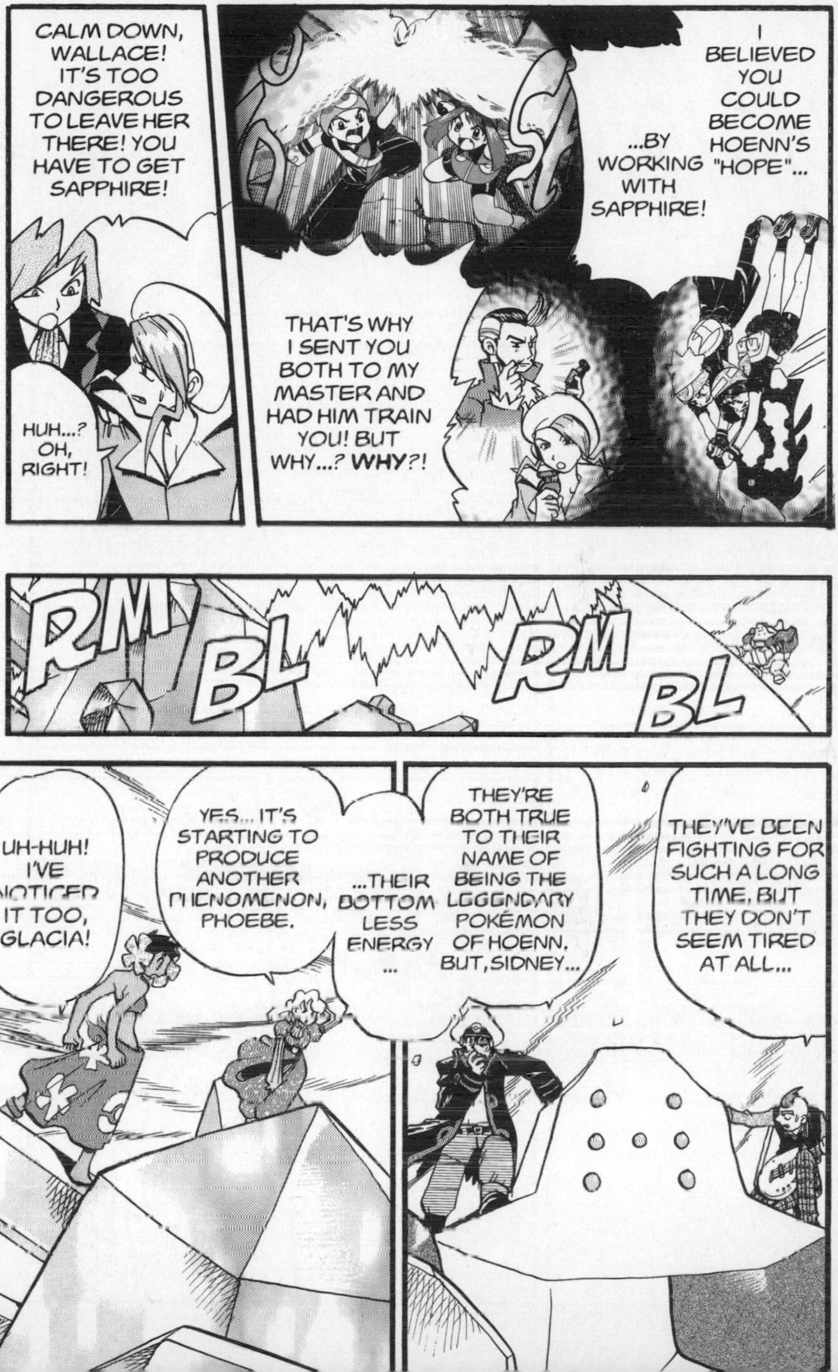
I BELIEVED YOU COULD BECOME HOENN'S "HOPE"...
...BY WORKING WITH SAPPHIRE!
THAT'S WHY I SENT YOU BOTH TO MY MASTER AND HAD HIM TRAIN YOU! BUT WHY...? **WHY**?!
CALM DOWN, WALLACE! IT'S TOO DANGEROUS TO LEAVE HER THERE! YOU HAVE TO GET SAPPHIRE!
HUH...? OH, RIGHT!
RM BL
RM BL
THEY'VE BEEN FIGHTING FOR SUCH A LONG TIME, BUT THEY DON'T SEEM TIRED AT ALL...
THEY'RE BOTH TRUE TO THEIR NAME OF BEING THE LEGENDARY POKÉMON OF HOENN. BUT, SIDNEY...
...THEIR BOTTOMLESS ENERGY...
YES... IT'S STARTING TO PRODUCE ANOTHER PHENOMENON, PHOEBE.
UH-HUH! I'VE NOTICED IT TOO, GLACIA!

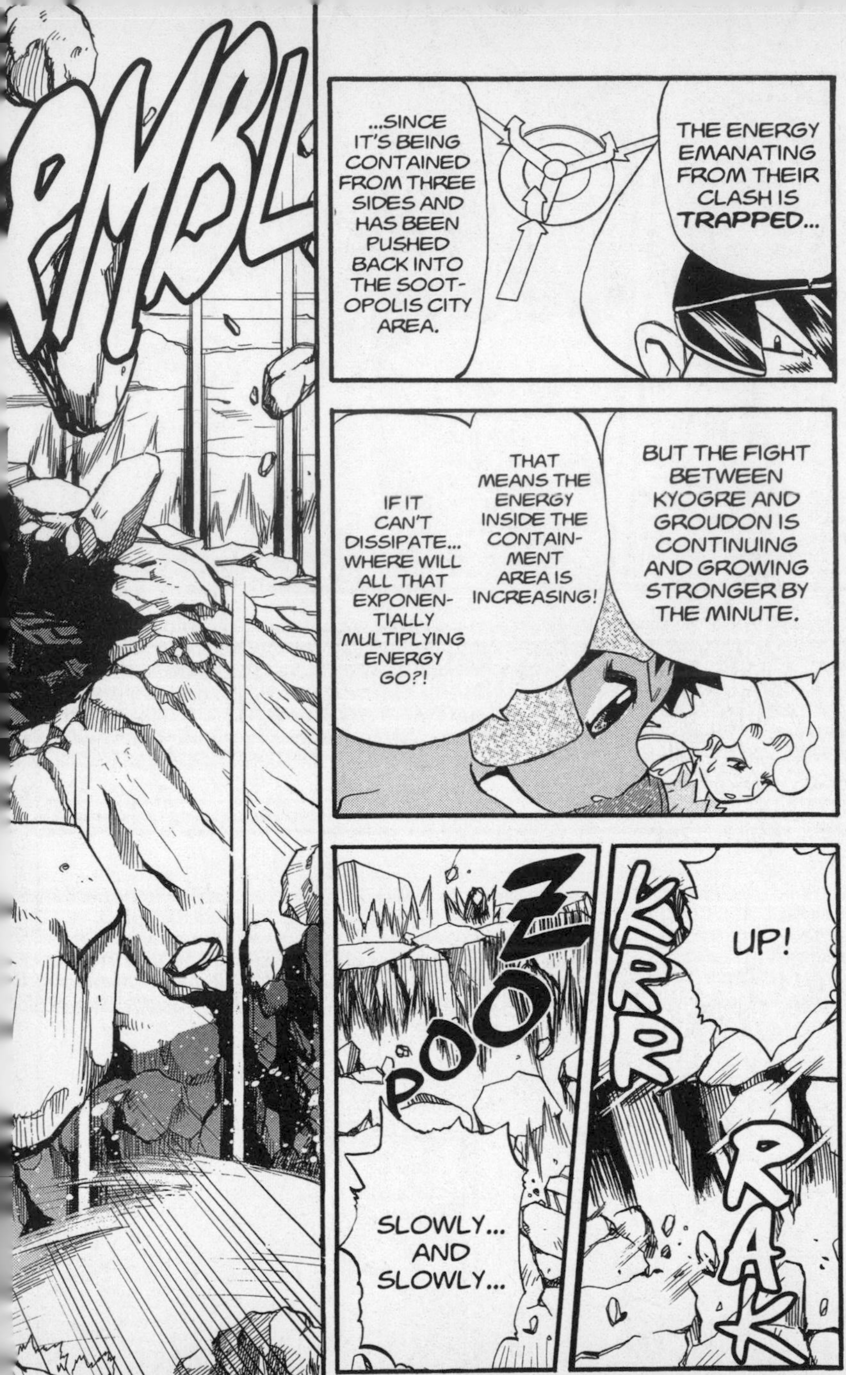
THE ENERGY EMANATING FROM THEIR CLASH IS TRAPPED...
...SINCE IT'S BEING CONTAINED FROM THREE SIDES AND HAS BEEN PUSHED BACK INTO THE SOOT-OPOLIS CITY AREA.
BUT THE FIGHT BETWEEN KYOGRE AND GROUDON IS CONTINUING AND GROWING STRONGER BY THE MINUTE.
THAT MEANS THE ENERGY INSIDE THE CONTAIN-MENT AREA IS INCREASING!
IF IT CAN'T DISSIPATE... WHERE WILL ALL THAT EXPONEN-TIALLY MULTIPLYING ENERGY GO?!
KRRRR
UP!
RAK
ZOOOP
SLOWLY... AND SLOWLY...

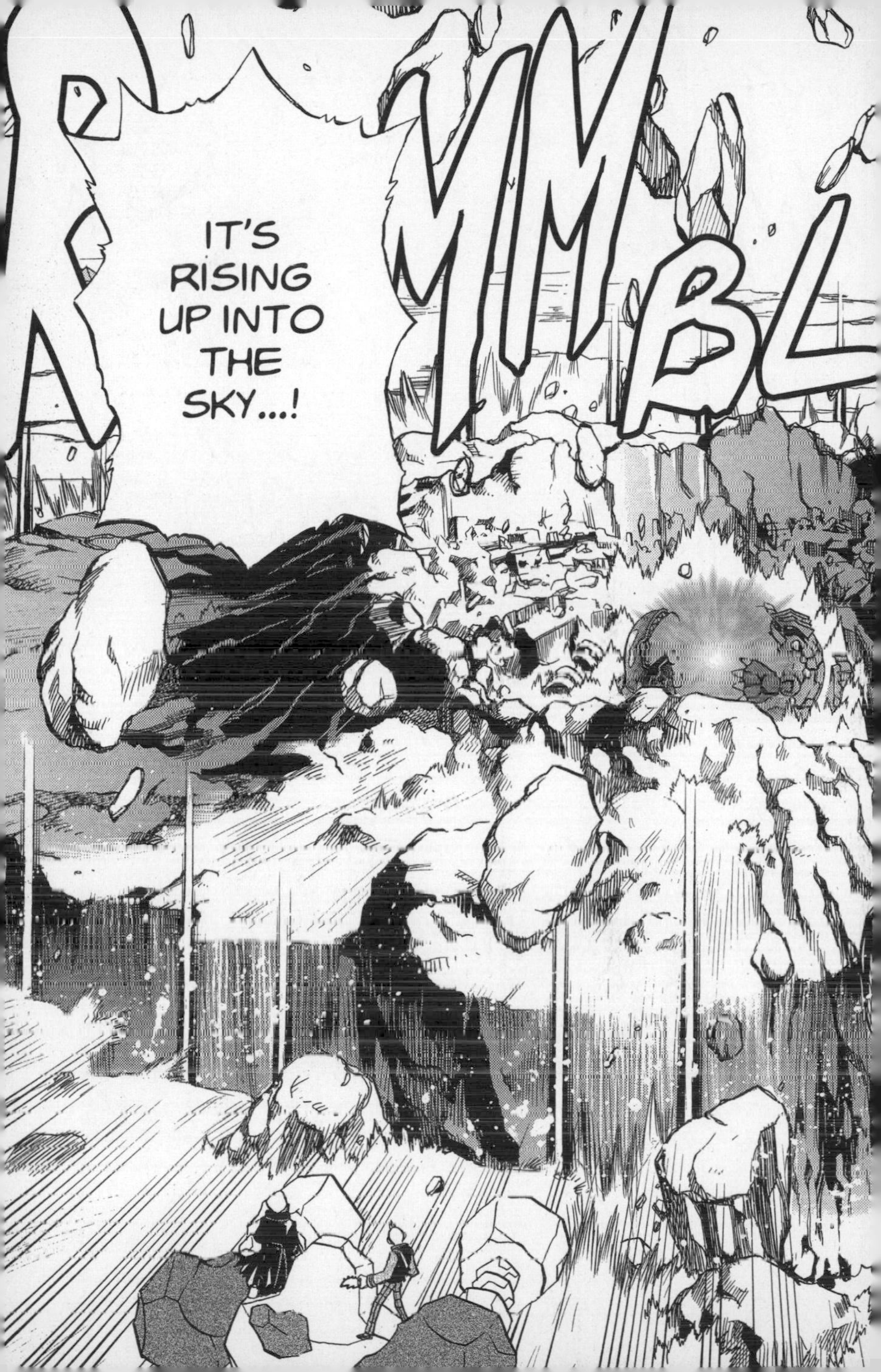
MMBL
IT'S RISING UP INTO THE SKY...!

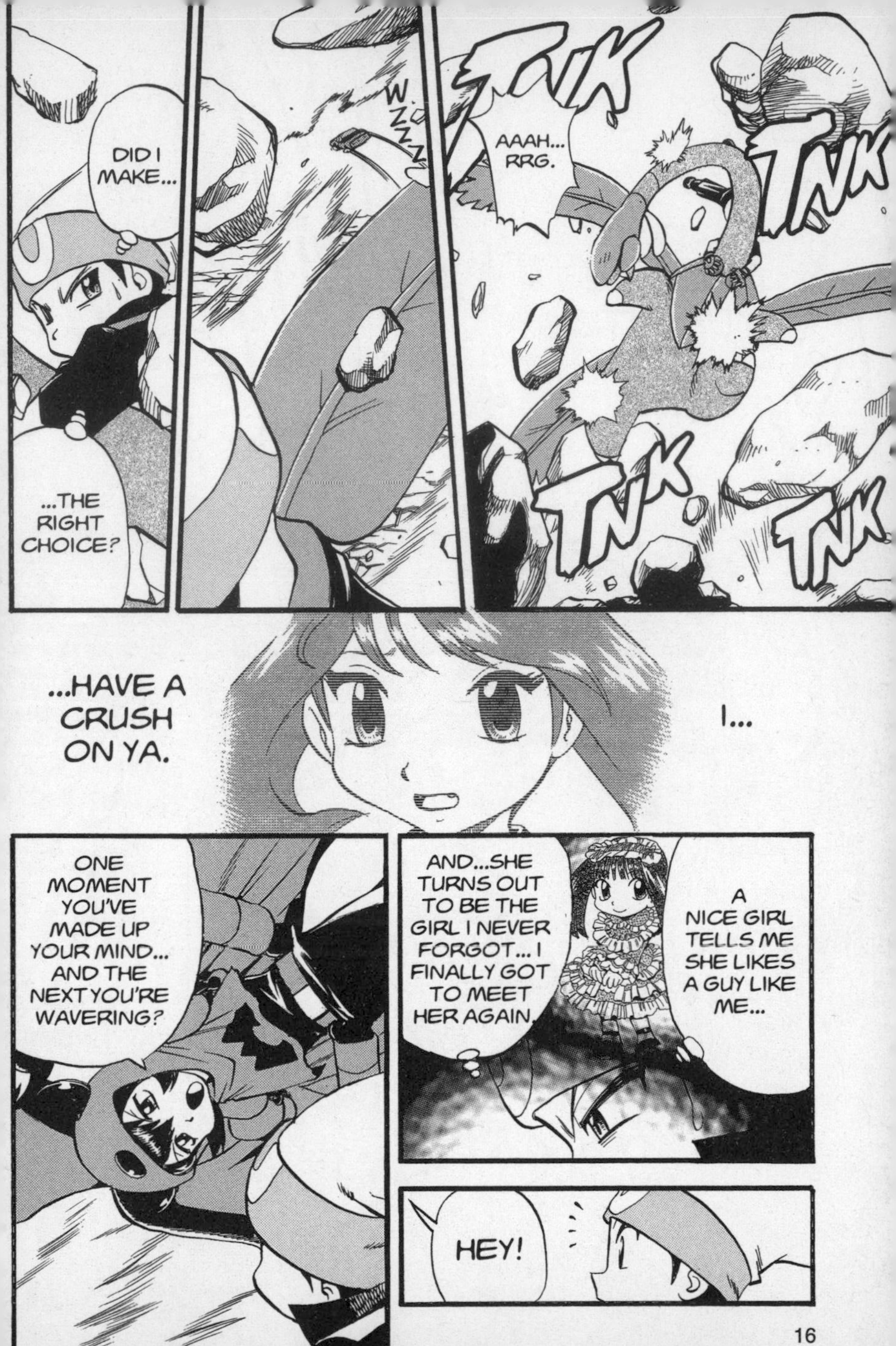
TNK
TNK
AAAH... RRG.
TNK
TNK
WZZZ
DID I MAKE...
...THE RIGHT CHOICE?
I...
...HAVE A CRUSH ON YA.
A NICE GIRL TELLS ME SHE LIKES A GUY LIKE ME...
AND...SHE TURNS OUT TO BE THE GIRL I NEVER FORGOT... I FINALLY GOT TO MEET HER AGAIN.
HEY!
ONE MOMENT YOU'VE MADE UP YOUR MIND... AND THE NEXT YOU'RE WAVERING?

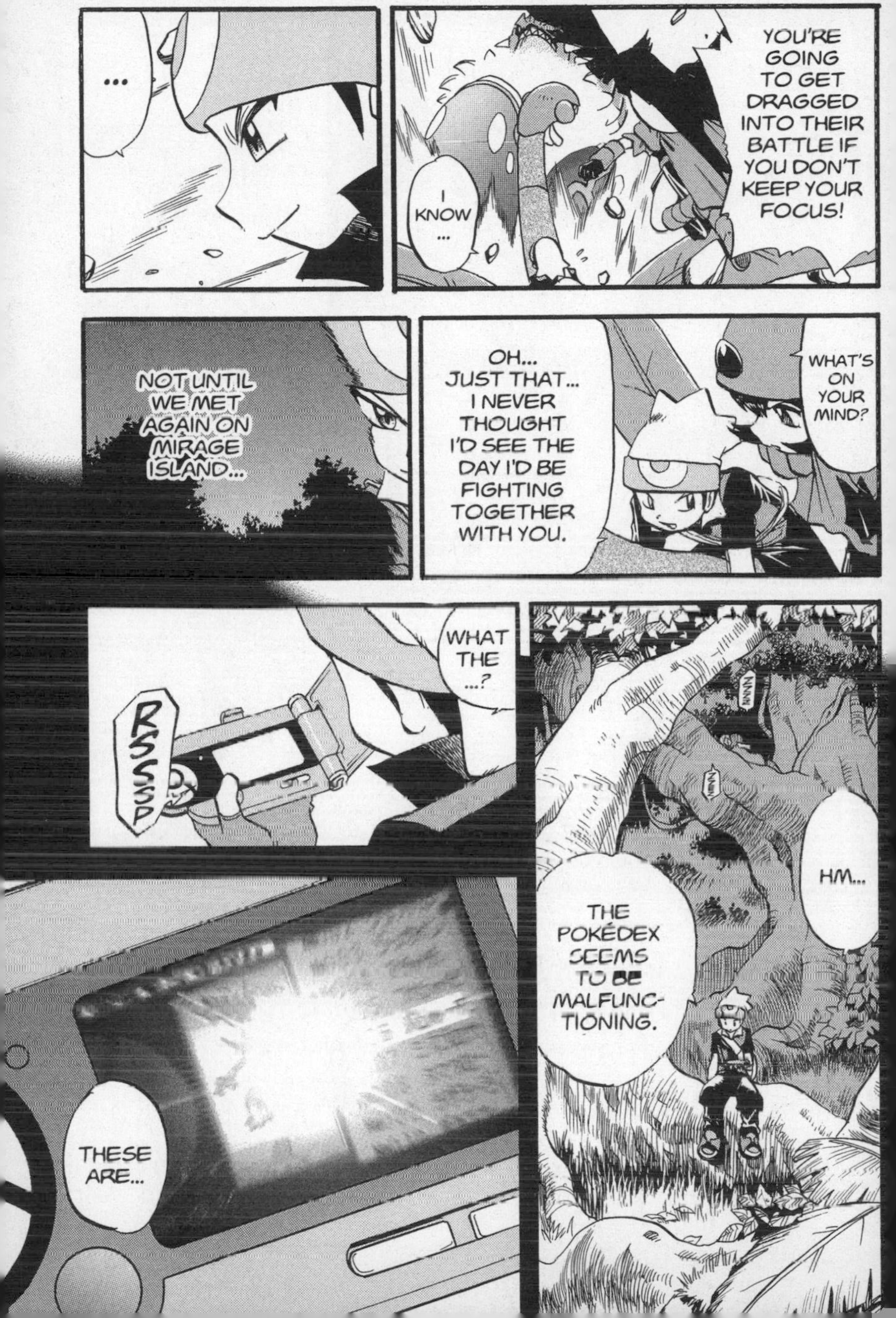
YOU'RE GOING TO GET DRAGGED INTO THEIR BATTLE IF YOU DON'T KEEP YOUR FOCUS!
I KNOW...
...
WHAT'S ON YOUR MIND?
OH... JUST THAT... I NEVER THOUGHT I'D SEE THE DAY I'D BE FIGHTING TOGETHER WITH YOU.
NOT UNTIL WE MET AGAIN ON MIRAGE ISLAND...
HM...
THE POKÉDEX SEEMS TO BE MALFUNCTIONING.
WHAT THE ...?
RSSSP
THESE ARE...

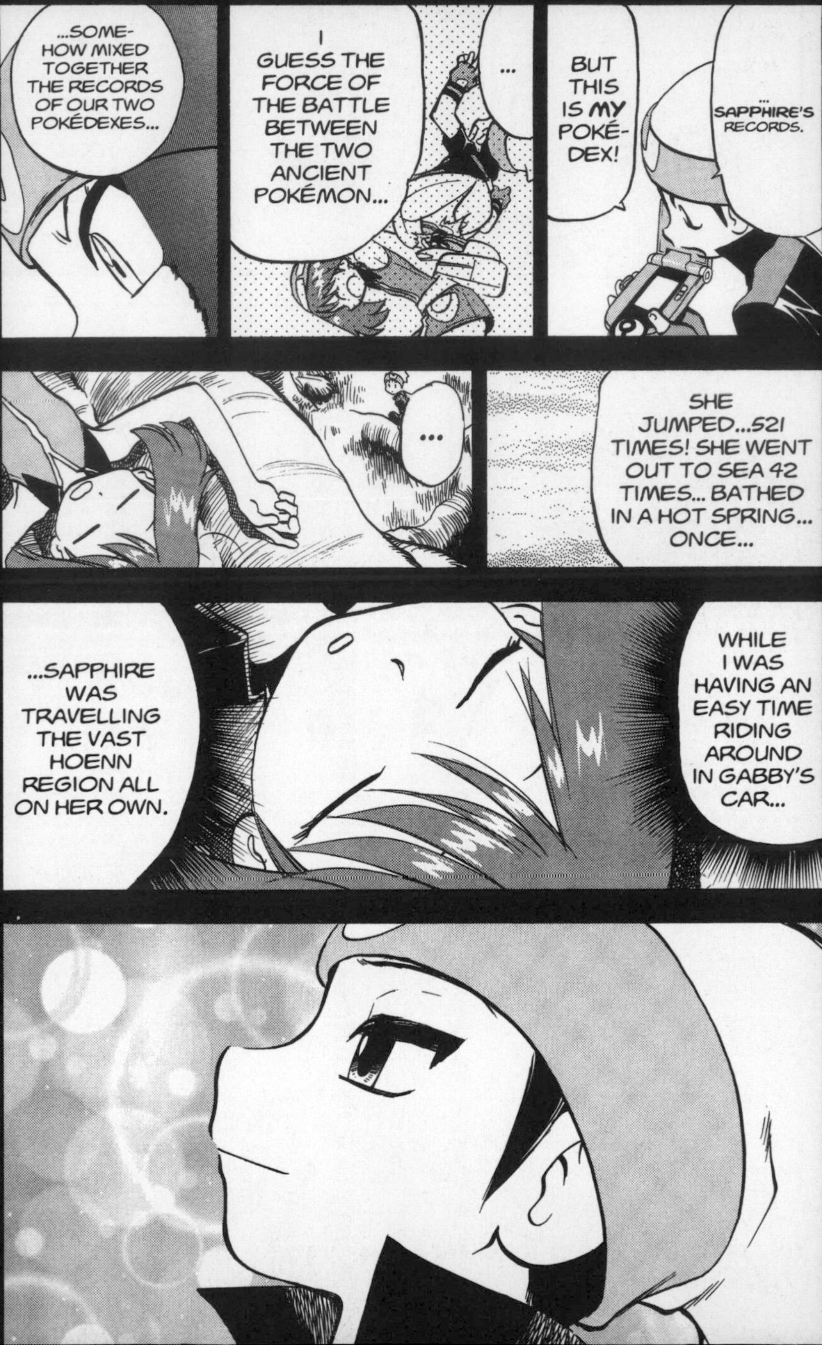
...SAPPHIRE'S RECORDS.
BUT THIS IS MY POKÉDEX!
...
I GUESS THE FORCE OF THE BATTLE BETWEEN THE TWO ANCIENT POKÉMON...
...SOMEHOW MIXED TOGETHER THE RECORDS OF OUR TWO POKÉDEXES...
SHE JUMPED...521 TIMES! SHE WENT OUT TO SEA 42 TIMES... BATHED IN A HOT SPRING... ONCE...
...
WHILE I WAS HAVING AN EASY TIME RIDING AROUND IN GABBY'S CAR...
...SAPPHIRE WAS TRAVELLING THE VAST HOENN REGION ALL ON HER OWN.

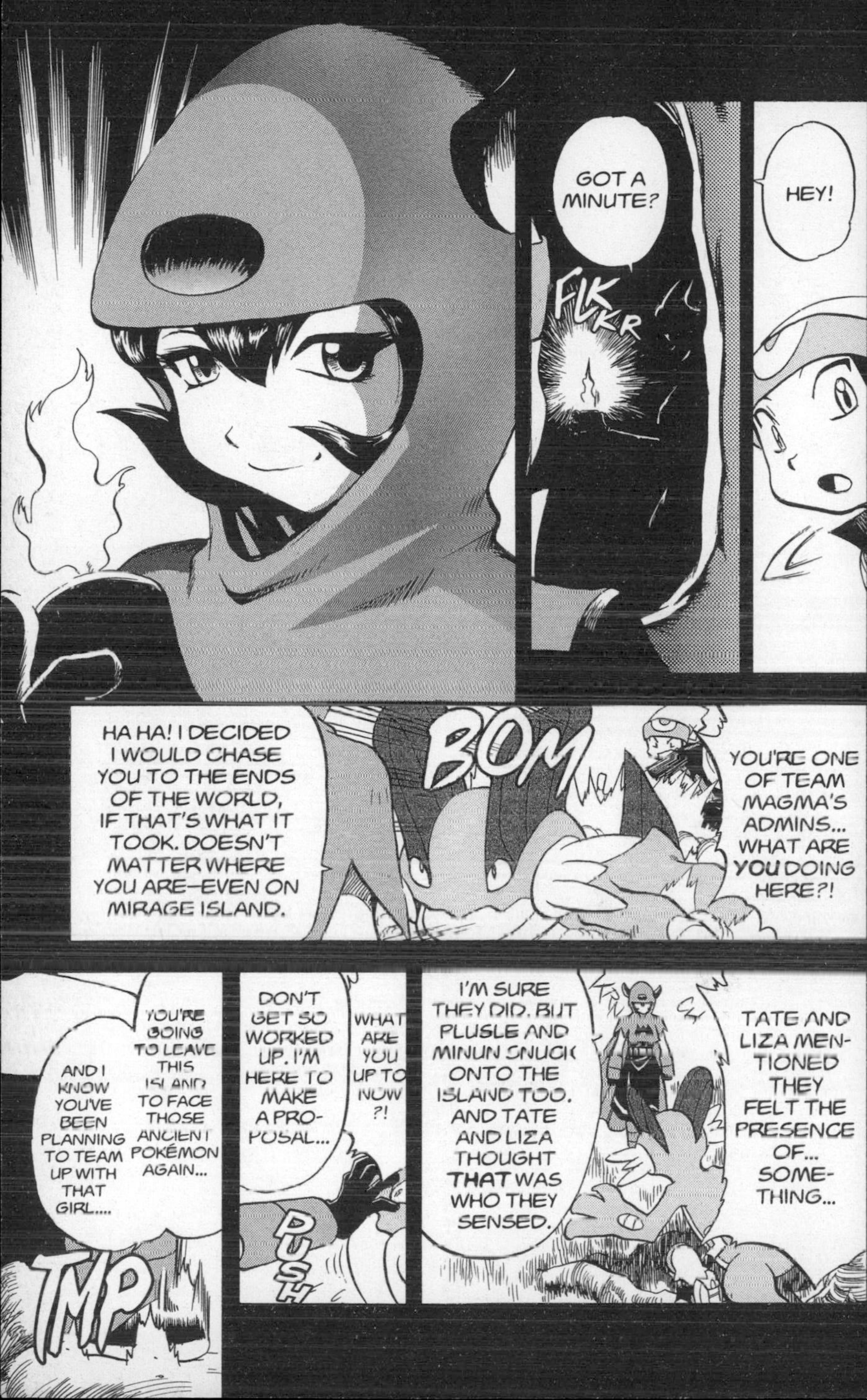
HEY!
GOT A MINUTE?
FLKKR
YOU'RE ONE OF TEAM MAGMA'S ADMINS... WHAT ARE YOU DOING HERE?!
BOM
HA HA! I DECIDED I WOULD CHASE YOU TO THE ENDS OF THE WORLD, IF THAT'S WHAT IT TOOK. DOESN'T MATTER WHERE YOU ARE—EVEN ON MIRAGE ISLAND.
TATE AND LIZA MENTIONED THEY FELT THE PRESENCE OF... SOMETHING...
I'M SURE THEY DID. BUT PLUSLE AND MINUN SNUCK ONTO THE ISLAND TOO. AND TATE AND LIZA THOUGHT THAT WAS WHO THEY SENSED.
WHAT ARE YOU UP TO NOW?!
DON'T GET SO WORKED UP. I'M HERE TO MAKE A PROPOSAL...
PUSH
YOU'RE GOING TO LEAVE THIS ISLAND TO FACE THOSE ANCIENT POKÉMON AGAIN...
AND I KNOW YOU'VE BEEN PLANNING TO TEAM UP WITH THAT GIRL....
TMP

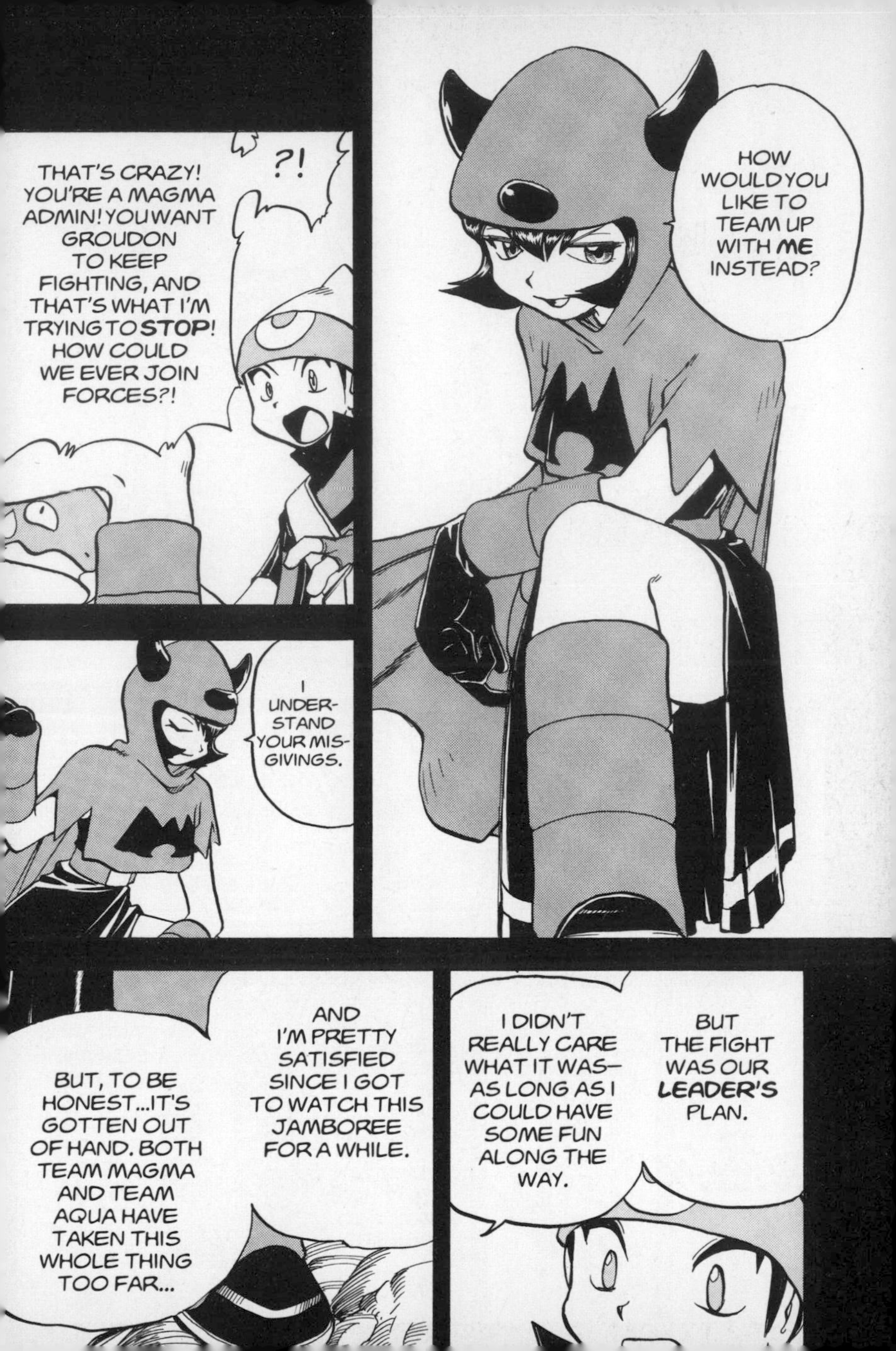
HOW WOULD YOU LIKE TO TEAM UP WITH **ME** INSTEAD?
?!
THAT'S CRAZY! YOU'RE A MAGMA ADMIN! YOU WANT GROUDON TO KEEP FIGHTING, AND THAT'S WHAT I'M TRYING TO **STOP**! HOW COULD WE EVER JOIN FORCES?!
I UNDER-STAND YOUR MIS-GIVINGS.
BUT THE FIGHT WAS OUR **LEADER'S** PLAN.
I DIDN'T REALLY CARE WHAT IT WAS— AS LONG AS I COULD HAVE SOME FUN ALONG THE WAY.
AND I'M PRETTY SATISFIED SINCE I GOT TO WATCH THIS JAMBOREE FOR A WHILE.
BUT, TO BE HONEST...IT'S GOTTEN OUT OF HAND. BOTH TEAM MAGMA AND TEAM AQUA HAVE TAKEN THIS WHOLE THING TOO FAR...

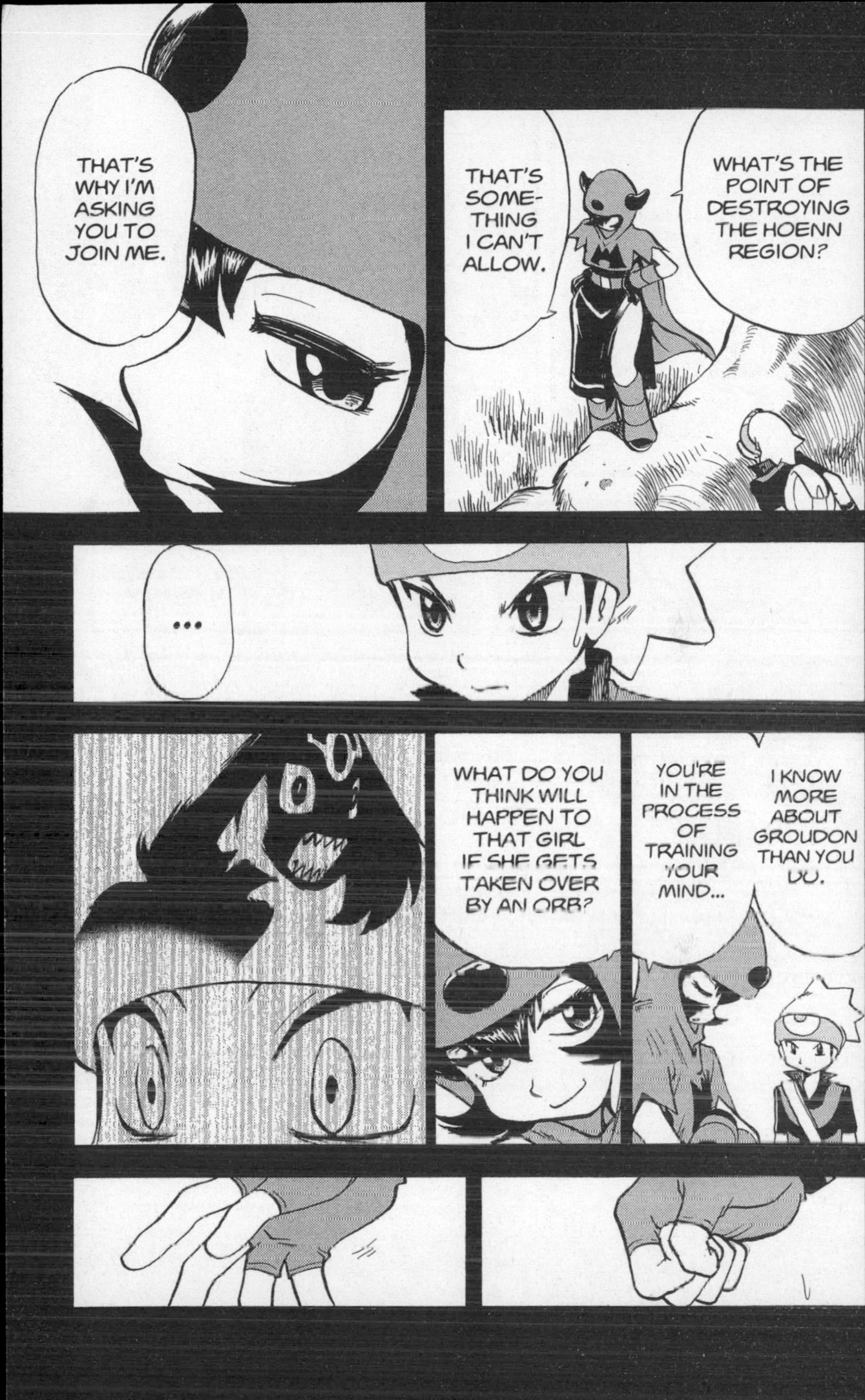
WHAT'S THE POINT OF DESTROYING THE HOENN REGION?
THAT'S SOME-THING I CAN'T ALLOW.
THAT'S WHY I'M ASKING YOU TO JOIN ME.
...
I KNOW MORE ABOUT GROUDON THAN YOU DO.
YOU'RE IN THE PROCESS OF TRAINING YOUR MIND...
WHAT DO YOU THINK WILL HAPPEN TO THAT GIRL IF SHE GETS TAKEN OVER BY AN ORB?

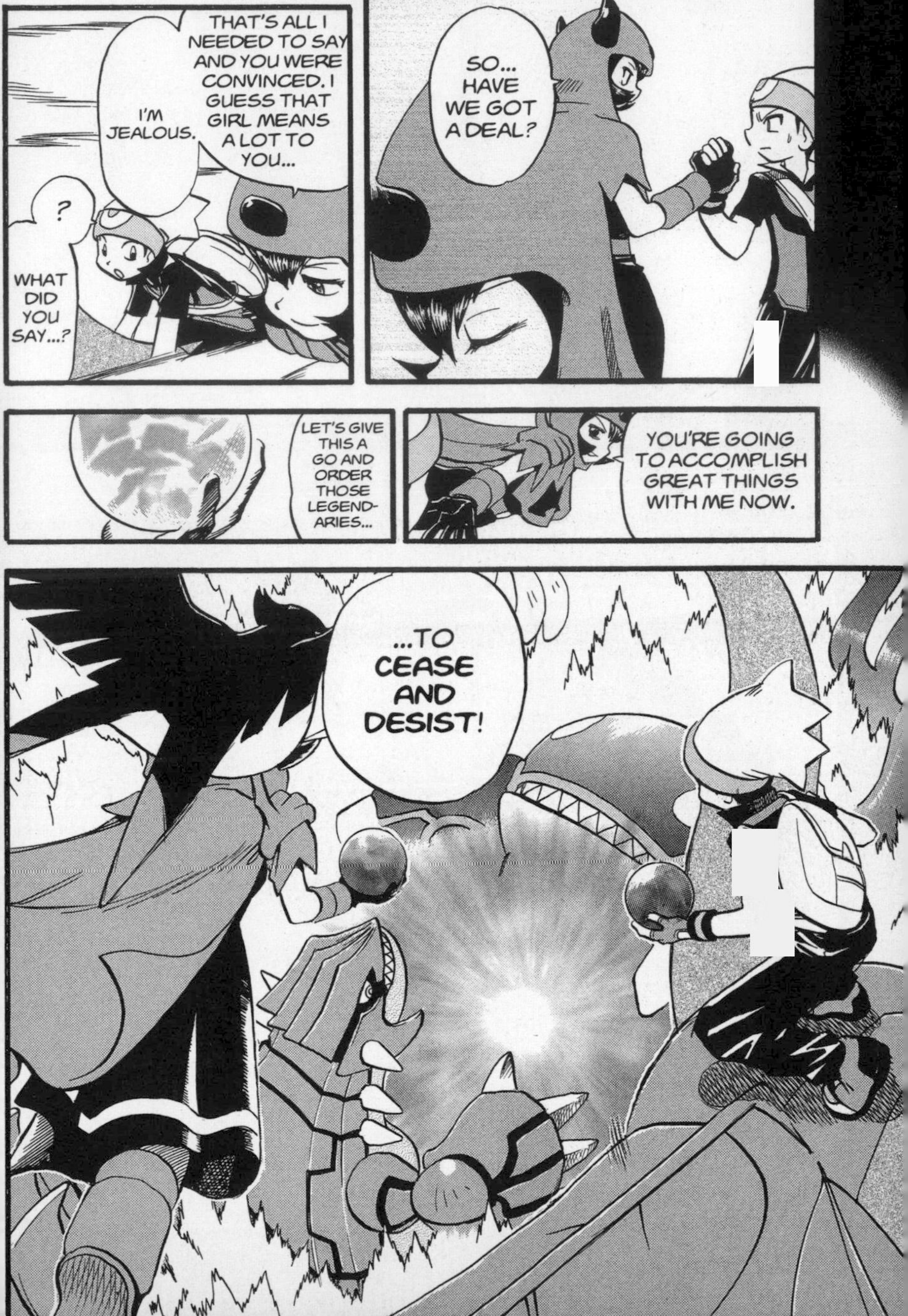
SO... HAVE WE GOT A DEAL?
THAT'S ALL I NEEDED TO SAY AND YOU WERE CONVINCED. I GUESS THAT GIRL MEANS A LOT TO YOU...
I'M JEALOUS.
?
WHAT DID YOU SAY...?
YOU'RE GOING TO ACCOMPLISH GREAT THINGS WITH ME NOW.
LET'S GIVE THIS A GO AND ORDER THOSE LEGEND-ARIES...
...TO CEASE AND DESIST!

ADVENTURE MAP

SAPPHIRE

RUBY

CHIC
Blaziken ♀
Lv59

RONO
Aggron ♂
Lv54

PHADO
Donphan ♂
Lv58

MINUN
Minun ♀
Lv52

PLUSLE
Plusle ♂
Lv52

Sootopolis City
↓
Mirage Island
↓
Sootopolis City

MUMU
Swampert ♂

NANA
Mightyena ♀

KIKI
Delcatty ♀

FOFO
Castform ♀

TROPPY
Tropius ♂

Stone Badge	Knuckle Badge	Dynamo Badge	Heat Badge
Balance Badge	Feather Badge	Mind Badge	Rain Badge

	Cool	Beauty	Cute	Smart	Tough
Normal	🎗	🎗	🎗	🎗	🎗
Super	🎗	🎗	🎗	🎗	🎗
Hyper	🎗		🎗	🎗	🎗
Master	🎗	🎗		🎗	🎗

● Chapter 261 ●
It All Ends Now II

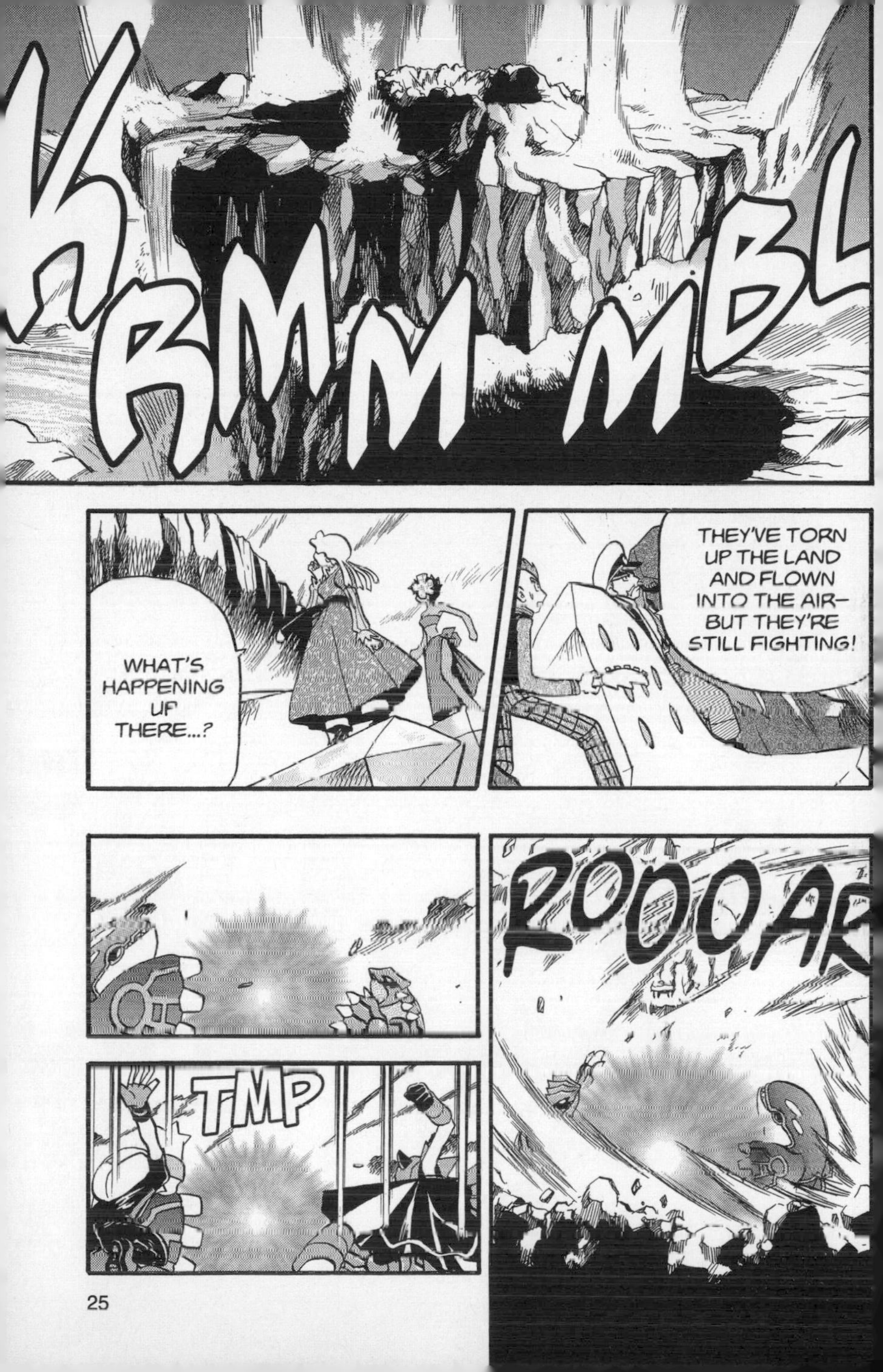
KRMMMBL
THEY'VE TORN UP THE LAND AND FLOWN INTO THE AIR—BUT THEY'RE STILL FIGHTING!
WHAT'S HAPPENING UP THERE...?
ROOOAR
TMP

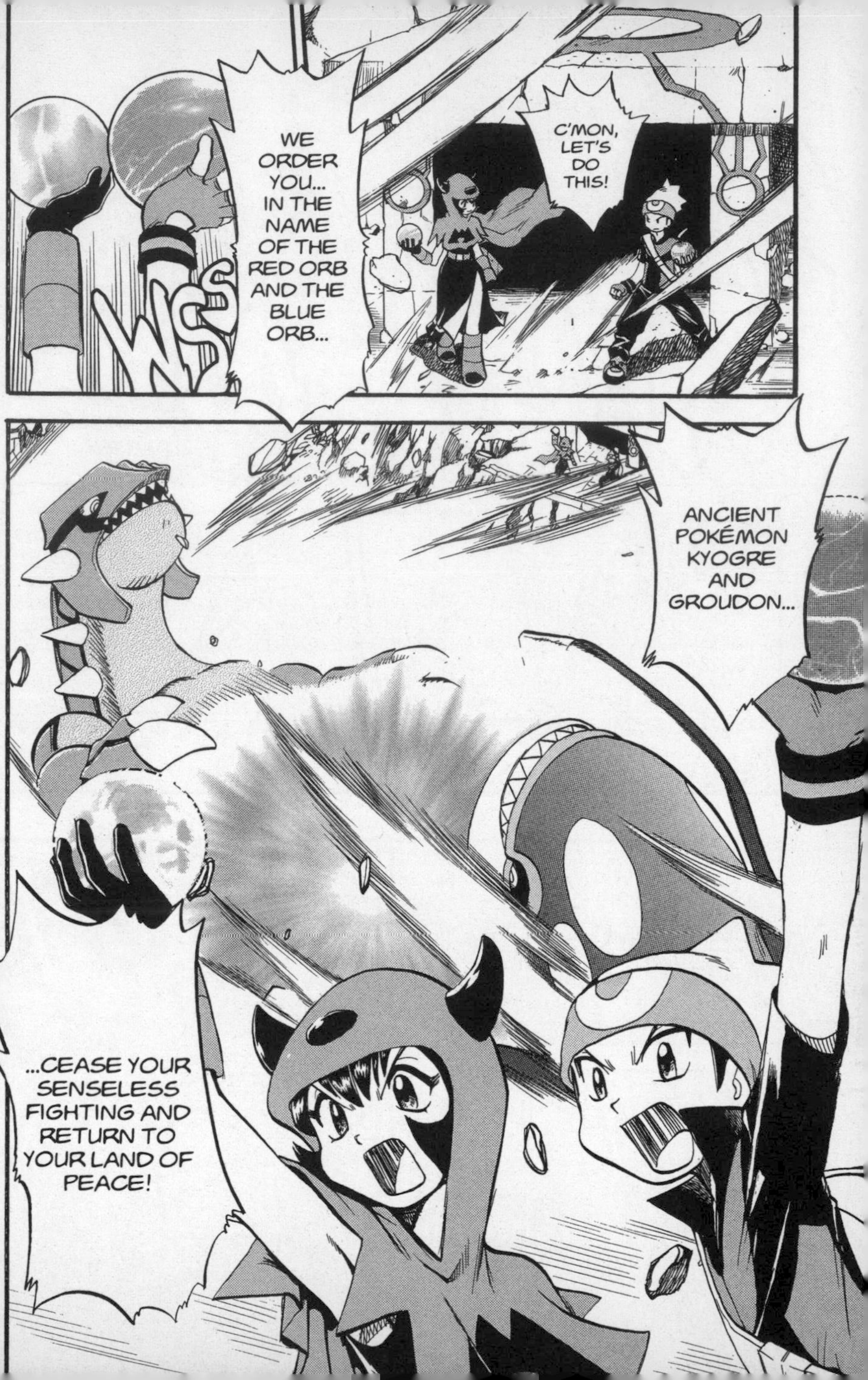
C'MON, LET'S DO THIS!
WE ORDER YOU... IN THE NAME OF THE RED ORB AND THE BLUE ORB...
ANCIENT POKÉMON KYOGRE AND GROUDON...
...CEASE YOUR SENSELESS FIGHTING AND RETURN TO YOUR LAND OF PEACE!

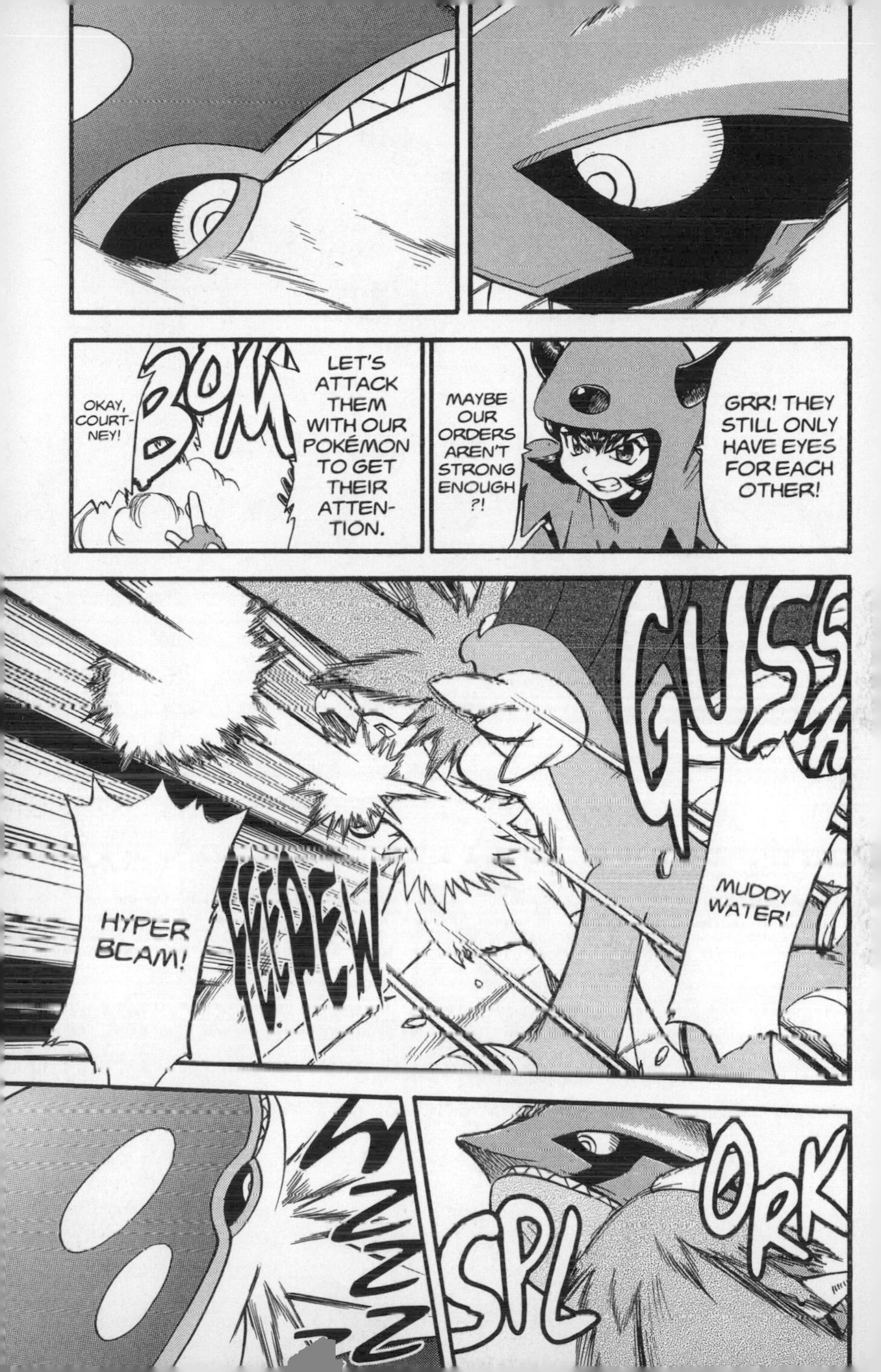
GRR! THEY STILL ONLY HAVE EYES FOR EACH OTHER!
MAYBE OUR ORDERS AREN'T STRONG ENOUGH?!
LET'S ATTACK THEM WITH OUR POKÉMON TO GET THEIR ATTENTION.
BOM
OKAY, COURTNEY!
MUDDY WATER!
HYPER BEAM!
SPLORK

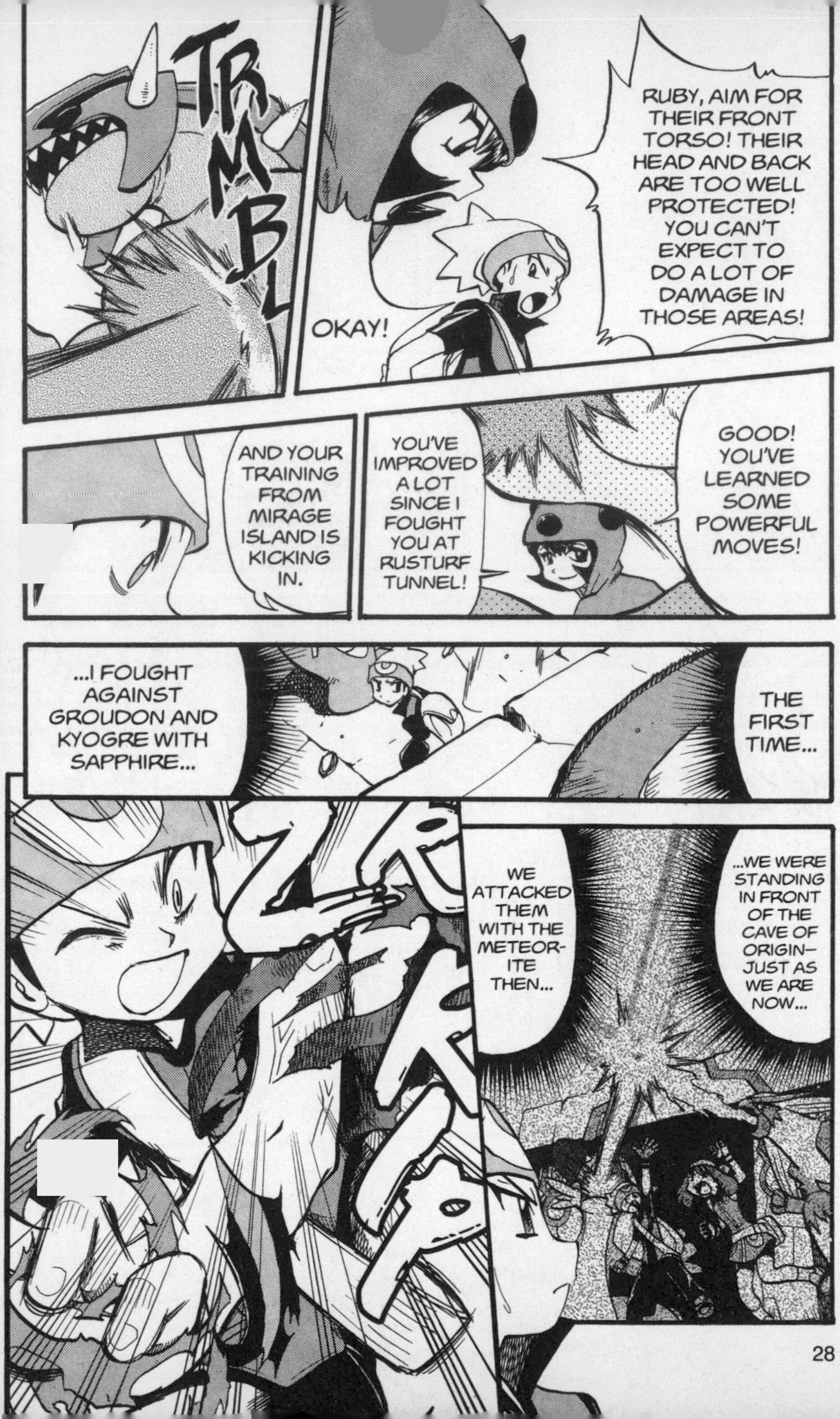
RUBY, AIM FOR THEIR FRONT TORSO! THEIR HEAD AND BACK ARE TOO WELL PROTECTED! YOU CAN'T EXPECT TO DO A LOT OF DAMAGE IN THOSE AREAS!
OKAY!
TRMBL
GOOD! YOU'VE LEARNED SOME POWERFUL MOVES!
YOU'VE IMPROVED A LOT SINCE I FOUGHT YOU AT RUSTURF TUNNEL!
AND YOUR TRAINING FROM MIRAGE ISLAND IS KICKING IN.
THE FIRST TIME...
...I FOUGHT AGAINST GROUDON AND KYOGRE WITH SAPPHIRE...
...WE WERE STANDING IN FRONT OF THE CAVE OF ORIGIN–JUST AS WE ARE NOW...
WE ATTACKED THEM WITH THE METEOR-ITE THEN...

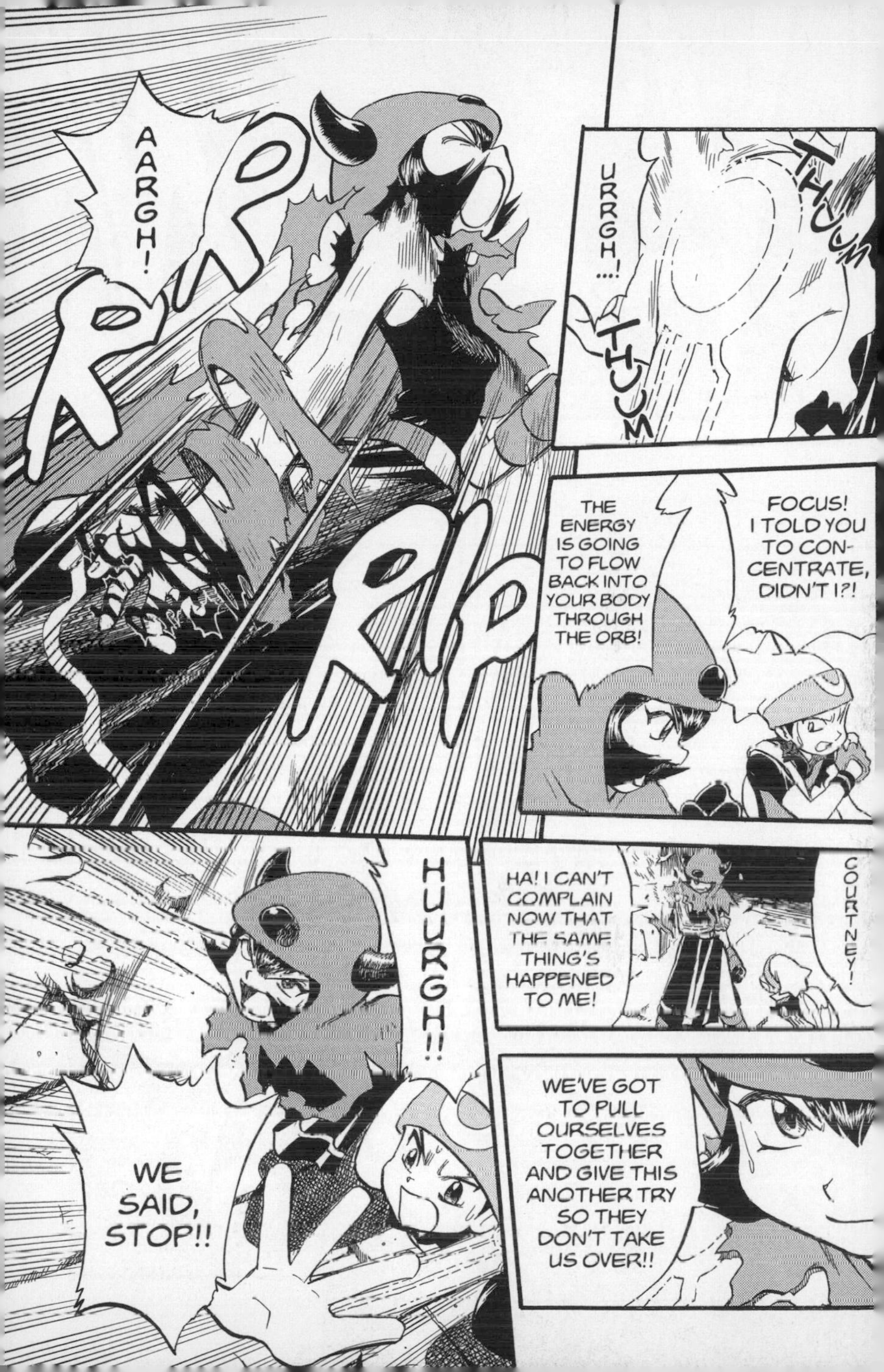
THUUM
URRGH...!
THUUM
FOCUS! I TOLD YOU TO CON-CENTRATE, DIDN'T I?!
THE ENERGY IS GOING TO FLOW BACK INTO YOUR BODY THROUGH THE ORB!
AARGH!
RIP
RIP
COURTNEY!
HA! I CAN'T COMPLAIN NOW THAT THE SAME THING'S HAPPENED TO ME!
WE'VE GOT TO PULL OURSELVES TOGETHER AND GIVE THIS ANOTHER TRY SO THEY DON'T TAKE US OVER!!
HUURGH!!
WE SAID, STOP!!

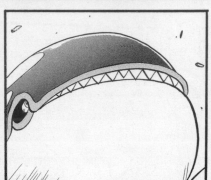

THEY
STOPPED
...

OH NO!

COURTNEY!

30

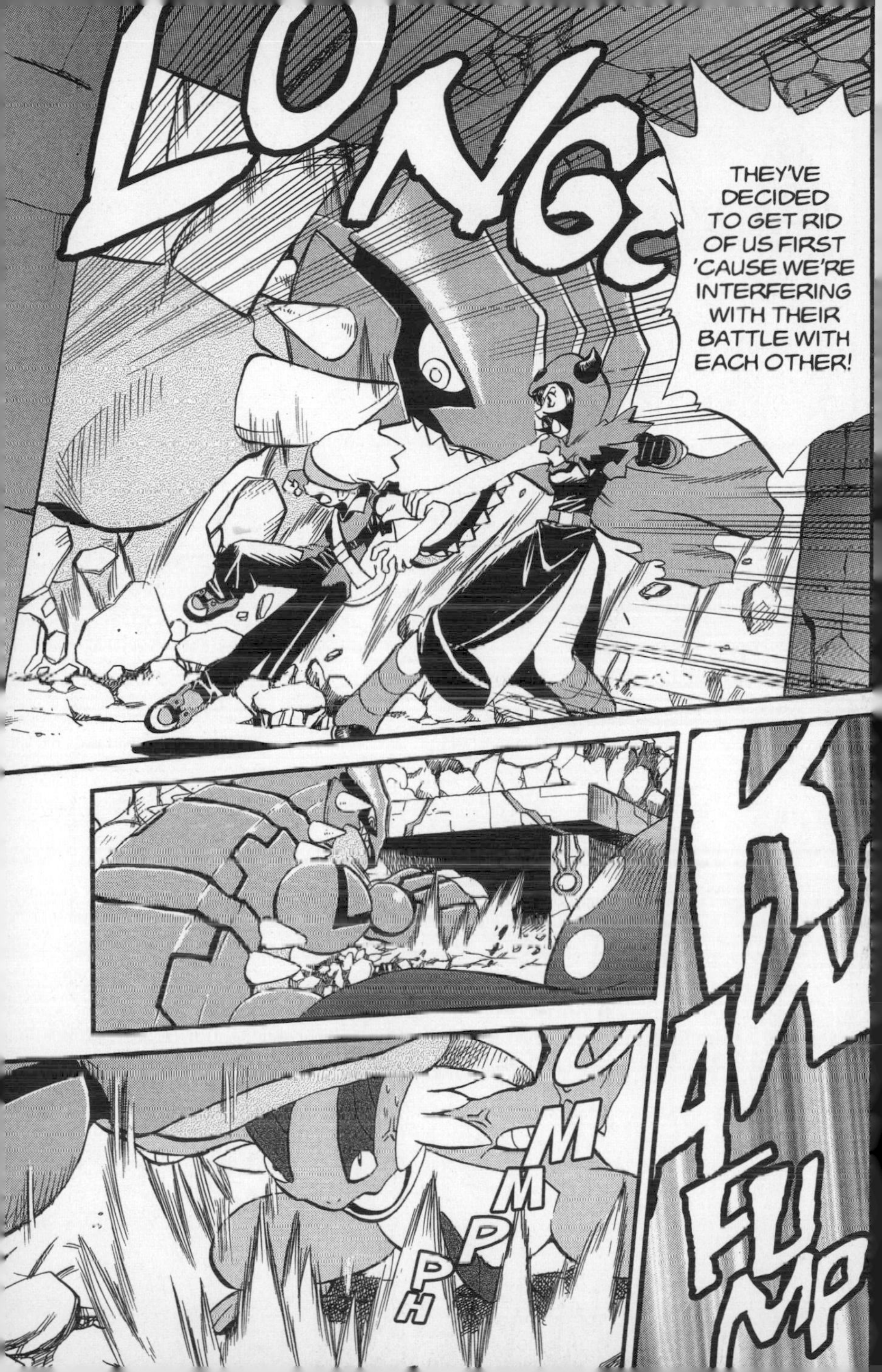
LONG
THEY'VE DECIDED TO GET RID OF US FIRST 'CAUSE WE'RE INTERFERING WITH THEIR BATTLE WITH EACH OTHER!
FUMP
MMPPH

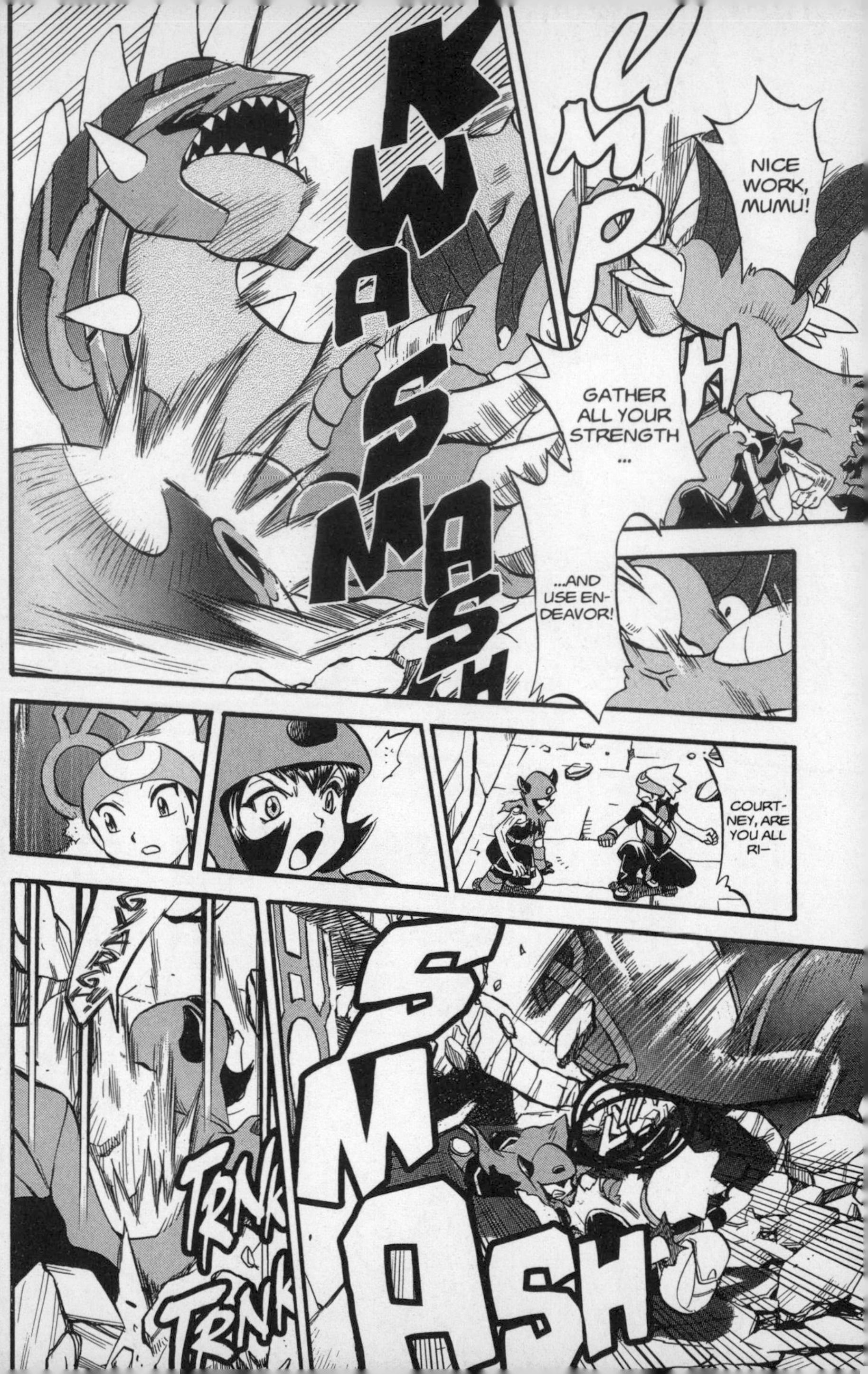
MUMP
NICE WORK, MUMU!
GATHER ALL YOUR STRENGTH...
...AND USE EN-DEAVOR!
KWASMASH
COURTNEY, ARE YOU ALL RI–
SMASH
TRNK TRNK

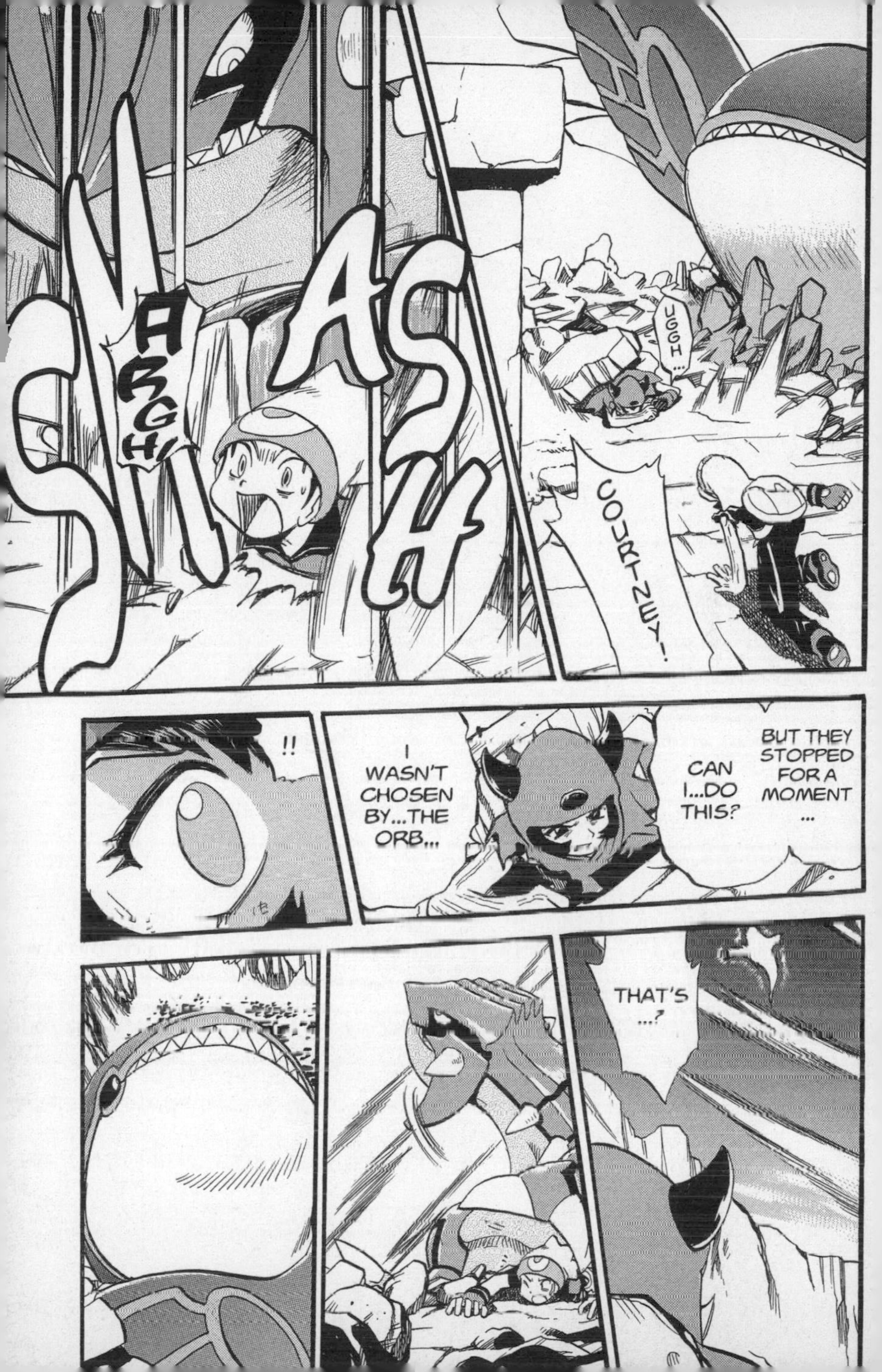
UGGH...
COURTNEY!
SMASH
ARGH!
BUT THEY STOPPED FOR A MOMENT ...
CAN I...DO THIS?
I WASN'T CHOSEN BY...THE ORB...
!!
THAT'S ...?

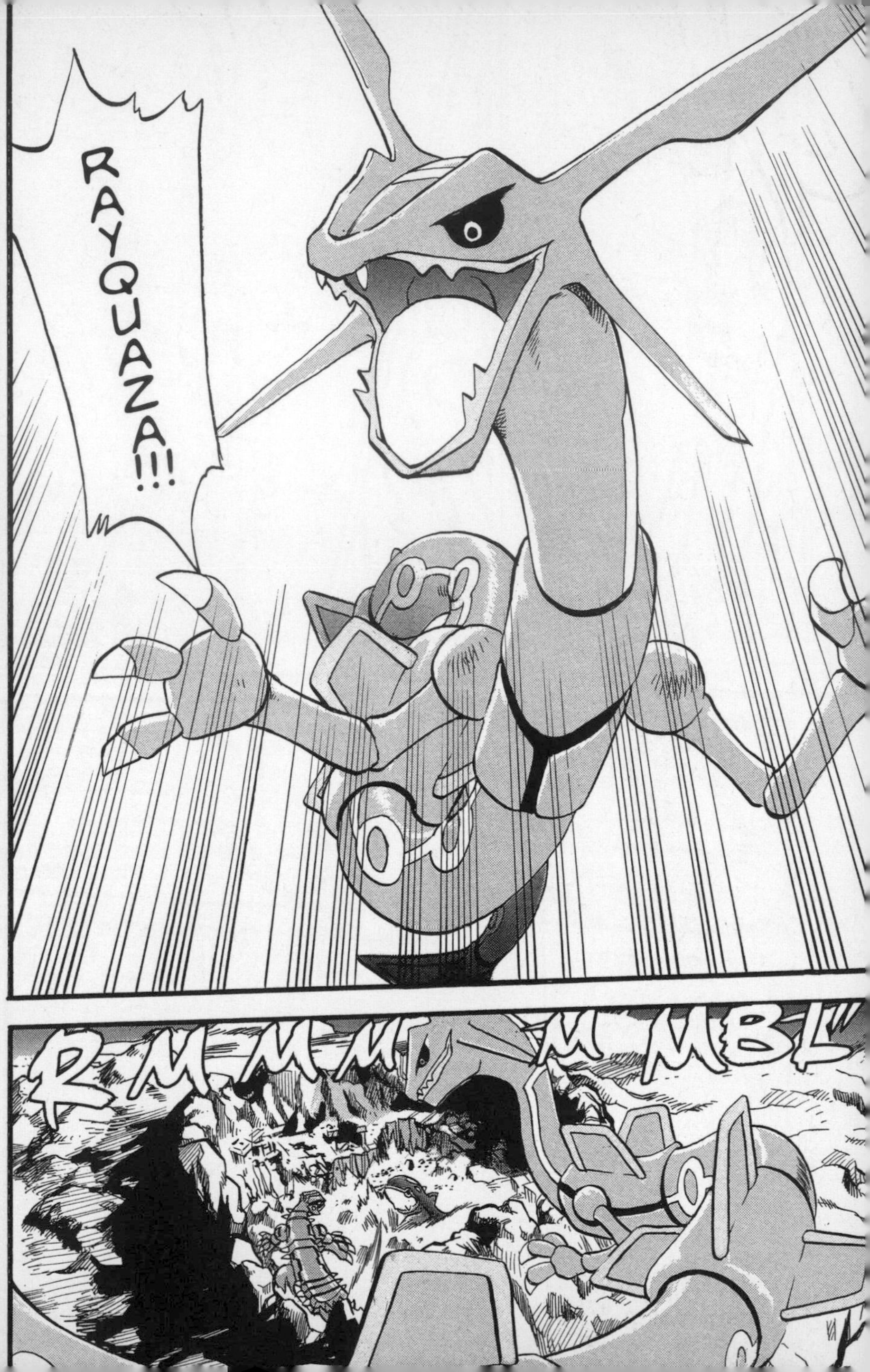
RAYQUAZA!!!
RMMM MMBL

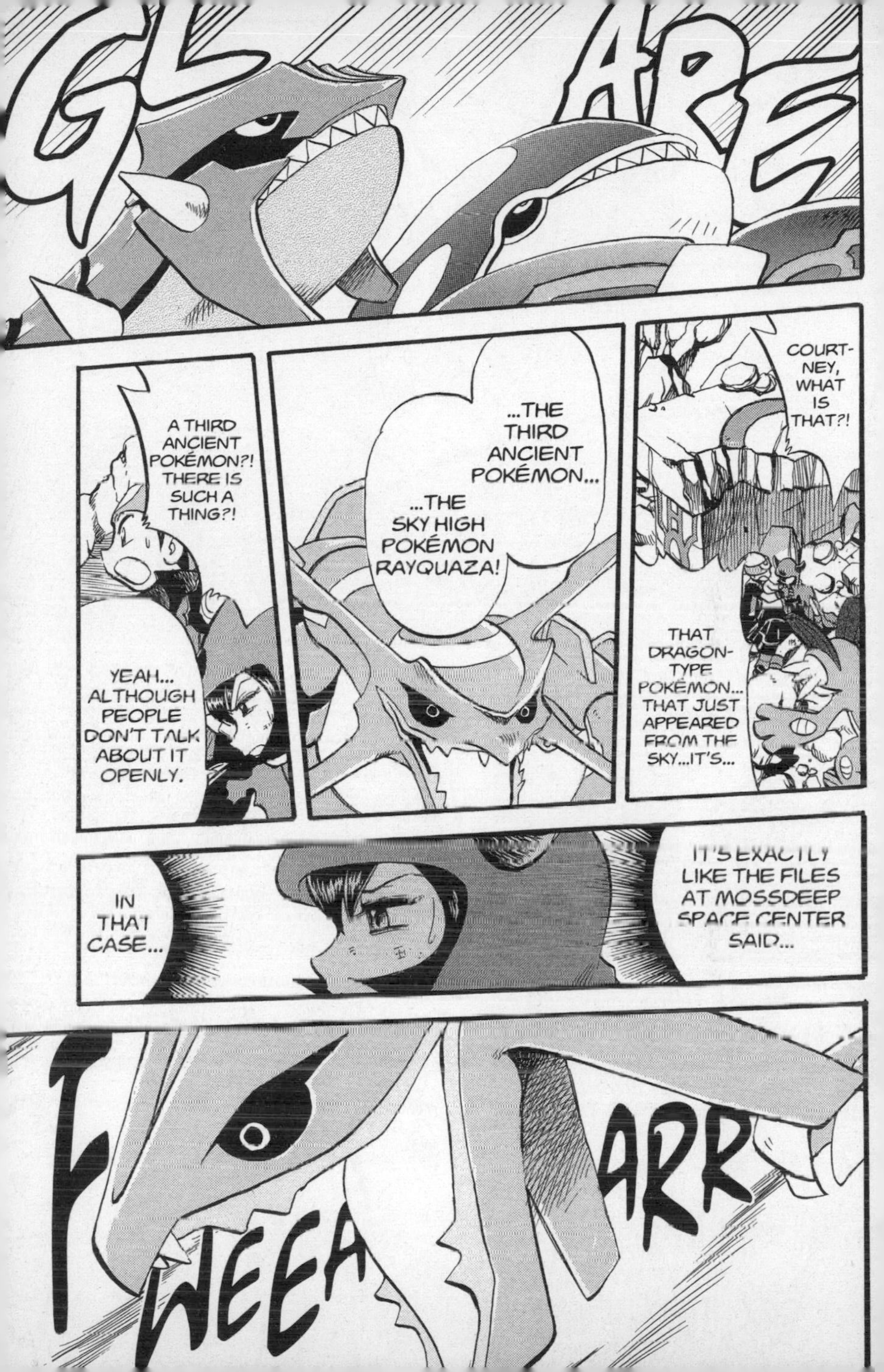
GLARE
COURTNEY, WHAT IS THAT?!
THAT DRAGON-TYPE POKÉMON... THAT JUST APPEARED FROM THE SKY...IT'S...
...THE THIRD ANCIENT POKÉMON...
...THE SKY HIGH POKÉMON RAYQUAZA!
A THIRD ANCIENT POKÉMON?! THERE IS SUCH A THING?!
YEAH... ALTHOUGH PEOPLE DON'T TALK ABOUT IT OPENLY.
IT'S EXACTLY LIKE THE FILES AT MOSSDEEP SPACE CENTER SAID...
IN THAT CASE...
FWEEAARR

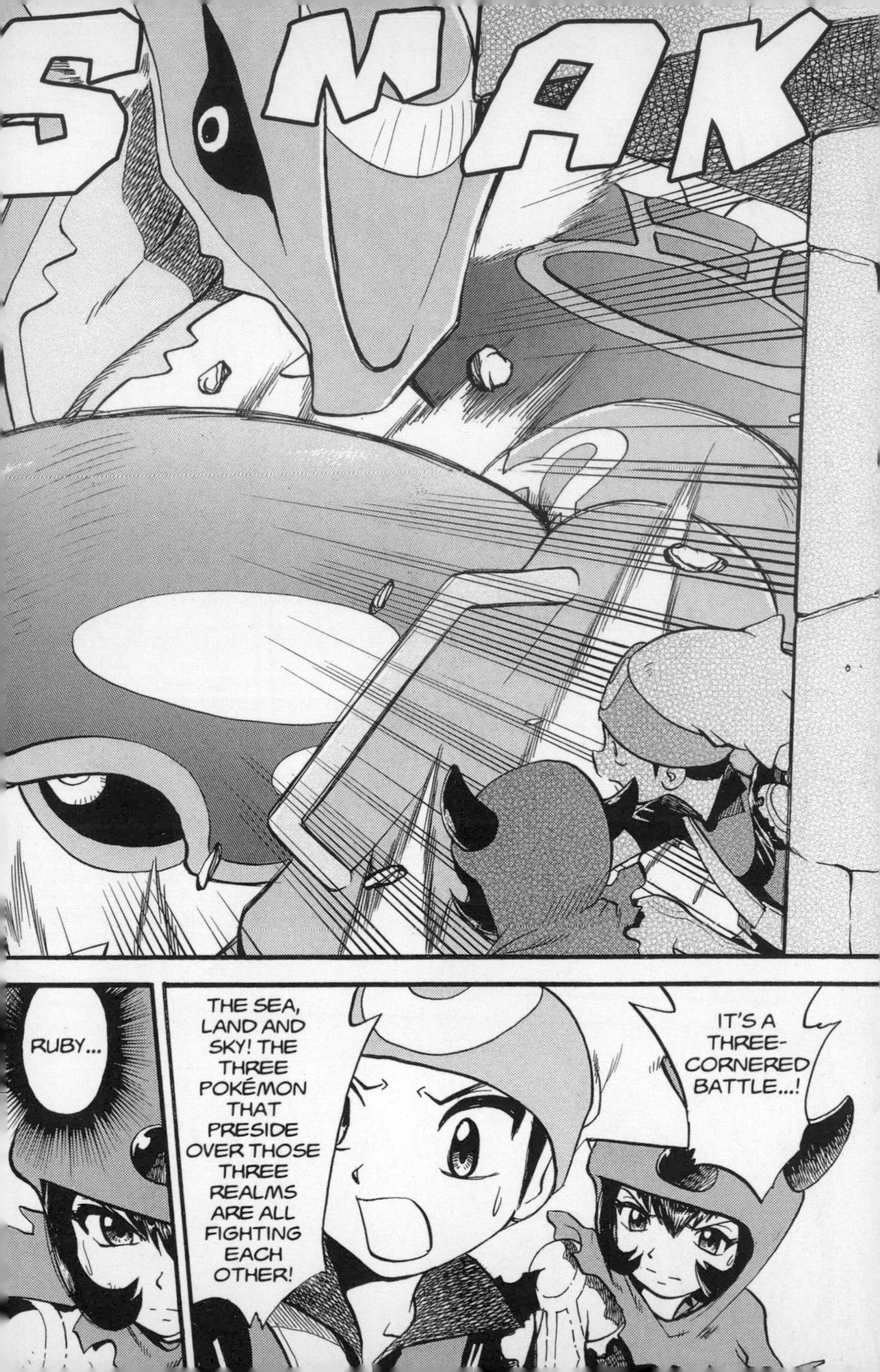
SMAK
IT'S A THREE-CORNERED BATTLE...!
THE SEA, LAND AND SKY! THE THREE POKÉMON THAT PRESIDE OVER THOSE THREE REALMS ARE ALL FIGHTING EACH OTHER!
RUBY...

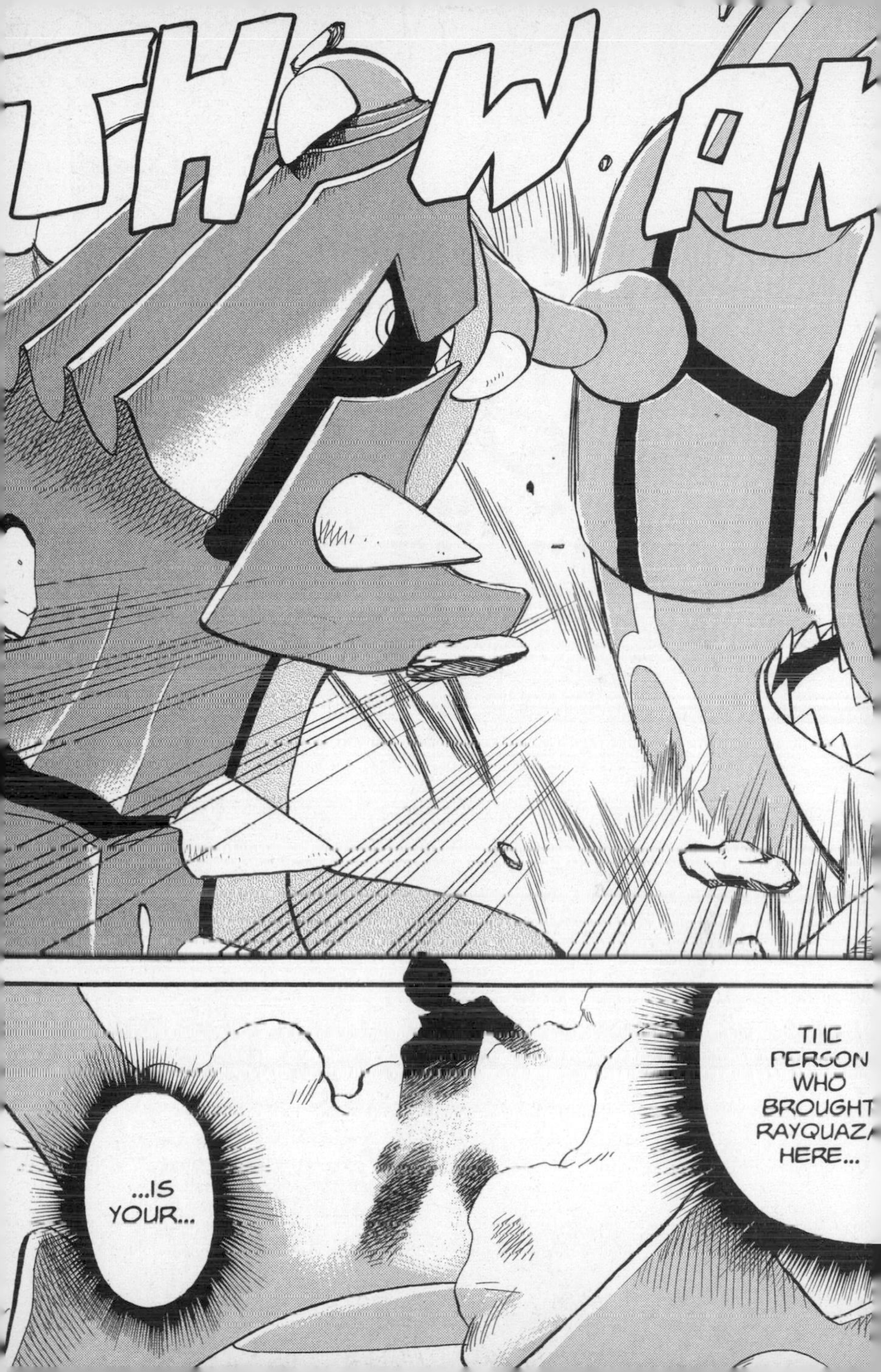
THE PERSON WHO BROUGHT RAYQUAZA HERE...
...IS YOUR...

● Chapter 262 ●

It All Ends Now III

Pokémon Adventures Ruby & Sapphire

The Fourth Chapter

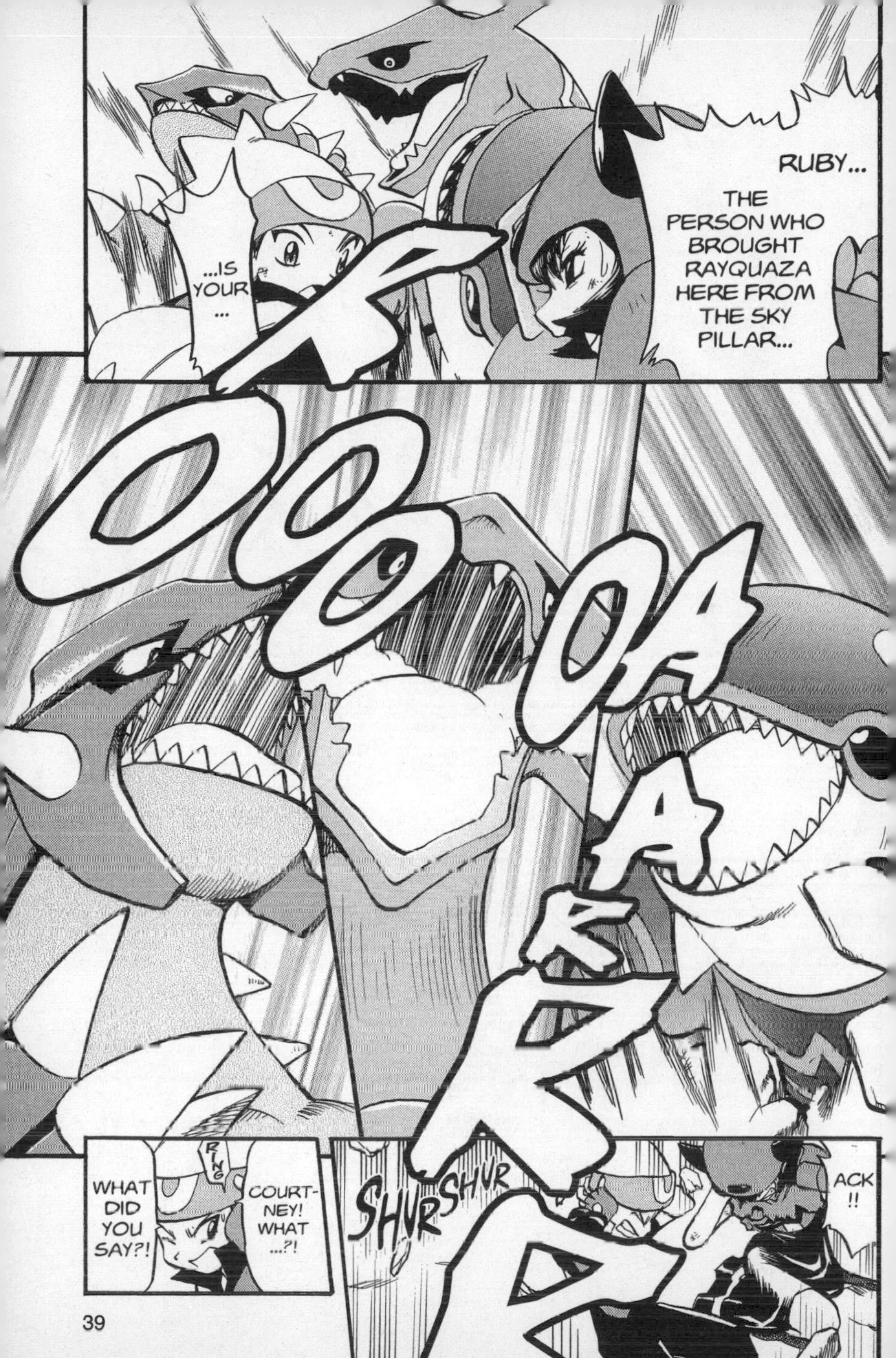
RUBY...
THE PERSON WHO BROUGHT RAYQUAZA HERE FROM THE SKY PILLAR...
...IS YOUR ...
ACK !!
SHURSHUR
RING
COURTNEY! WHAT ...?!
WHAT DID YOU SAY?!

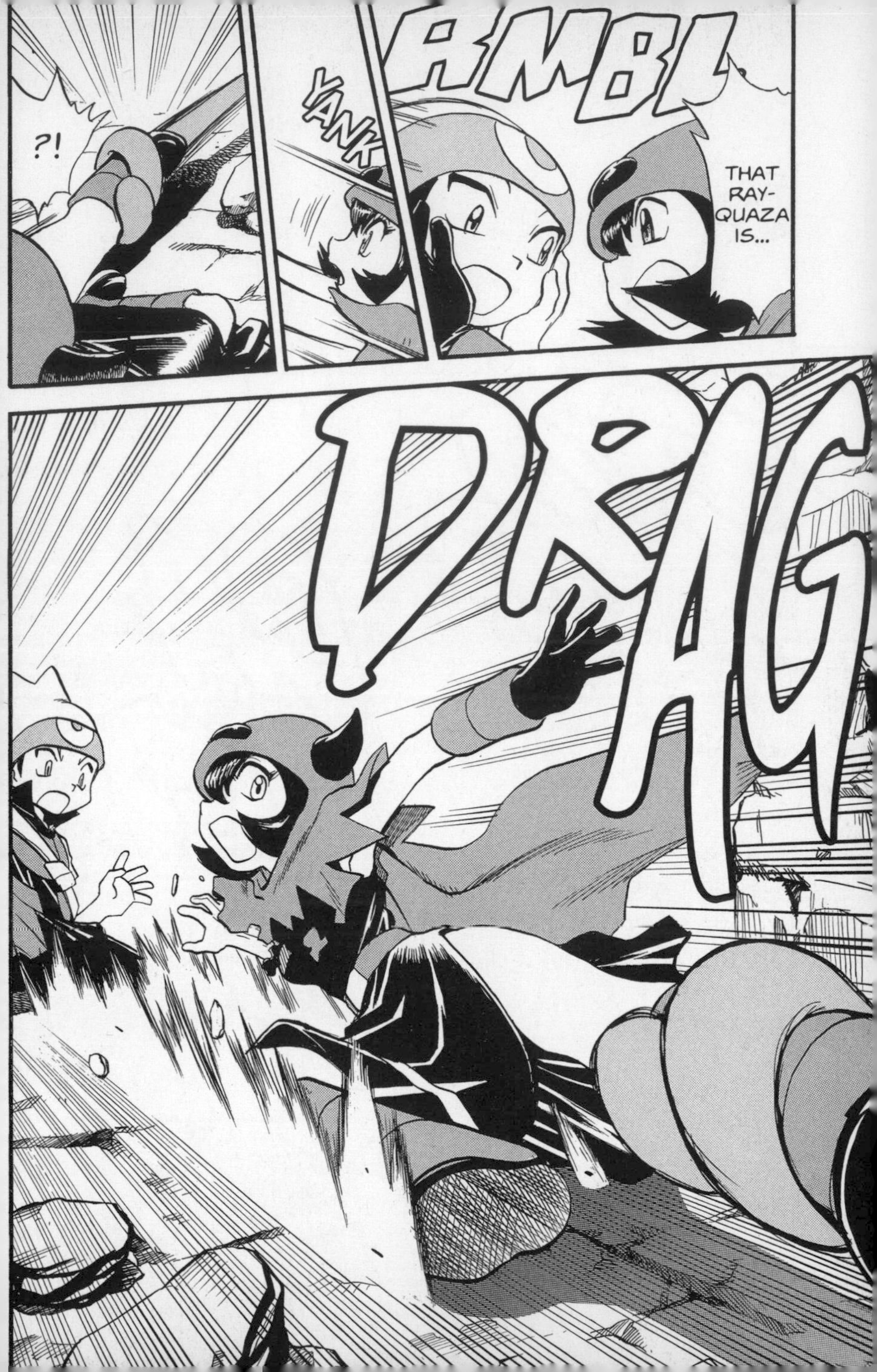
RMBL
THAT RAY-QUAZA IS...
YANK
?!
DRAG

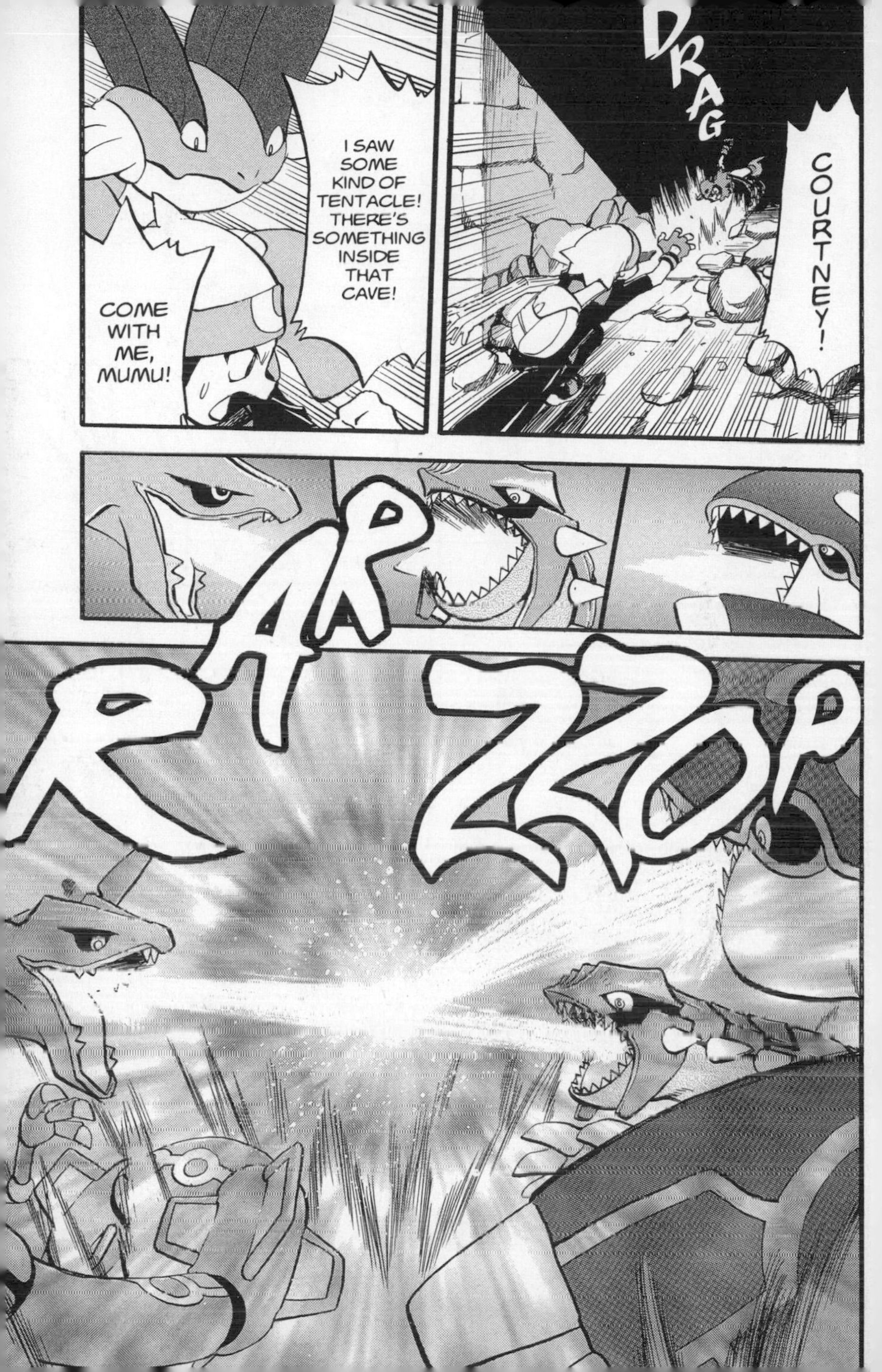
DRAG
COURTNEY!
I SAW SOME KIND OF TENTACLE! THERE'S SOMETHING INSIDE THAT CAVE!
COME WITH ME, MUMU!
RAR
ZZOP

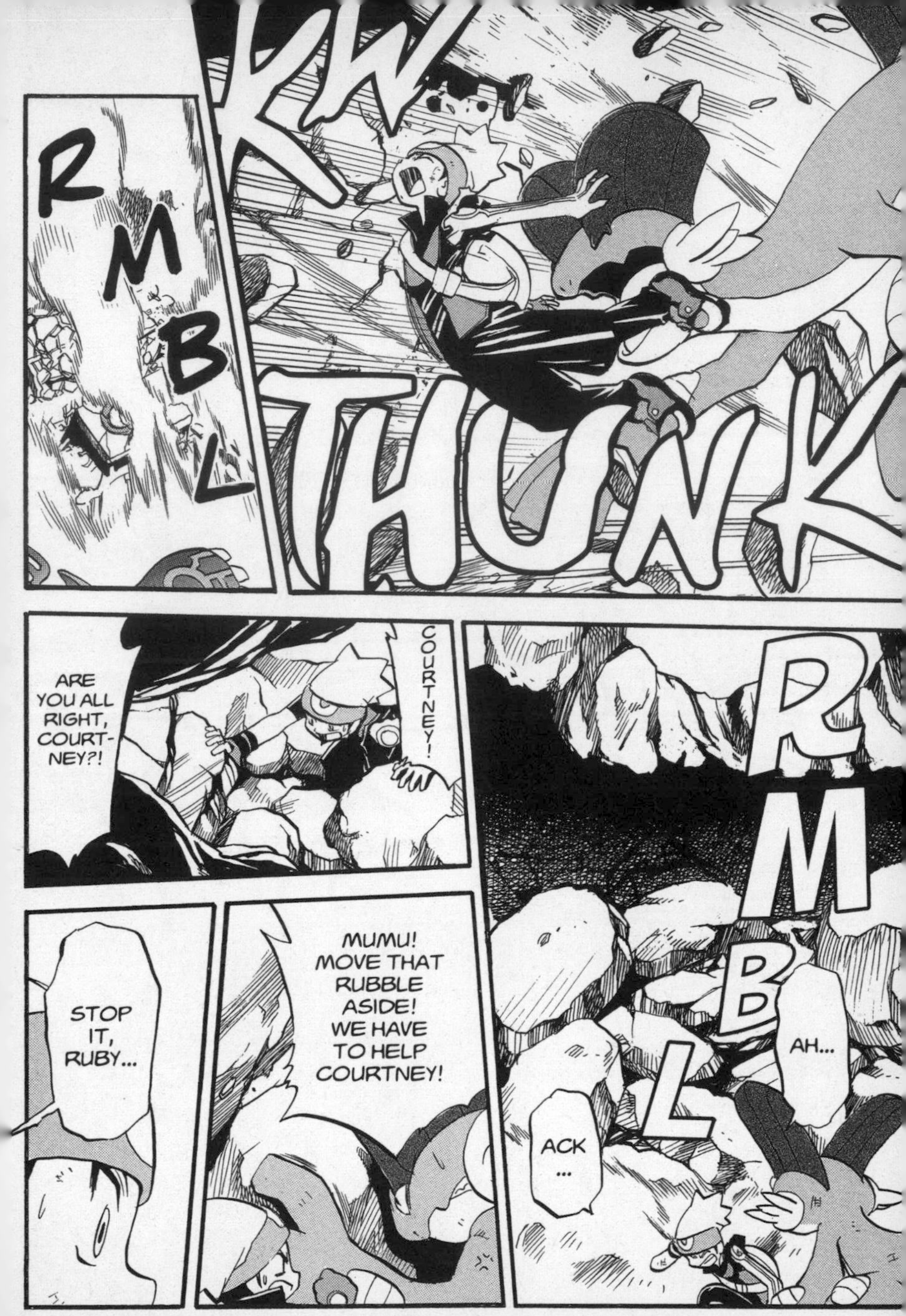
KW
THUNK
RMBL
RMBL
AH...
ACK ...
COURTNEY!
ARE YOU ALL RIGHT, COURT-NEY?!
MUMU! MOVE THAT RUBBLE ASIDE! WE HAVE TO HELP COURTNEY!
STOP IT, RUBY...

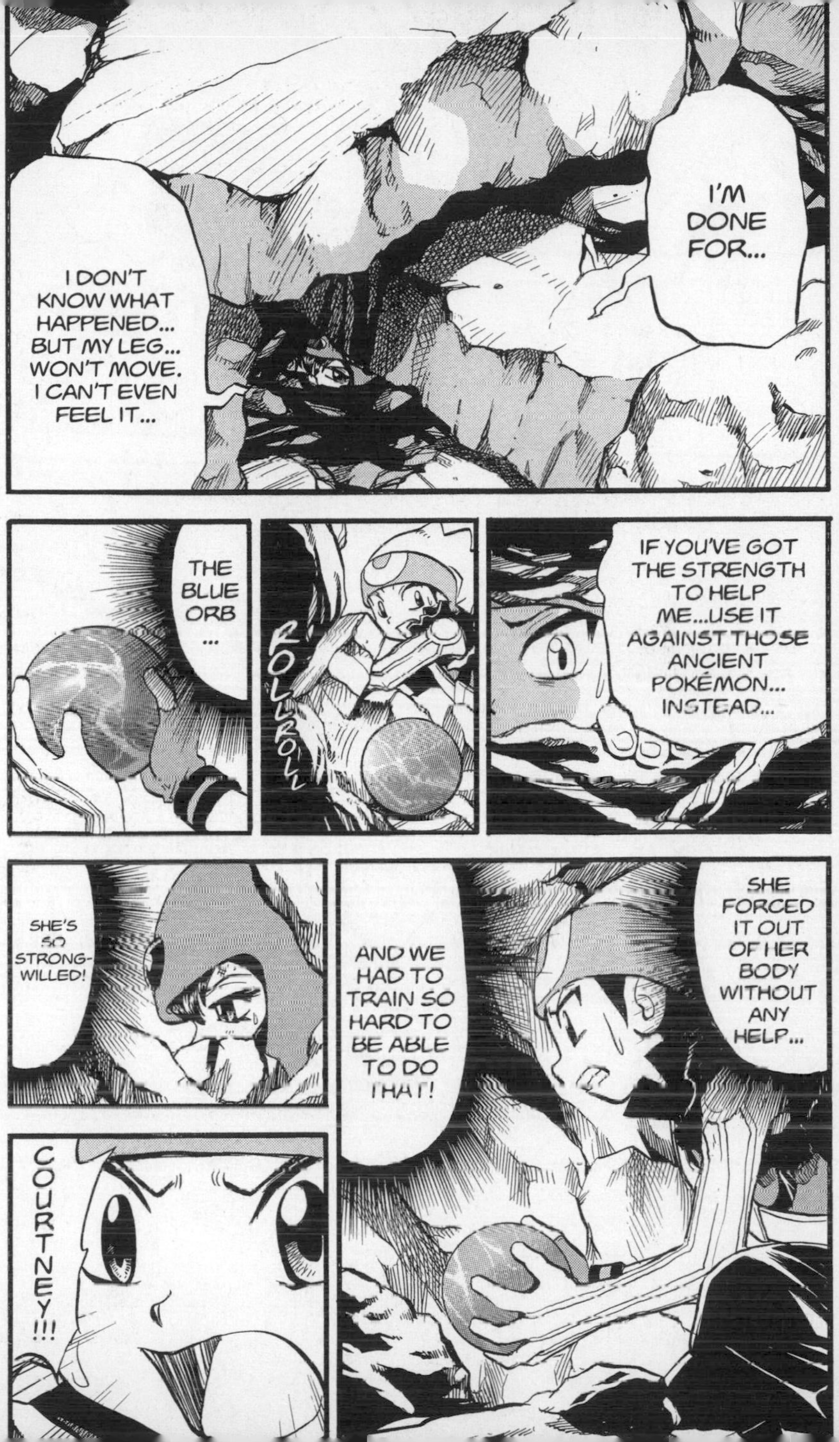
I'M DONE FOR...
I DON'T KNOW WHAT HAPPENED... BUT MY LEG... WON'T MOVE. I CAN'T EVEN FEEL IT...
IF YOU'VE GOT THE STRENGTH TO HELP ME...USE IT AGAINST THOSE ANCIENT POKÉMON... INSTEAD...
ROLL ROLL
THE BLUE ORB ...
SHE FORCED IT OUT OF HER BODY WITHOUT ANY HELP...
AND WE HAD TO TRAIN SO HARD TO BE ABLE TO DO THAT!
SHE'S SO STRONG-WILLED!
COURTNEY!!!

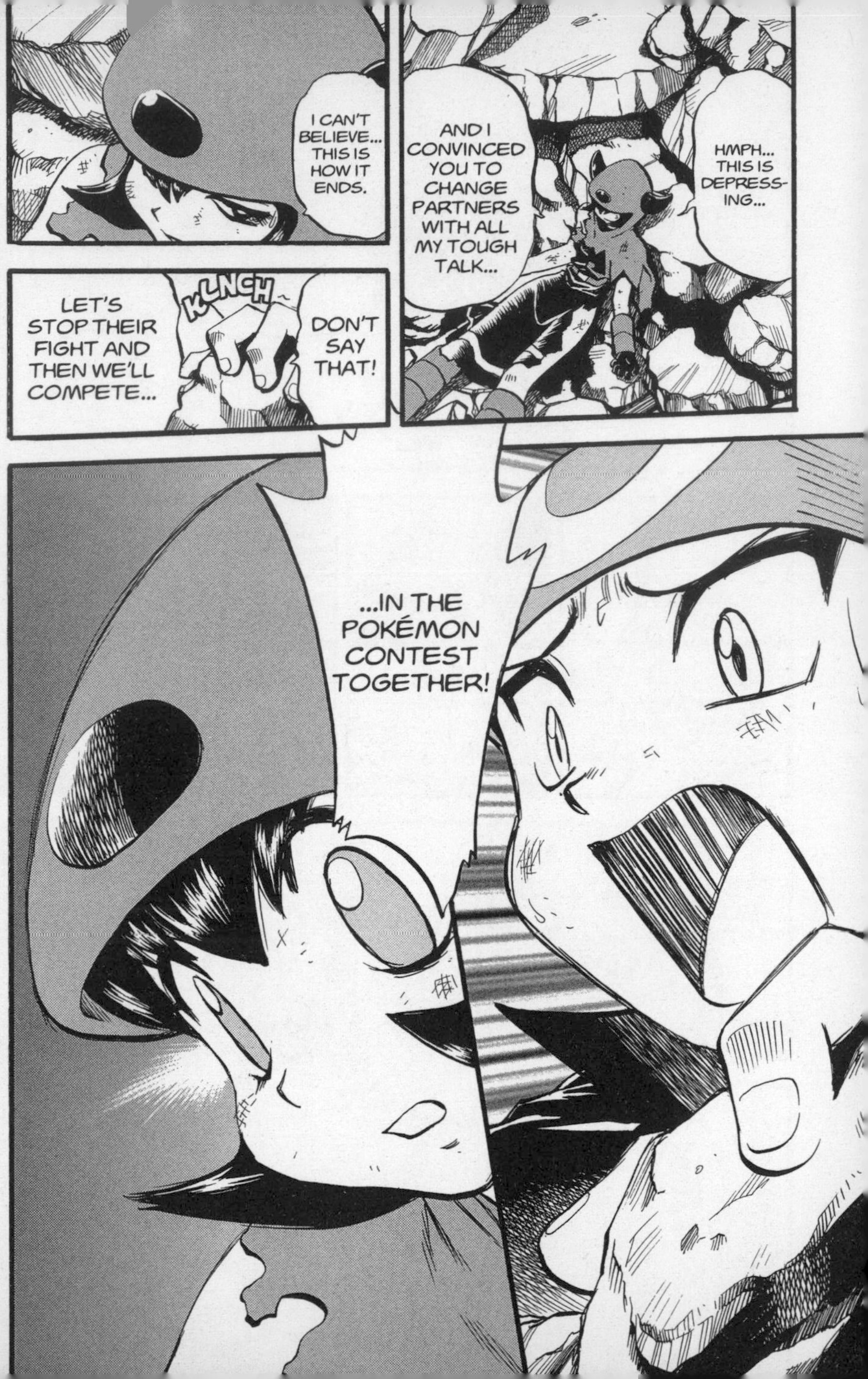
HMPH... THIS IS DEPRESS-ING...
AND I CONVINCED YOU TO CHANGE PARTNERS WITH ALL MY TOUGH TALK...
I CAN'T BELIEVE... THIS IS HOW IT ENDS.
DON'T SAY THAT!
KLNCH
LET'S STOP THEIR FIGHT AND THEN WE'LL COMPETE...
...IN THE POKÉMON CONTEST TOGETHER!

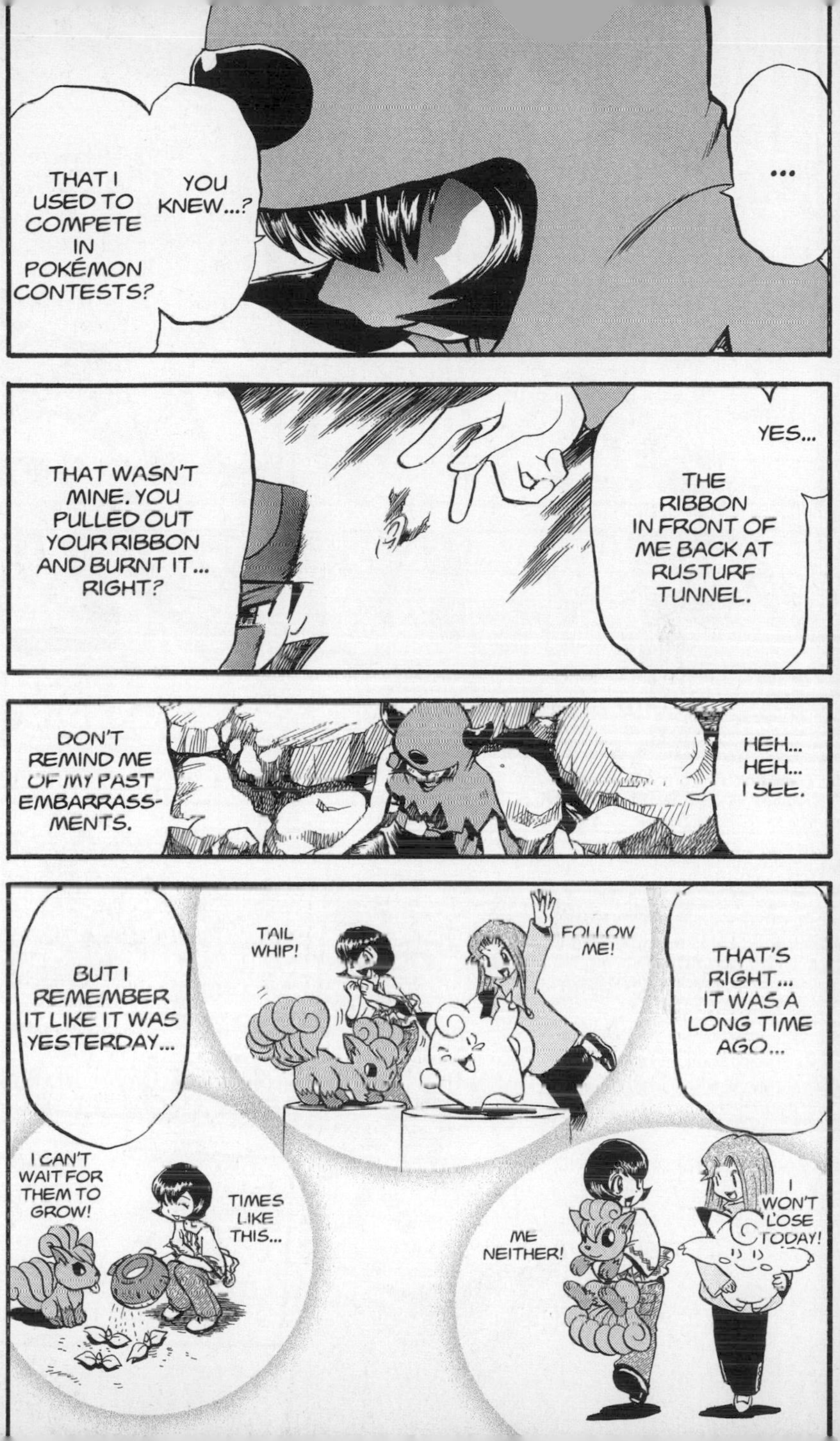
...
YOU KNEW...? THAT I USED TO COMPETE IN POKÉMON CONTESTS?
YES... THE RIBBON IN FRONT OF ME BACK AT RUSTURF TUNNEL.
THAT WASN'T MINE. YOU PULLED OUT YOUR RIBBON AND BURNT IT... RIGHT?
HEH... HEH... I SEE.
DON'T REMIND ME OF MY PAST EMBARRASS-MENTS.
THAT'S RIGHT... IT WAS A LONG TIME AGO...
BUT I REMEMBER IT LIKE IT WAS YESTERDAY...
FOLLOW ME!
TAIL WHIP!
I WON'T LOSE TODAY!
ME NEITHER!
TIMES LIKE THIS...
I CAN'T WAIT FOR THEM TO GROW!

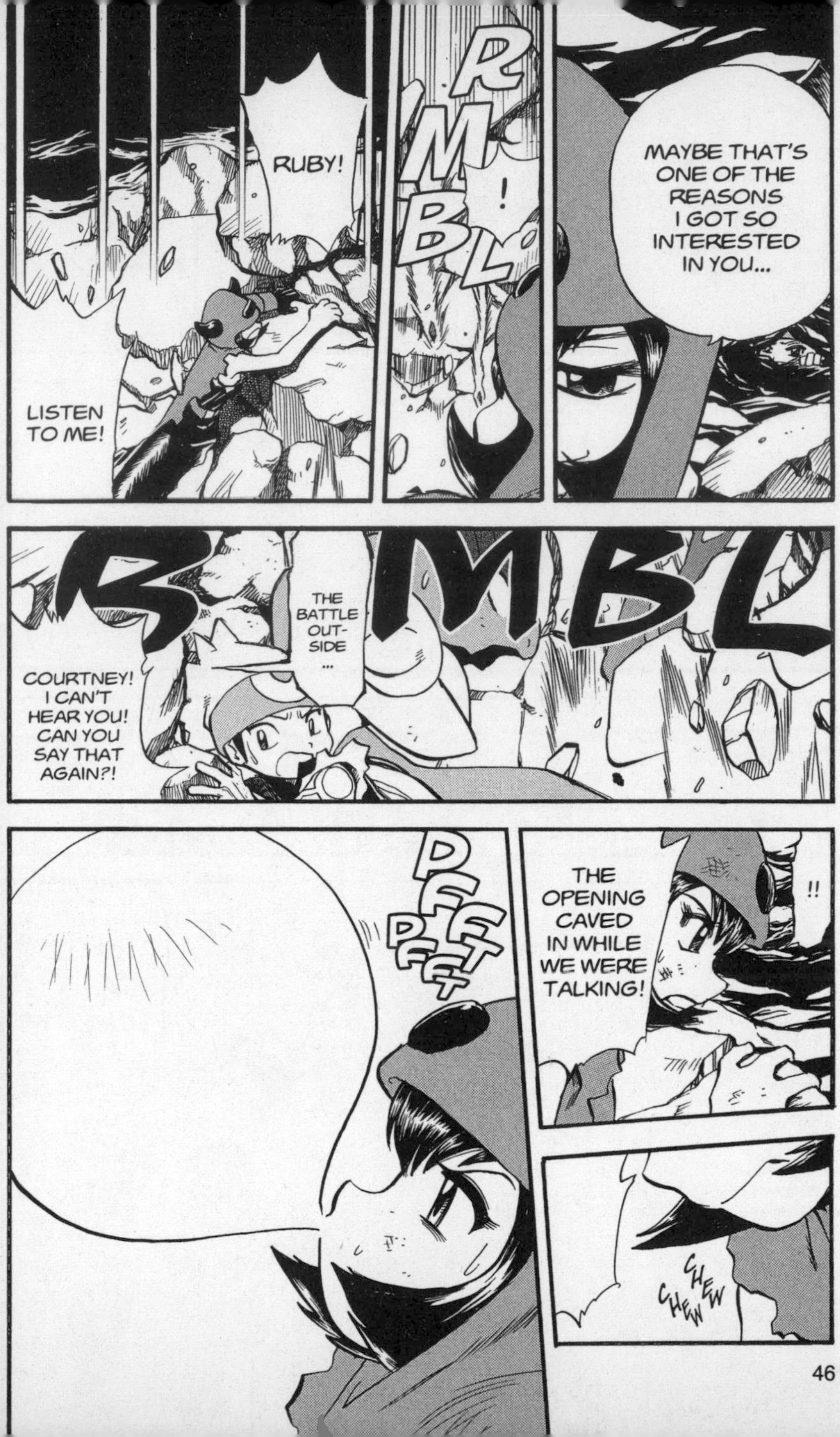
MAYBE THAT'S ONE OF THE REASONS I GOT SO INTERESTED IN YOU...
RMMBL
!
RUBY!
LISTEN TO ME!
RMBL
THE BATTLE OUT-SIDE ...
COURTNEY! I CAN'T HEAR YOU! CAN YOU SAY THAT AGAIN?!
!!
THE OPENING CAVED IN WHILE WE WERE TALKING!
CHEW CHEW
PFFT PFFT

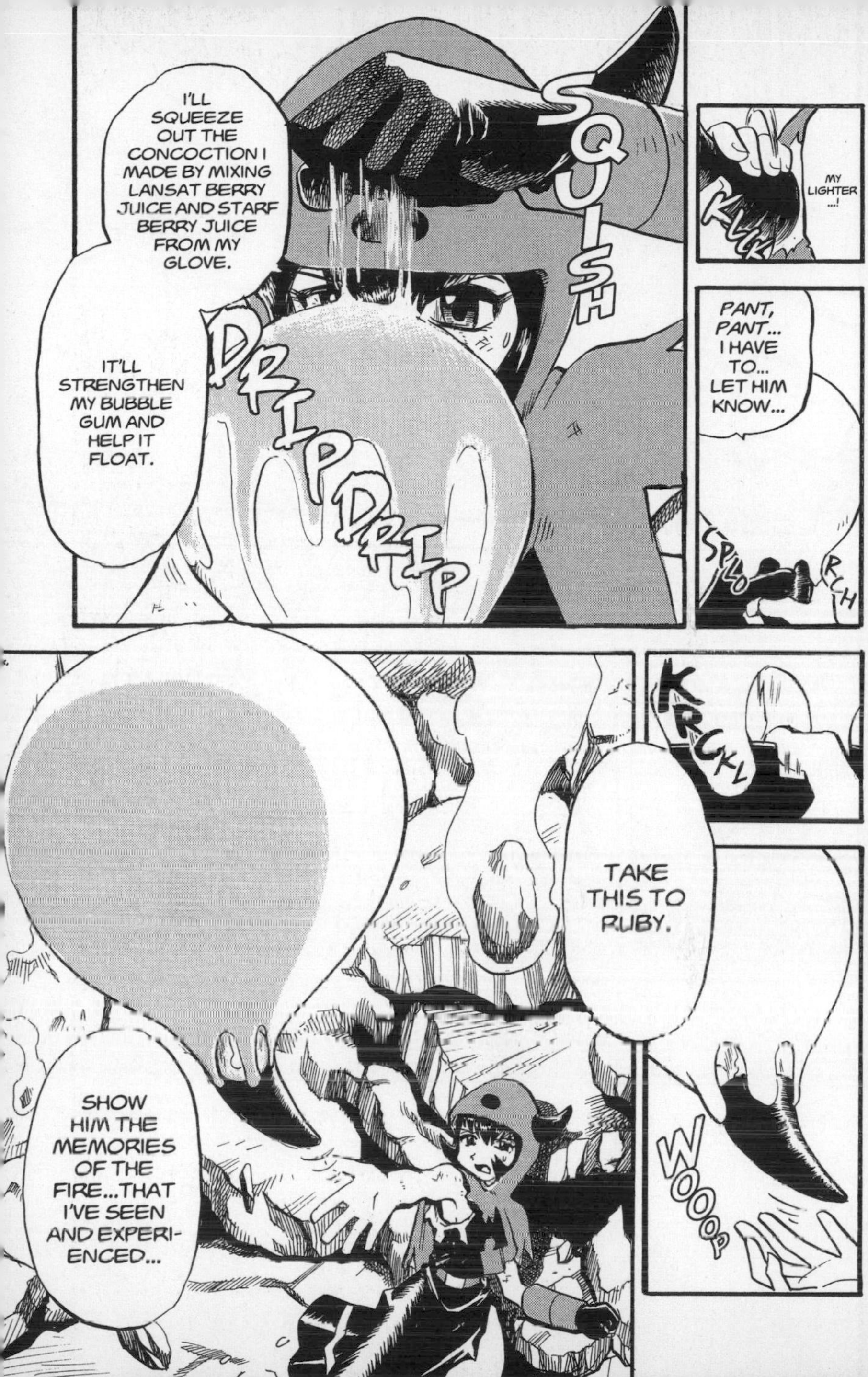
MY LIGHTER ...!
KLICK
PANT, PANT... I HAVE TO... LET HIM KNOW...
SPLORCH
I'LL SQUEEZE OUT THE CONCOCTION I MADE BY MIXING LANSAT BERRY JUICE AND STARF BERRY JUICE FROM MY GLOVE.
SQUISH
IT'LL STRENGTHEN MY BUBBLE GUM AND HELP IT FLOAT.
DRIP DRIP
KRCKL
TAKE THIS TO RUBY.
WOOOP
SHOW HIM THE MEMORIES OF THE FIRE...THAT I'VE SEEN AND EXPERI-ENCED...

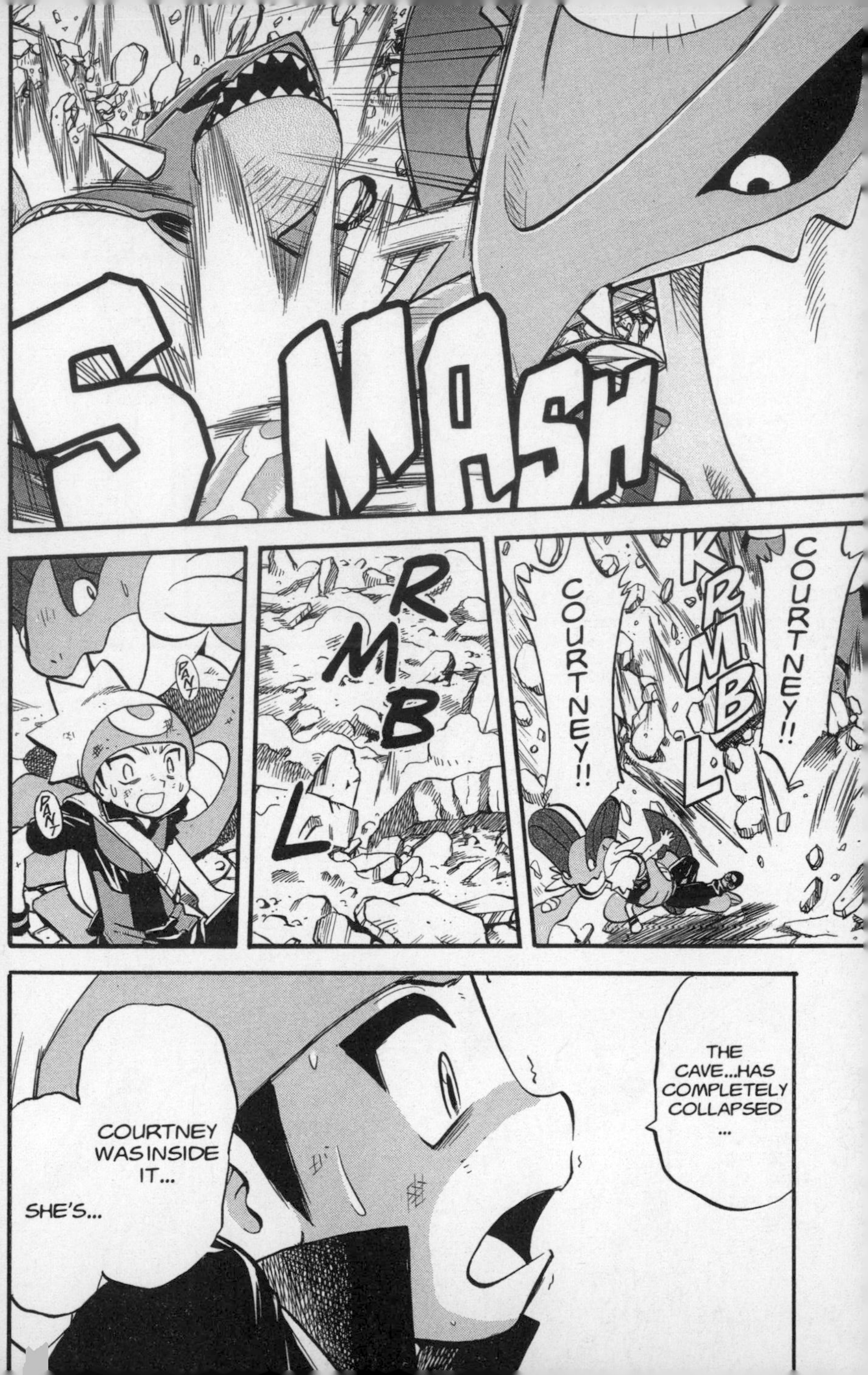
SMASH
COURTNEY!!
KRMBL
COURTNEY!!
RMBL
PANT
PANT
THE CAVE...HAS COMPLETELY COLLAPSED ...
COURTNEY WAS INSIDE IT...
SHE'S...

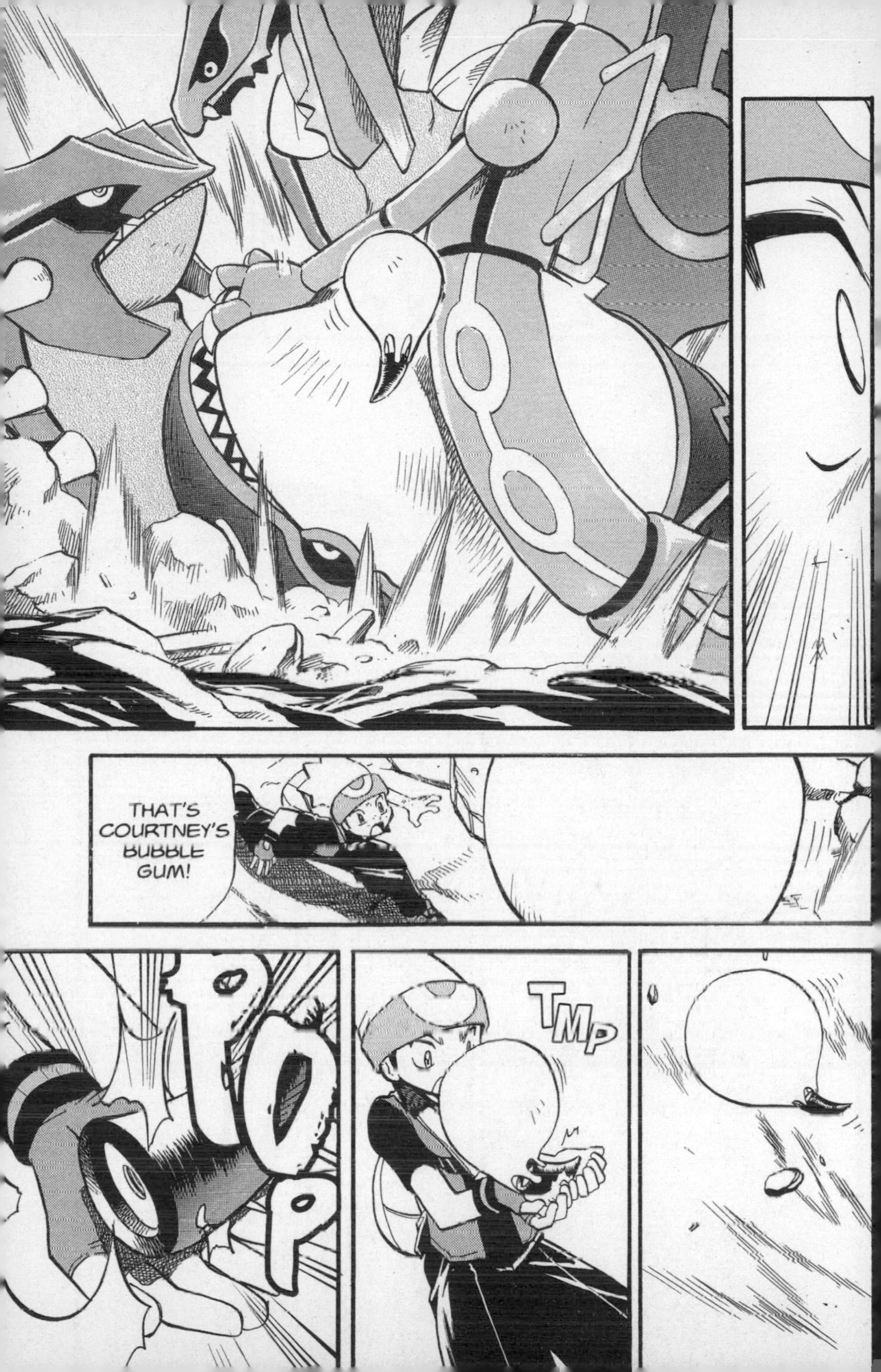
THAT'S COURTNEY'S BUBBLE GUM!
TMP

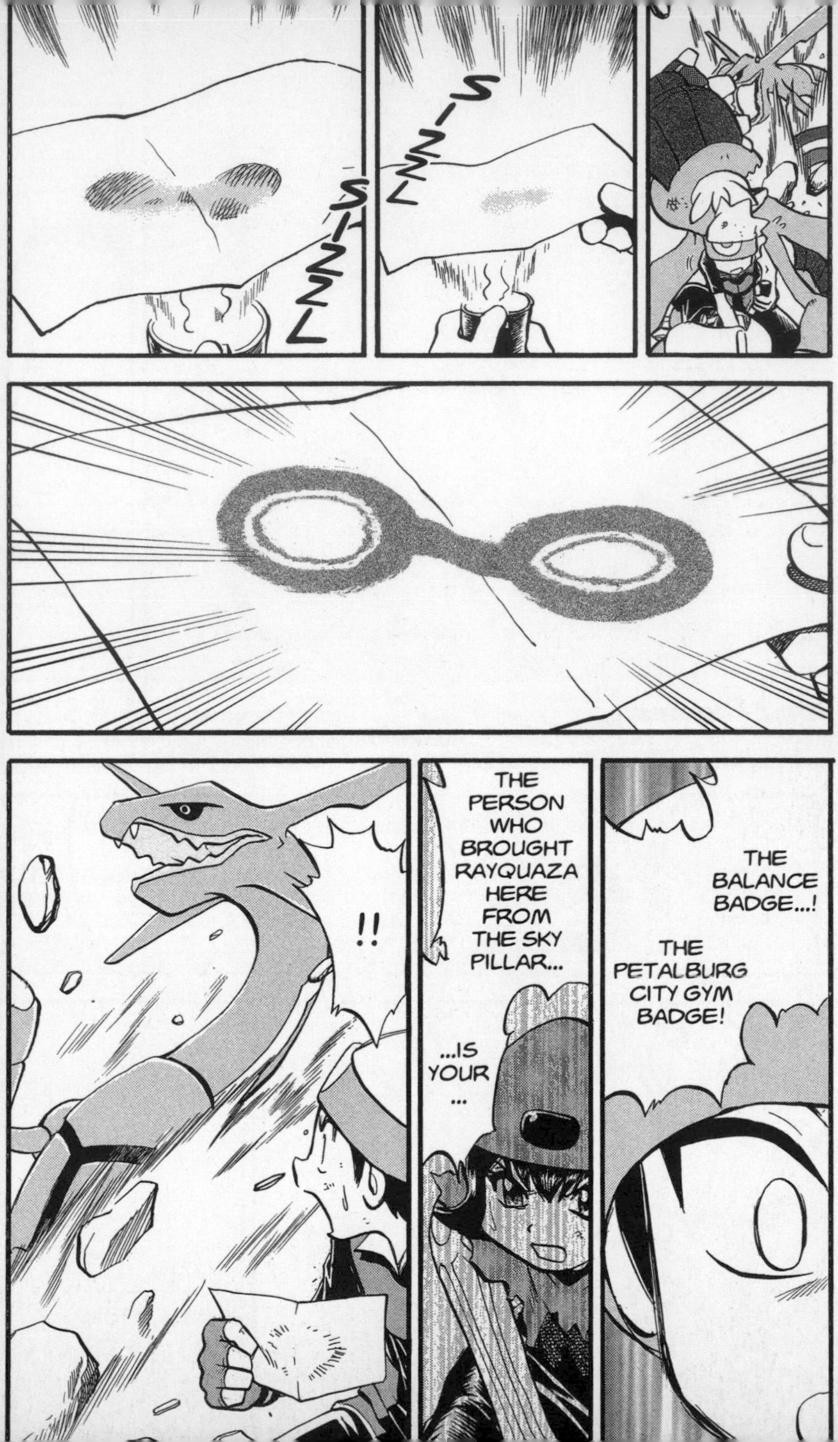
SIZZL
SIZZL
THE BALANCE BADGE...!
THE PETALBURG CITY GYM BADGE!
THE PERSON WHO BROUGHT RAYQUAZA HERE FROM THE SKY PILLAR...
...IS YOUR ...
!!

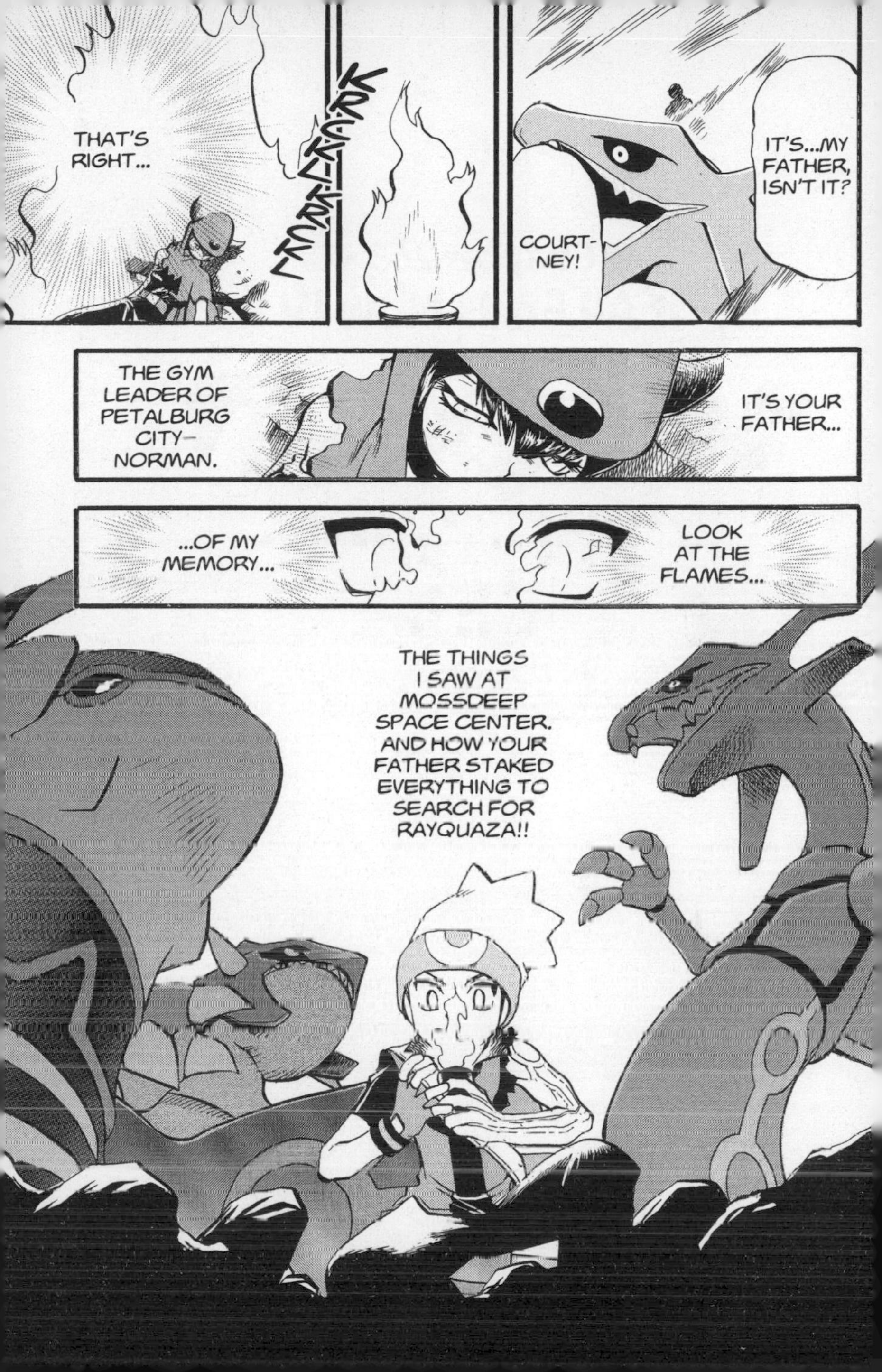
IT'S...MY FATHER, ISN'T IT?
COURT-NEY!
KRCKLKRCKL
THAT'S RIGHT...
IT'S YOUR FATHER...
THE GYM LEADER OF PETALBURG CITY—NORMAN.
LOOK AT THE FLAMES...
...OF MY MEMORY...
THE THINGS I SAW AT MOSSDEEP SPACE CENTER. AND HOW YOUR FATHER STAKED EVERYTHING TO SEARCH FOR RAYQUAZA!!

● Chapter 263 ●

It All Ends Now IV

Pokémon™ Adventures Ruby & Sapphire

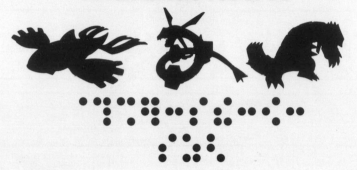

The Fourth Chapter

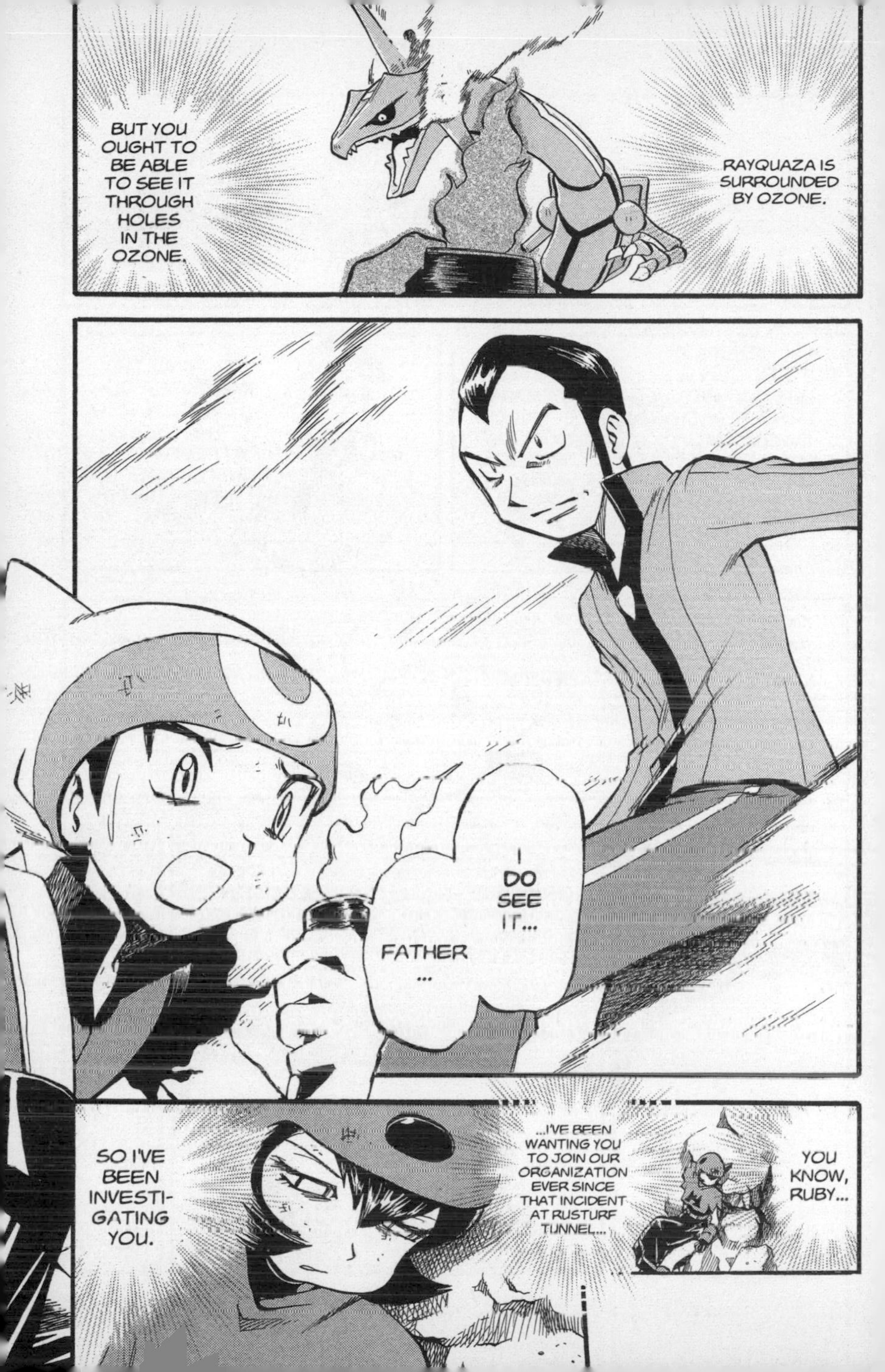
RAYQUAZA IS SURROUNDED BY OZONE.
BUT YOU OUGHT TO BE ABLE TO SEE IT THROUGH HOLES IN THE OZONE.
I DO SEE IT...
FATHER ...
YOU KNOW, RUBY...
...I'VE BEEN WANTING YOU TO JOIN OUR ORGANIZATION EVER SINCE THAT INCIDENT AT RUSTURF TUNNEL...
SO I'VE BEEN INVESTI-GATING YOU.

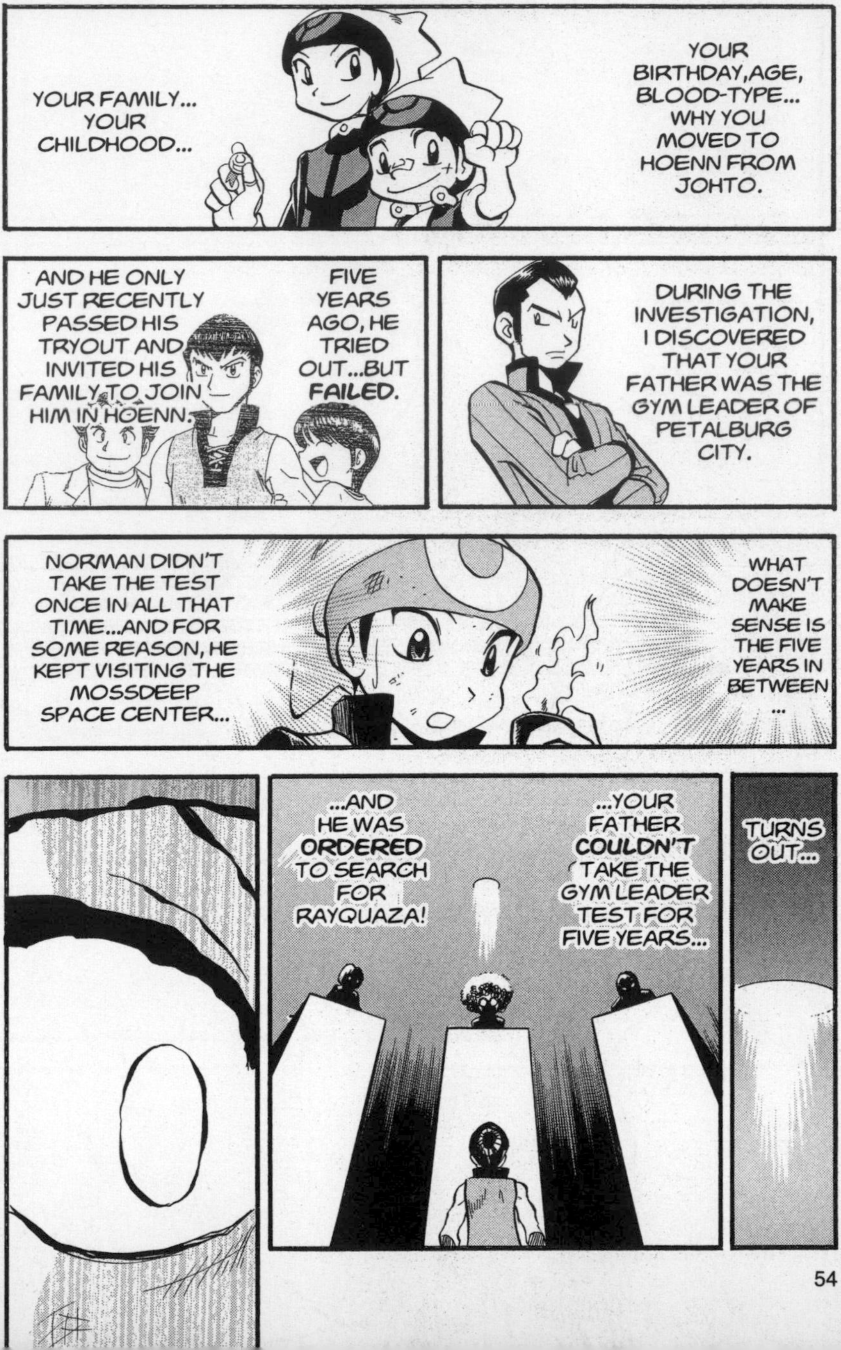
YOUR BIRTHDAY, AGE, BLOOD-TYPE... WHY YOU MOVED TO HOENN FROM JOHTO.
YOUR FAMILY... YOUR CHILDHOOD...
DURING THE INVESTIGATION, I DISCOVERED THAT YOUR FATHER WAS THE GYM LEADER OF PETALBURG CITY.
FIVE YEARS AGO, HE TRIED OUT...BUT FAILED.
AND HE ONLY JUST RECENTLY PASSED HIS TRYOUT AND INVITED HIS FAMILY TO JOIN HIM IN HOENN.
WHAT DOESN'T MAKE SENSE IS THE FIVE YEARS IN BETWEEN...
NORMAN DIDN'T TAKE THE TEST ONCE IN ALL THAT TIME...AND FOR SOME REASON, HE KEPT VISITING THE MOSSDEEP SPACE CENTER...
TURNS OUT...
...YOUR FATHER COULDN'T TAKE THE GYM LEADER TEST FOR FIVE YEARS...
...AND HE WAS ORDERED TO SEARCH FOR RAYQUAZA!

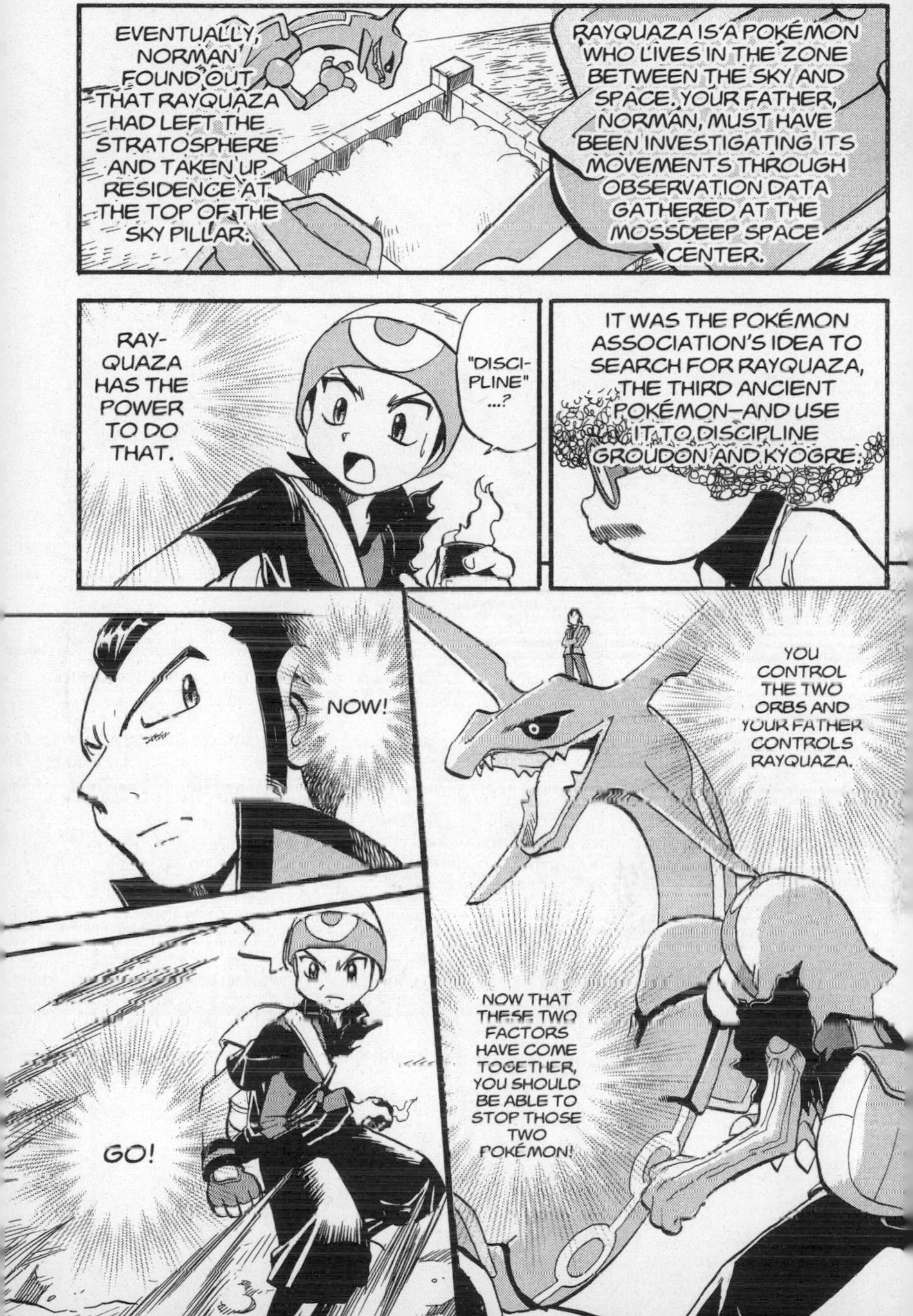
RAYQUAZA IS A POKÉMON WHO LIVES IN THE ZONE BETWEEN THE SKY AND SPACE. YOUR FATHER, NORMAN, MUST HAVE BEEN INVESTIGATING ITS MOVEMENTS THROUGH OBSERVATION DATA GATHERED AT THE MOSSDEEP SPACE CENTER.
EVENTUALLY, NORMAN FOUND OUT THAT RAYQUAZA HAD LEFT THE STRATOSPHERE AND TAKEN UP RESIDENCE AT THE TOP OF THE SKY PILLAR.
IT WAS THE POKÉMON ASSOCIATION'S IDEA TO SEARCH FOR RAYQUAZA, THE THIRD ANCIENT POKÉMON—AND USE IT TO DISCIPLINE GROUDON AND KYOGRE.
"DISCIPLINE" ...?
RAYQUAZA HAS THE POWER TO DO THAT.
YOU CONTROL THE TWO ORBS AND YOUR FATHER CONTROLS RAYQUAZA.
NOW THAT THESE TWO FACTORS HAVE COME TOGETHER, YOU SHOULD BE ABLE TO STOP THOSE TWO POKÉMON!
NOW!
GO!

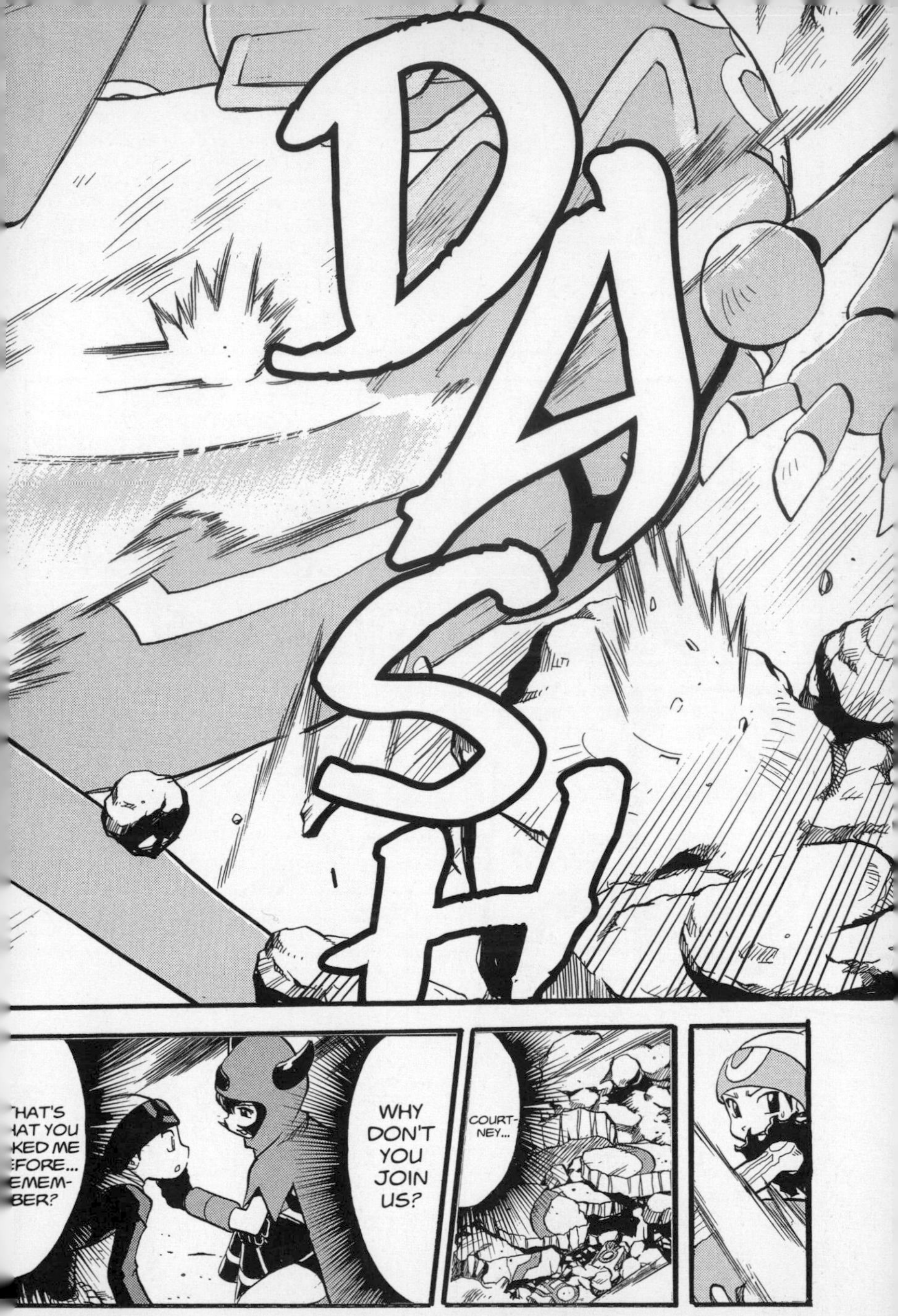
DASH
COURT-NEY...
WHY DON'T YOU JOIN US?
THAT'S HAT YOU KED ME EFORE... EMEM-BER?

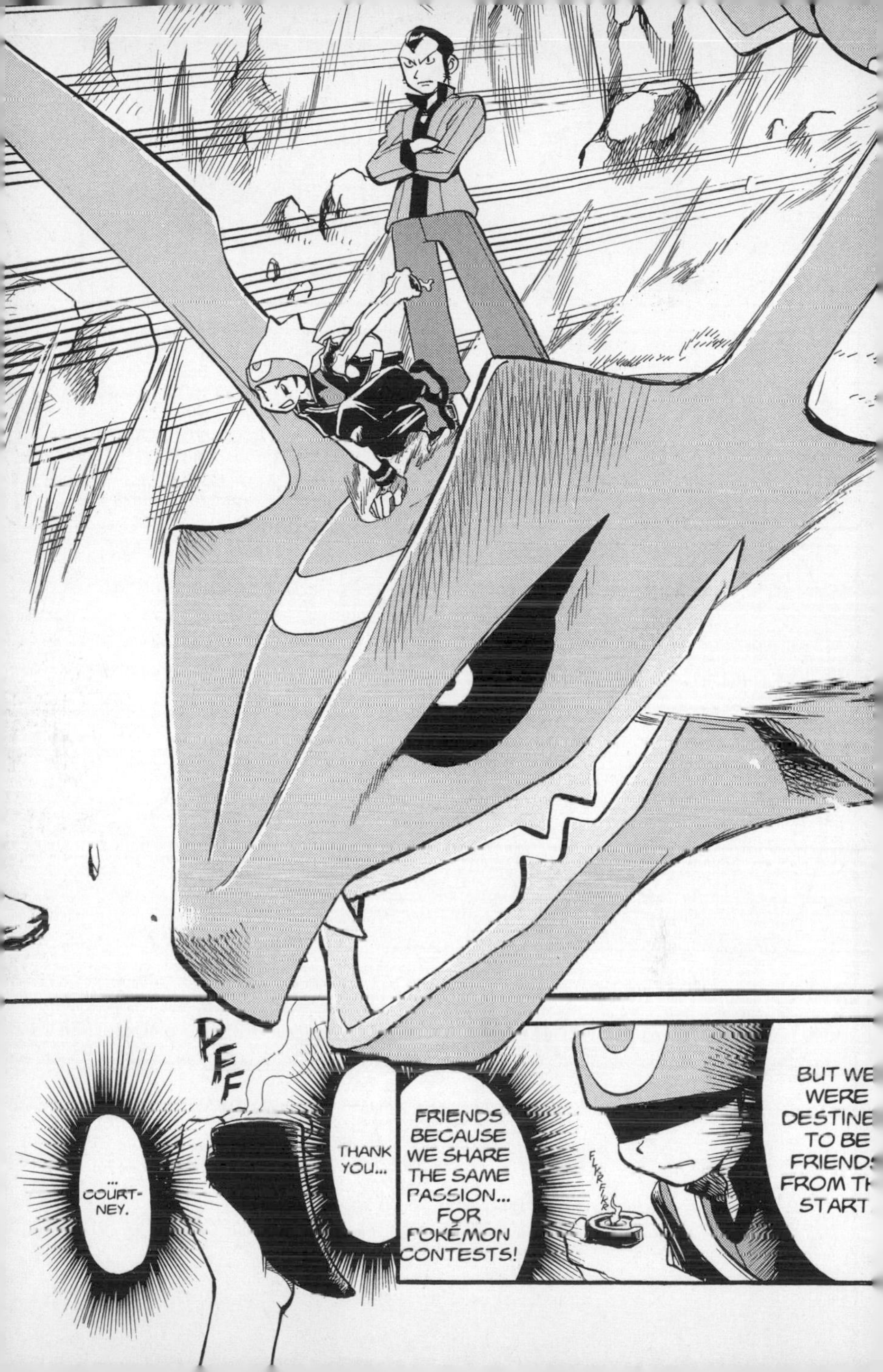
BUT WE WERE DESTINE TO BE FRIENDS FROM TH START
FRIENDS BECAUSE WE SHARE THE SAME PASSION... FOR POKÉMON CONTESTS!
THANK YOU...
PFF
... COURTNEY.

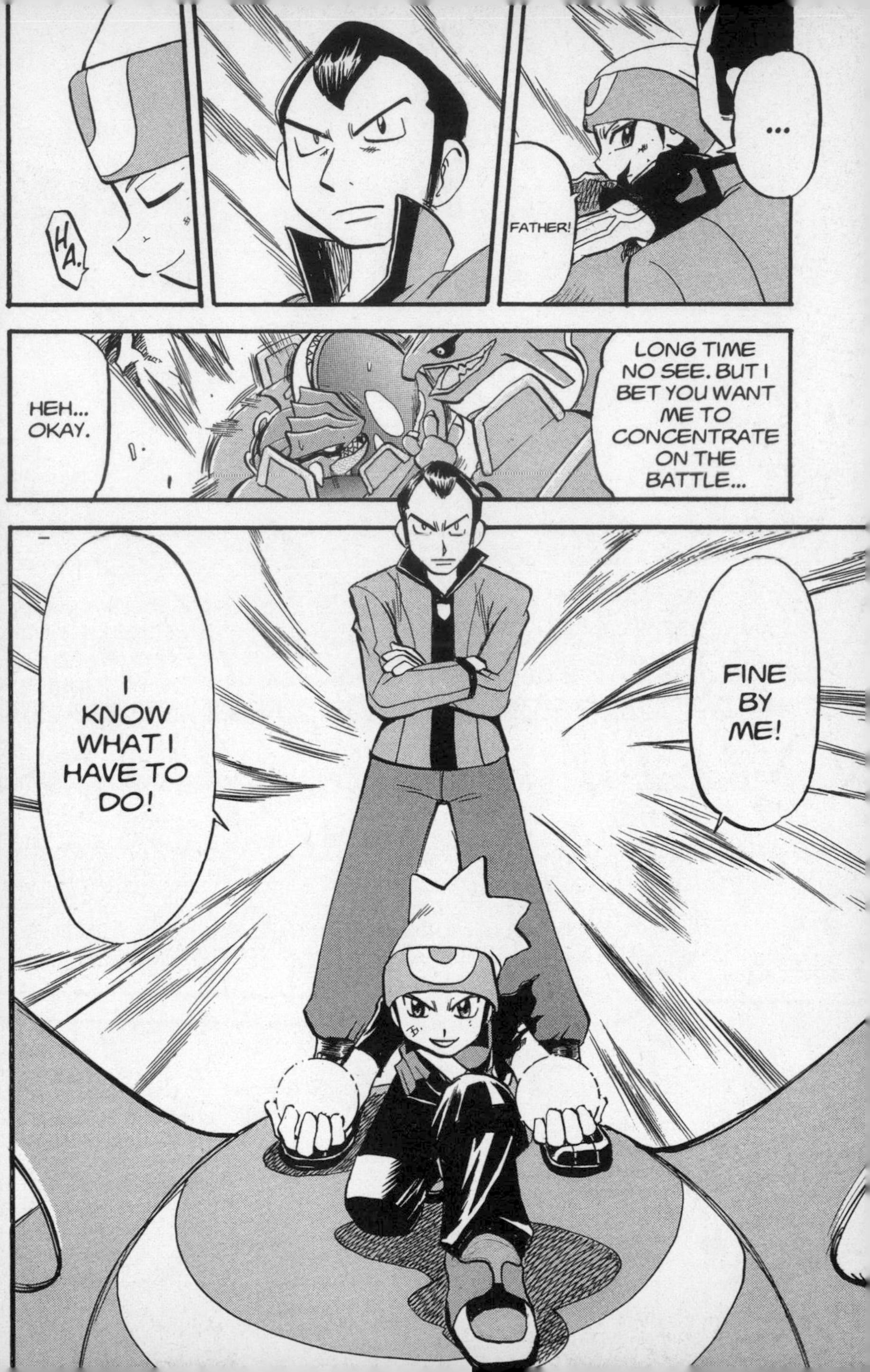
...
FATHER!
HA.
LONG TIME NO SEE. BUT I BET YOU WANT ME TO CONCENTRATE ON THE BATTLE...
HEH... OKAY.
FINE BY ME!
I KNOW WHAT I HAVE TO DO!

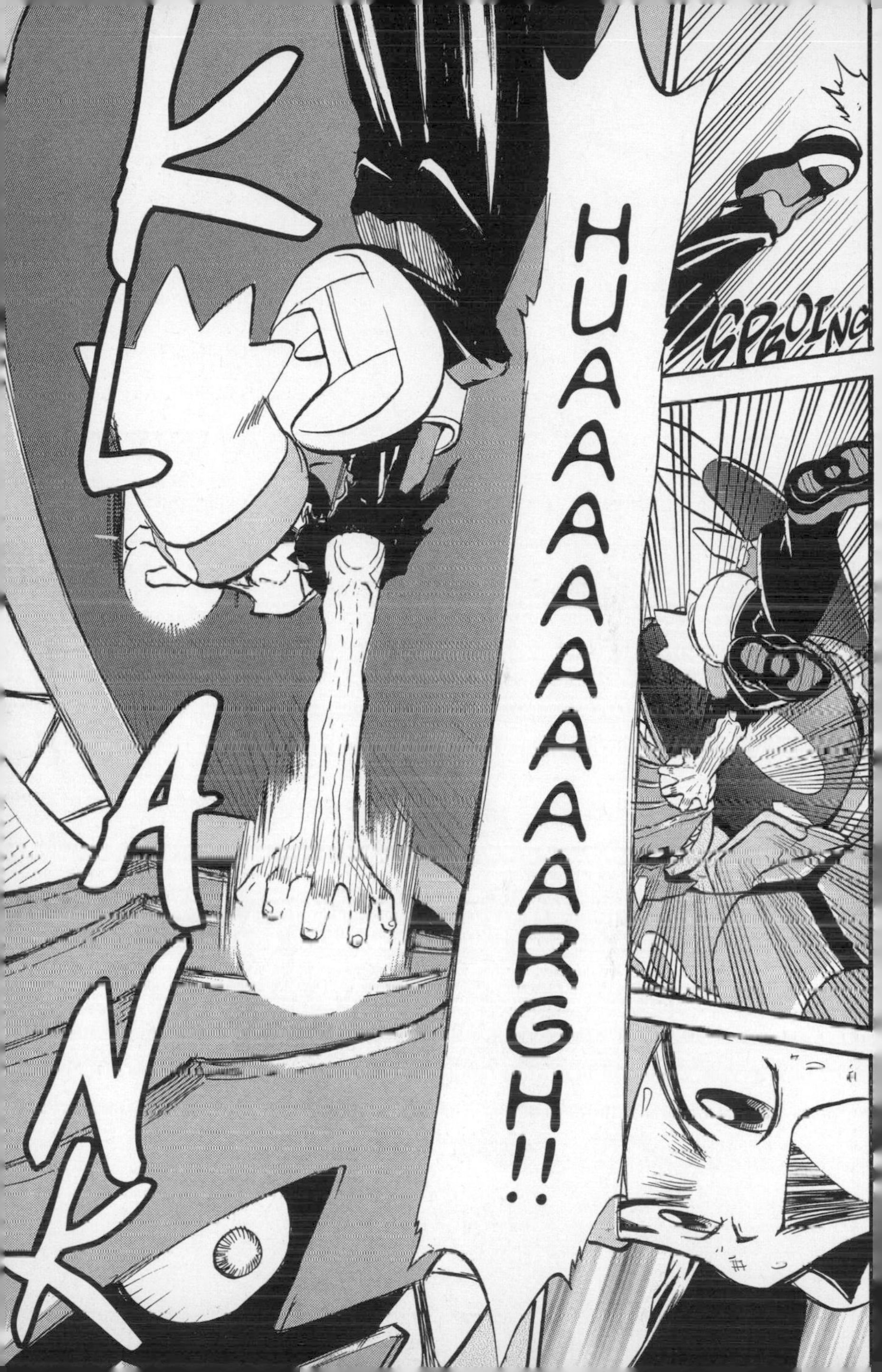
SPROING
HUAAAAAAAARGH!!
KLANK

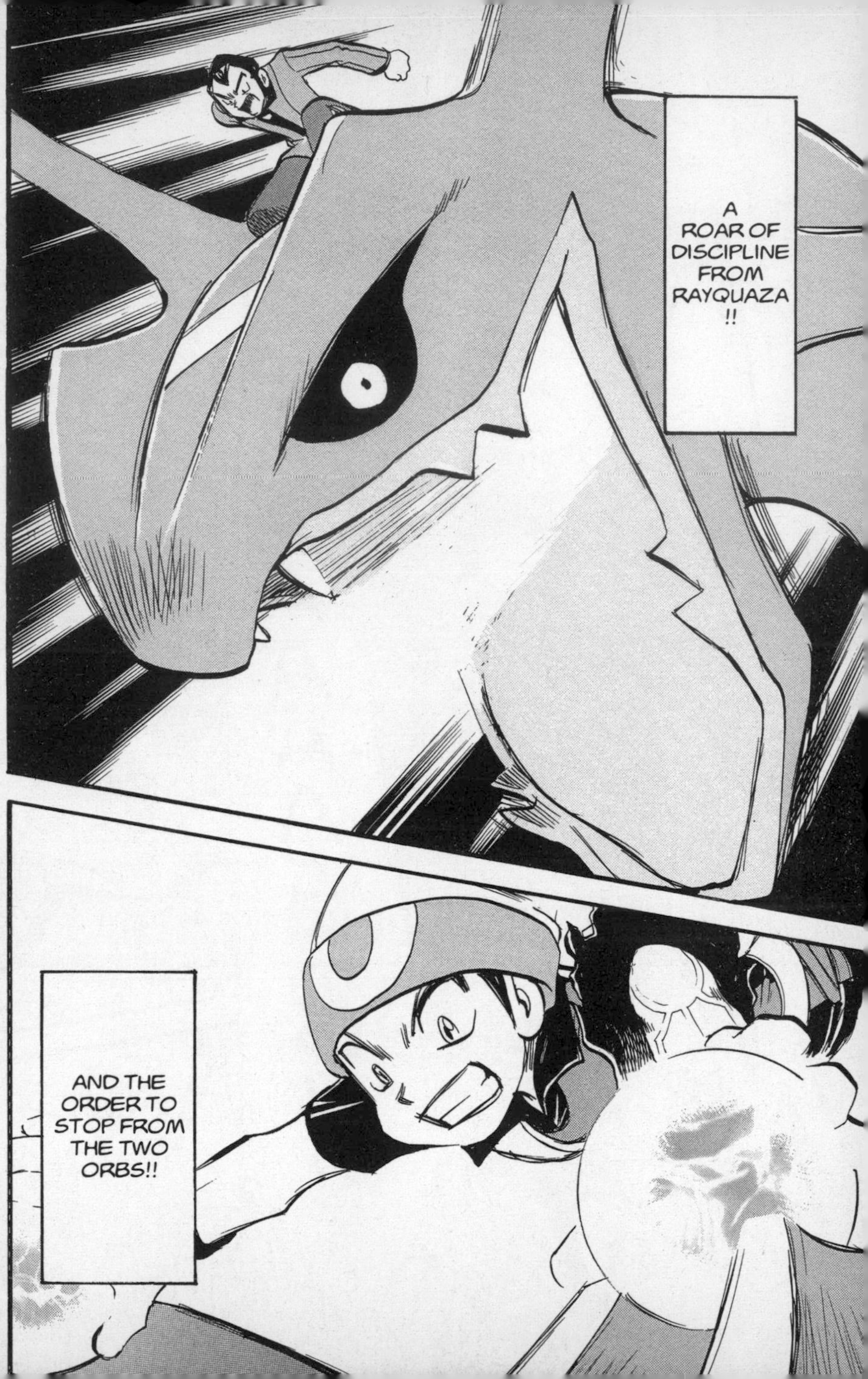
A ROAR OF DISCIPLINE FROM RAYQUAZA !!
AND THE ORDER TO STOP FROM THE TWO ORBS!!

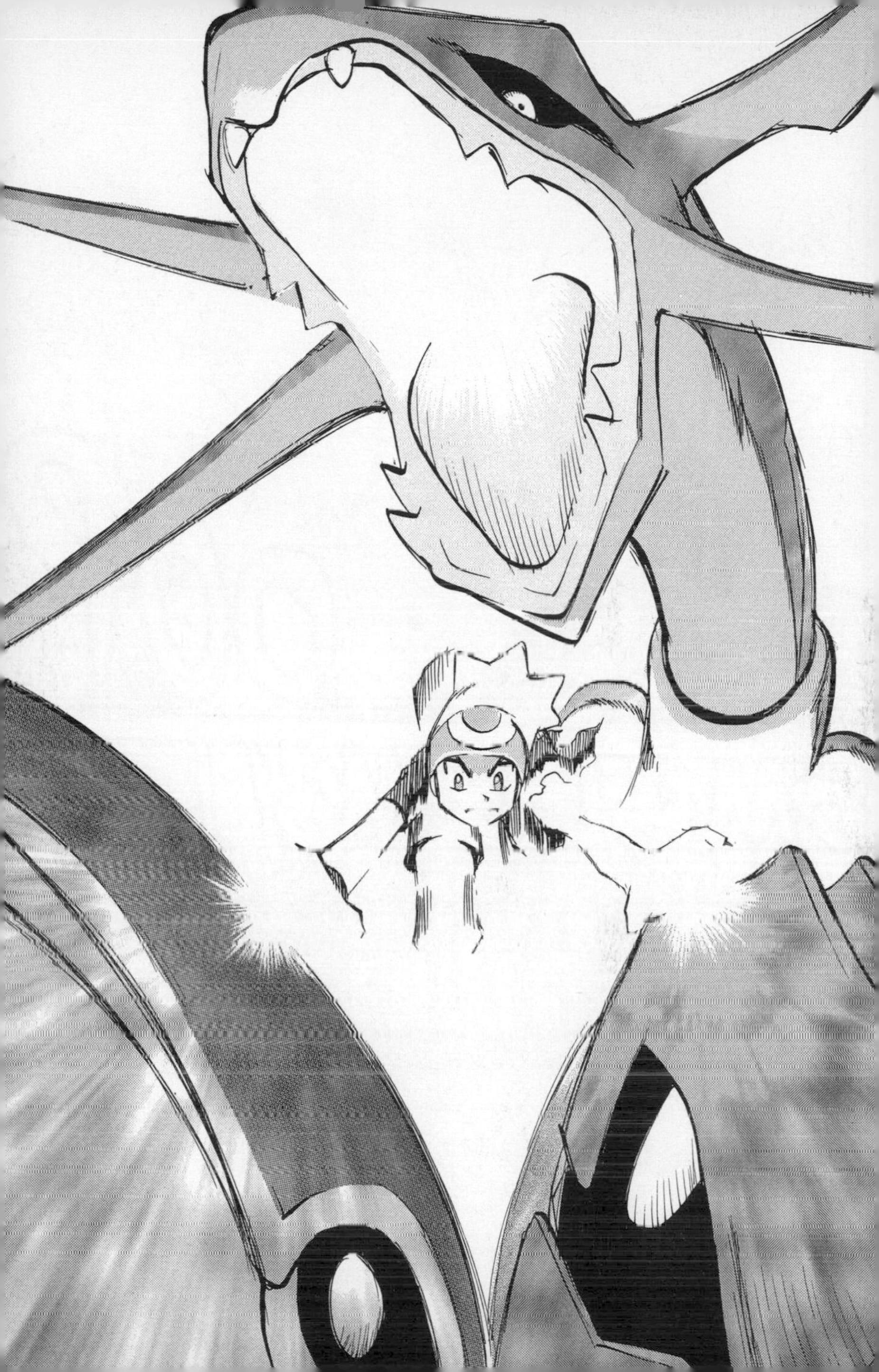

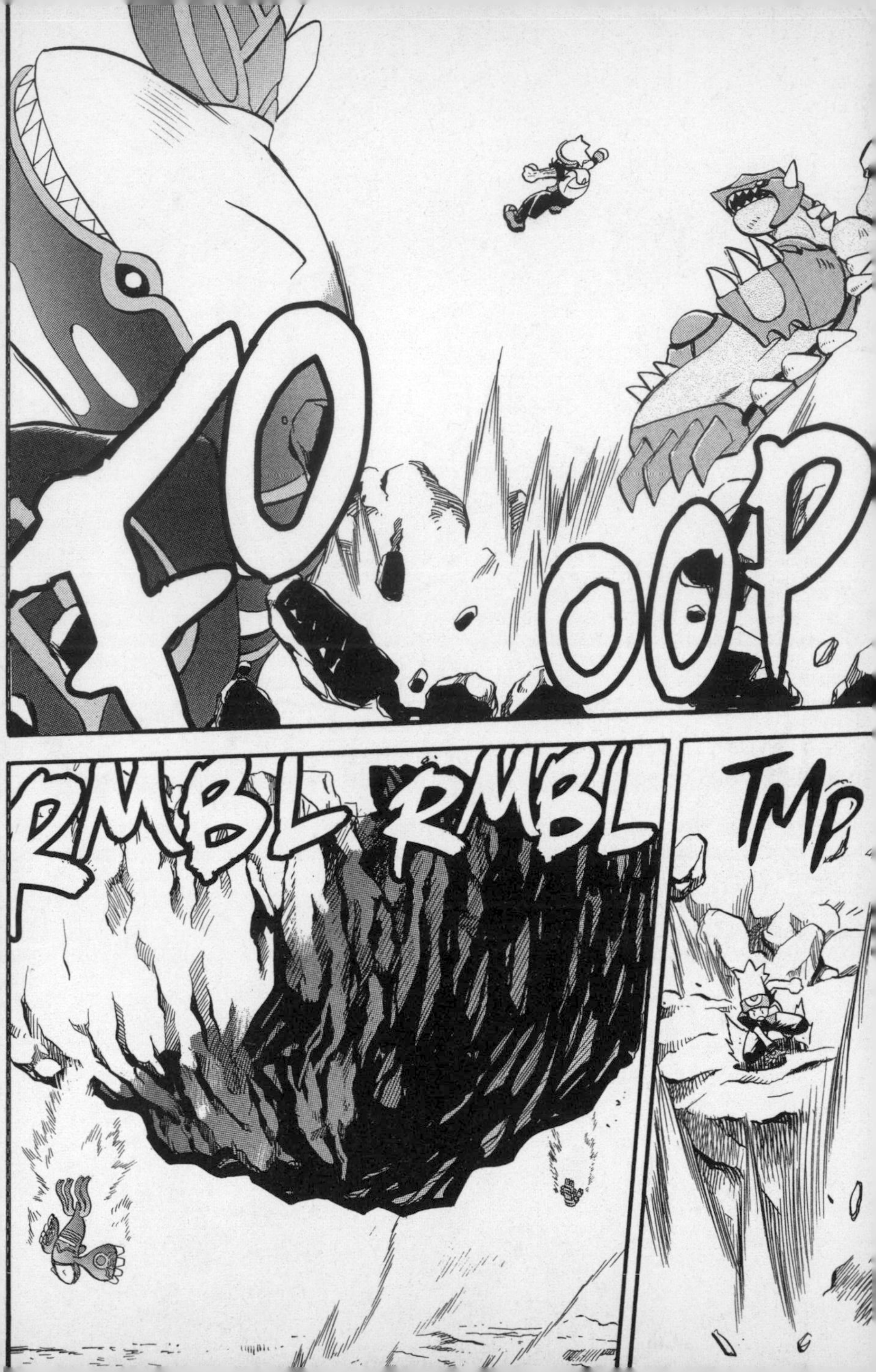
O
OOP
TMP
RMBL RMBL

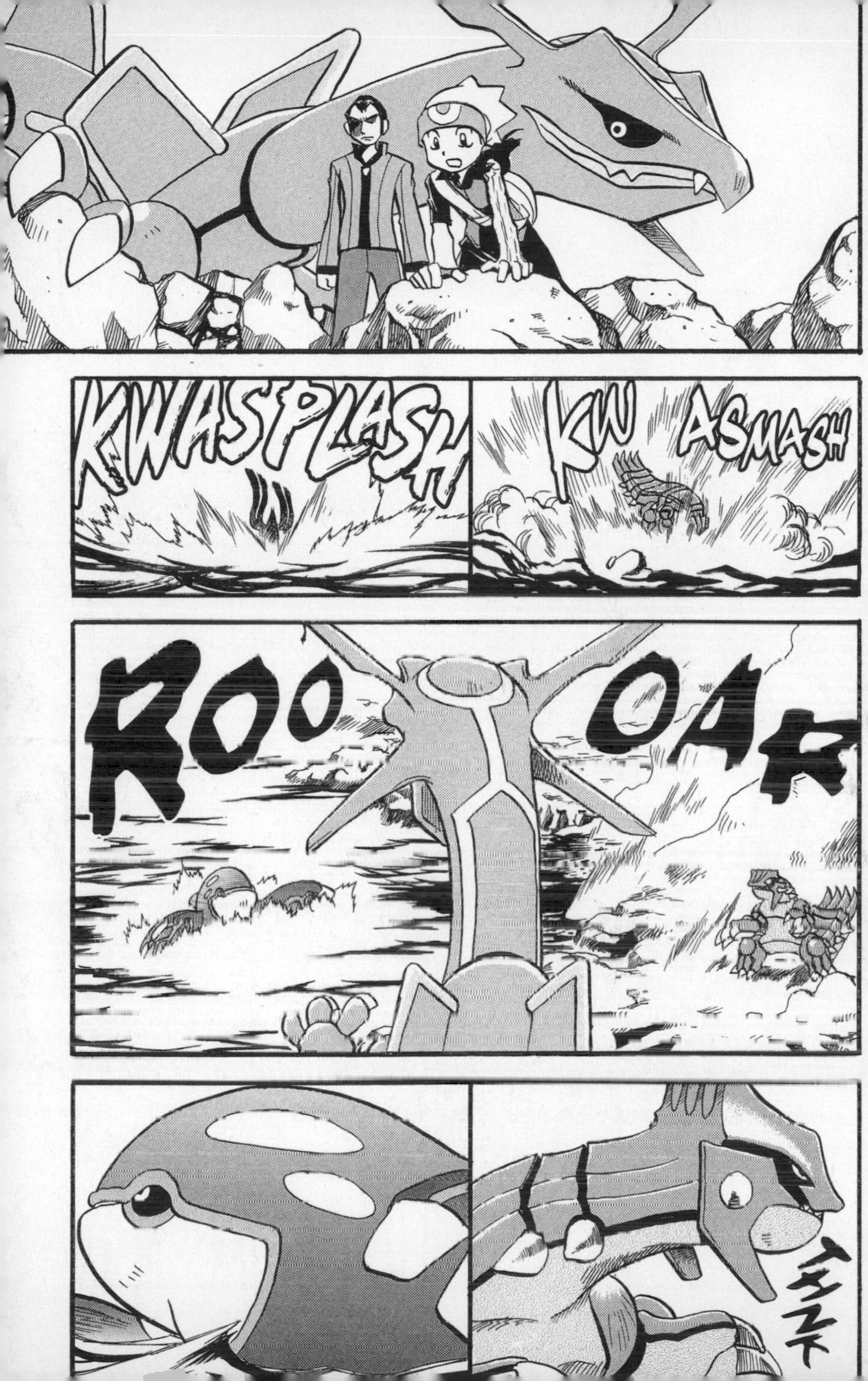
KW ASMASH
KWASPLASH
ROO OAR

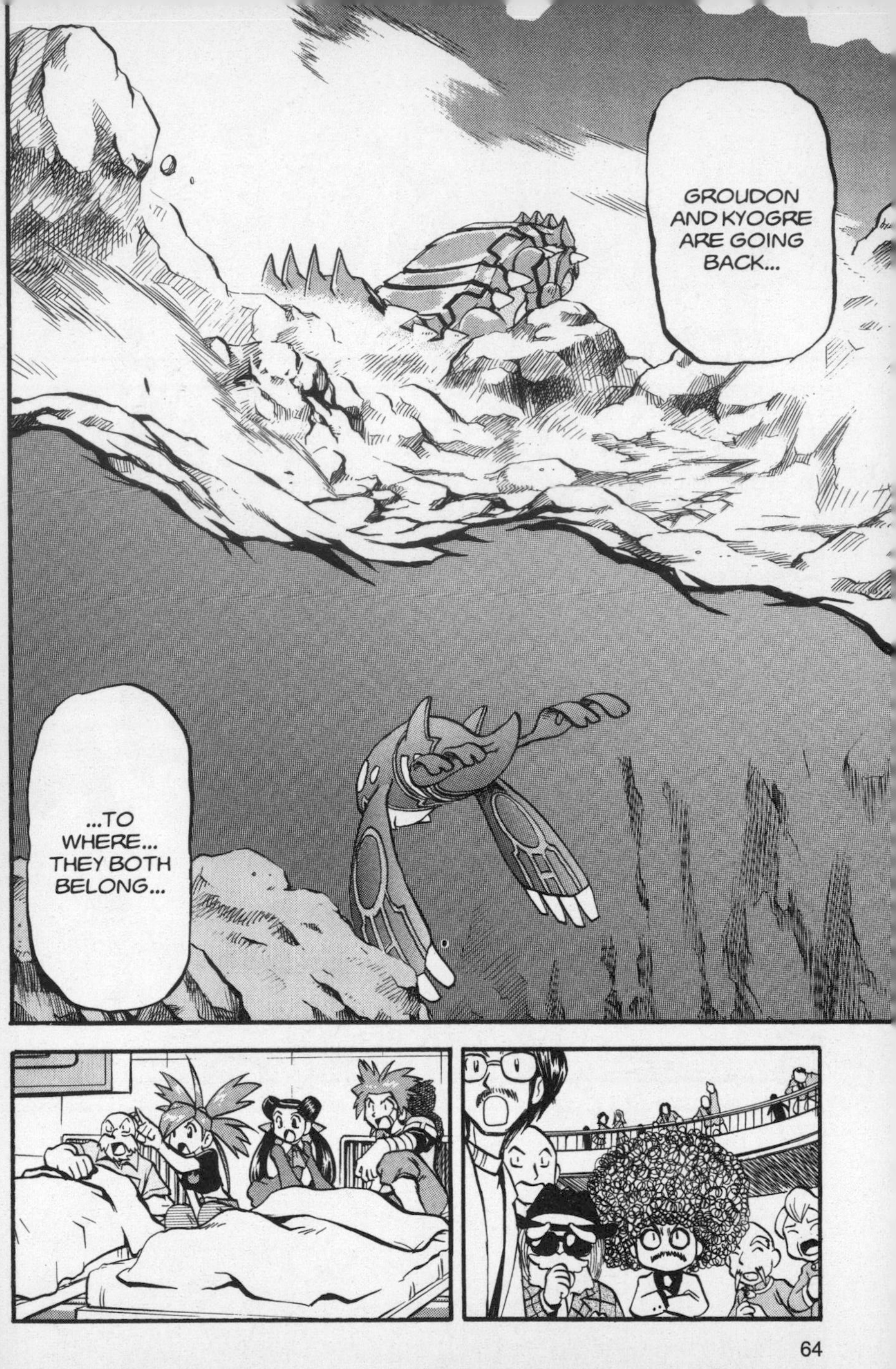
GROUDON AND KYOGRE ARE GOING BACK...
...TO WHERE... THEY BOTH BELONG...

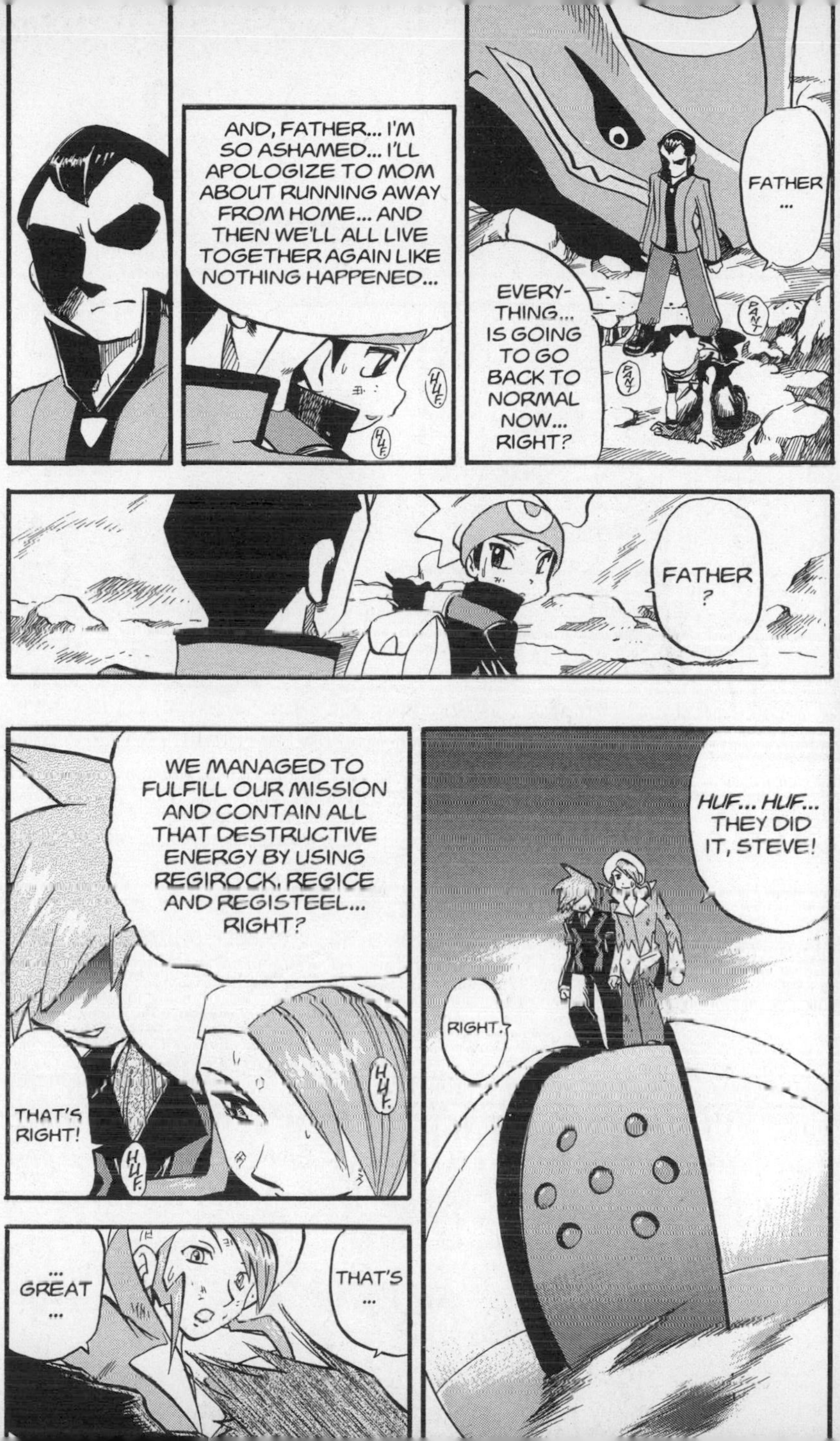
FATHER ...
EVERY-THING... IS GOING TO GO BACK TO NORMAL NOW... RIGHT?
PANT
PANT
AND, FATHER... I'M SO ASHAMED... I'LL APOLOGIZE TO MOM ABOUT RUNNING AWAY FROM HOME... AND THEN WE'LL ALL LIVE TOGETHER AGAIN LIKE NOTHING HAPPENED...
HUF
HUF
FATHER ?
HUF... HUF... THEY DID IT, STEVE!
RIGHT.
WE MANAGED TO FULFILL OUR MISSION AND CONTAIN ALL THAT DESTRUCTIVE ENERGY BY USING REGIROCK, REGICE AND REGISTEEL... RIGHT?
HUF
THAT'S RIGHT!
HUF
THAT'S ...
... GREAT ...

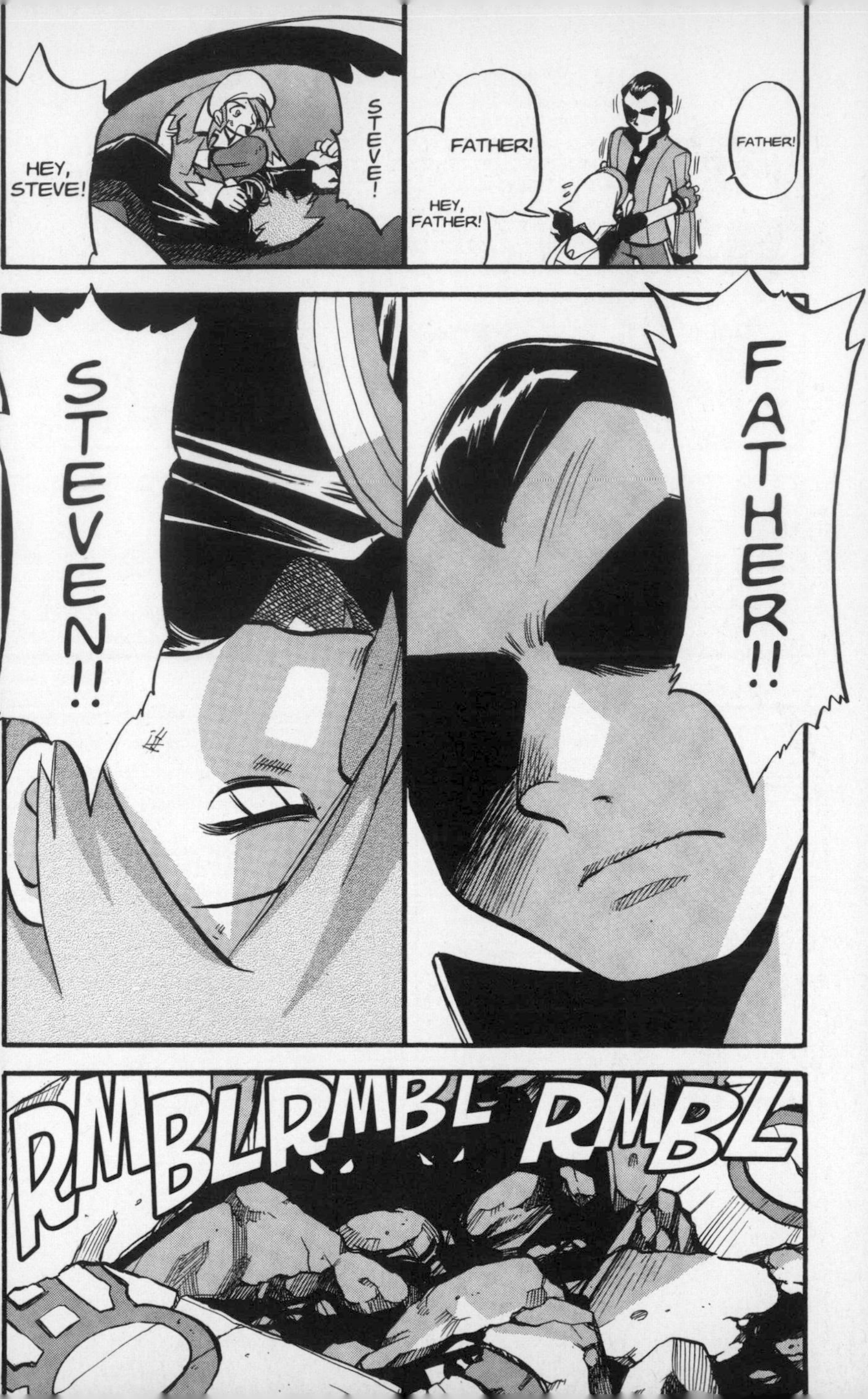
FATHER!
FATHER!
HEY, FATHER!
STEVE!
HEY, STEVE!
FATHER!!
STEVEN!!
RMBLRMBL RMBL

ADVENTURE MAP

SAPPHIRE

CHIC	Blaziken ♀ Lv59
RONO	Aggron ♂ Lv54
PHADO	Donphan ♂ Lv58
MINUN	Minun ♀ Lv52
PLUSLE	Plusle ♂ Lv52

RUBY

MUMU	Swampert ♂
NANA	Mightyena ♀
KIKI	Delcatty ♀
FOFO	Castform ♀
TROPPY	Tropius ♂

Mirage Island

▼

Sootopolis City

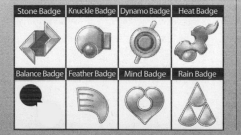

Stone Badge	Knuckle Badge	Dynamo Badge	Heat Badge
Balance Badge	**Feather Badge**	**Mind Badge**	**Rain Badge**

	Cool	Beauty	Cute	Smart	Toug
Normal					
Super					
Hyper					
Master					

● Chapter 264 ●
It All Ends Now V

Pokémon™ Adventures Ruby & Sapphire
The Fourth Chapter

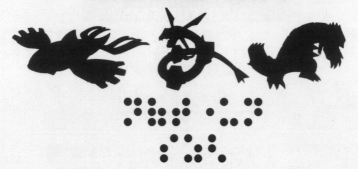

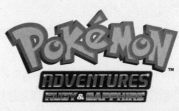

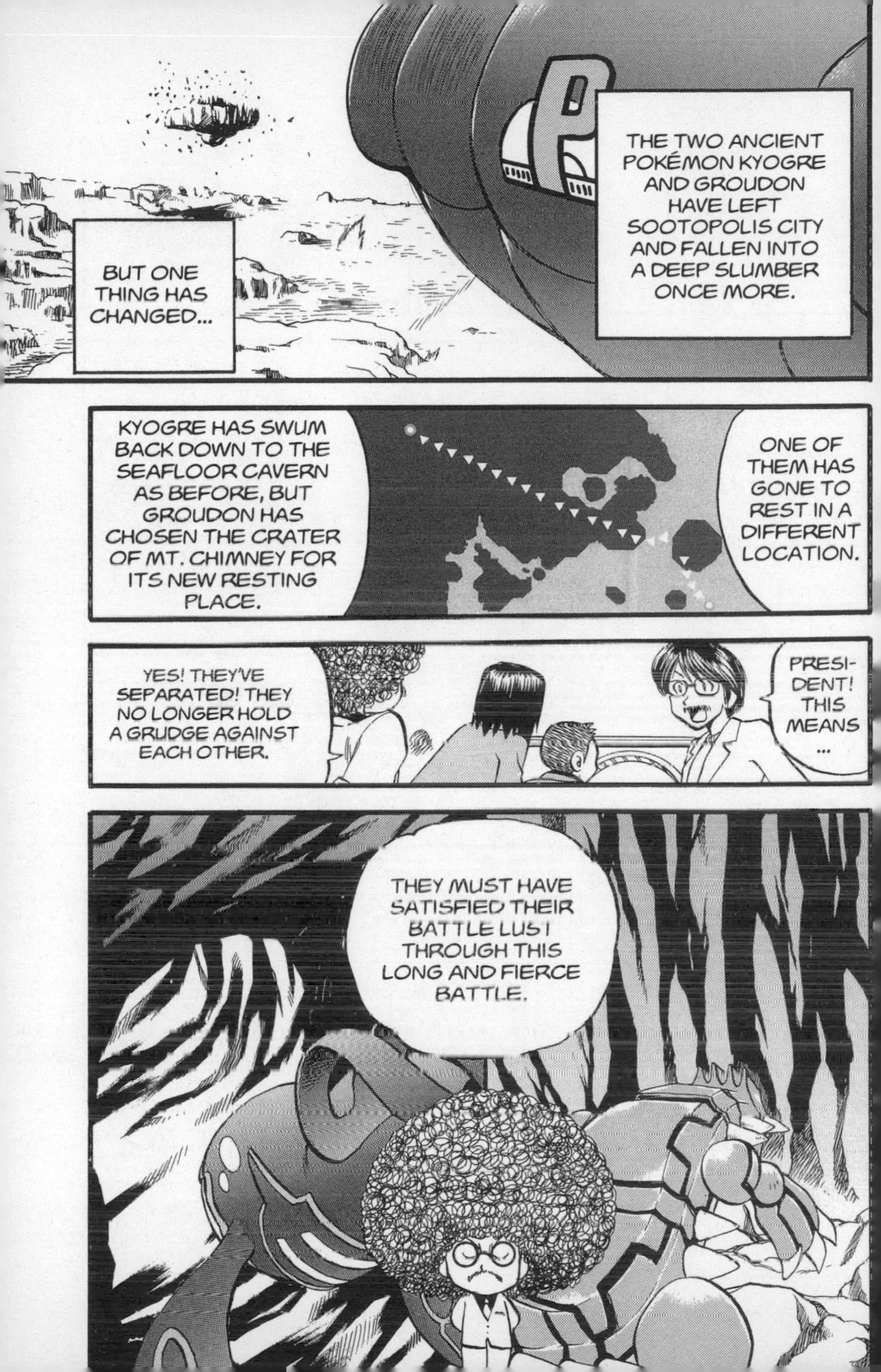
THE TWO ANCIENT POKÉMON KYOGRE AND GROUDON HAVE LEFT SOOTOPOLIS CITY AND FALLEN INTO A DEEP SLUMBER ONCE MORE.
BUT ONE THING HAS CHANGED...
ONE OF THEM HAS GONE TO REST IN A DIFFERENT LOCATION.
KYOGRE HAS SWUM BACK DOWN TO THE SEAFLOOR CAVERN AS BEFORE, BUT GROUDON HAS CHOSEN THE CRATER OF MT. CHIMNEY FOR ITS NEW RESTING PLACE.
PRESI-DENT! THIS MEANS ...
YES! THEY'VE SEPARATED! THEY NO LONGER HOLD A GRUDGE AGAINST EACH OTHER.
THEY MUST HAVE SATISFIED THEIR BATTLE LUST THROUGH THIS LONG AND FIERCE BATTLE.

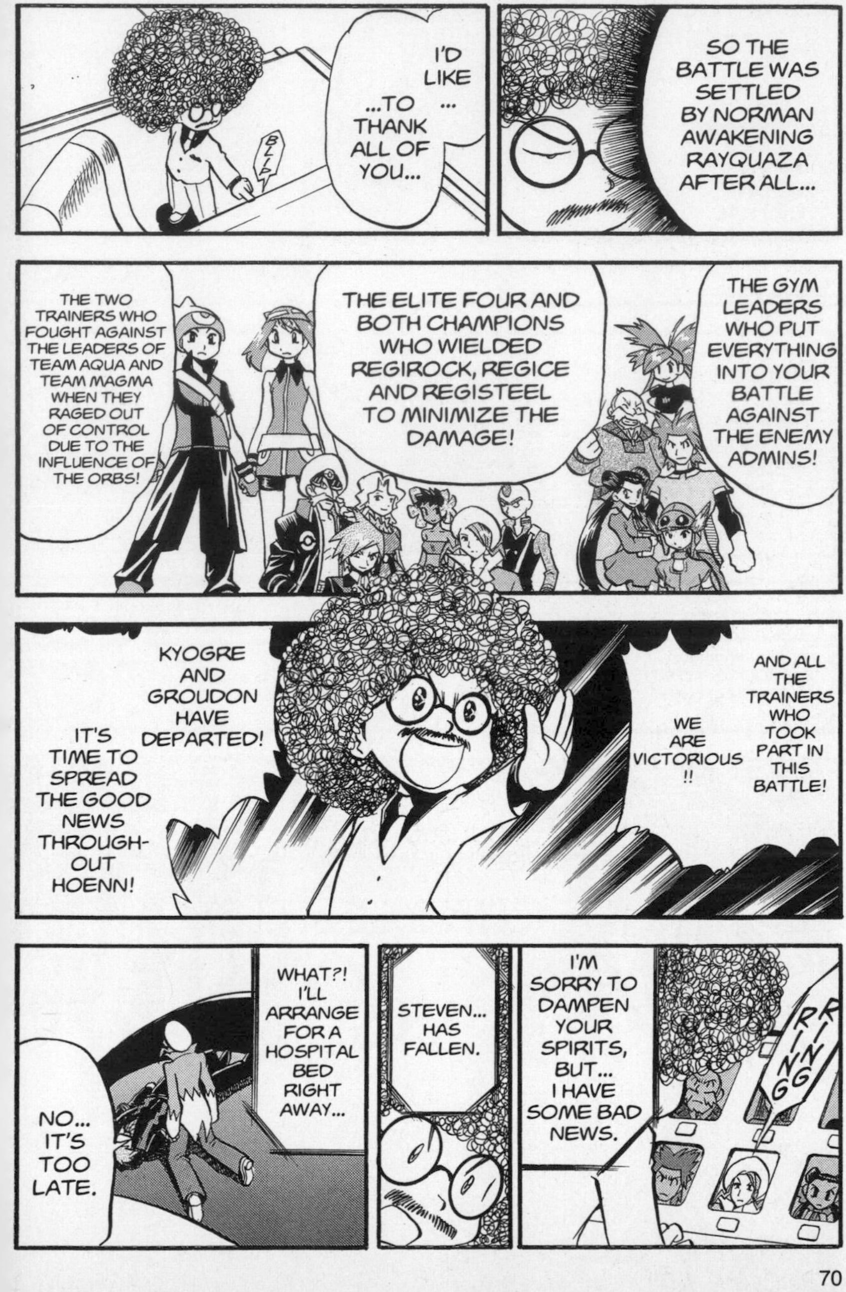
SO THE BATTLE WAS SETTLED BY NORMAN AWAKENING RAYQUAZA AFTER ALL...
I'D LIKE ...
...TO THANK ALL OF YOU...
BLIP
THE GYM LEADERS WHO PUT EVERYTHING INTO YOUR BATTLE AGAINST THE ENEMY ADMINS!
THE ELITE FOUR AND BOTH CHAMPIONS WHO WIELDED REGIROCK, REGICE AND REGISTEEL TO MINIMIZE THE DAMAGE!
THE TWO TRAINERS WHO FOUGHT AGAINST THE LEADERS OF TEAM AQUA AND TEAM MAGMA WHEN THEY RAGED OUT OF CONTROL DUE TO THE INFLUENCE OF THE ORBS!
AND ALL THE TRAINERS WHO TOOK PART IN THIS BATTLE!
WE ARE VICTORIOUS !!
KYOGRE AND GROUDON HAVE DEPARTED!
IT'S TIME TO SPREAD THE GOOD NEWS THROUGH-OUT HOENN!
RING RING
I'M SORRY TO DAMPEN YOUR SPIRITS, BUT... I HAVE SOME BAD NEWS.
STEVEN... HAS FALLEN.
WHAT?! I'LL ARRANGE FOR A HOSPITAL BED RIGHT AWAY...
NO... IT'S TOO LATE.

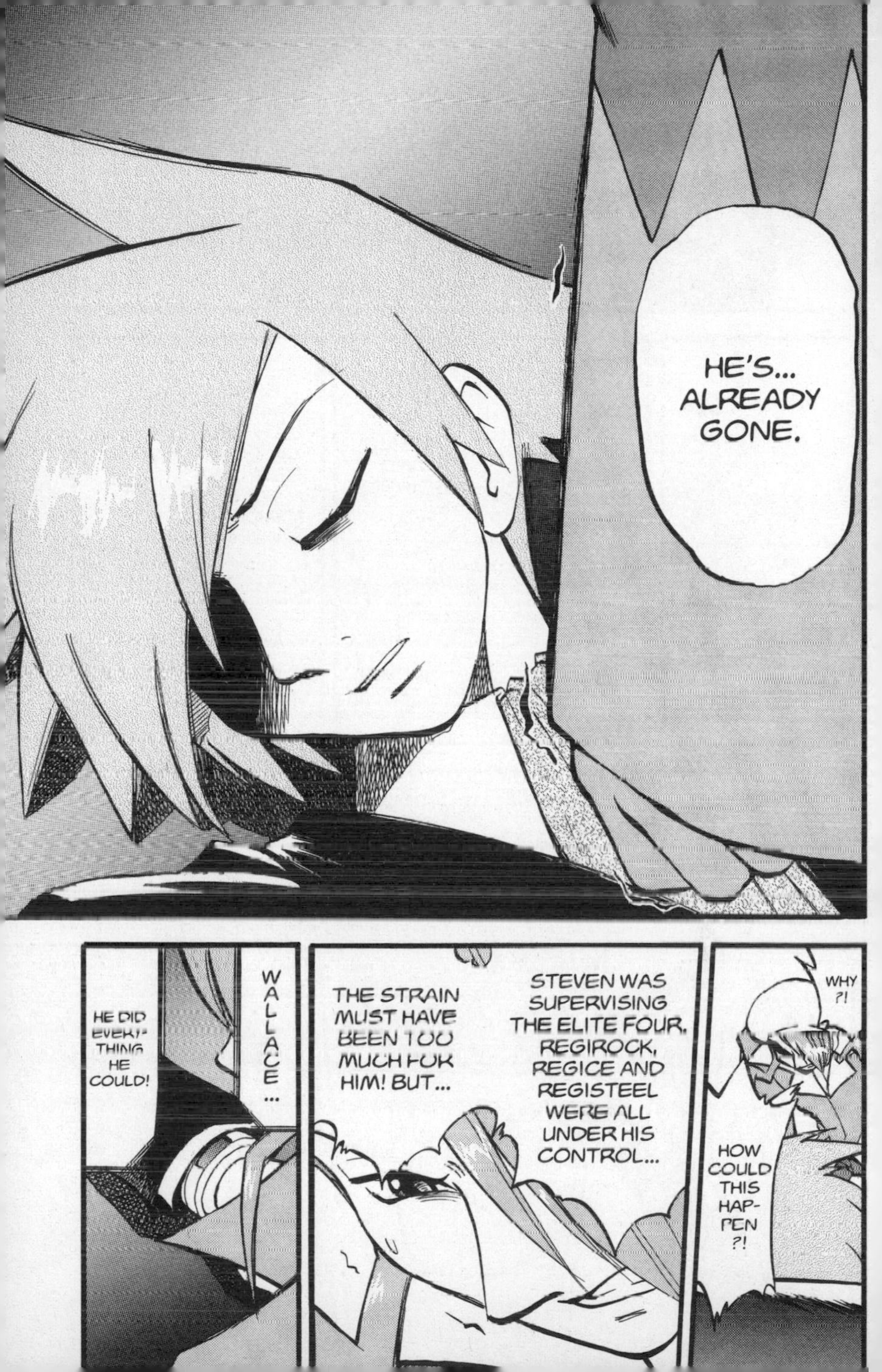
HE'S... ALREADY GONE.
WHY?!
HOW COULD THIS HAP-PEN?!
STEVEN WAS SUPERVISING THE ELITE FOUR. REGIROCK, REGICE AND REGISTEEL WERE ALL UNDER HIS CONTROL...
THE STRAIN MUST HAVE BEEN TOO MUCH FOR HIM! BUT...
WALLACE...
HE DID EVERY-THING HE COULD!

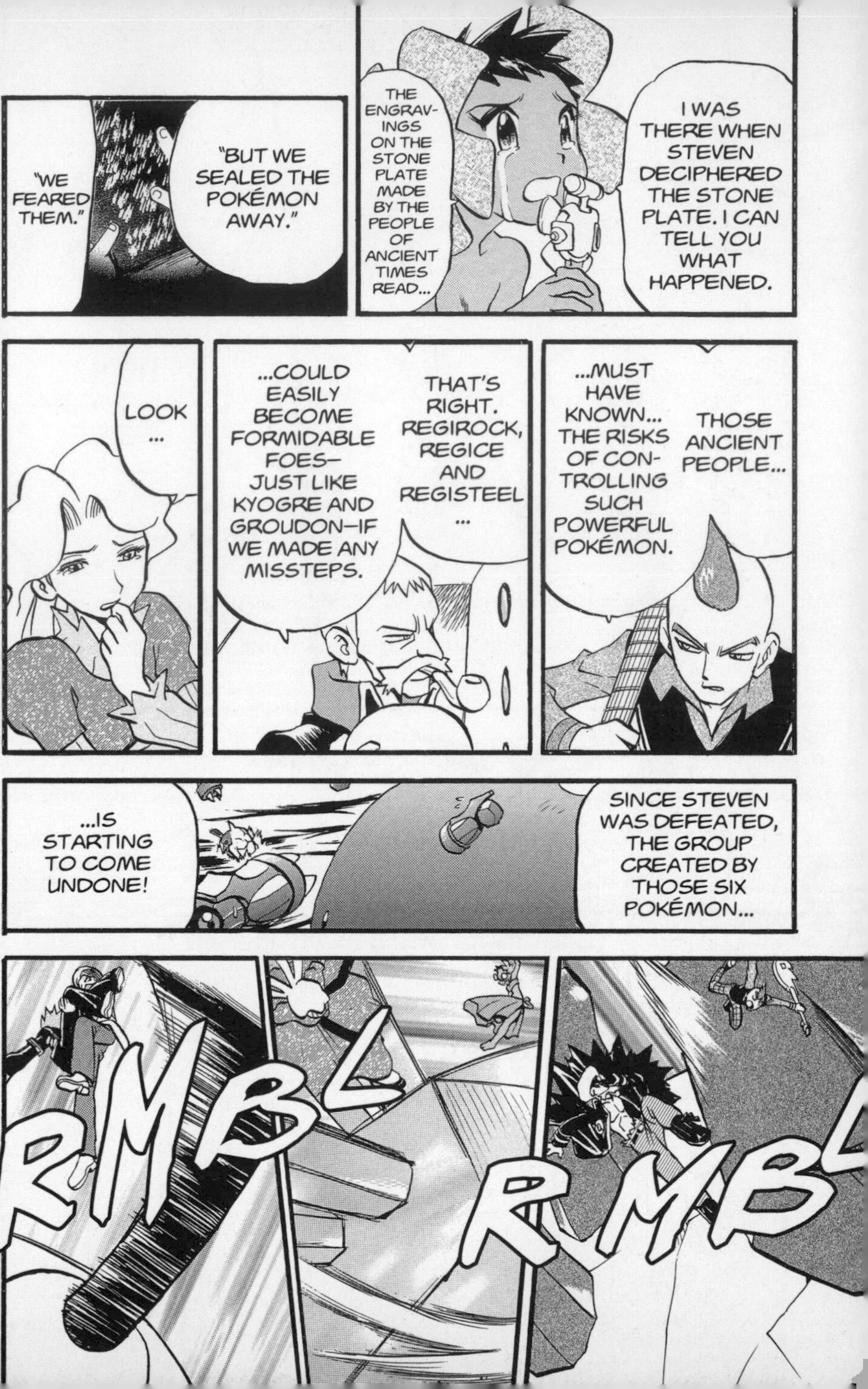
I WAS THERE WHEN STEVEN DECIPHERED THE STONE PLATE. I CAN TELL YOU WHAT HAPPENED.
THE ENGRAV-INGS ON THE STONE PLATE MADE BY THE PEOPLE OF ANCIENT TIMES READ...
"BUT WE SEALED THE POKÉMON AWAY."
"WE FEARED THEM."
THOSE ANCIENT PEOPLE...
...MUST HAVE KNOWN... THE RISKS OF CON-TROLLING SUCH POWERFUL POKÉMON.
THAT'S RIGHT. REGIROCK, REGICE AND REGISTEEL ...
...COULD EASILY BECOME FORMIDABLE FOES– JUST LIKE KYOGRE AND GROUDON–IF WE MADE ANY MISSTEPS.
LOOK ...
SINCE STEVEN WAS DEFEATED, THE GROUP CREATED BY THOSE SIX POKÉMON...
...IS STARTING TO COME UNDONE!
RMBL
RMBL

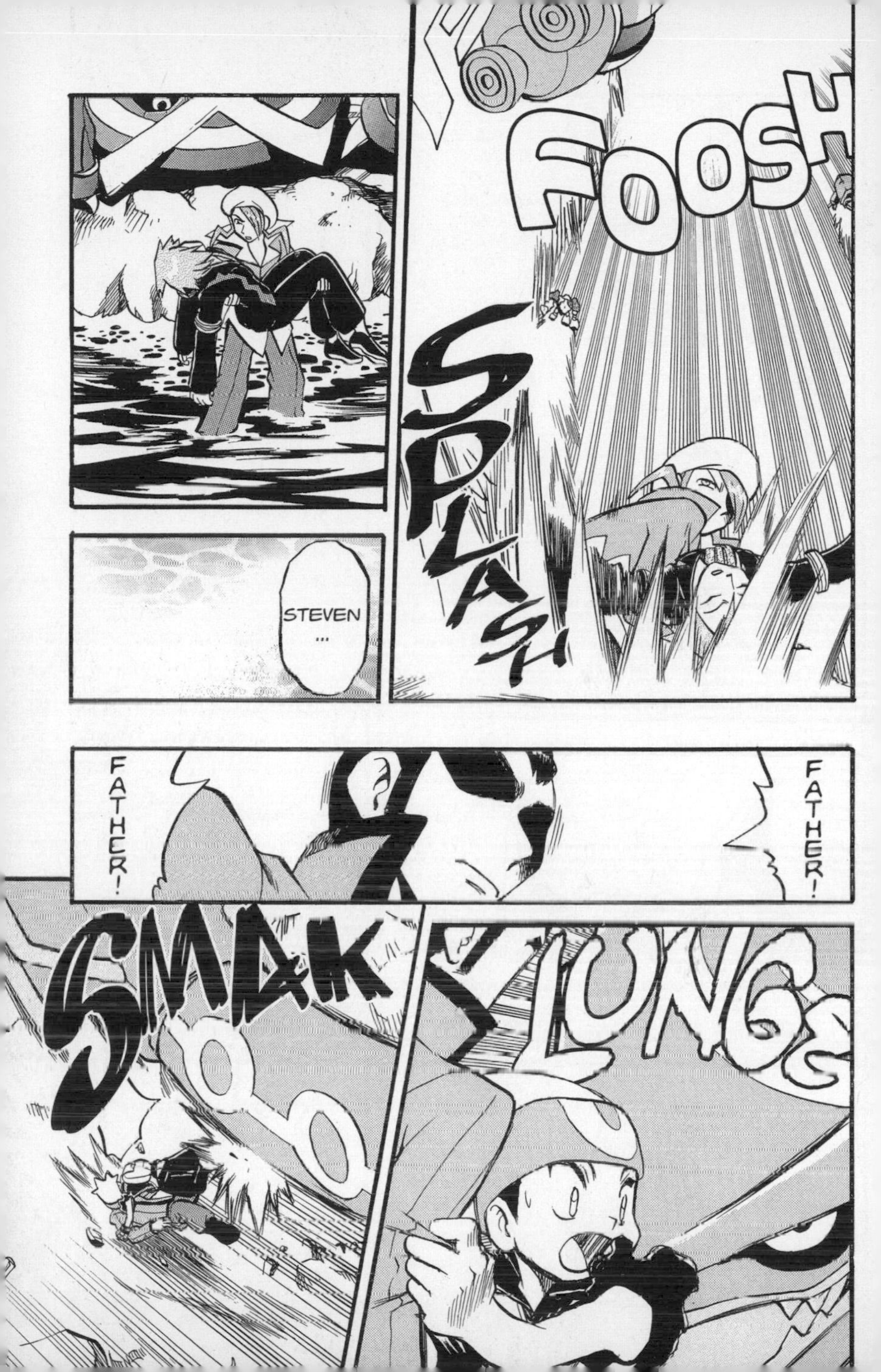
FOOSH
SPLASH
STEVEN
...
FATHER!
FATHER!
LUNGE
SMAK

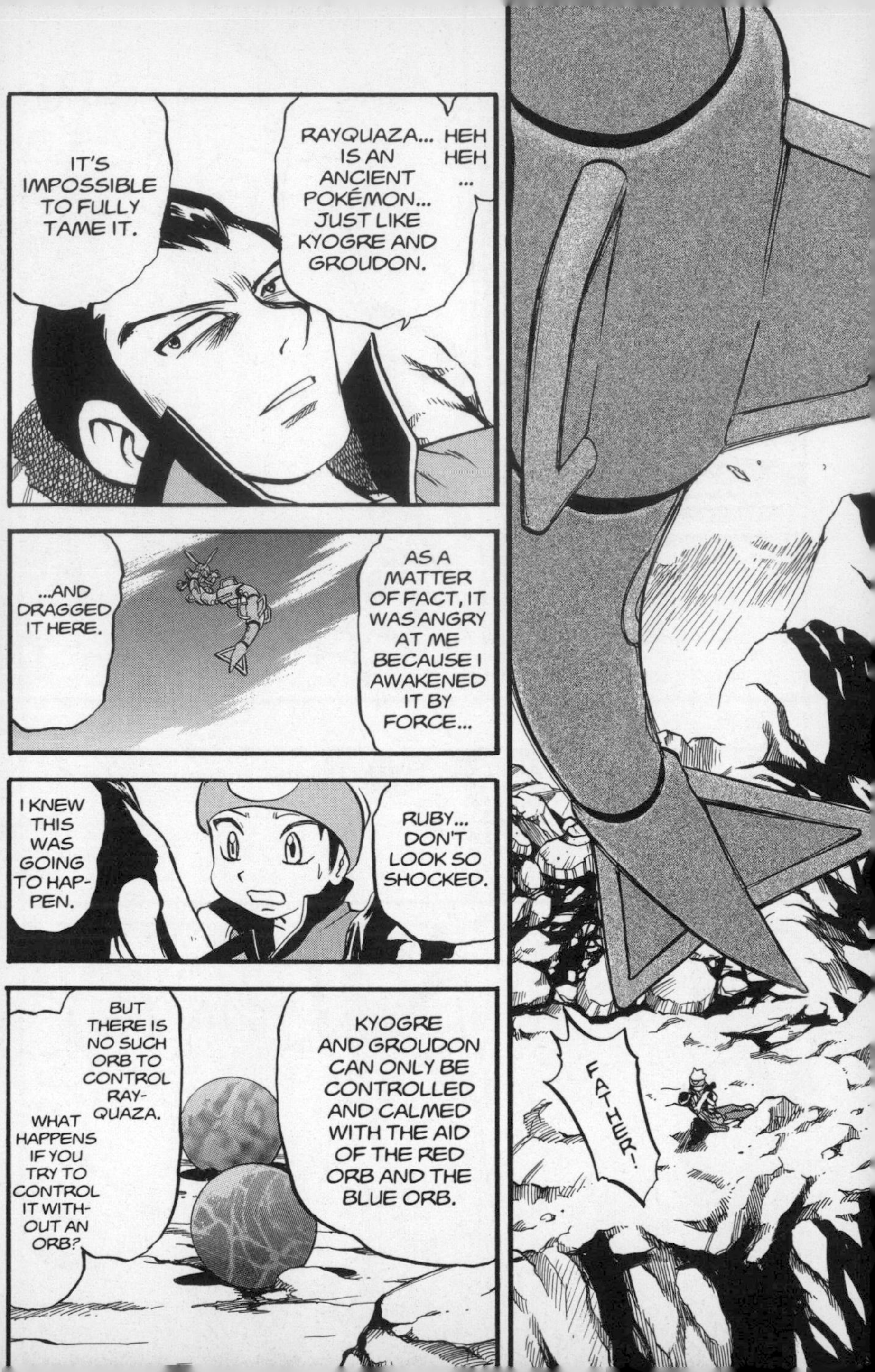
FATHER!
HEH HEH ...
RAYQUAZA... IS AN ANCIENT POKÉMON... JUST LIKE KYOGRE AND GROUDON.
IT'S IMPOSSIBLE TO FULLY TAME IT.
AS A MATTER OF FACT, IT WAS ANGRY AT ME BECAUSE I AWAKENED IT BY FORCE...
...AND DRAGGED IT HERE.
RUBY... DON'T LOOK SO SHOCKED.
I KNEW THIS WAS GOING TO HAP-PEN.
KYOGRE AND GROUDON CAN ONLY BE CONTROLLED AND CALMED WITH THE AID OF THE RED ORB AND THE BLUE ORB.
BUT THERE IS NO SUCH ORB TO CONTROL RAY-QUAZA.
WHAT HAPPENS IF YOU TRY TO CONTROL IT WITH-OUT AN ORB?

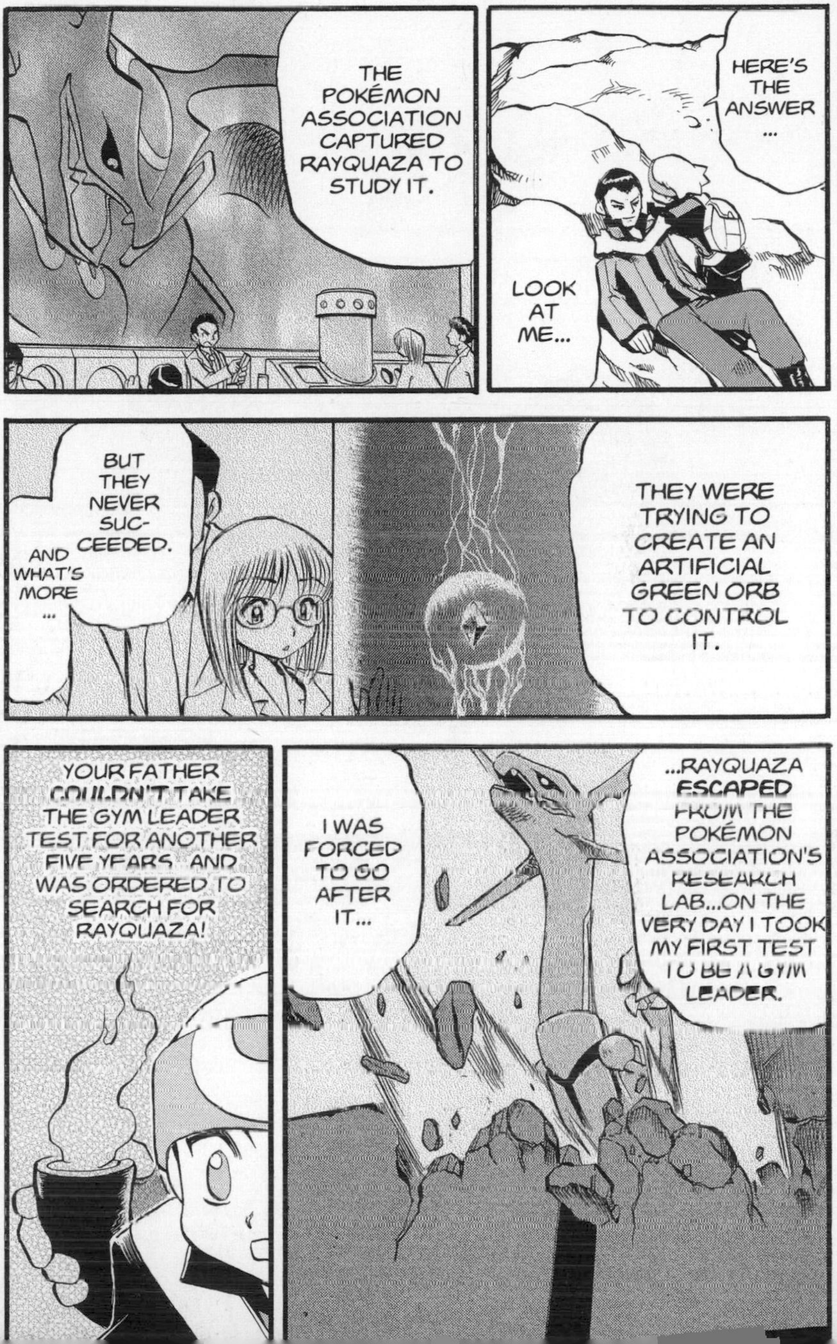
HERE'S THE ANSWER ...
LOOK AT ME...
THE POKÉMON ASSOCIATION CAPTURED RAYQUAZA TO STUDY IT.
THEY WERE TRYING TO CREATE AN ARTIFICIAL GREEN ORB TO CONTROL IT.
BUT THEY NEVER SUC-CEEDED.
AND WHAT'S MORE ...
...RAYQUAZA ESCAPED FROM THE POKÉMON ASSOCIATION'S RESEARCH LAB...ON THE VERY DAY I TOOK MY FIRST TEST TO BE A GYM LEADER.
I WAS FORCED TO GO AFTER IT...
YOUR FATHER COULDN'T TAKE THE GYM LEADER TEST FOR ANOTHER FIVE YEARS AND WAS ORDERED TO SEARCH FOR RAYQUAZA!

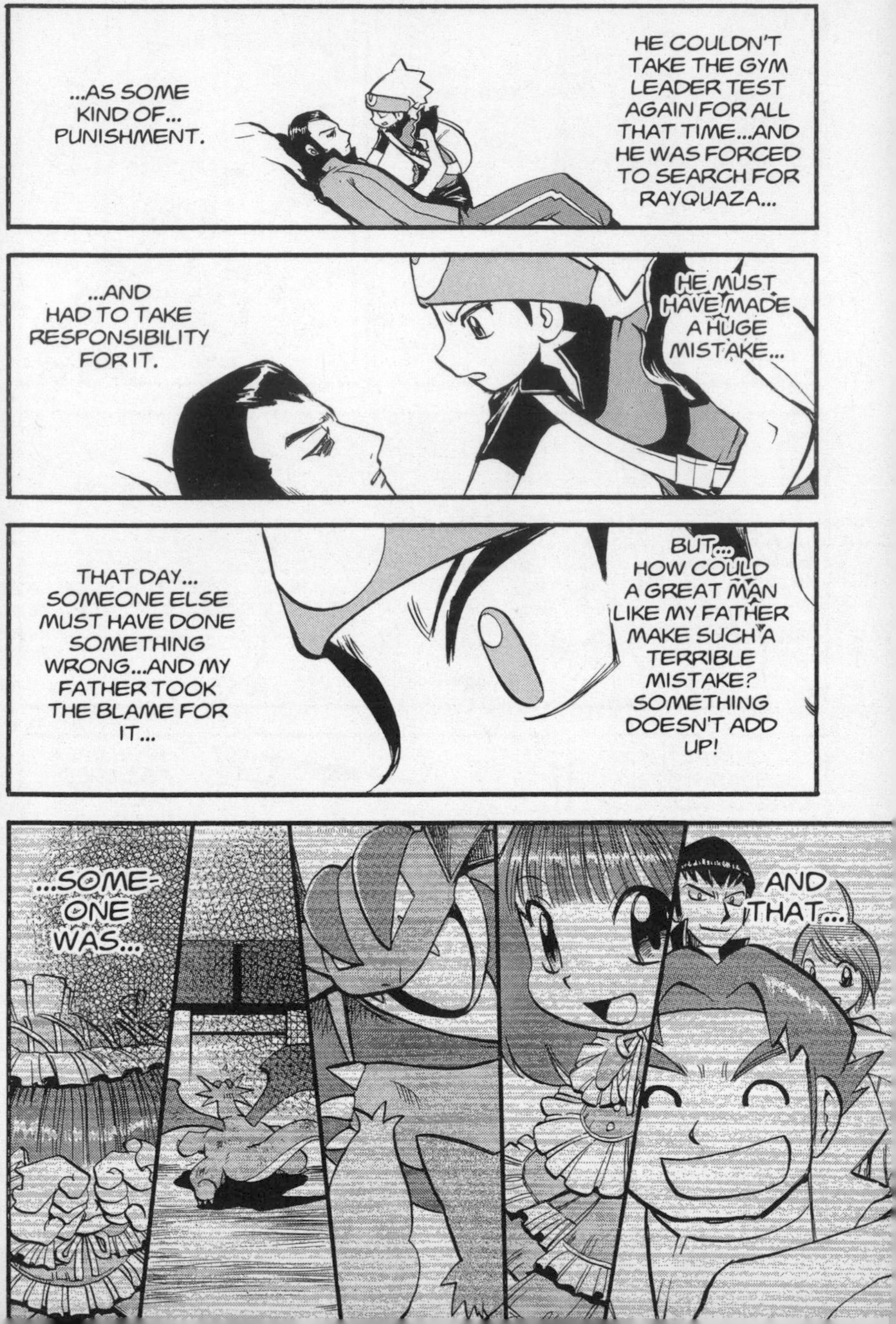
HE COULDN'T TAKE THE GYM LEADER TEST AGAIN FOR ALL THAT TIME...AND HE WAS FORCED TO SEARCH FOR RAYQUAZA...
...AS SOME KIND OF... PUNISHMENT.
HE MUST HAVE MADE A HUGE MISTAKE...
...AND HAD TO TAKE RESPONSIBILITY FOR IT.
BUT... HOW COULD A GREAT MAN LIKE MY FATHER MAKE SUCH A TERRIBLE MISTAKE? SOMETHING DOESN'T ADD UP!
THAT DAY... SOMEONE ELSE MUST HAVE DONE SOMETHING WRONG...AND MY FATHER TOOK THE BLAME FOR IT...
AND THAT...
...SOME-ONE WAS...

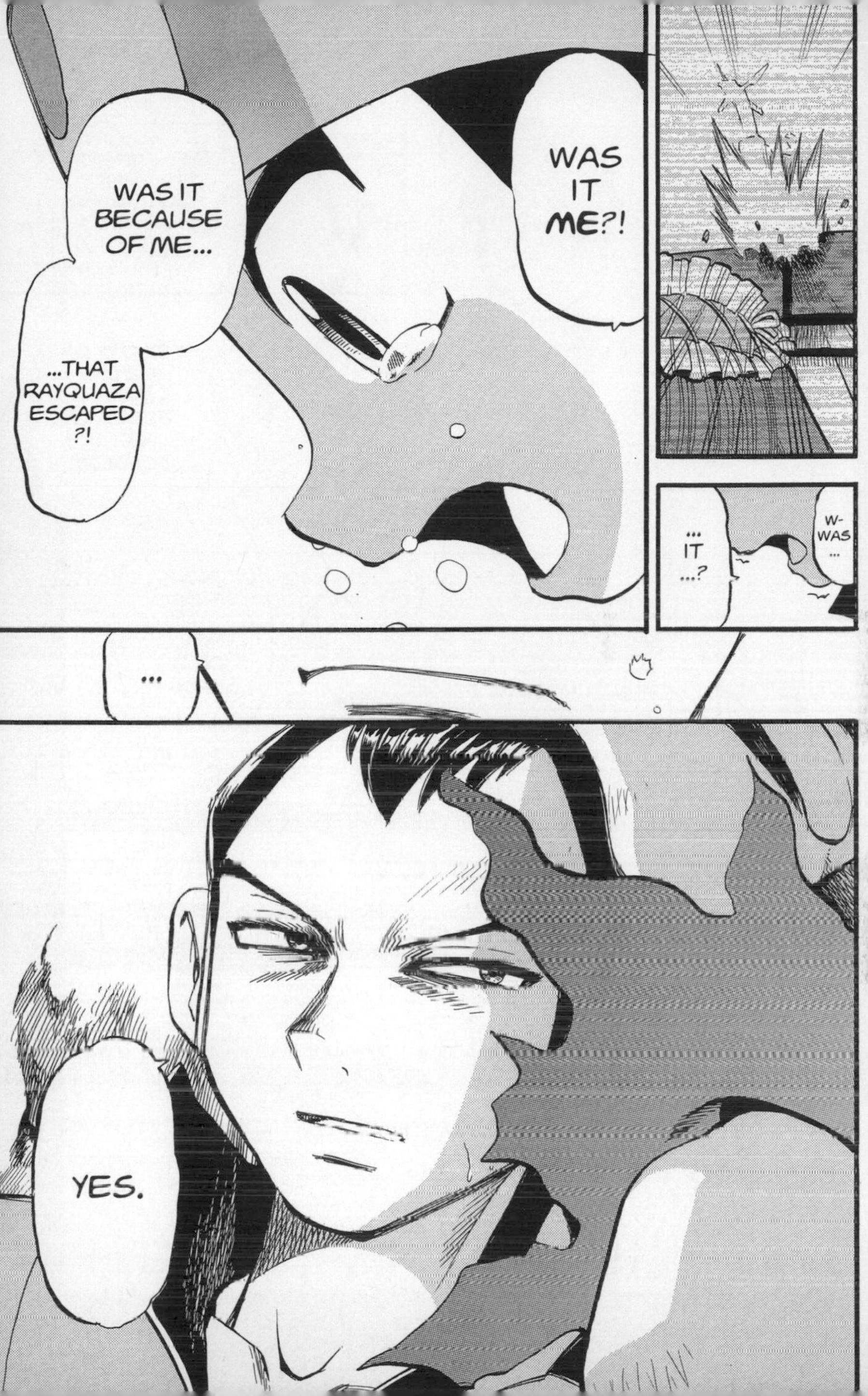
W-WAS...
...IT...?
WAS IT ME?!
WAS IT BECAUSE OF ME...
...THAT RAYQUAZA ESCAPED?!
...
YES.

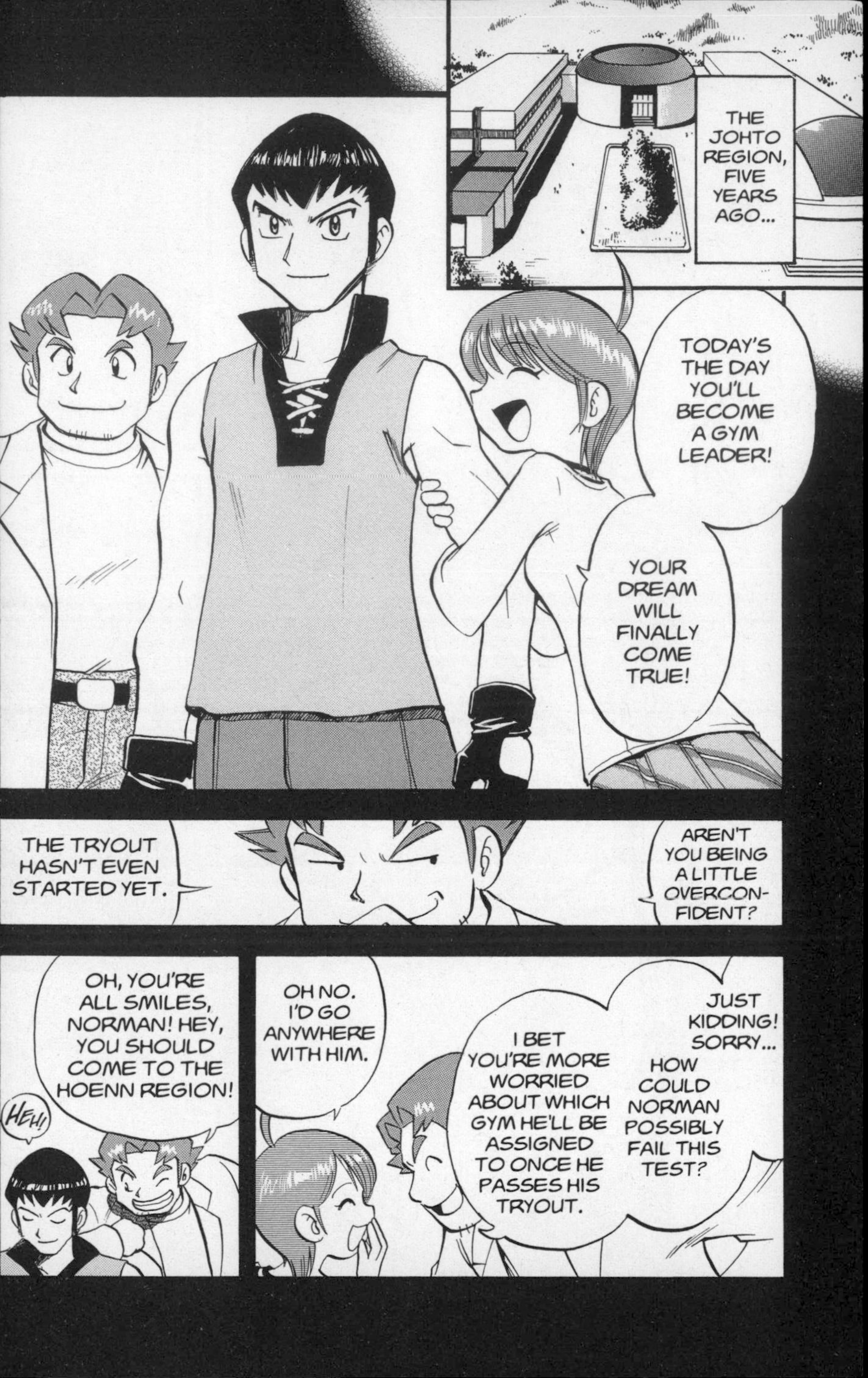
THE JOHTO REGION, FIVE YEARS AGO...
TODAY'S THE DAY YOU'LL BECOME A GYM LEADER!
YOUR DREAM WILL FINALLY COME TRUE!
AREN'T YOU BEING A LITTLE OVERCON-FIDENT?
THE TRYOUT HASN'T EVEN STARTED YET.
JUST KIDDING! SORRY...
HOW COULD NORMAN POSSIBLY FAIL THIS TEST?
I BET YOU'RE MORE WORRIED ABOUT WHICH GYM HE'LL BE ASSIGNED TO ONCE HE PASSES HIS TRYOUT.
OH NO. I'D GO ANYWHERE WITH HIM.
OH, YOU'RE ALL SMILES, NORMAN! HEY, YOU SHOULD COME TO THE HOENN REGION!
HEH!

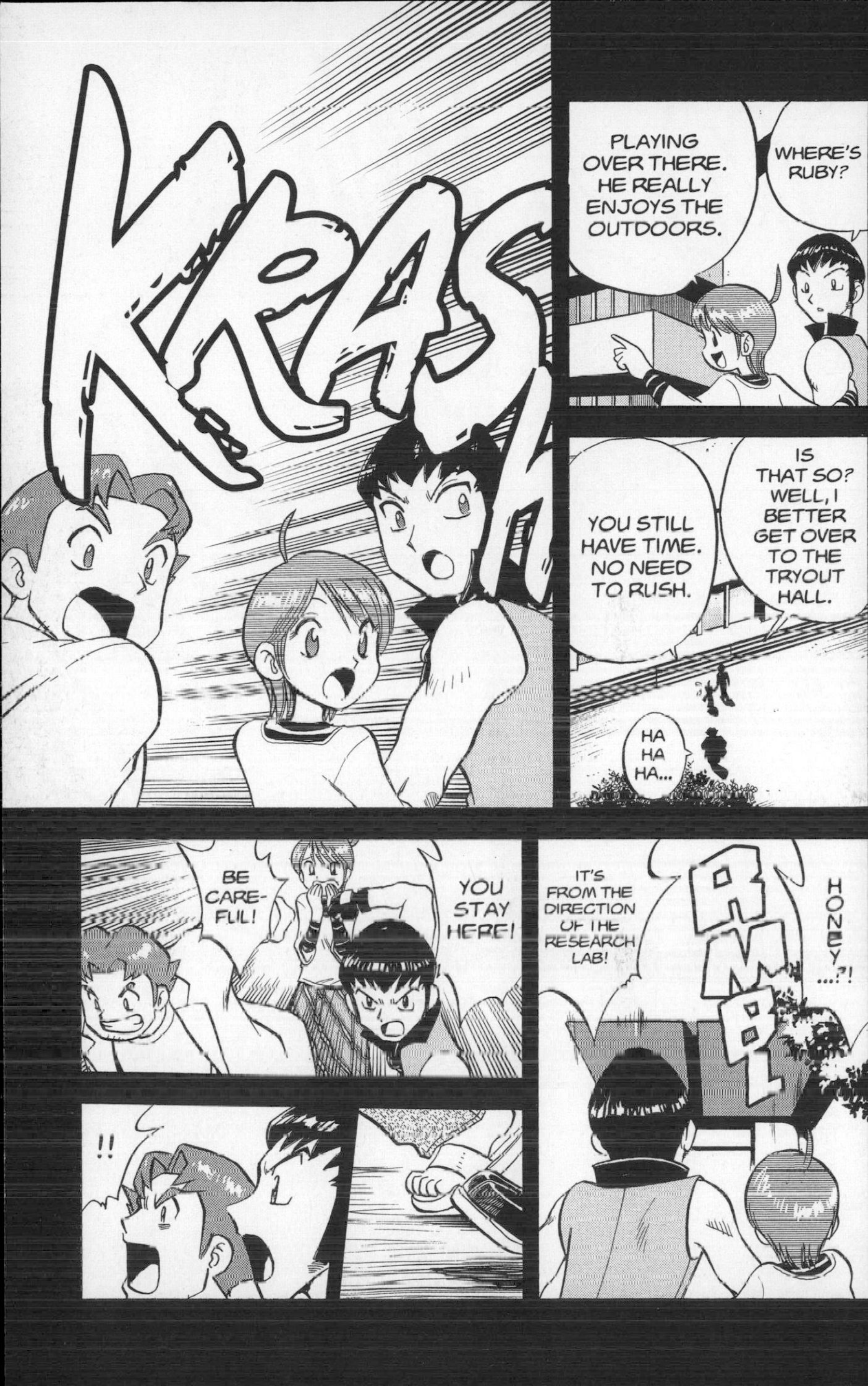
WHERE'S RUBY?
PLAYING OVER THERE. HE REALLY ENJOYS THE OUTDOORS.
IS THAT SO? WELL, I BETTER GET OVER TO THE TRYOUT HALL.
YOU STILL HAVE TIME. NO NEED TO RUSH.
HA HA HA...
KRASH
HONEY...?!
RMBL
IT'S FROM THE DIRECTION OF THE RESEARCH LAB!
YOU STAY HERE!
BE CARE-FUL!
!!

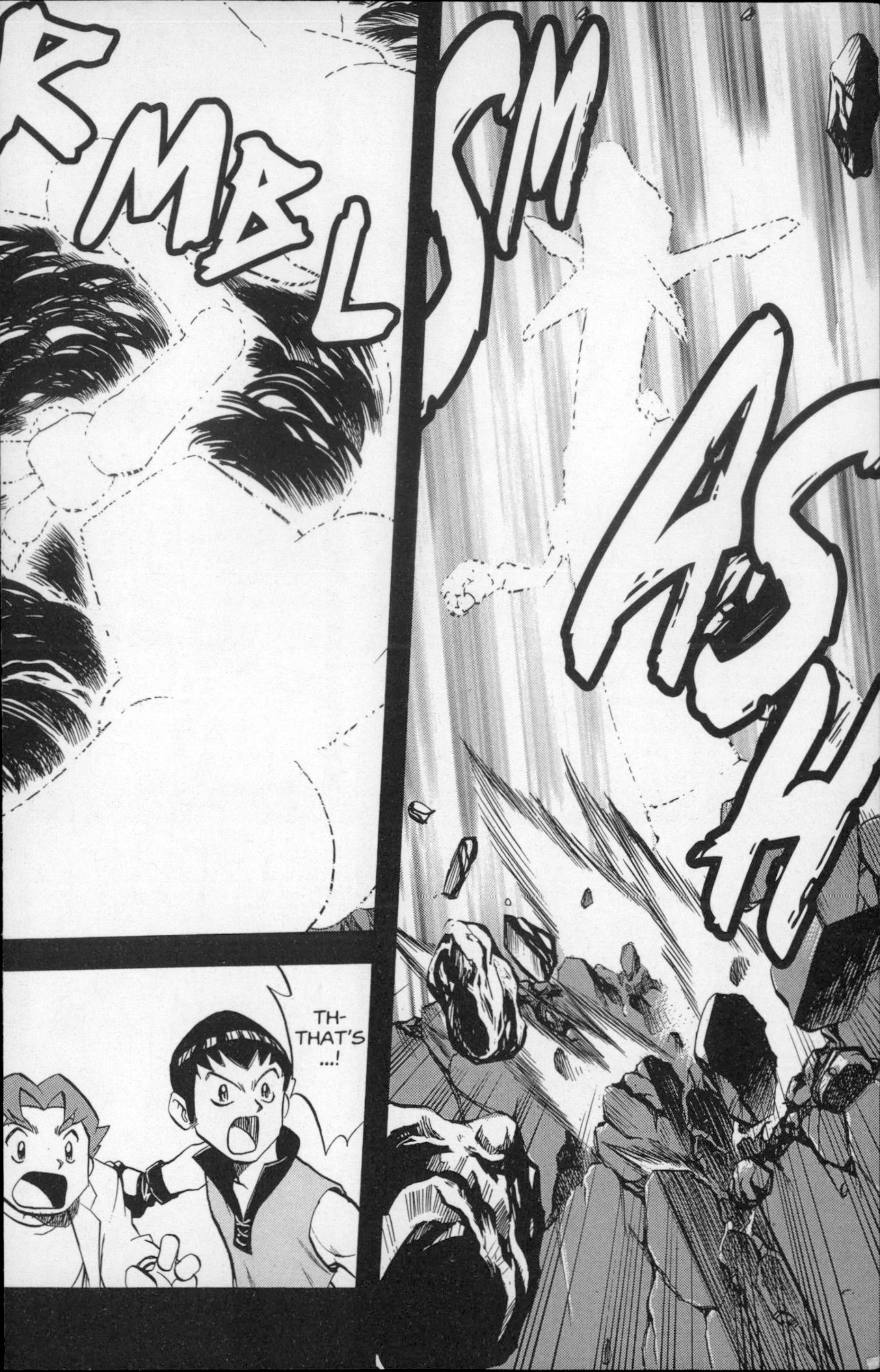
SMASH
RMBL
TH-THAT'S ...!

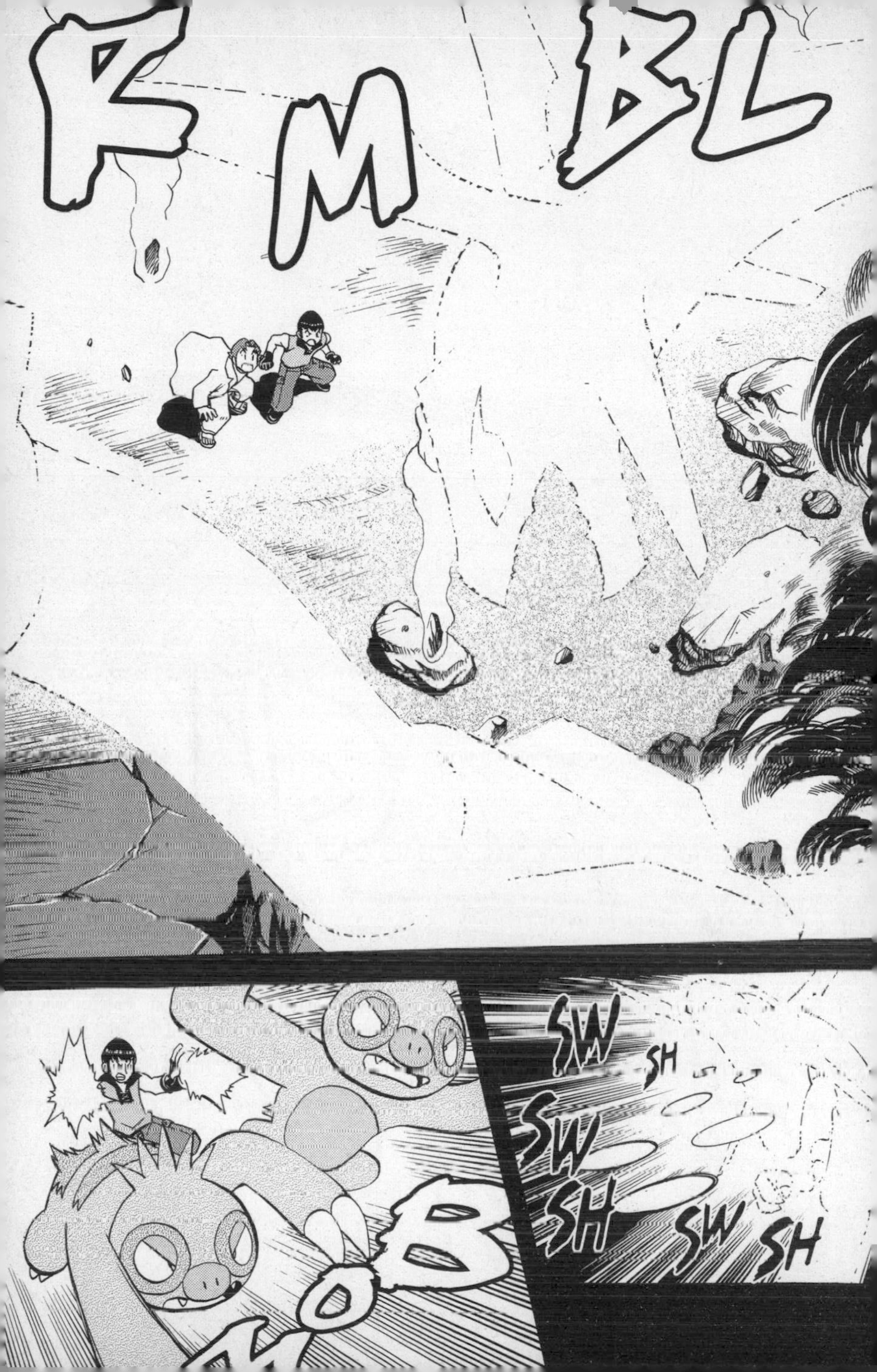
RMBL
SWSH
SWSH
SWSH

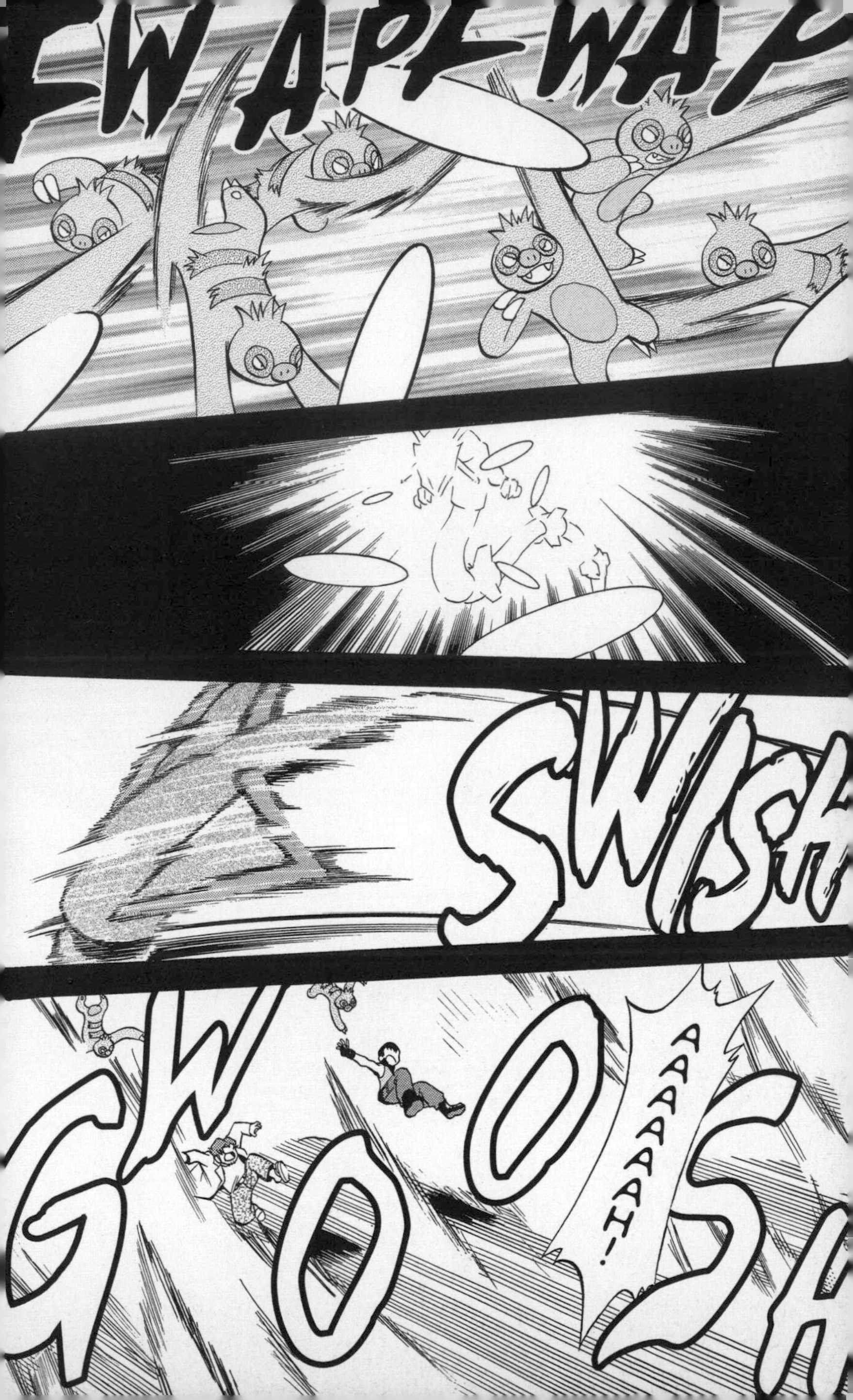
SWAP SWAP
SWISH
AAAAAAAH-!
SWOOSH

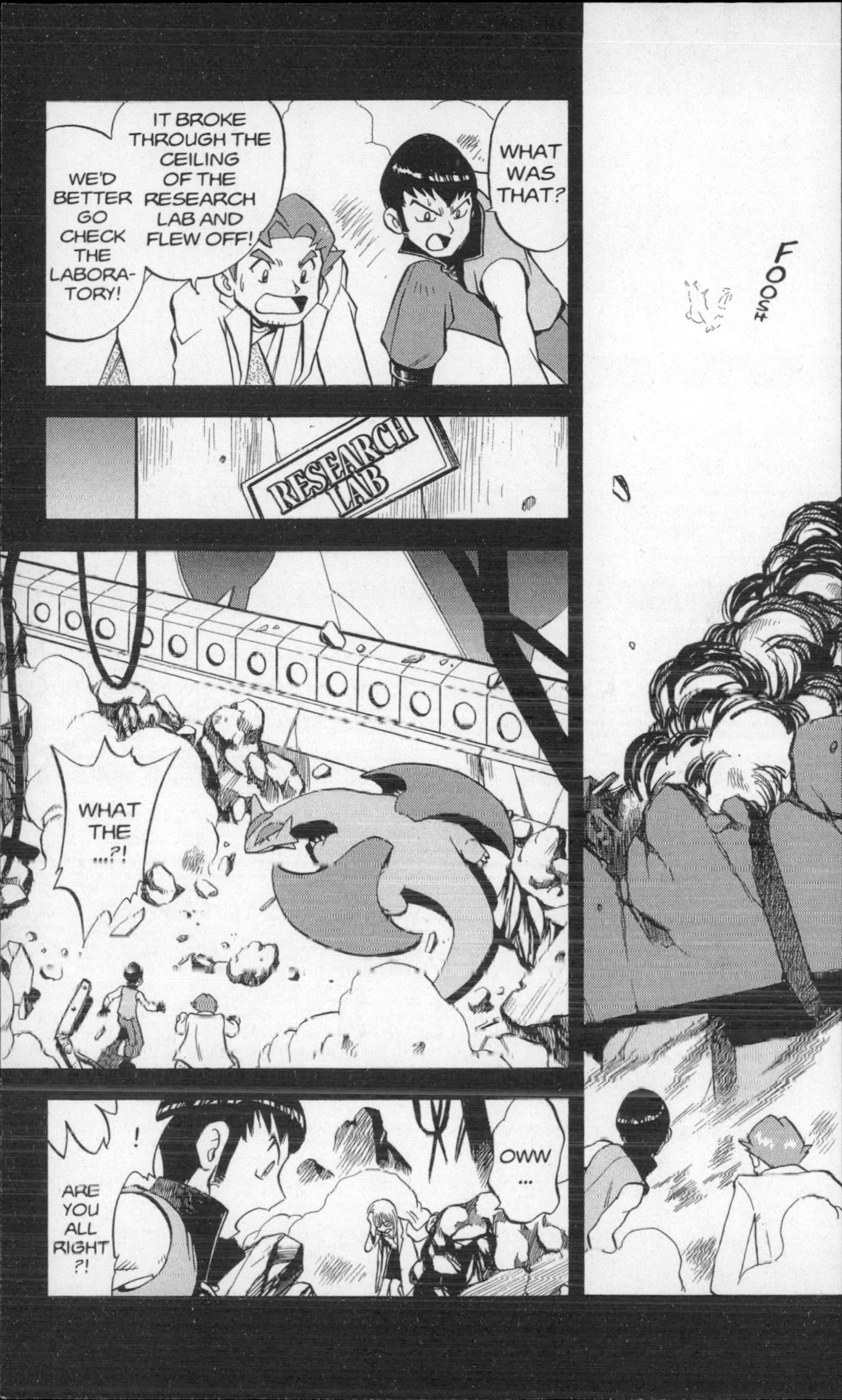
FOOSH
WHAT WAS THAT?
IT BROKE THROUGH THE CEILING OF THE RESEARCH LAB AND FLEW OFF!
WE'D BETTER GO CHECK THE LABORA-TORY!
RESEARCH LAB
WHAT THE ...?!
OWW ...
!
ARE YOU ALL RIGHT ?!

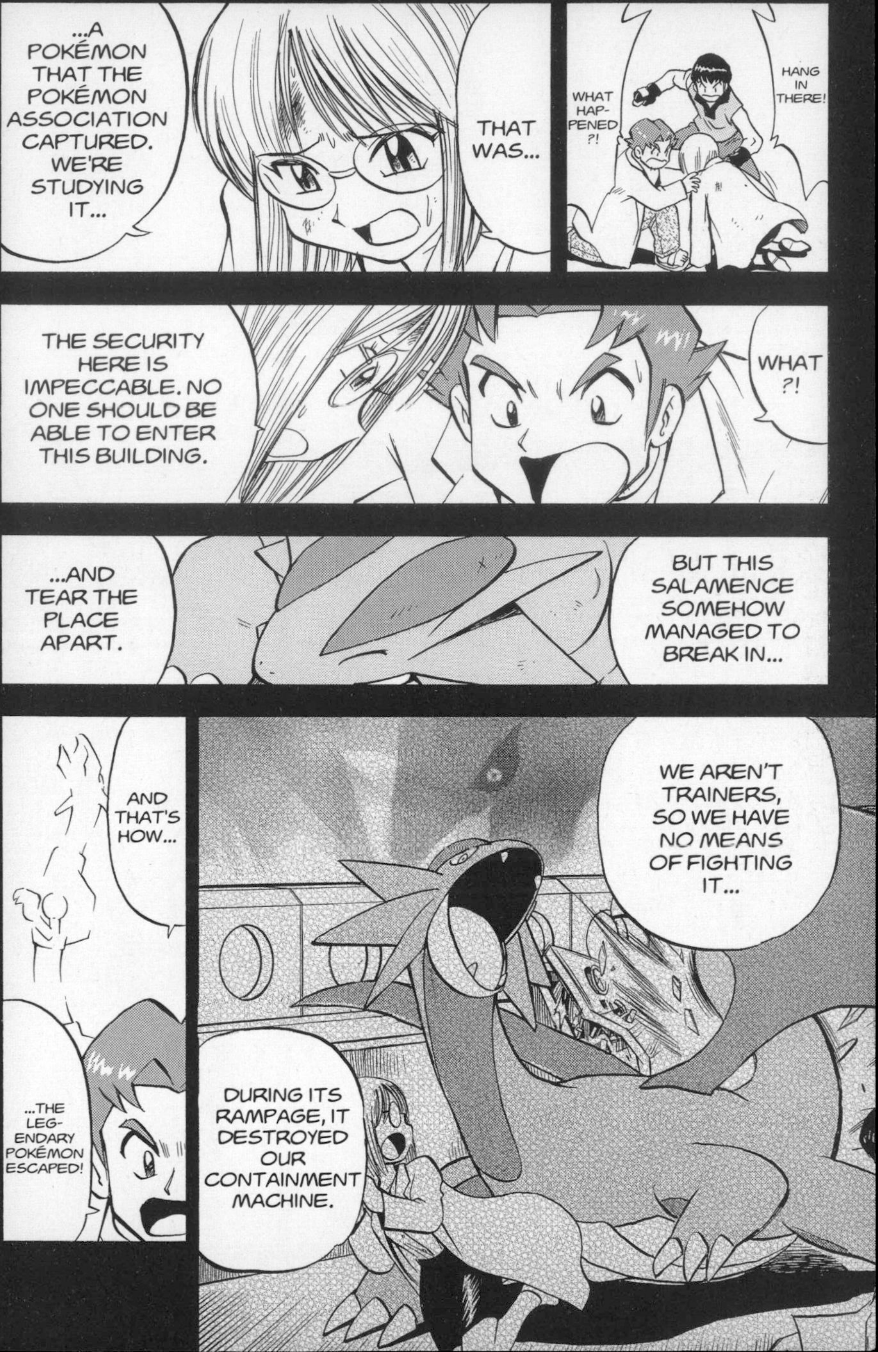
HANG IN THERE!
WHAT HAPPENED?!
THAT WAS...
...A POKÉMON THAT THE POKÉMON ASSOCIATION CAPTURED. WE'RE STUDYING IT...
WHAT?!
THE SECURITY HERE IS IMPECCABLE. NO ONE SHOULD BE ABLE TO ENTER THIS BUILDING.
BUT THIS SALAMENCE SOMEHOW MANAGED TO BREAK IN...
...AND TEAR THE PLACE APART.
WE AREN'T TRAINERS, SO WE HAVE NO MEANS OF FIGHTING IT...
DURING ITS RAMPAGE, IT DESTROYED OUR CONTAINMENT MACHINE.
AND THAT'S HOW...
...THE LEGENDARY POKÉMON ESCAPED!

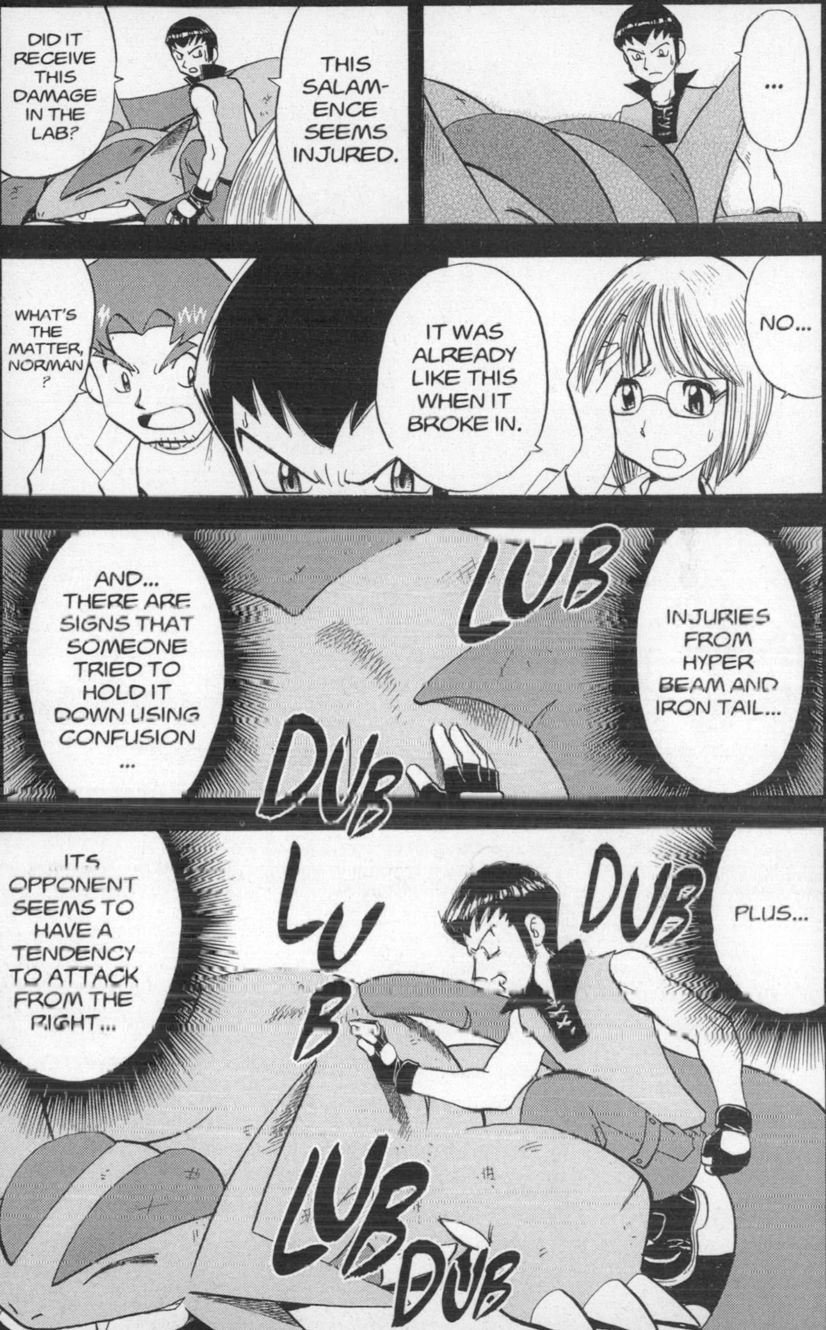
...
THIS SALAM-ENCE SEEMS INJURED.
DID IT RECEIVE THIS DAMAGE IN THE LAB?
NO...
IT WAS ALREADY LIKE THIS WHEN IT BROKE IN.
WHAT'S THE MATTER, NORMAN?
INJURIES FROM HYPER BEAM AND IRON TAIL...
LUB
AND... THERE ARE SIGNS THAT SOMEONE TRIED TO HOLD IT DOWN USING CONFUSION...
DUB
PLUS...
DUB
ITS OPPONENT SEEMS TO HAVE A TENDENCY TO ATTACK FROM THE RIGHT...
LUB
LUB
DUB

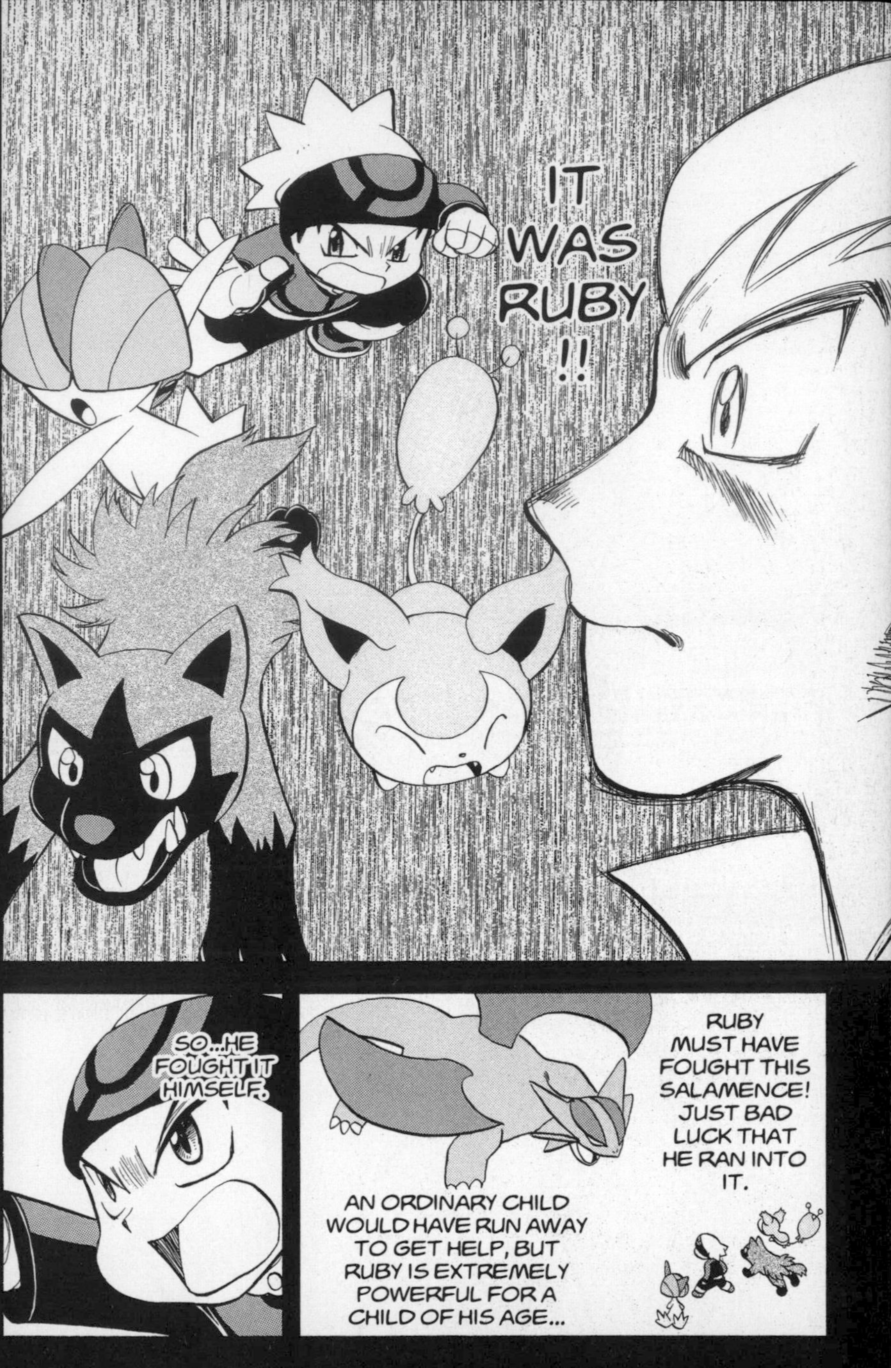
IT WAS RUBY!!
RUBY MUST HAVE FOUGHT THIS SALAMENCE! JUST BAD LUCK THAT HE RAN INTO IT.
AN ORDINARY CHILD WOULD HAVE RUN AWAY TO GET HELP, BUT RUBY IS EXTREMELY POWERFUL FOR A CHILD OF HIS AGE...
SO...HE FOUGHT IT HIMSELF.

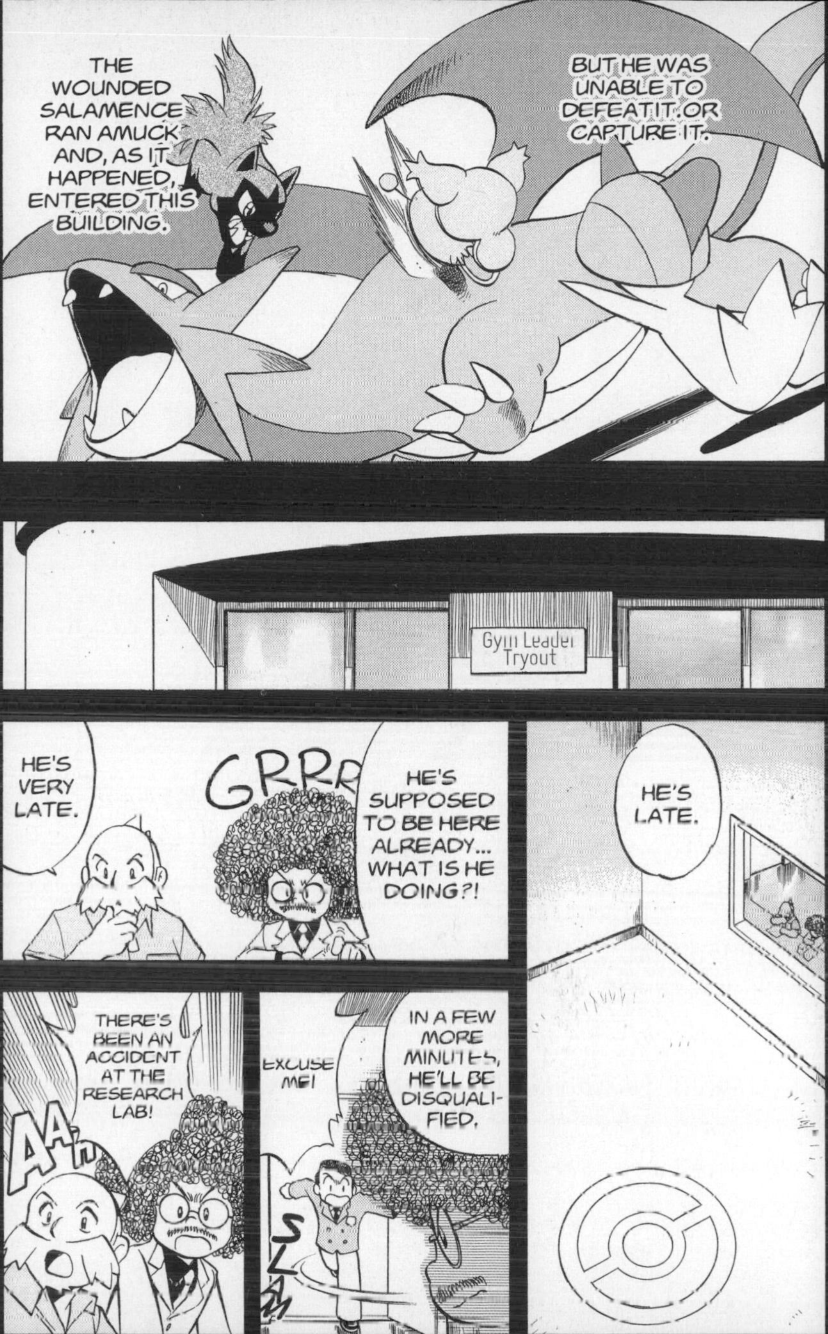
BUT HE WAS UNABLE TO DEFEAT IT OR CAPTURE IT.
THE WOUNDED SALAMENCE RAN AMUCK AND, AS IT HAPPENED, ENTERED THIS BUILDING.
Gym Leader Tryout
HE'S LATE.
HE'S SUPPOSED TO BE HERE ALREADY... WHAT IS HE DOING?!
GRRR
HE'S VERY LATE.
IN A FEW MORE MINUTES, HE'LL BE DISQUALIFIED.
EXCUSE ME!
SLAM
THERE'S BEEN AN ACCIDENT AT THE RESEARCH LAB!
AAh

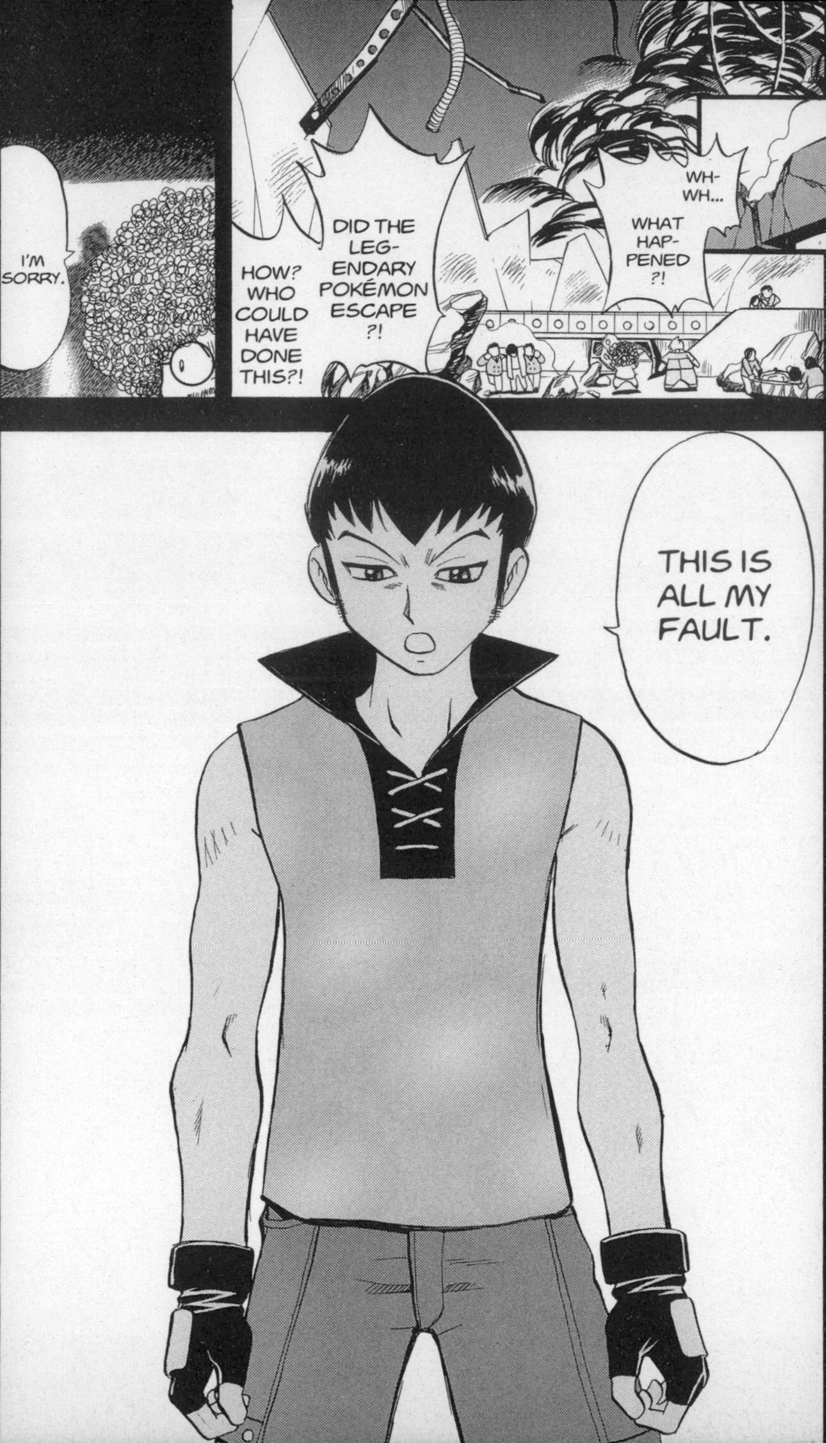
WH-WH... WHAT HAPPENED?!
DID THE LEGENDARY POKÉMON ESCAPE?!
HOW? WHO COULD HAVE DONE THIS?!
I'M SORRY.
THIS IS ALL MY FAULT.

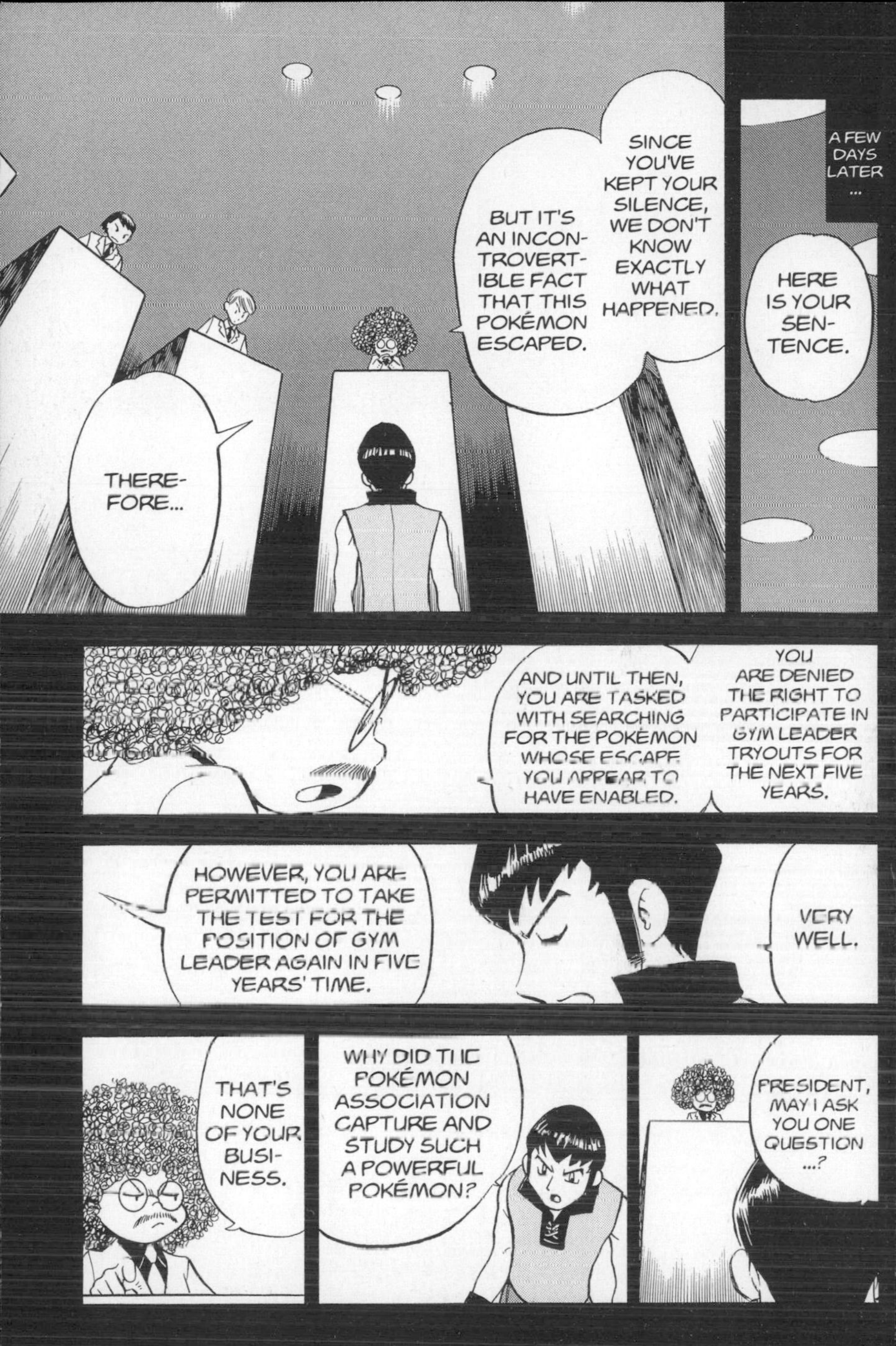
A FEW DAYS LATER...
HERE IS YOUR SENTENCE.
SINCE YOU'VE KEPT YOUR SILENCE, WE DON'T KNOW EXACTLY WHAT HAPPENED.
BUT IT'S AN INCONTROVERTIBLE FACT THAT THIS POKÉMON ESCAPED.
THEREFORE...
YOU ARE DENIED THE RIGHT TO PARTICIPATE IN GYM LEADER TRYOUTS FOR THE NEXT FIVE YEARS.
AND UNTIL THEN, YOU ARE TASKED WITH SEARCHING FOR THE POKÉMON WHOSE ESCAPE YOU APPEAR TO HAVE ENABLED.
HOWEVER, YOU ARE PERMITTED TO TAKE THE TEST FOR THE POSITION OF GYM LEADER AGAIN IN FIVE YEARS' TIME.
VERY WELL.
PRESIDENT, MAY I ASK YOU ONE QUESTION...?
WHY DID THE POKÉMON ASSOCIATION CAPTURE AND STUDY SUCH A POWERFUL POKÉMON?
THAT'S NONE OF YOUR BUSINESS.

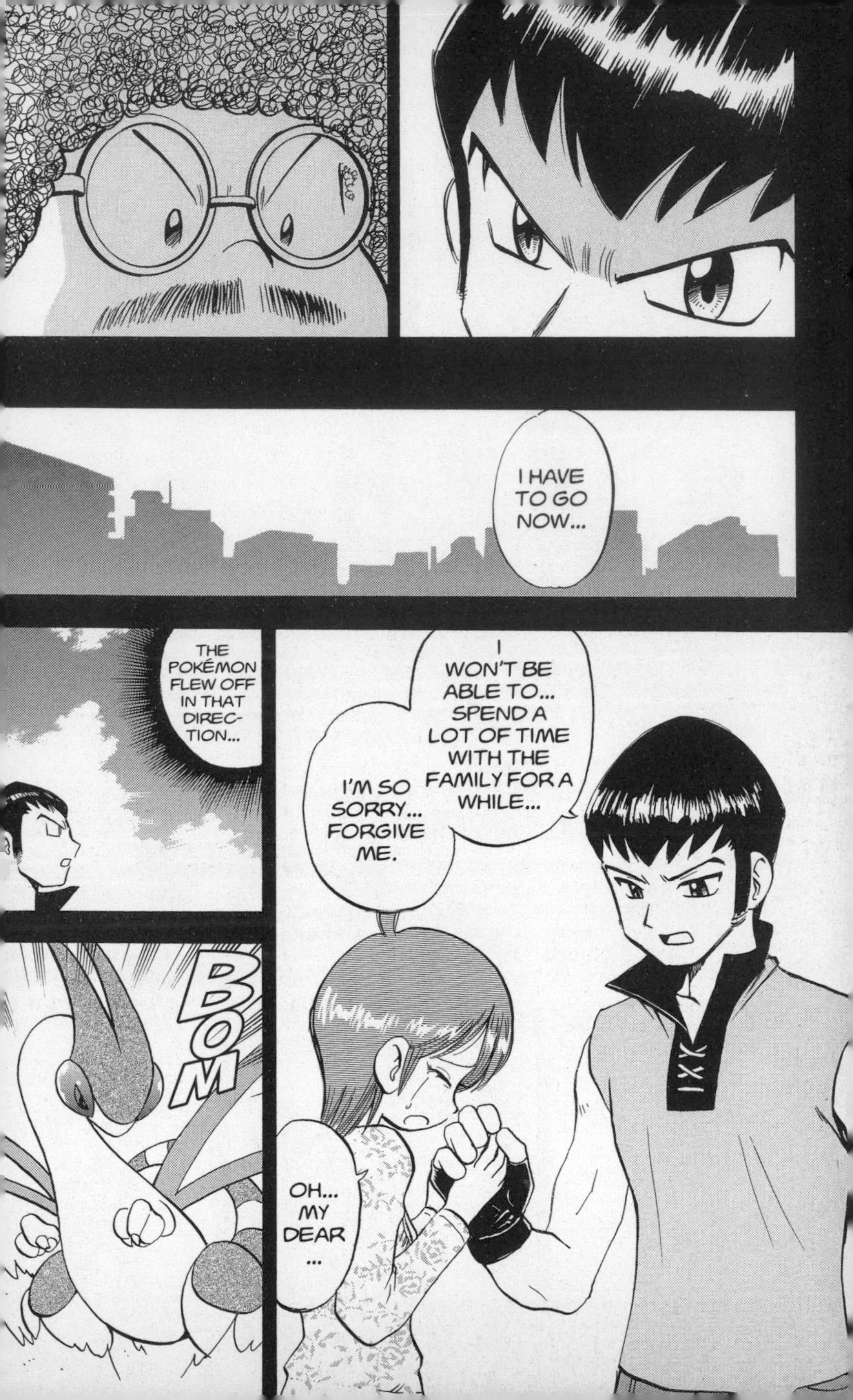
I HAVE TO GO NOW...
I WON'T BE ABLE TO... SPEND A LOT OF TIME WITH THE FAMILY FOR A WHILE...
I'M SO SORRY... FORGIVE ME.
OH... MY DEAR ...
THE POKÉMON FLEW OFF IN THAT DIREC- TION...
BOM

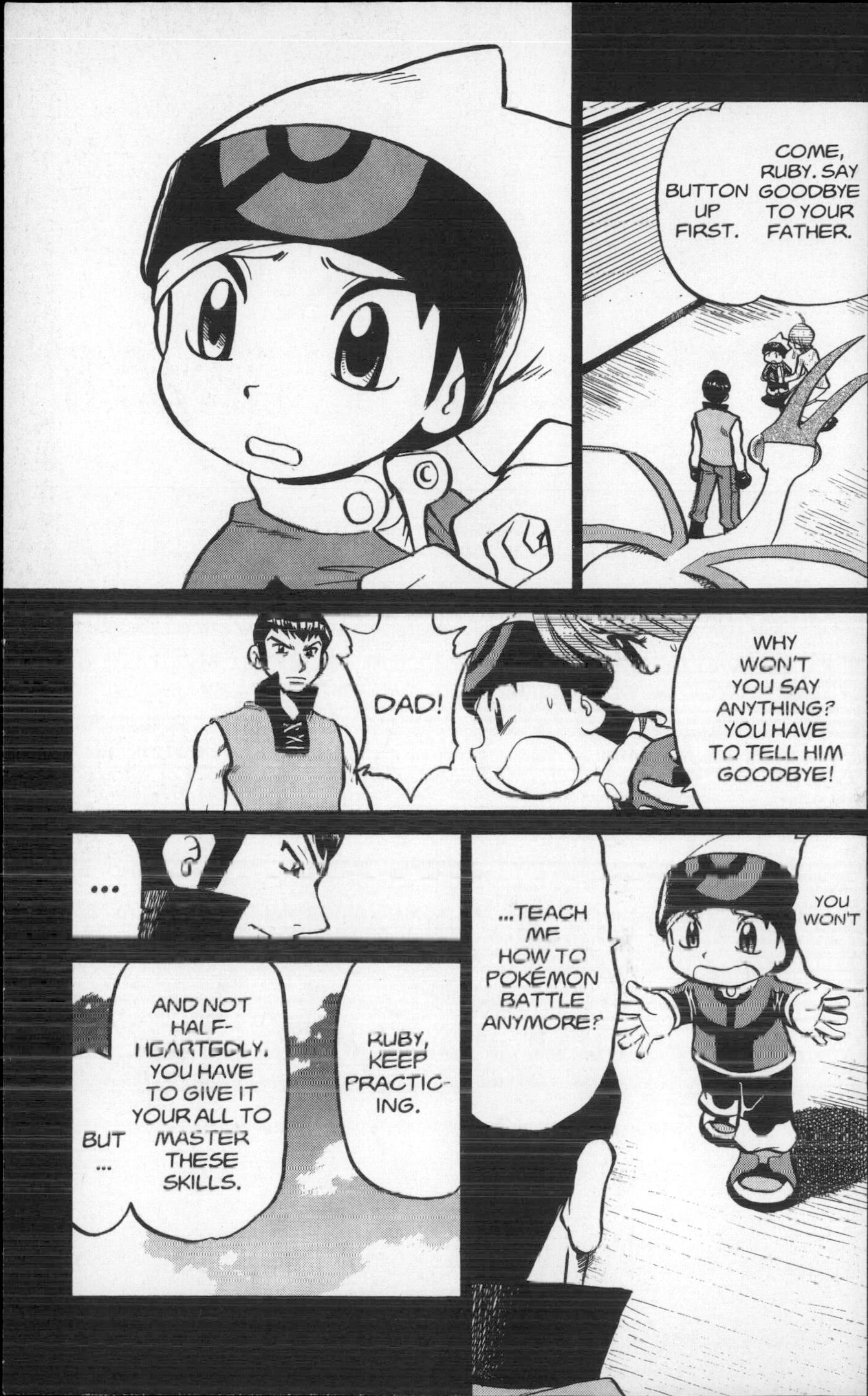
COME, RUBY. SAY GOODBYE TO YOUR FATHER.
BUTTON UP FIRST.
WHY WON'T YOU SAY ANYTHING? YOU HAVE TO TELL HIM GOODBYE!
DAD!
YOU WON'T
...TEACH ME HOW TO POKÉMON BATTLE ANYMORE?
...
RUBY, KEEP PRACTIC-ING.
AND NOT HALF-HEARTEDLY. YOU HAVE TO GIVE IT YOUR ALL TO MASTER THESE SKILLS.
BUT ...

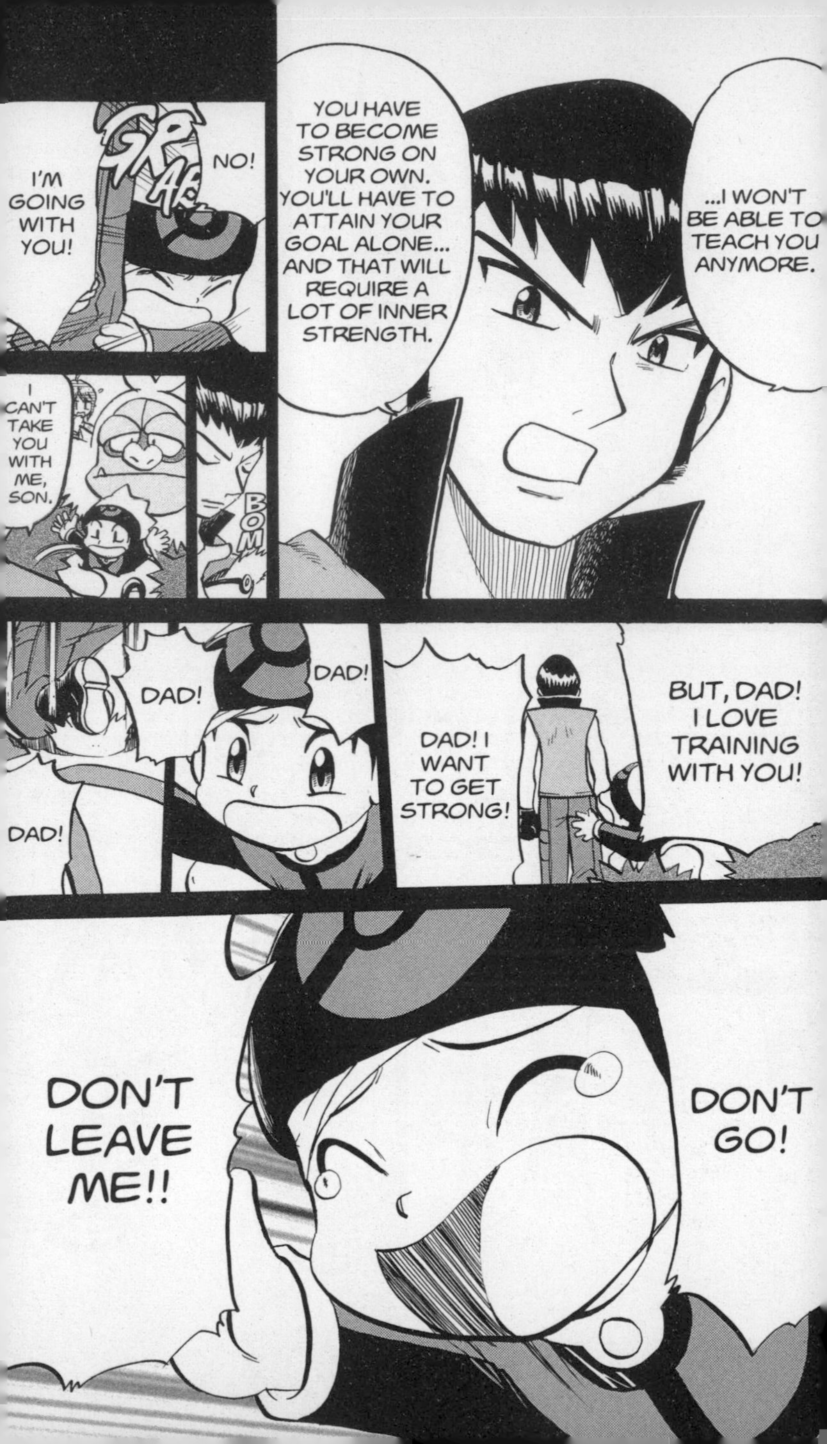
...I WON'T BE ABLE TO TEACH YOU ANYMORE.
YOU HAVE TO BECOME STRONG ON YOUR OWN. YOU'LL HAVE TO ATTAIN YOUR GOAL ALONE... AND THAT WILL REQUIRE A LOT OF INNER STRENGTH.
NO!
GRAB
I'M GOING WITH YOU!
BOM
I CAN'T TAKE YOU WITH ME, SON.
BUT, DAD! I LOVE TRAINING WITH YOU!
DAD! I WANT TO GET STRONG!
DAD!
DAD!
DAD!
DON'T GO!
DON'T LEAVE ME!!

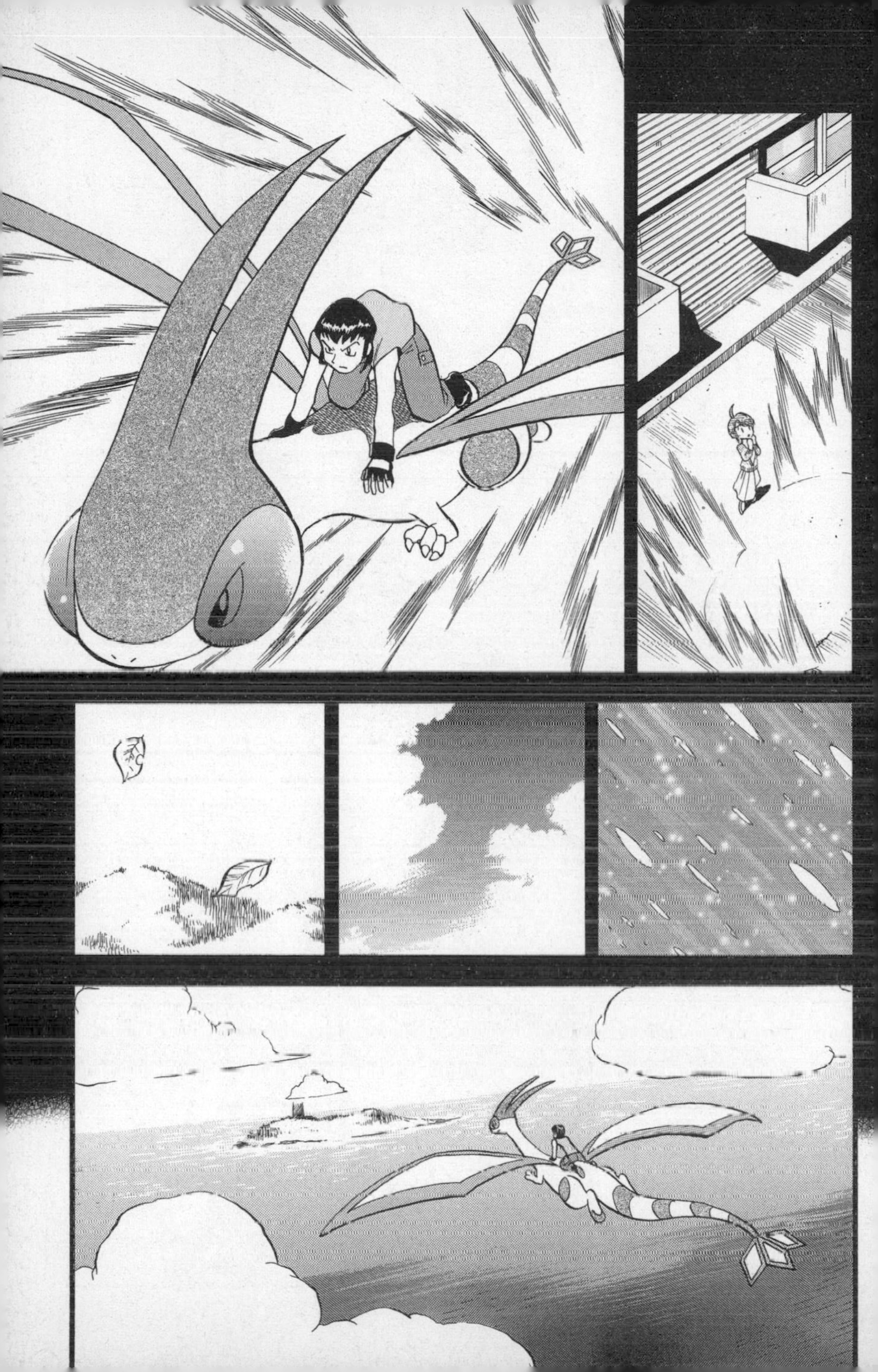

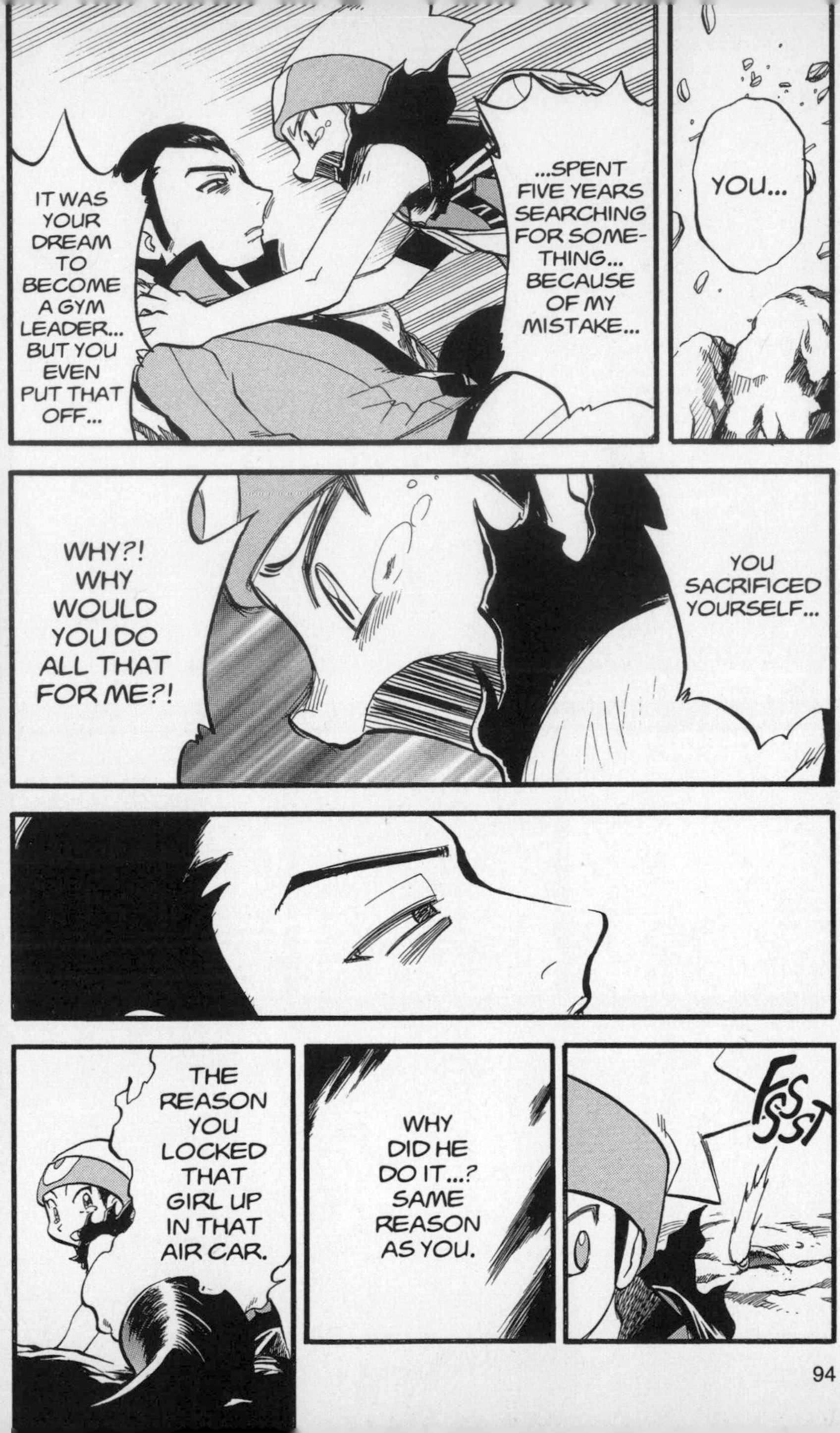
YOU...
...SPENT FIVE YEARS SEARCHING FOR SOMETHING... BECAUSE OF MY MISTAKE...
IT WAS YOUR DREAM TO BECOME A GYM LEADER... BUT YOU EVEN PUT THAT OFF...
YOU SACRIFICED YOURSELF...
WHY?! WHY WOULD YOU DO ALL THAT FOR ME?!
FSSST
WHY DID HE DO IT...? SAME REASON AS YOU.
THE REASON YOU LOCKED THAT GIRL UP IN THAT AIR CAR.

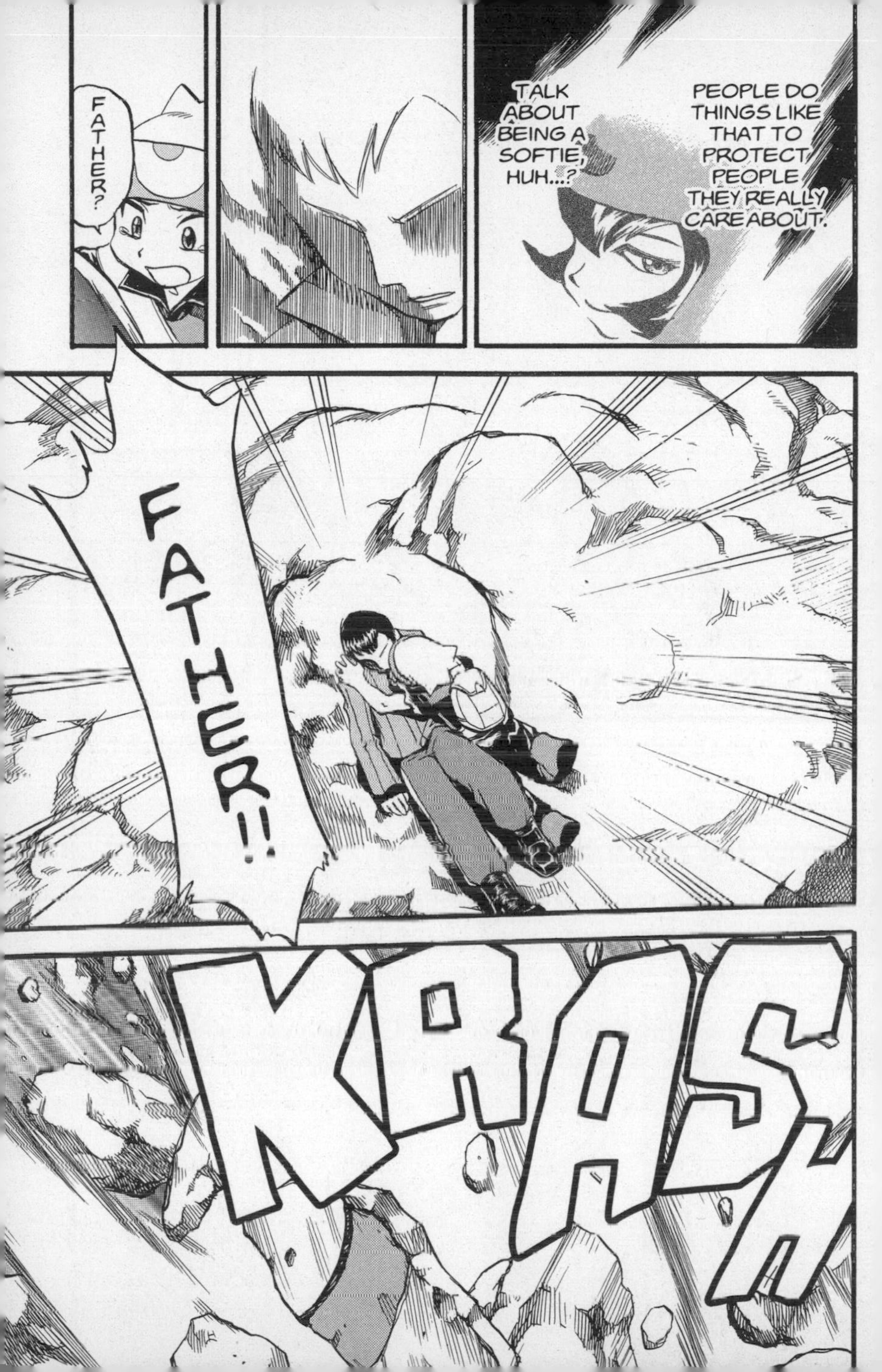
PEOPLE DO THINGS LIKE THAT TO PROTECT PEOPLE THEY REALLY CARE ABOUT.
TALK ABOUT BEING A SOFTIE, HUH...?
FATHER?
FATHER!!
KRASH

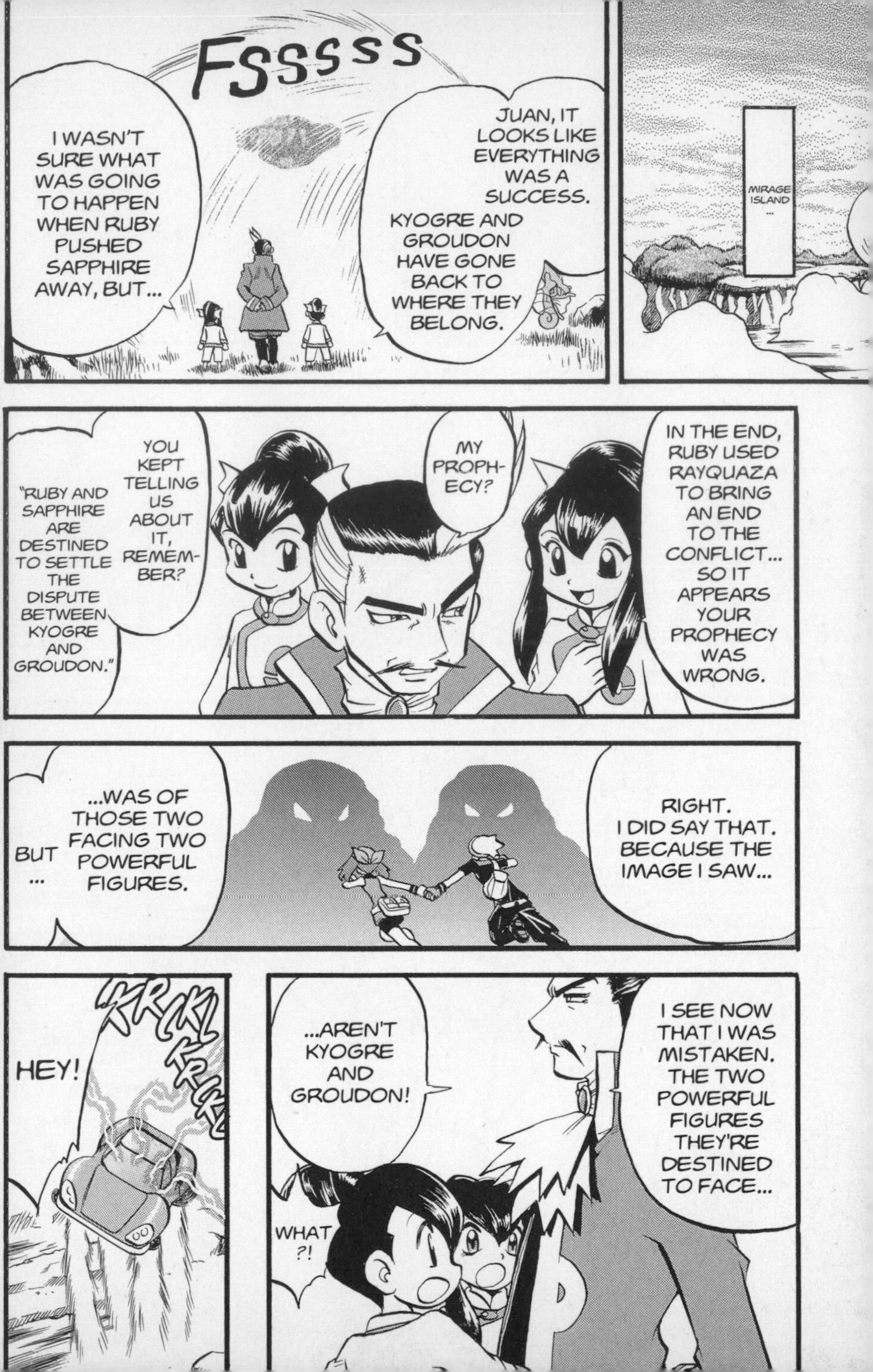
MIRAGE ISLAND ...
FSSSSS
JUAN, IT LOOKS LIKE EVERYTHING WAS A SUCCESS.
KYOGRE AND GROUDON HAVE GONE BACK TO WHERE THEY BELONG.
I WASN'T SURE WHAT WAS GOING TO HAPPEN WHEN RUBY PUSHED SAPPHIRE AWAY, BUT...
IN THE END, RUBY USED RAYQUAZA TO BRING AN END TO THE CONFLICT... SO IT APPEARS YOUR PROPHECY WAS WRONG.
MY PROPHECY?
YOU KEPT TELLING US ABOUT IT, REMEMBER?
"RUBY AND SAPPHIRE ARE DESTINED TO SETTLE THE DISPUTE BETWEEN KYOGRE AND GROUDON."
RIGHT. I DID SAY THAT. BECAUSE THE IMAGE I SAW...
...WAS OF THOSE TWO FACING TWO POWERFUL FIGURES.
BUT ...
I SEE NOW THAT I WAS MISTAKEN. THE TWO POWERFUL FIGURES THEY'RE DESTINED TO FACE...
...AREN'T KYOGRE AND GROUDON!
WHAT ?!
KRIKL KRIKL
HEY!

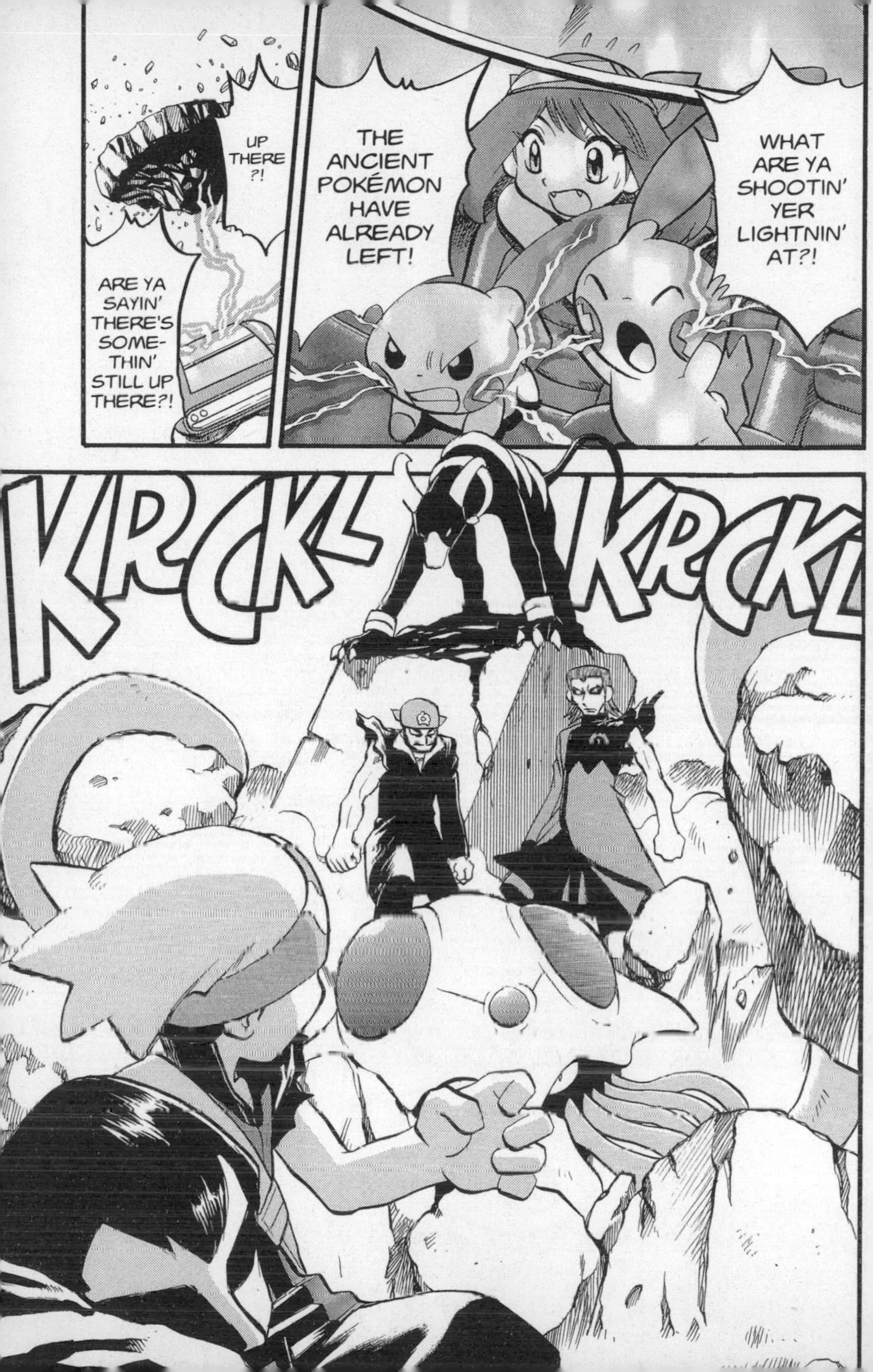
WHAT ARE YA SHOOTIN' YER LIGHTNIN' AT?!
THE ANCIENT POKÉMON HAVE ALREADY LEFT!
UP THERE?!
ARE YA SAYIN' THERE'S SOME-THIN' STILL UP THERE?!
KRCKL
KRCKL

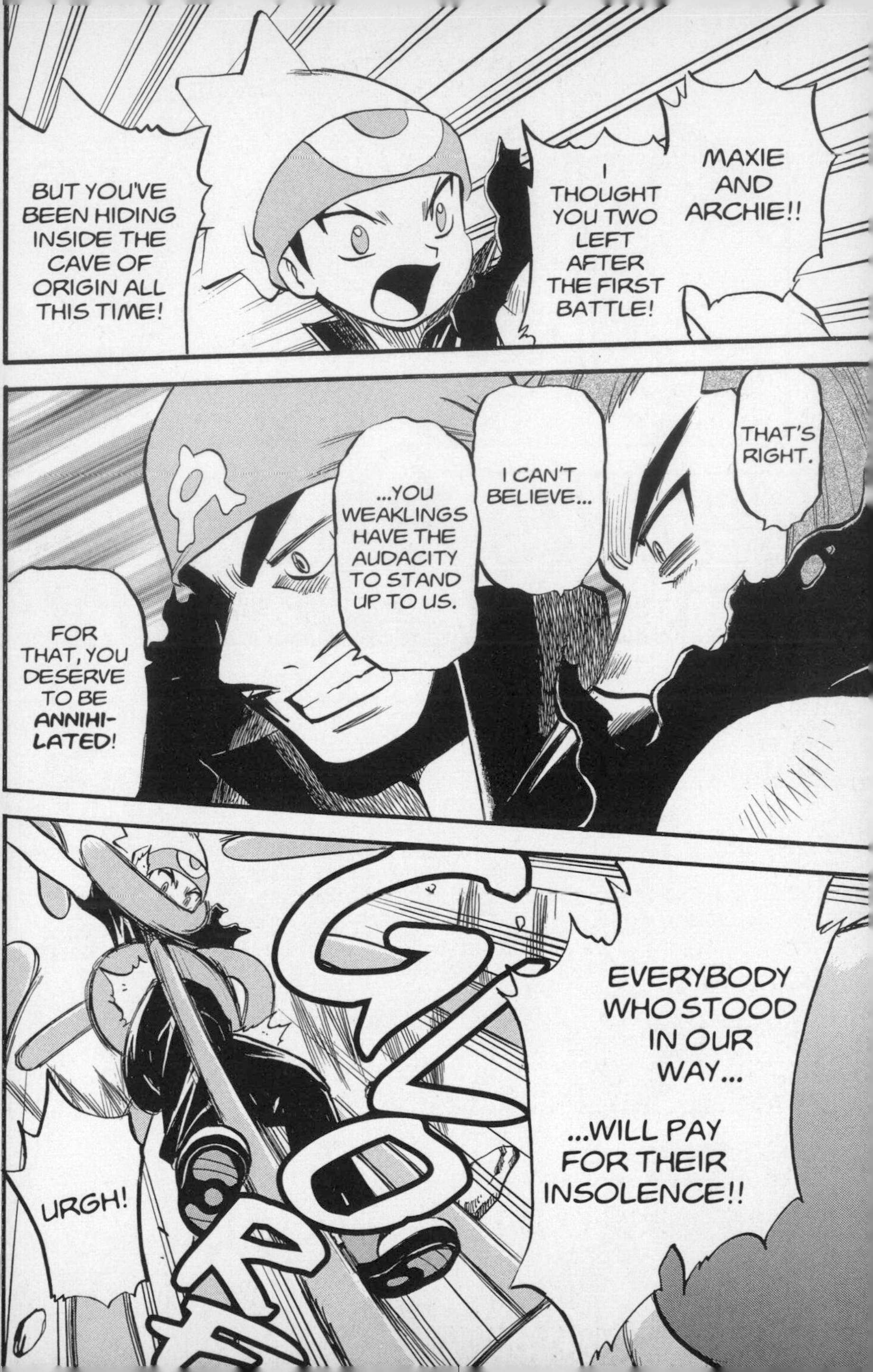
MAXIE AND ARCHIE!!
I THOUGHT YOU TWO LEFT AFTER THE FIRST BATTLE!
BUT YOU'VE BEEN HIDING INSIDE THE CAVE OF ORIGIN ALL THIS TIME!
THAT'S RIGHT.
I CAN'T BELIEVE...
...YOU WEAKLINGS HAVE THE AUDACITY TO STAND UP TO US.
FOR THAT, YOU DESERVE TO BE **ANNIHILATED**!
EVERYBODY WHO STOOD IN OUR WAY...
...WILL PAY FOR THEIR INSOLENCE!!
URGH!

ADVENTURE MAP

● Sootopolis City ●

SAPPHIRE

CHIC
Blaziken ♀
Lv59

RONO
Aggron ♂
Lv54

PHADO
Donphan ♂
Lv58

MINUN
Minun ♀
Lv52

PLUSLE
Plusle ♂
Lv52

RUBY

MUMU
Swampert ♂

NANA
Mightyena ♀

KIKI
Delcatty ♀

FOFO
Castform ♀

TROPPY
Tropius ♂

Stone Badge	Knuckle Badge	Dynamo Badge	Heat Badge
Balance Badge	Feather Badge	Mind Badge	Rain Badge

	Cool	Beauty	Cute	Smart	Tough
Normal	○	○	○	○	○
Super	○	○	○	○	○
Hyper	○	✦	○	○	○
Master	✦	✦	..	✦	○

● Chapter 265 ●
It All Ends Now VI

Pokémon™ Adventures Ruby & Sapphire

The Fourth Chapter

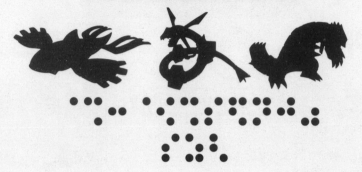

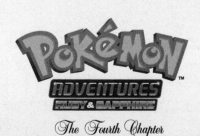

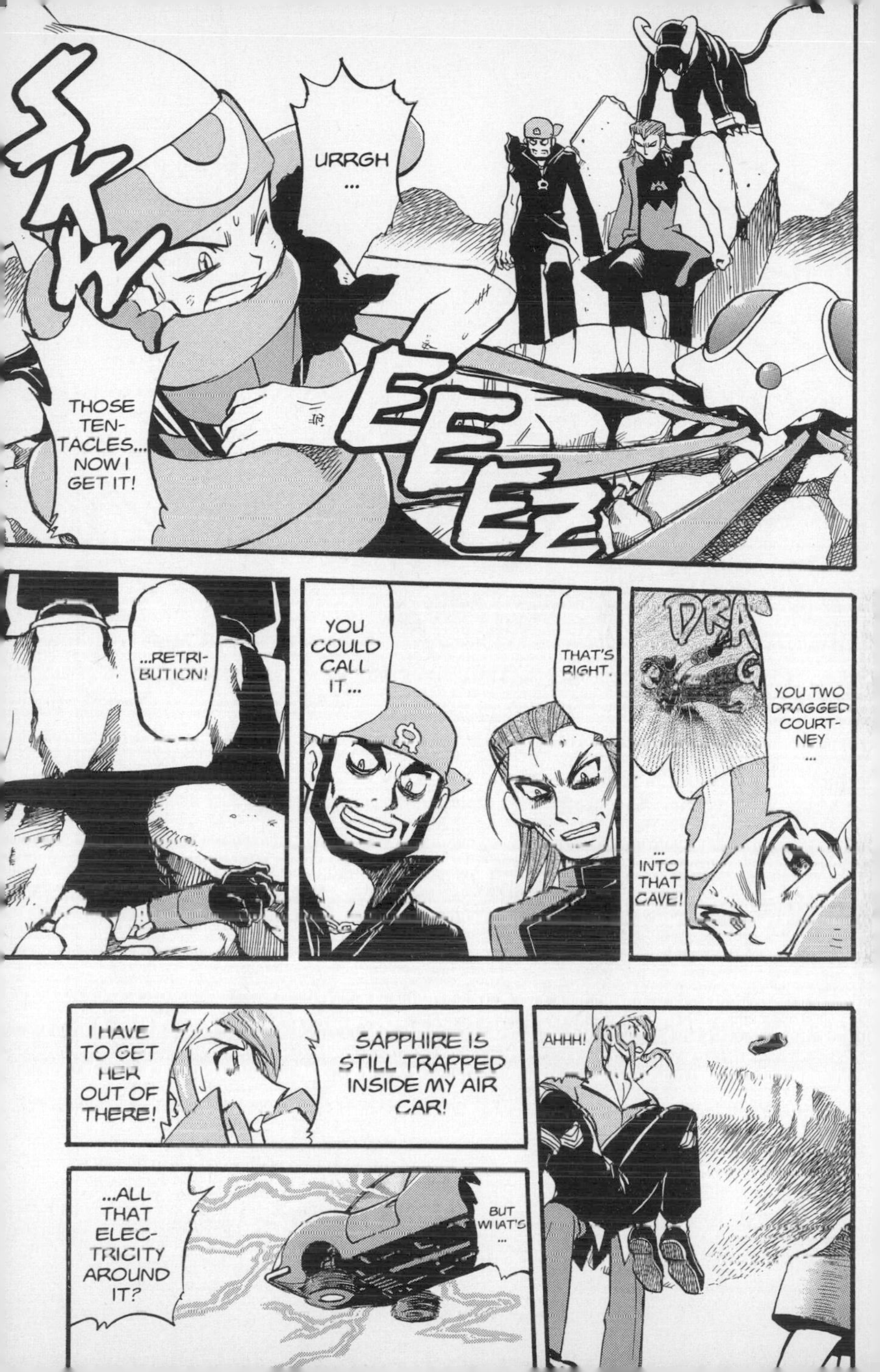
URRGH ...
EEEZ
SKW
THOSE TENTACLES... NOW I GET IT!
DRA
YOU TWO DRAGGED COURTNEY ...
... INTO THAT CAVE!
THAT'S RIGHT.
YOU COULD CALL IT...
...RETRIBUTION!
AHHH!
SAPPHIRE IS STILL TRAPPED INSIDE MY AIR CAR!
I HAVE TO GET HER OUT OF THERE!
BUT WHAT'S ...
...ALL THAT ELECTRICITY AROUND IT?

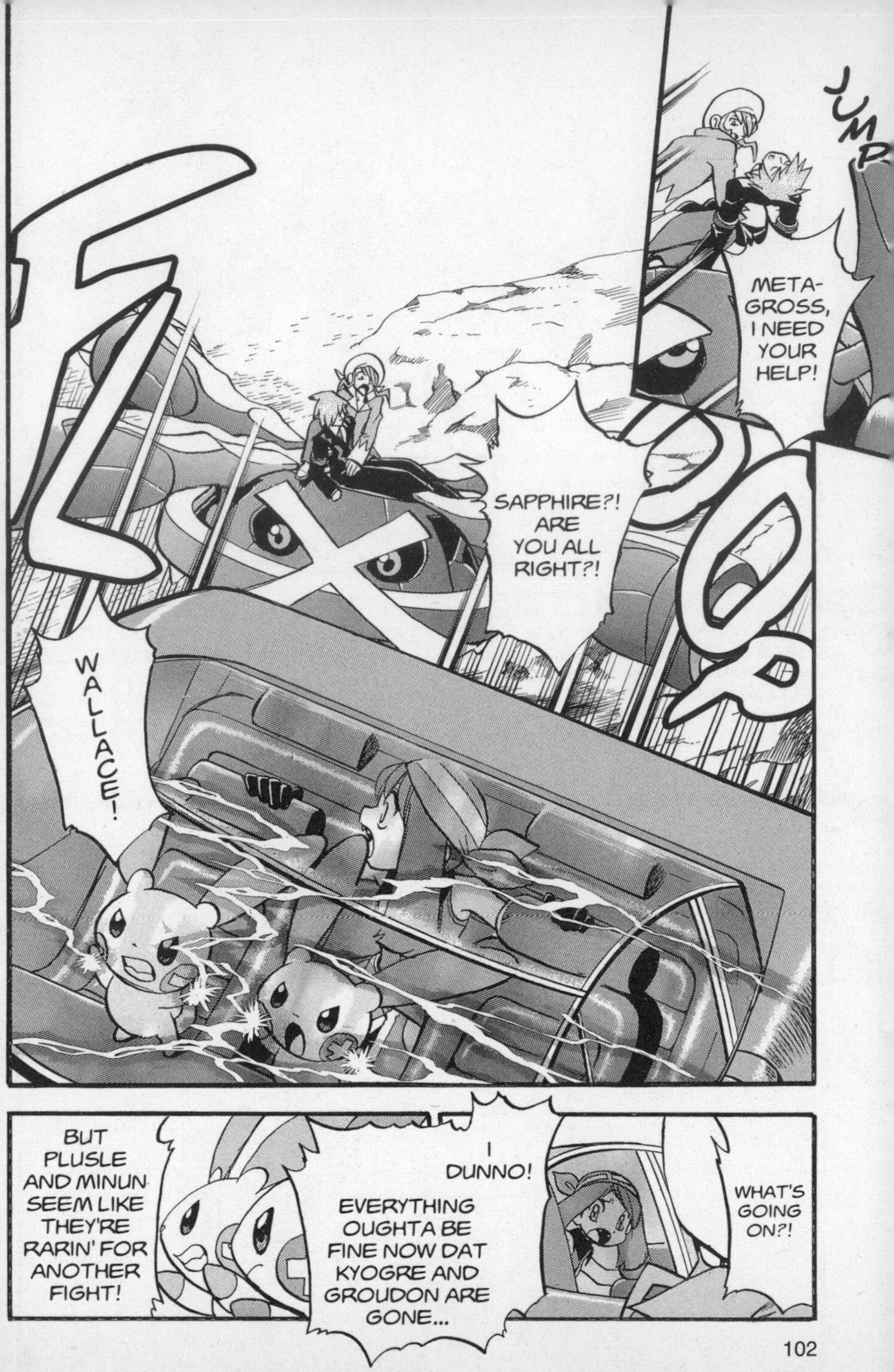
JUMP
METAGROSS, I NEED YOUR HELP!
SAPPHIRE?! ARE YOU ALL RIGHT?!
WALLACE!
WHAT'S GOING ON?!
I DUNNO!
EVERYTHING OUGHTA BE FINE NOW DAT KYOGRE AND GROUDON ARE GONE...
BUT PLUSLE AND MINUN SEEM LIKE THEY'RE RARIN' FOR ANOTHER FIGHT!

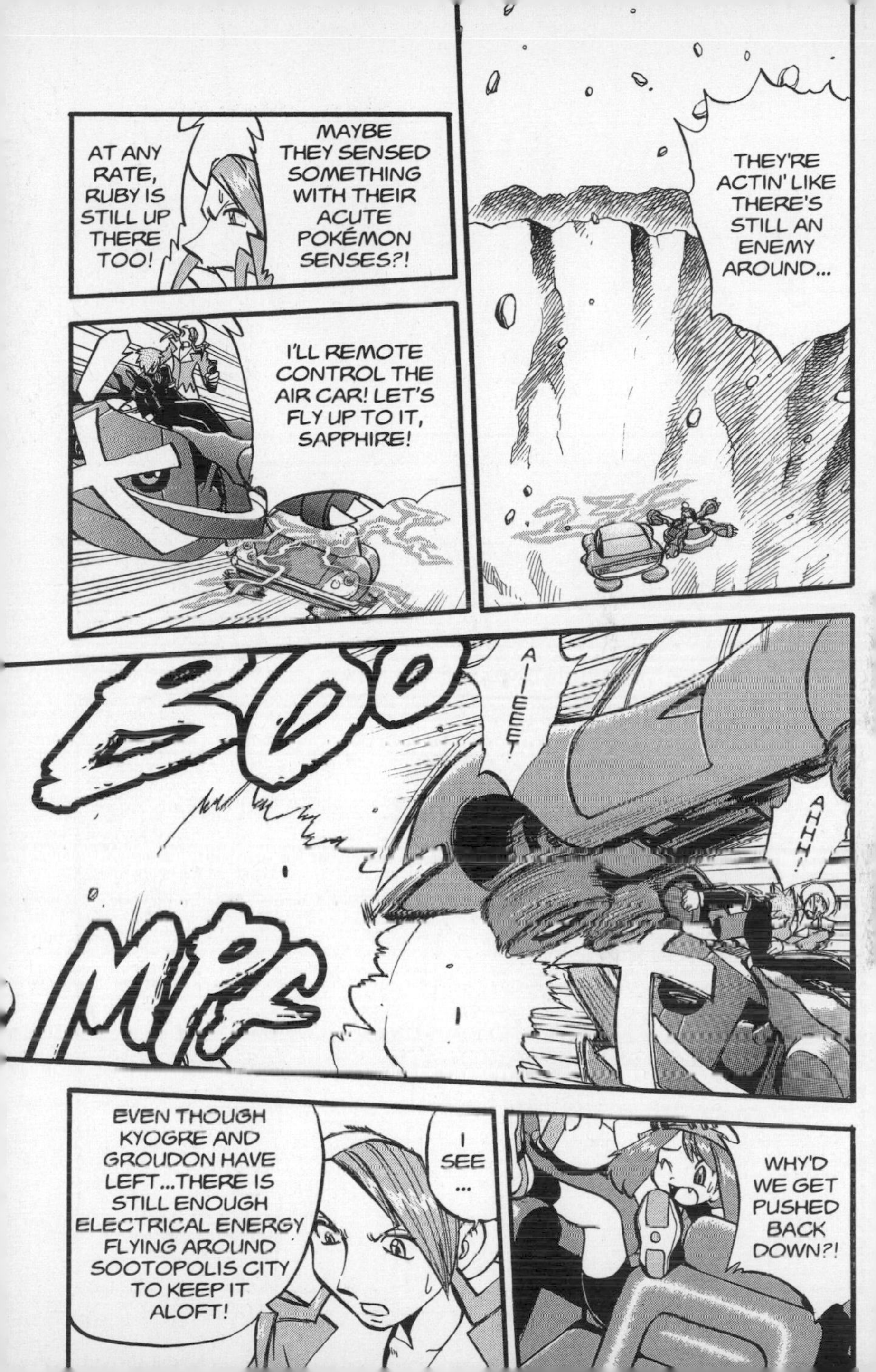
THEY'RE ACTIN' LIKE THERE'S STILL AN ENEMY AROUND...
MAYBE THEY SENSED SOMETHING WITH THEIR ACUTE POKÉMON SENSES?!
AT ANY RATE, RUBY IS STILL UP THERE TOO!
I'LL REMOTE CONTROL THE AIR CAR! LET'S FLY UP TO IT, SAPPHIRE!
AHHH!
AIEEET!
BOOMPF
WHY'D WE GET PUSHED BACK DOWN?!
I SEE...
EVEN THOUGH KYOGRE AND GROUDON HAVE LEFT...THERE IS STILL ENOUGH ELECTRICAL ENERGY FLYING AROUND SOOTOPOLIS CITY TO KEEP IT ALOFT!

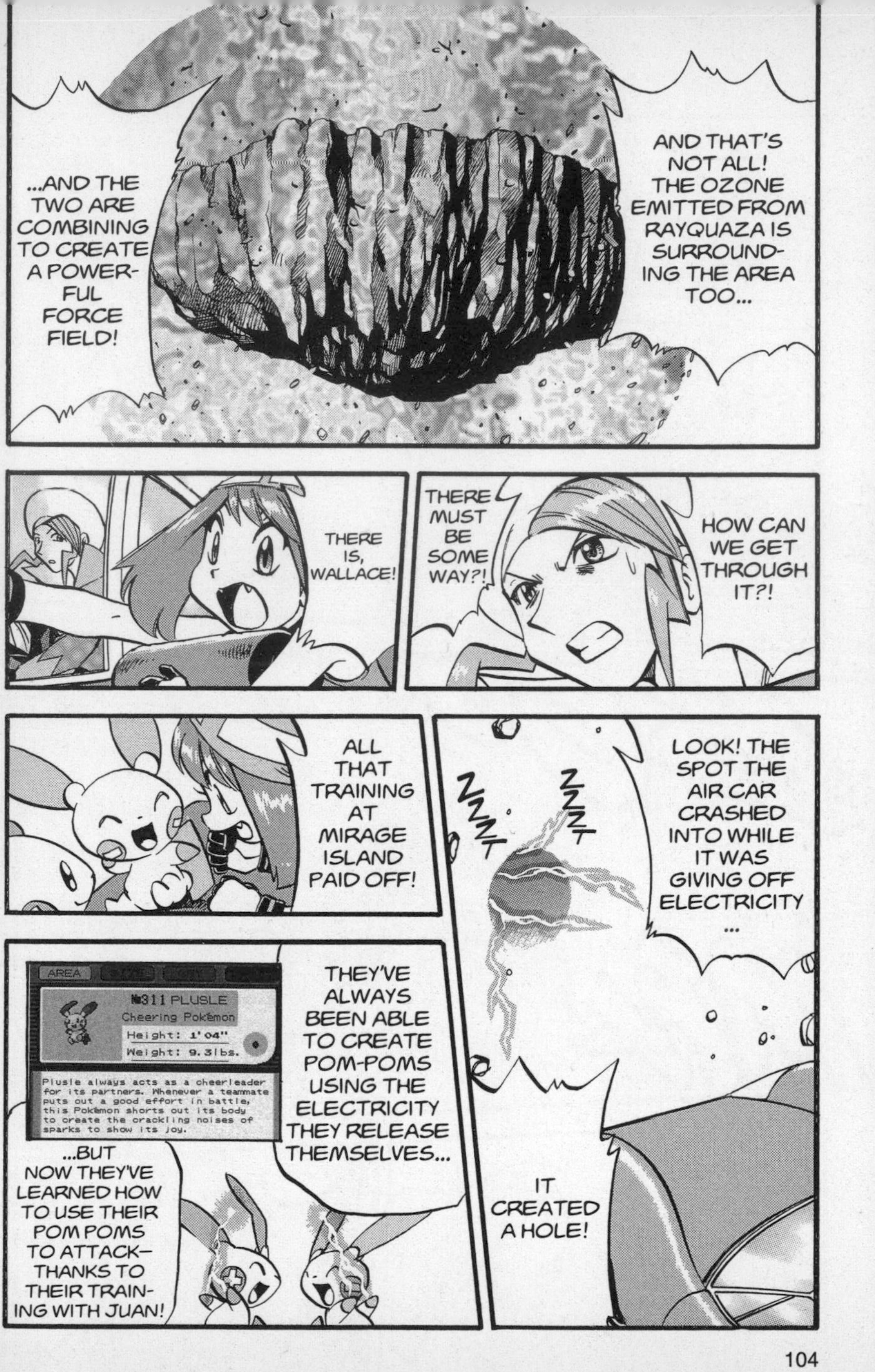
AND THAT'S NOT ALL! THE OZONE EMITTED FROM RAYQUAZA IS SURROUNDING THE AREA TOO...
...AND THE TWO ARE COMBINING TO CREATE A POWERFUL FORCE FIELD!
HOW CAN WE GET THROUGH IT?!
THERE MUST BE SOME WAY?!
THERE IS, WALLACE!
LOOK! THE SPOT THE AIR CAR CRASHED INTO WHILE IT WAS GIVING OFF ELECTRICITY...
ZZZT
ZZZT
IT CREATED A HOLE!
ALL THAT TRAINING AT MIRAGE ISLAND PAID OFF!
AREA
№311 PLUSLE
Cheering Pokémon
Height: 1'04"
Weight: 9.3lbs.
Plusle always acts as a cheerleader for its partners. Whenever a teammate puts out a good effort in battle, this Pokémon shorts out its body to create the crackling noises of sparks to show its joy.
THEY'VE ALWAYS BEEN ABLE TO CREATE POM-POMS USING THE ELECTRICITY THEY RELEASE THEMSELVES...
...BUT NOW THEY'VE LEARNED HOW TO USE THEIR POM POMS TO ATTACK— THANKS TO THEIR TRAINING WITH JUAN!

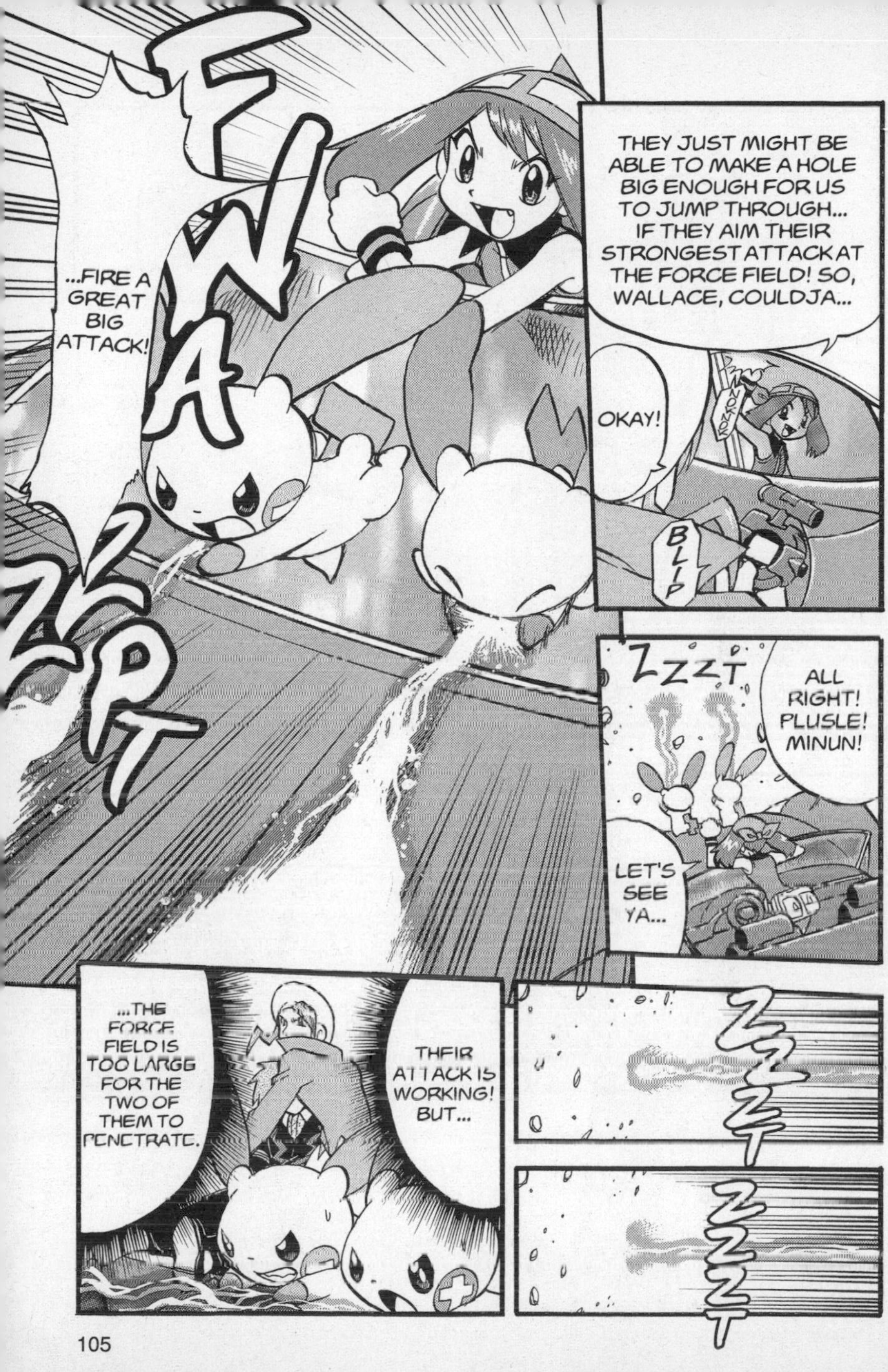
THEY JUST MIGHT BE ABLE TO MAKE A HOLE BIG ENOUGH FOR US TO JUMP THROUGH... IF THEY AIM THEIR STRONGEST ATTACK AT THE FORCE FIELD! SO, WALLACE, COULDJA...
OKAY!
KNOK KNOK
BLIP
ZZZT
ALL RIGHT! PLUSLE! MINUN!
LET'S SEE YA...
...FIRE A GREAT BIG ATTACK!
FWA
ZZPT
ZZZZT
ZZZZT
THEIR ATTACK IS WORKING! BUT...
...THE FORCE FIELD IS TOO LARGE FOR THE TWO OF THEM TO PENETRATE.

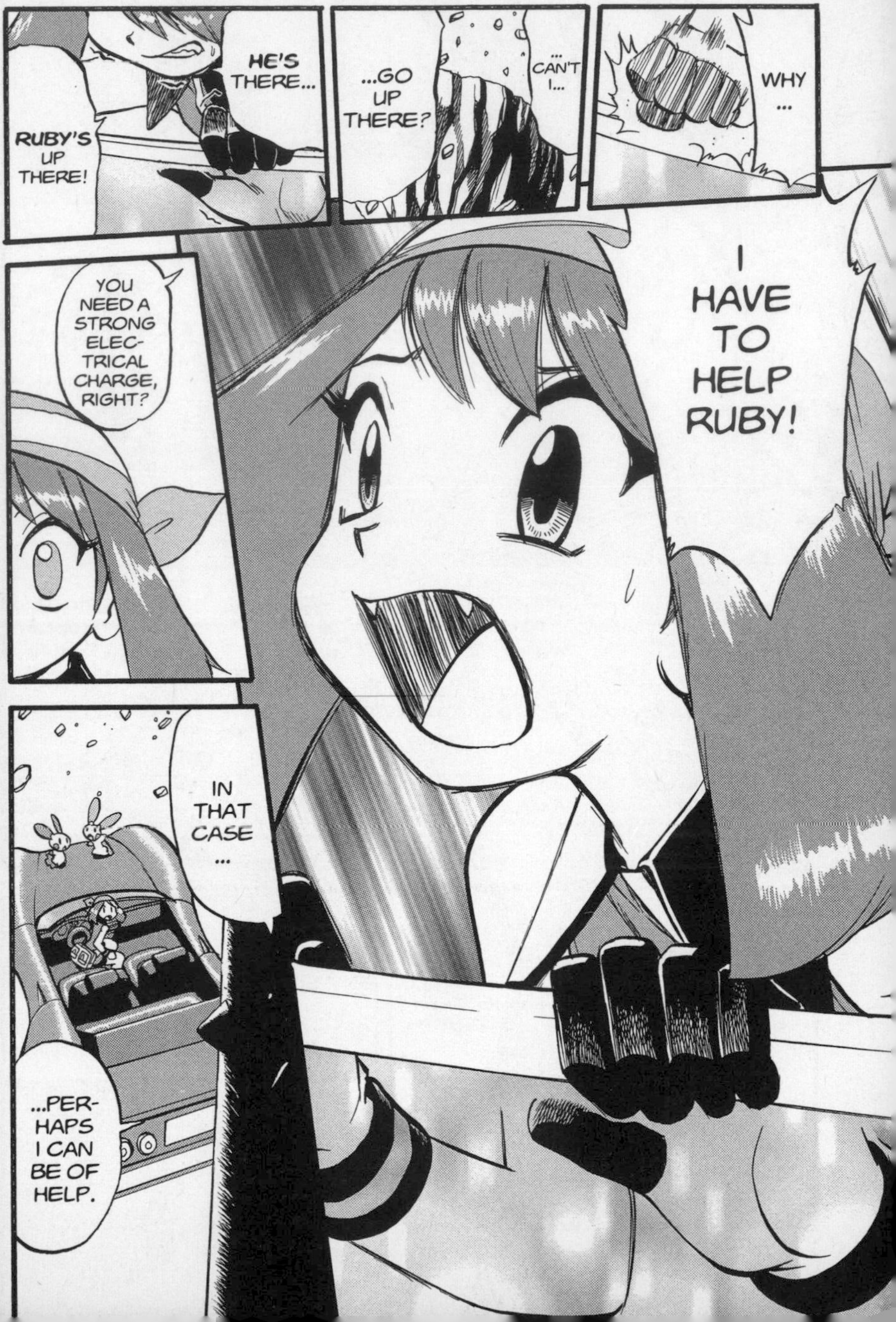
WHY ...
... CAN'T I...
...GO UP THERE?
HE'S THERE...
RUBY'S UP THERE!
I HAVE TO HELP RUBY!
YOU NEED A STRONG ELEC-TRICAL CHARGE, RIGHT?
IN THAT CASE ...
...PER-HAPS I CAN BE OF HELP.

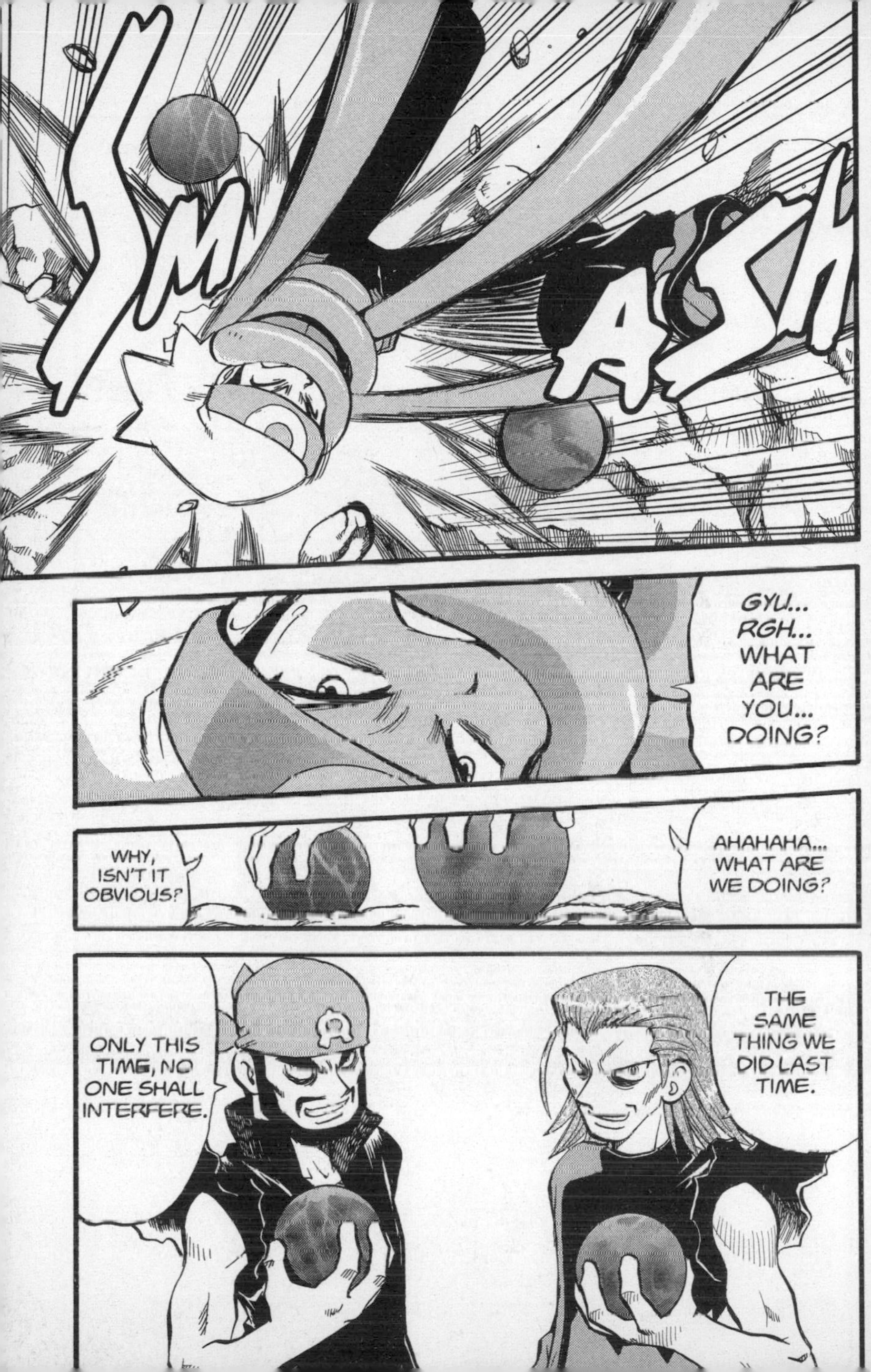
SMASH
GYU... RGH... WHAT ARE YOU... DOING?
AHAHAHA... WHAT ARE WE DOING?
WHY, ISN'T IT OBVIOUS?
THE SAME THING WE DID LAST TIME.
ONLY THIS TIME, NO ONE SHALL INTERFERE.

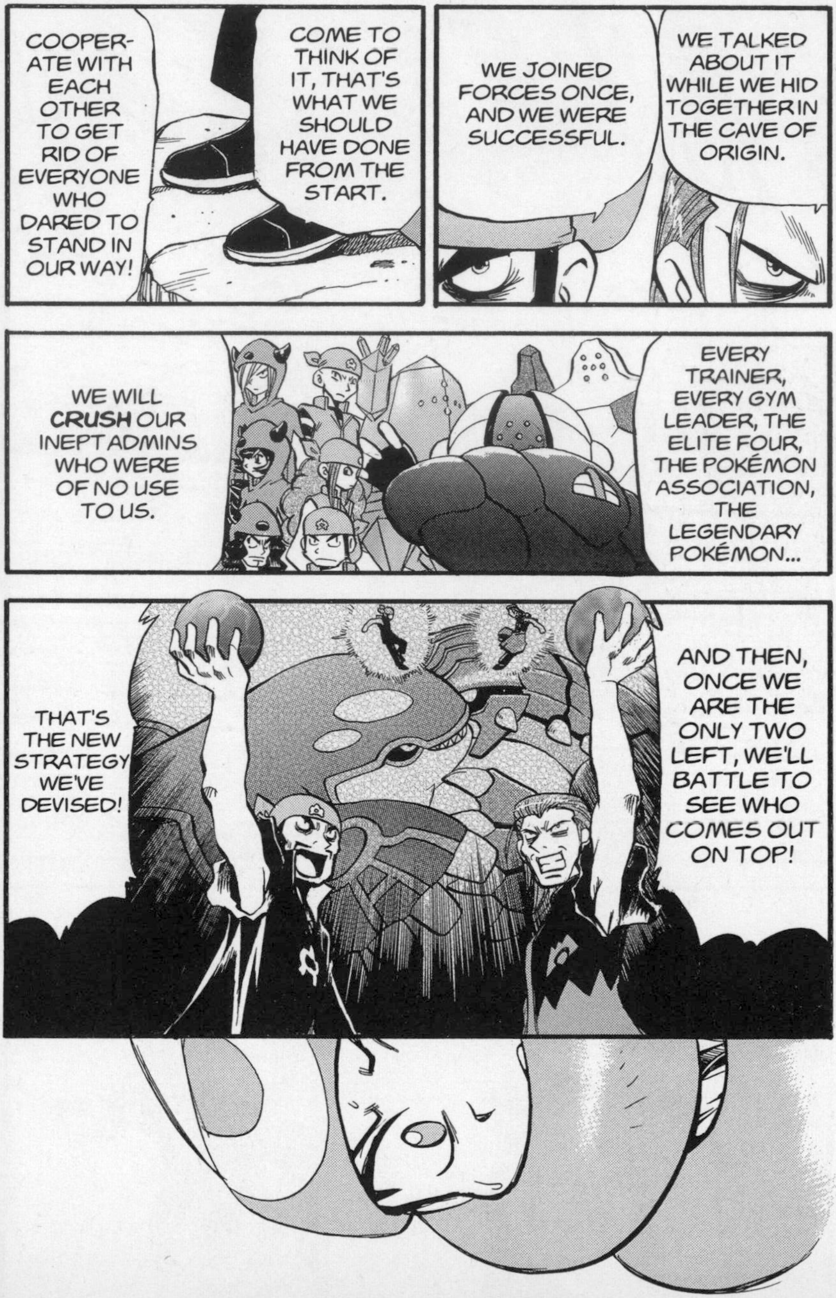
WE TALKED ABOUT IT WHILE WE HID TOGETHER IN THE CAVE OF ORIGIN.
WE JOINED FORCES ONCE, AND WE WERE SUCCESSFUL.
COME TO THINK OF IT, THAT'S WHAT WE SHOULD HAVE DONE FROM THE START.
COOPER-ATE WITH EACH OTHER TO GET RID OF EVERYONE WHO DARED TO STAND IN OUR WAY!
EVERY TRAINER, EVERY GYM LEADER, THE ELITE FOUR, THE POKÉMON ASSOCIATION, THE LEGENDARY POKÉMON...
WE WILL **CRUSH** OUR INEPT ADMINS WHO WERE OF NO USE TO US.
AND THEN, ONCE WE ARE THE ONLY TWO LEFT, WE'LL BATTLE TO SEE WHO COMES OUT ON TOP!
THAT'S THE NEW STRATEGY WE'VE DEVISED!

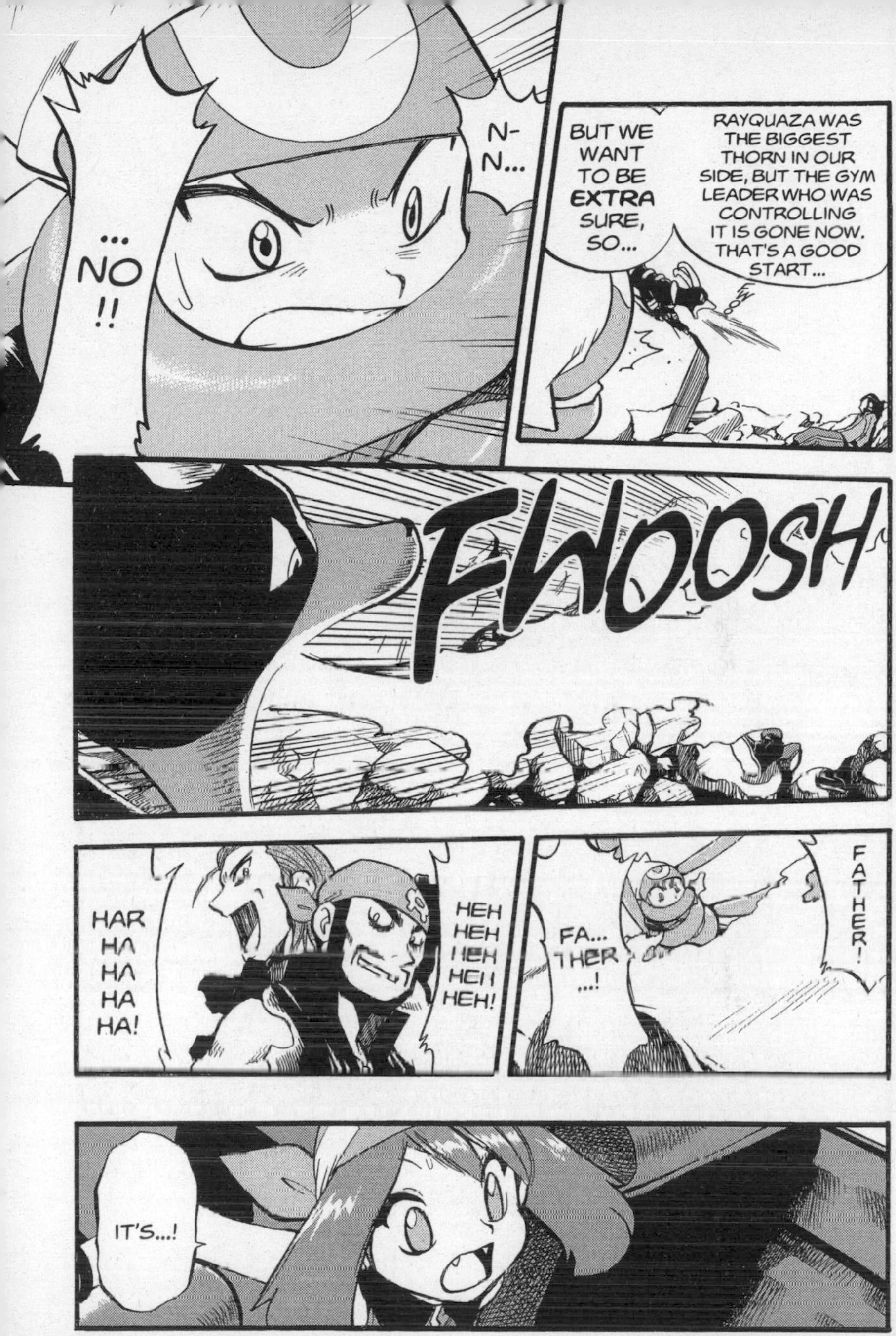
RAYQUAZA WAS THE BIGGEST THORN IN OUR SIDE, BUT THE GYM LEADER WHO WAS CONTROLLING IT IS GONE NOW. THAT'S A GOOD START...
BUT WE WANT TO BE **EXTRA** SURE, SO...
N- N...
... NO !!
FWOOSH
FATHER!
FA... THER ...!
HEH HEH HEH HEH HEH!
HAR HA HA HA HA!
IT'S...!

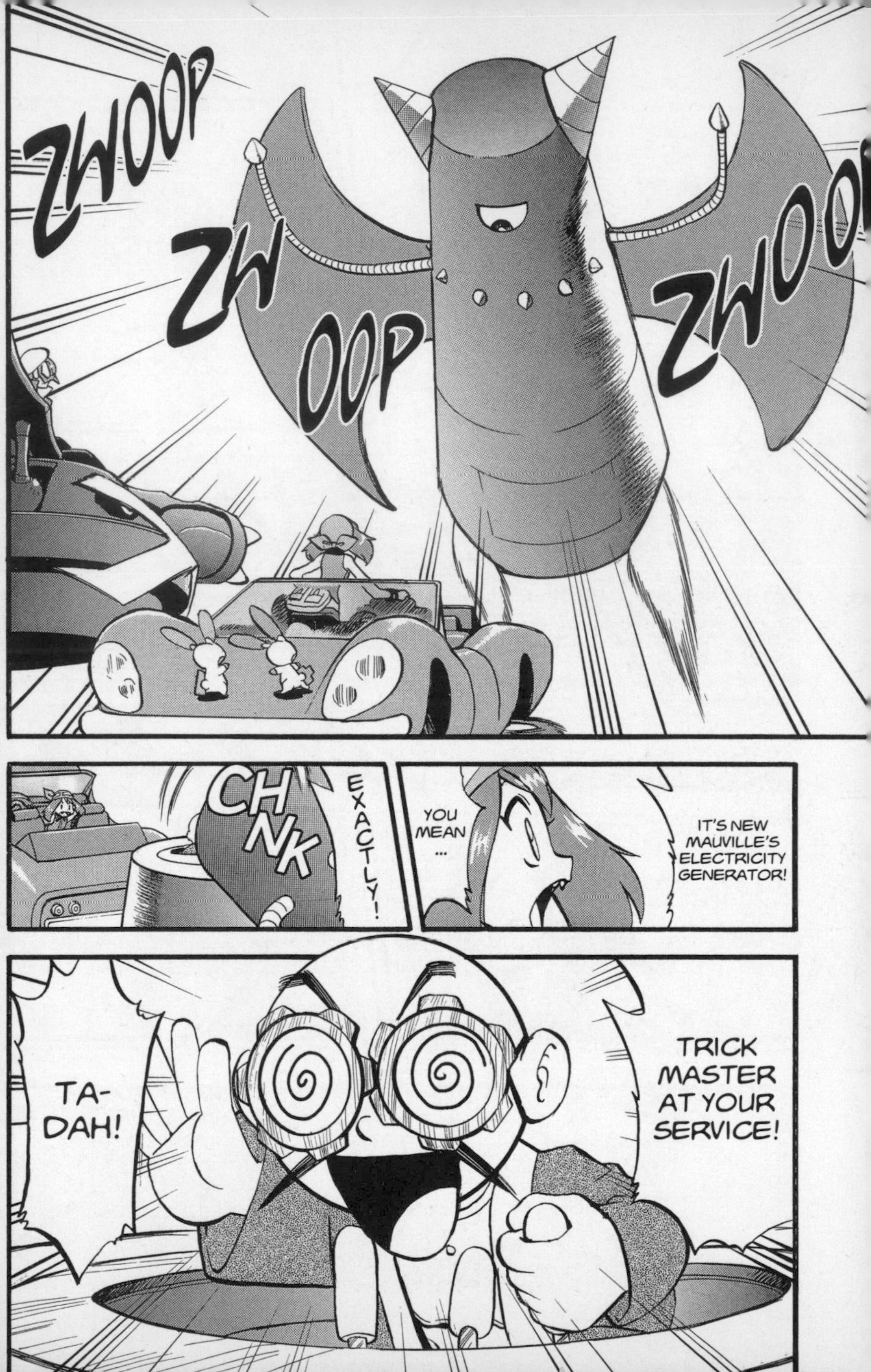
ZWOOP
ZWOOP
ZWOO
IT'S NEW MAUVILLE'S ELECTRICITY GENERATOR!
YOU MEAN...
CHNK
EXACTLY!
TRICK MASTER AT YOUR SERVICE!
TA-DAH!

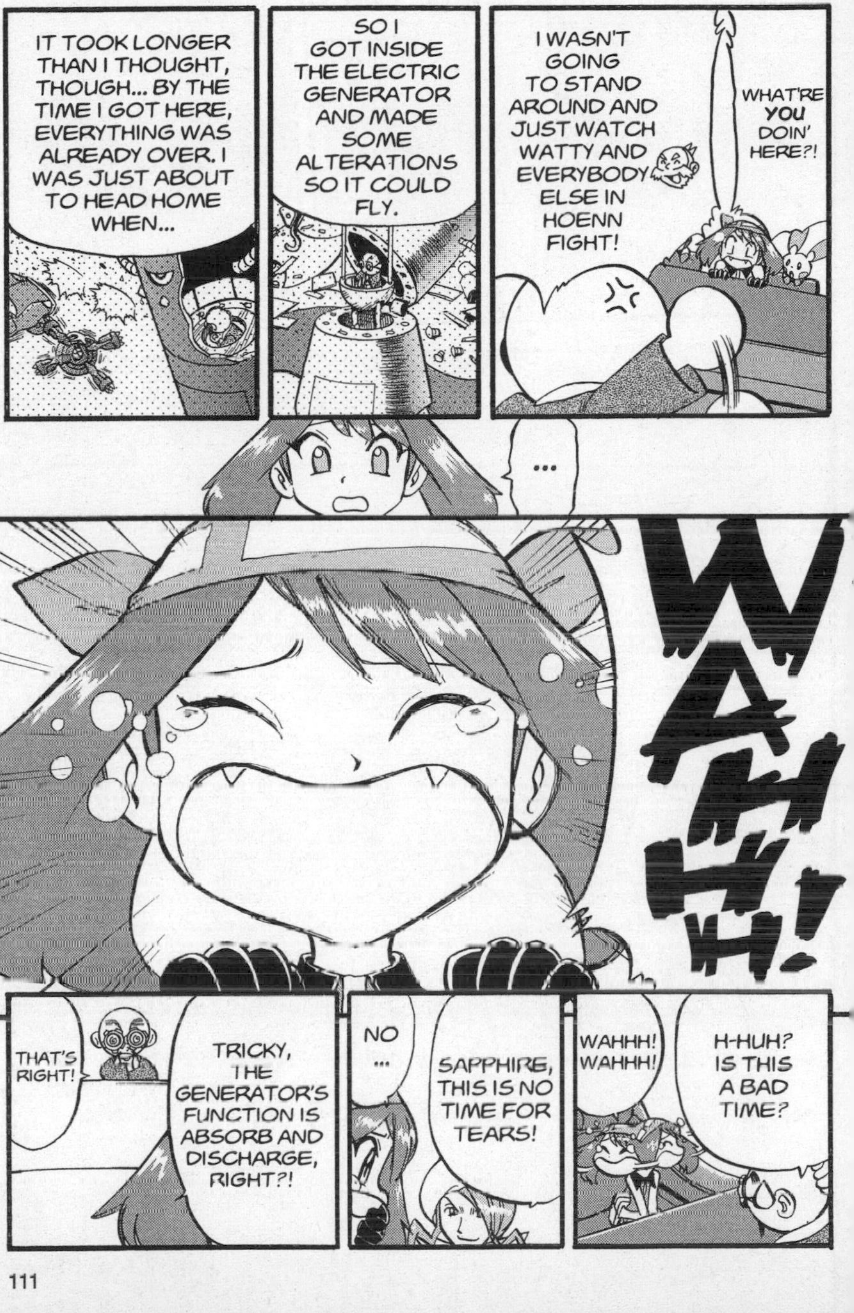
IT TOOK LONGER THAN I THOUGHT, THOUGH... BY THE TIME I GOT HERE, EVERYTHING WAS ALREADY OVER. I WAS JUST ABOUT TO HEAD HOME WHEN...
SO I GOT INSIDE THE ELECTRIC GENERATOR AND MADE SOME ALTERATIONS SO IT COULD FLY.
I WASN'T GOING TO STAND AROUND AND JUST WATCH WATTY AND EVERYBODY ELSE IN HOENN FIGHT!
WHAT'RE YOU DOIN' HERE?!
...
WAHHH!
TRICKY, THE GENERATOR'S FUNCTION IS ABSORB AND DISCHARGE, RIGHT?!
THAT'S RIGHT!
NO ...
SAPPHIRE, THIS IS NO TIME FOR TEARS!
WAHHH! WAHHH!
H-HUH? IS THIS A BAD TIME?

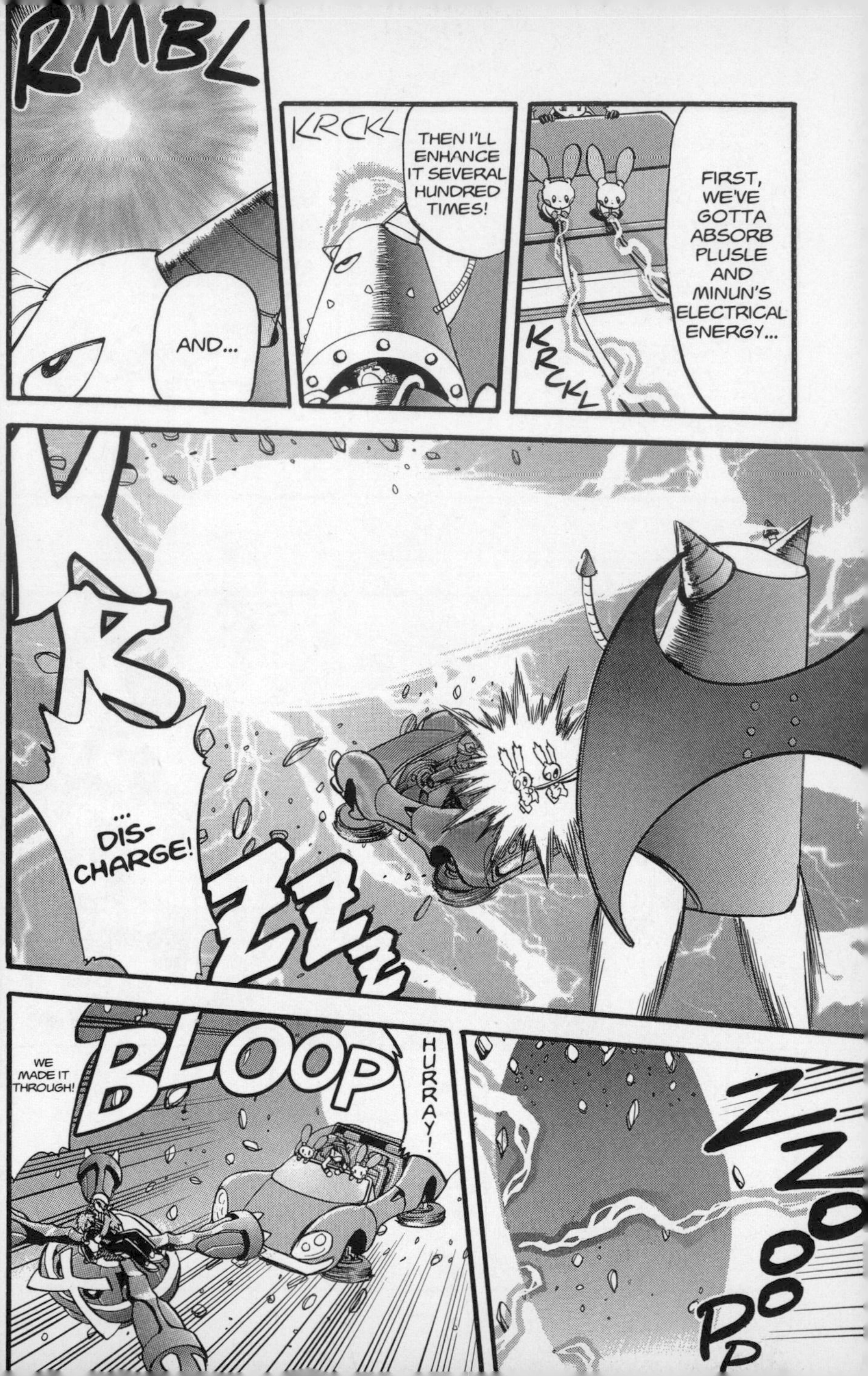
KRCKL
FIRST, WE'VE GOTTA ABSORB PLUSLE AND MINUN'S ELECTRICAL ENERGY...
KRCKL
THEN I'LL ENHANCE IT SEVERAL HUNDRED TIMES!
RMBL
AND...
R
...DIS-CHARGE!
ZZZZ
ZZOOOOOPP
BLOOP
HURRAY!
WE MADE IT THROUGH!

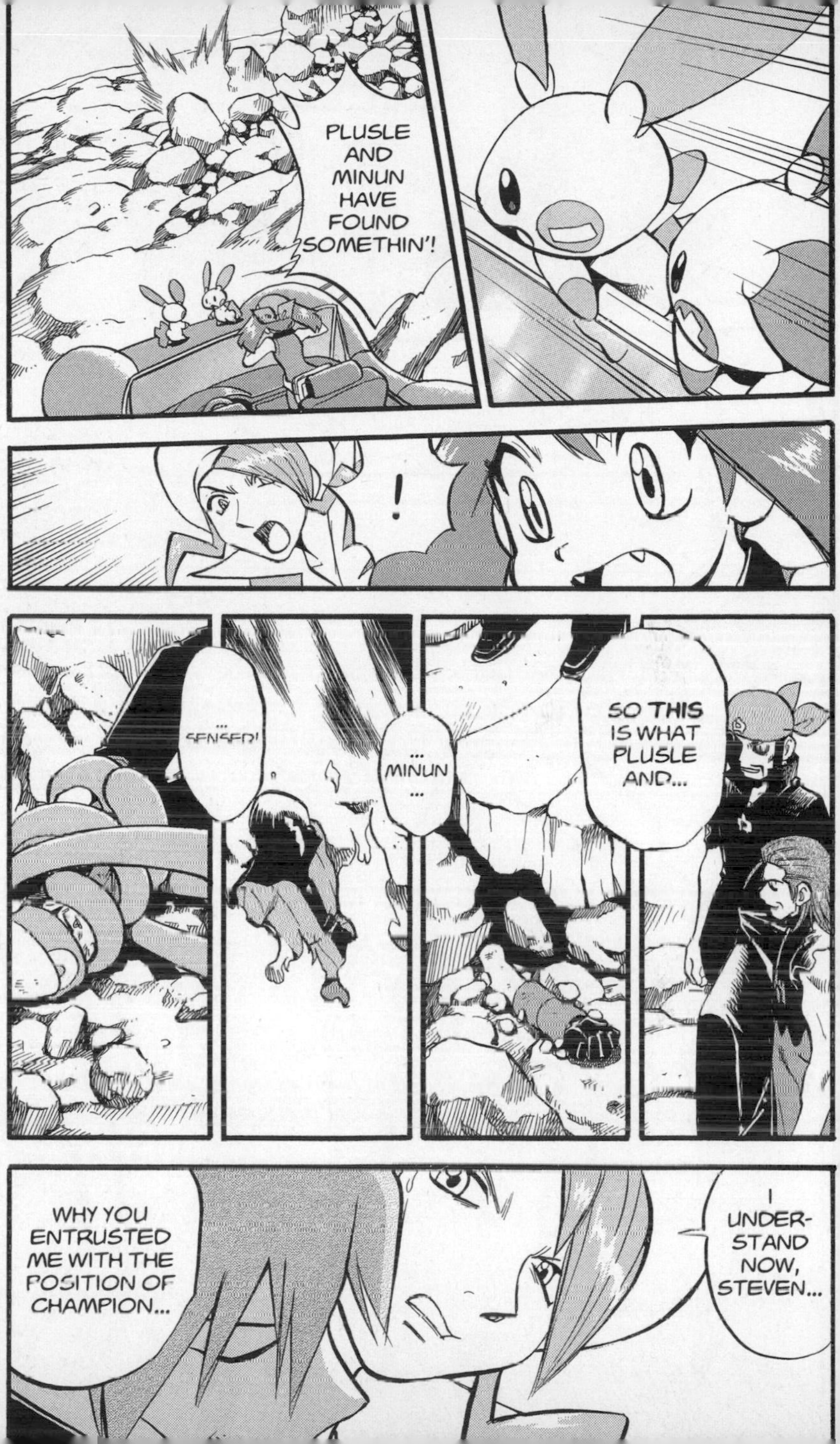
PLUSLE AND MINUN HAVE FOUND SOMETHIN'!
!
SO THIS IS WHAT PLUSLE AND...
...MINUN...
...SENSED!
I UNDER-STAND NOW, STEVEN...
WHY YOU ENTRUSTED ME WITH THE POSITION OF CHAMPION...

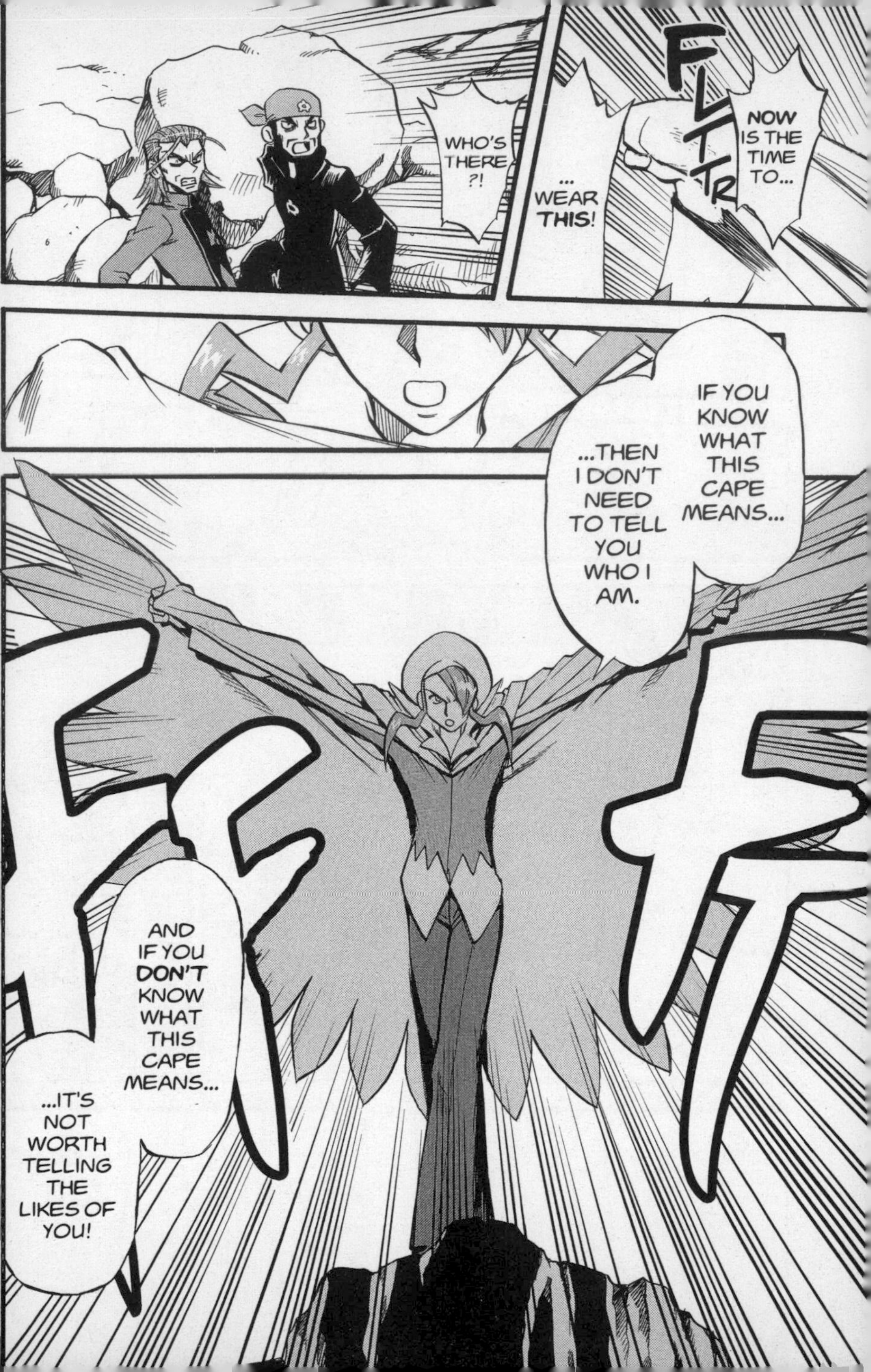
FLTTR
NOW IS THE TIME TO...
... WEAR THIS!
WHO'S THERE ?!
IF YOU KNOW WHAT THIS CAPE MEANS...
...THEN I DON'T NEED TO TELL YOU WHO I AM.
AND IF YOU DON'T KNOW WHAT THIS CAPE MEANS...
...IT'S NOT WORTH TELLING THE LIKES OF YOU!

ADVENTURE MAP

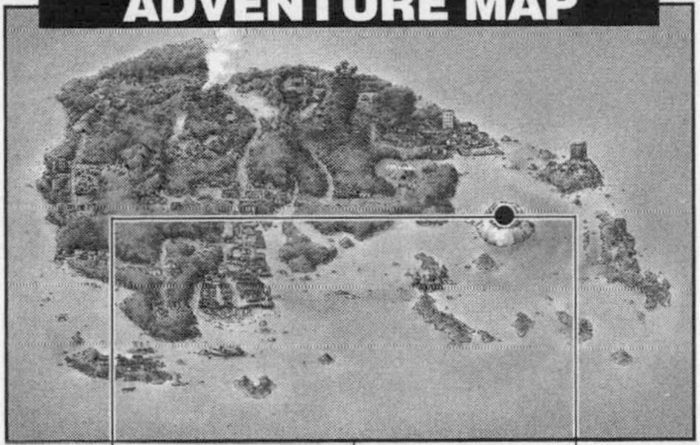

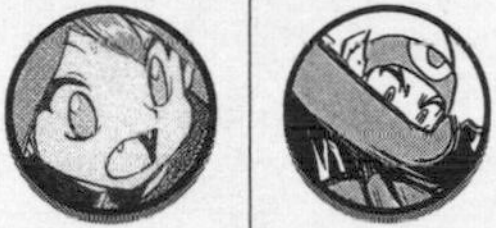

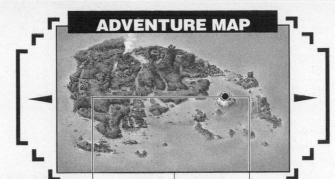

Sootopolis City

SAPPHIRE

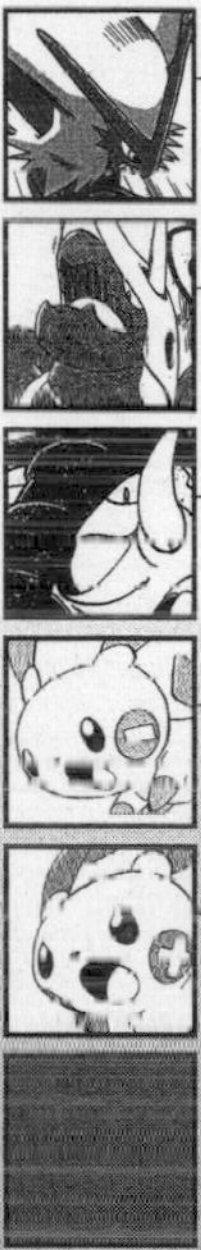

CHIC
Blaziken♀
Lv59

RONO
Aggron♂
Lv54

PHADO
Donphan♂
Lv58

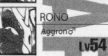

MINUN
Minun♀
Lv52

PLUSLE
Plusle♂
Lv52

RUBY

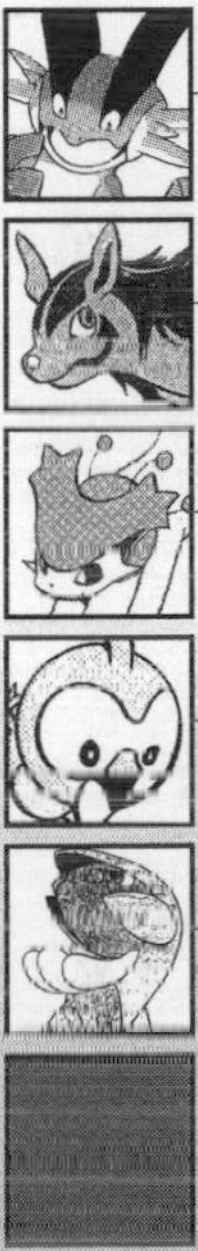

MUMU
Swampert ♂

NANA
Mightyena ♀

KIKI
Delcatty ♀

FOFO
Castform ♀

TROPPY
Tropius ♂

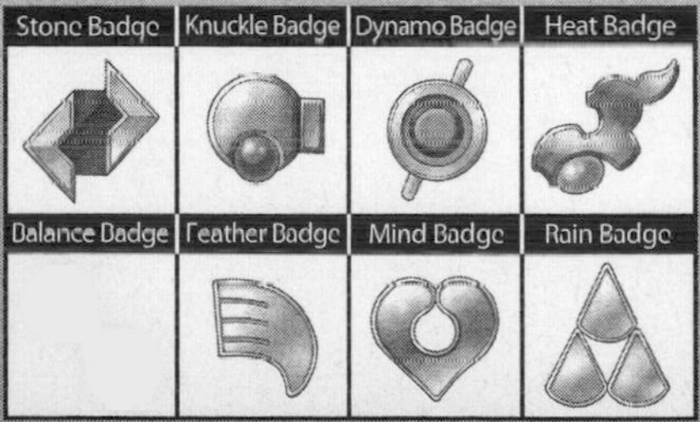
Stone Badge
Knuckle Badge
Dynamo Badge
Heat Badge
Balance Badge
Feather Badge
Mind Badge
Rain Badge

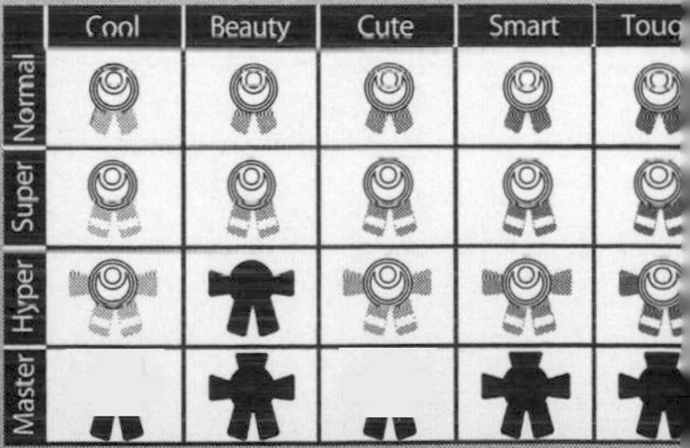
Cool
Beauty
Cute
Smart
Toug
Normal
Super
Hyper
Master

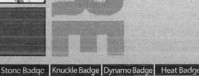

● Chapter 266 ●
It All Ends Now VII

Pokémon™ Adventures Ruby & Sapphire

The Fourth Chapter

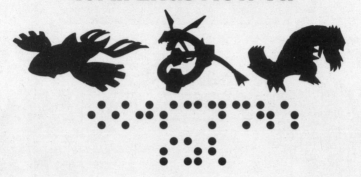

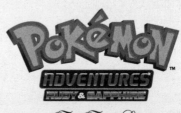

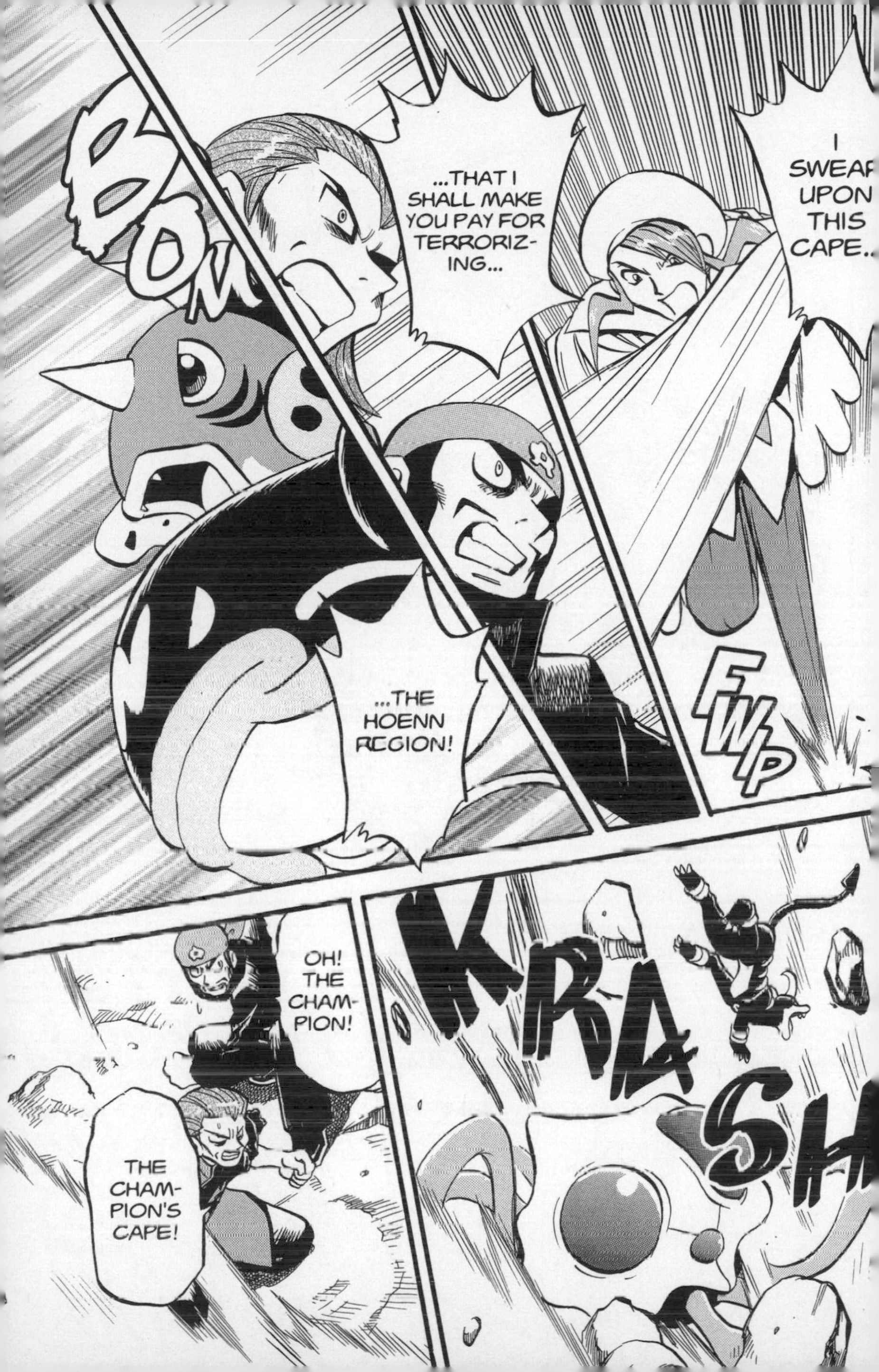
I SWEAR UPON THIS CAPE...
...THAT I SHALL MAKE YOU PAY FOR TERRORIZ-ING...
...THE HOENN REGION!
FWIP
KRASH
OH! THE CHAM-PION!
THE CHAM-PION'S CAPE!

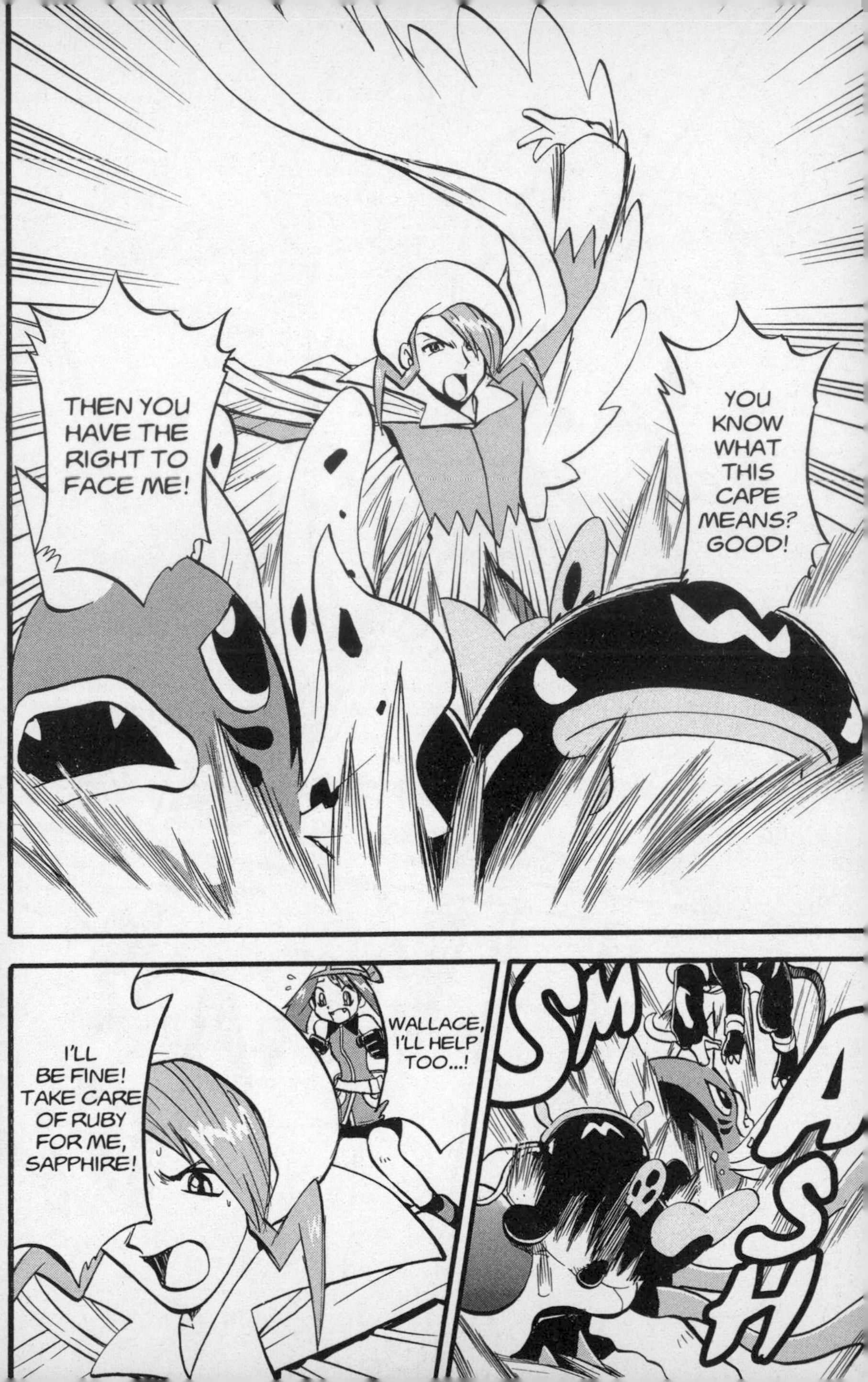
YOU KNOW WHAT THIS CAPE MEANS? GOOD!
THEN YOU HAVE THE RIGHT TO FACE ME!
SMASH
WALLACE, I'LL HELP TOO...!
I'LL BE FINE! TAKE CARE OF RUBY FOR ME, SAPPHIRE!

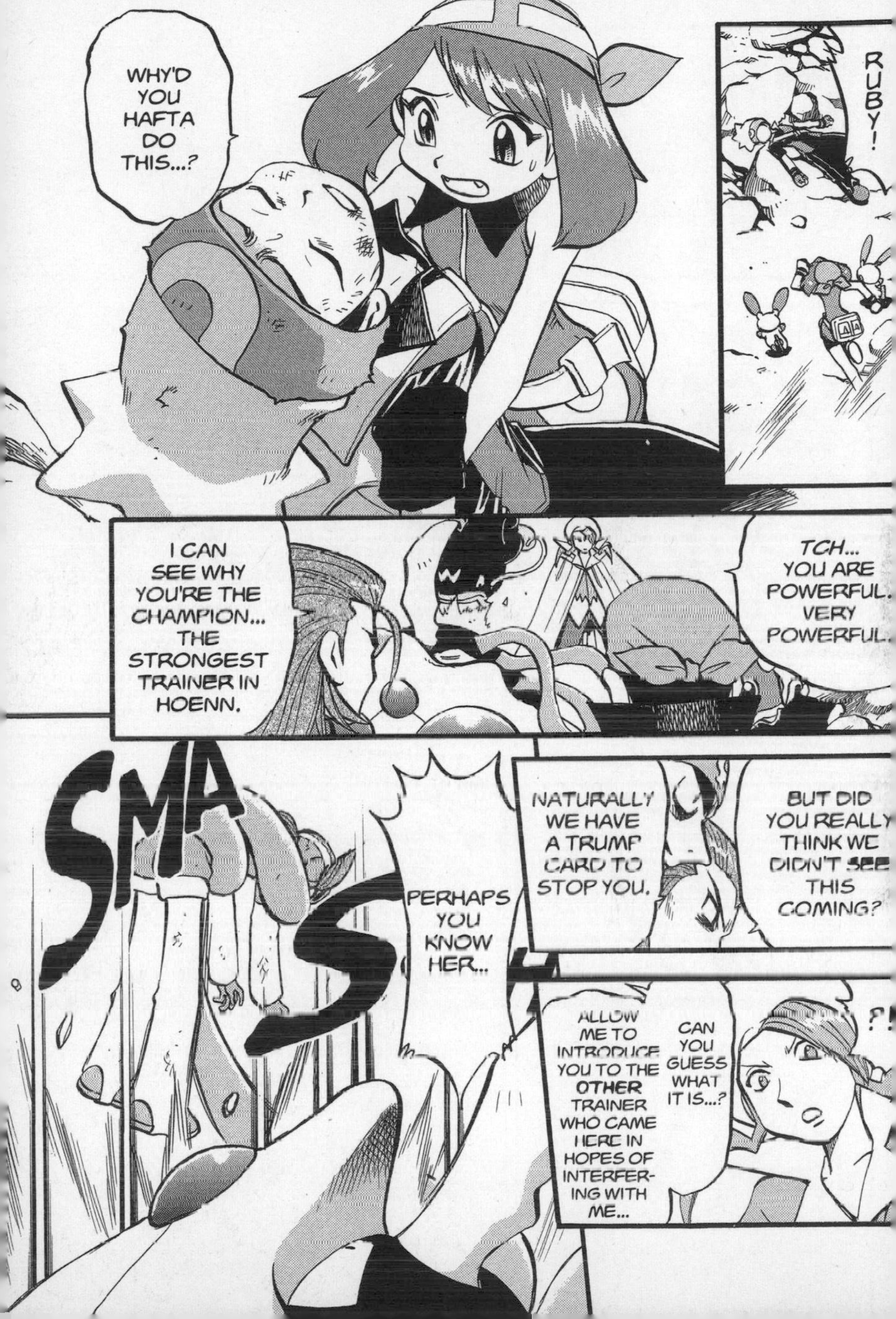
RUBY!
WHY'D YOU HAFTA DO THIS...?
TCH... YOU ARE POWERFUL. VERY POWERFUL.
I CAN SEE WHY YOU'RE THE CHAMPION... THE STRONGEST TRAINER IN HOENN.
BUT DID YOU REALLY THINK WE DIDN'T SEE THIS COMING?
NATURALLY WE HAVE A TRUMP CARD TO STOP YOU.
?!
CAN YOU GUESS WHAT IT IS...?
ALLOW ME TO INTRODUCE YOU TO THE **OTHER** TRAINER WHO CAME HERE IN HOPES OF INTERFERING WITH ME...
PERHAPS YOU KNOW HER...
SMASH

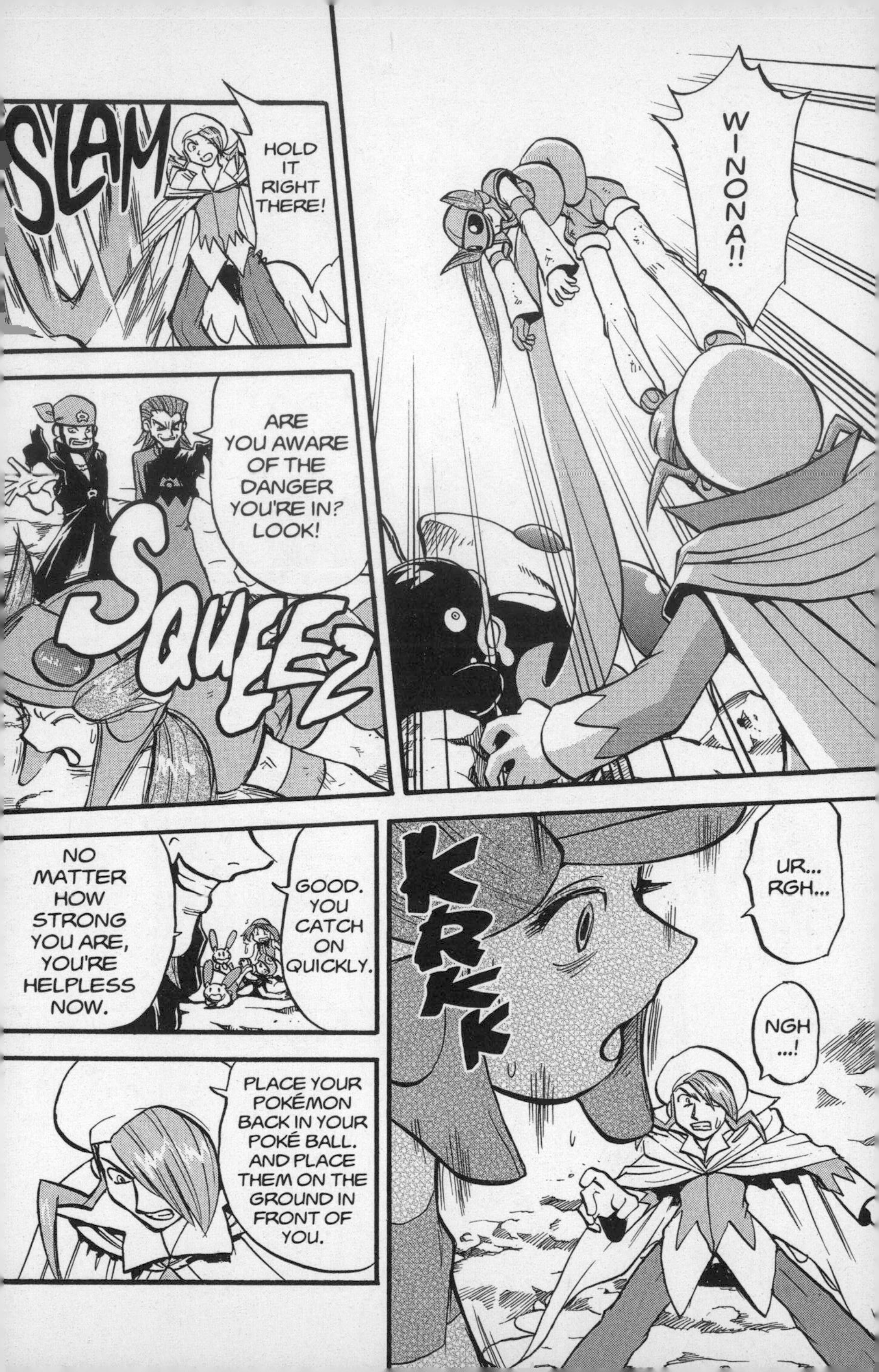
WINONA!!
SLAM
HOLD IT RIGHT THERE!
ARE YOU AWARE OF THE DANGER YOU'RE IN? LOOK!
SQUEEZ
UR... RGH...
KRKK
NGH ...!
GOOD. YOU CATCH ON QUICKLY.
NO MATTER HOW STRONG YOU ARE, YOU'RE HELPLESS NOW.
PLACE YOUR POKÉMON BACK IN YOUR POKÉ BALL. AND PLACE THEM ON THE GROUND IN FRONT OF YOU.

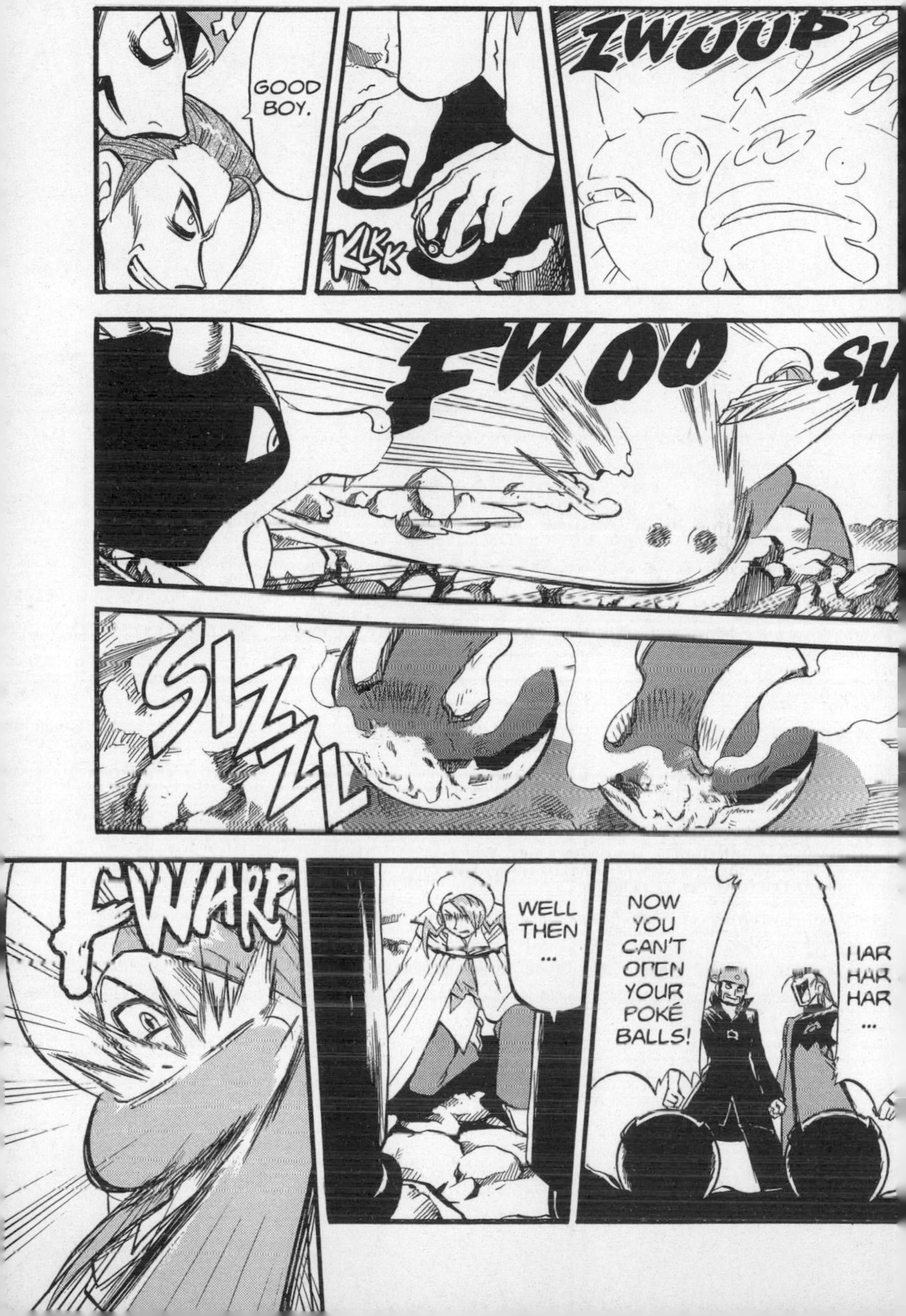
ZWUUP
KLIK
GOOD BOY.
FWOOSH
SIZZZL
NOW YOU CAN'T OPEN YOUR POKÉ BALLS!
HAR HAR HAR ...
WELL THEN ...
FWARP

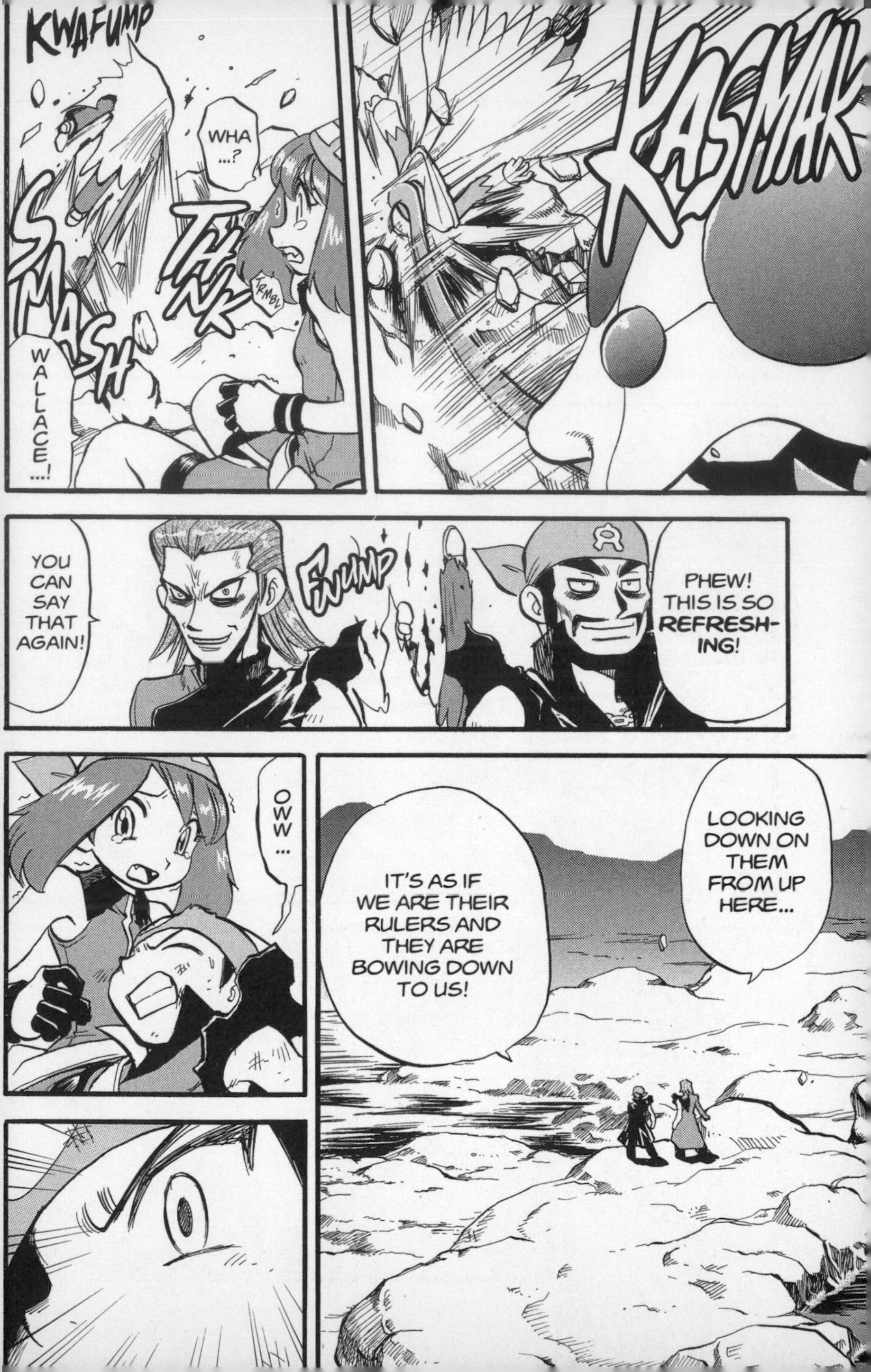
KASMAK
KWAFUMP
WHA ...?
SMASH
THINK
TRMBL
WALLACE ...!
PHEW! THIS IS SO REFRESHING!
FWUMP
YOU CAN SAY THAT AGAIN!
LOOKING DOWN ON THEM FROM UP HERE...
IT'S AS IF WE ARE THEIR RULERS AND THEY ARE BOWING DOWN TO US!
OWW ...

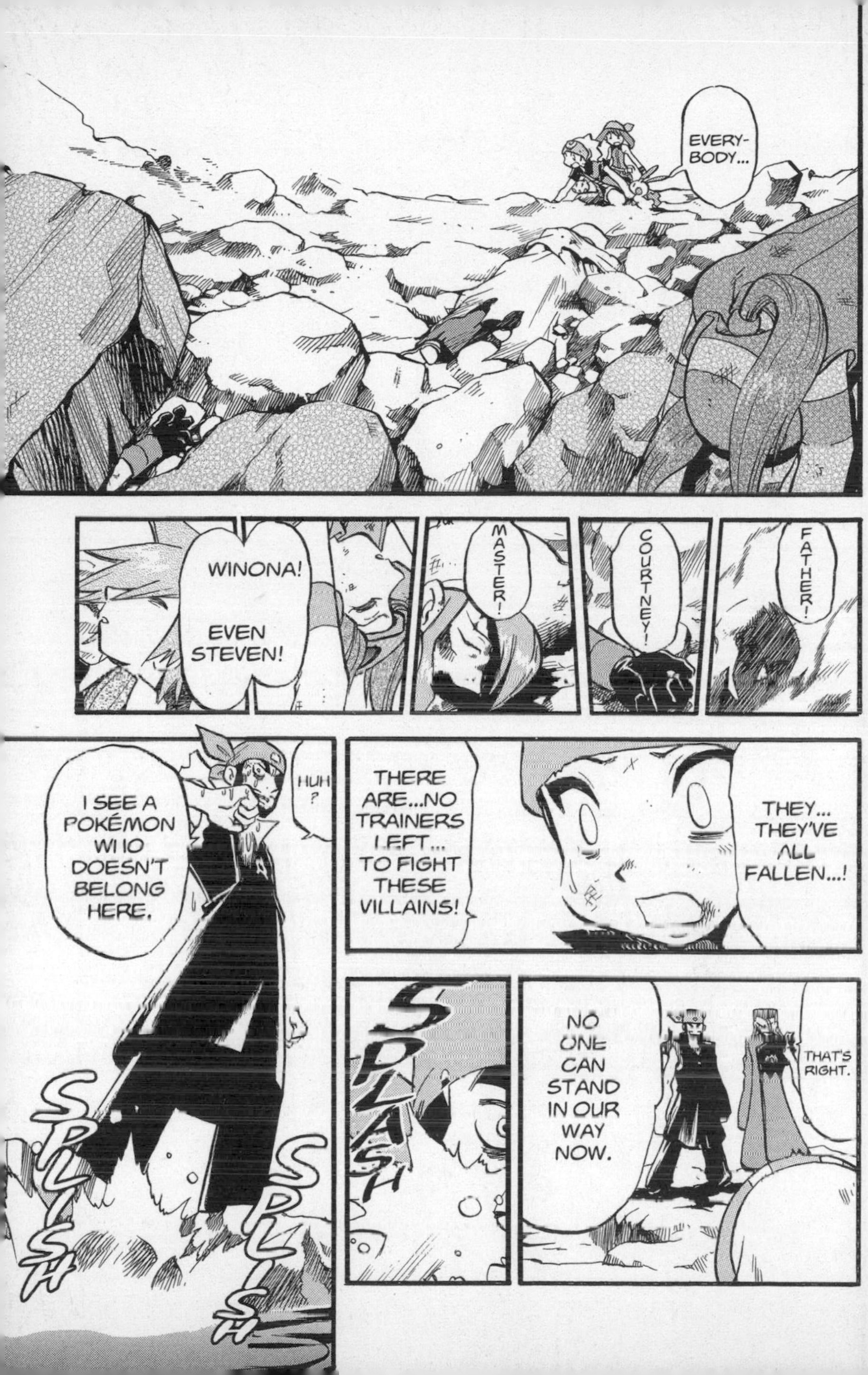
EVERY-BODY...
FATHER!
COURTNEY!
MASTER!
WINONA!
EVEN STEVEN!
THEY... THEY'VE ALL FALLEN...!
THERE ARE...NO TRAINERS LEFT... TO FIGHT THESE VILLAINS!
NO ONE CAN STAND IN OUR WAY NOW.
THAT'S RIGHT.
SPLASH
HUH?
I SEE A POKÉMON WHO DOESN'T BELONG HERE.
SPLISH
SPLISH

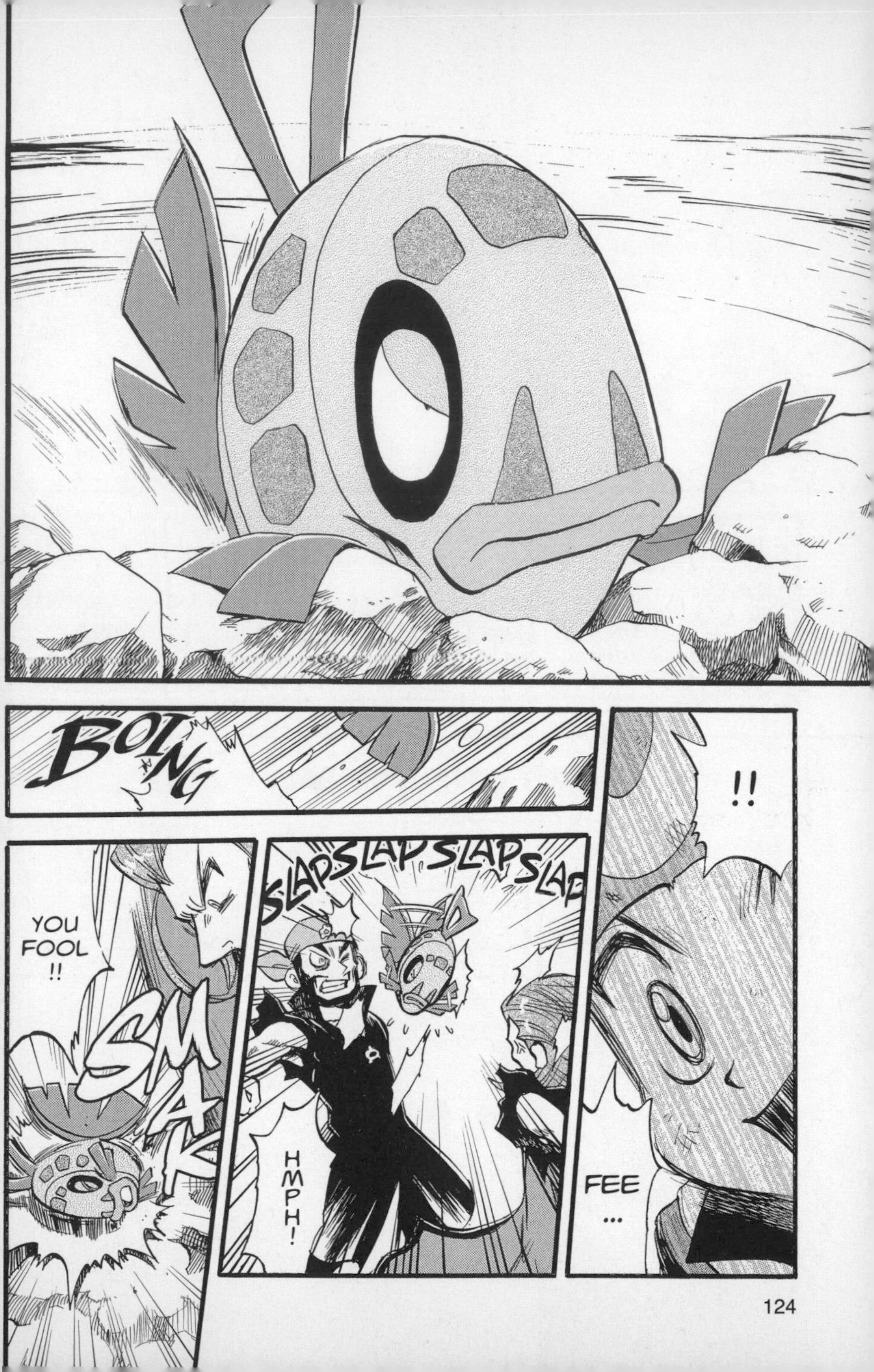
!!
FEE ...
BOING
SLAPSLAPSLAPSLAP
HMPH!
YOU FOOL !!
SMACK

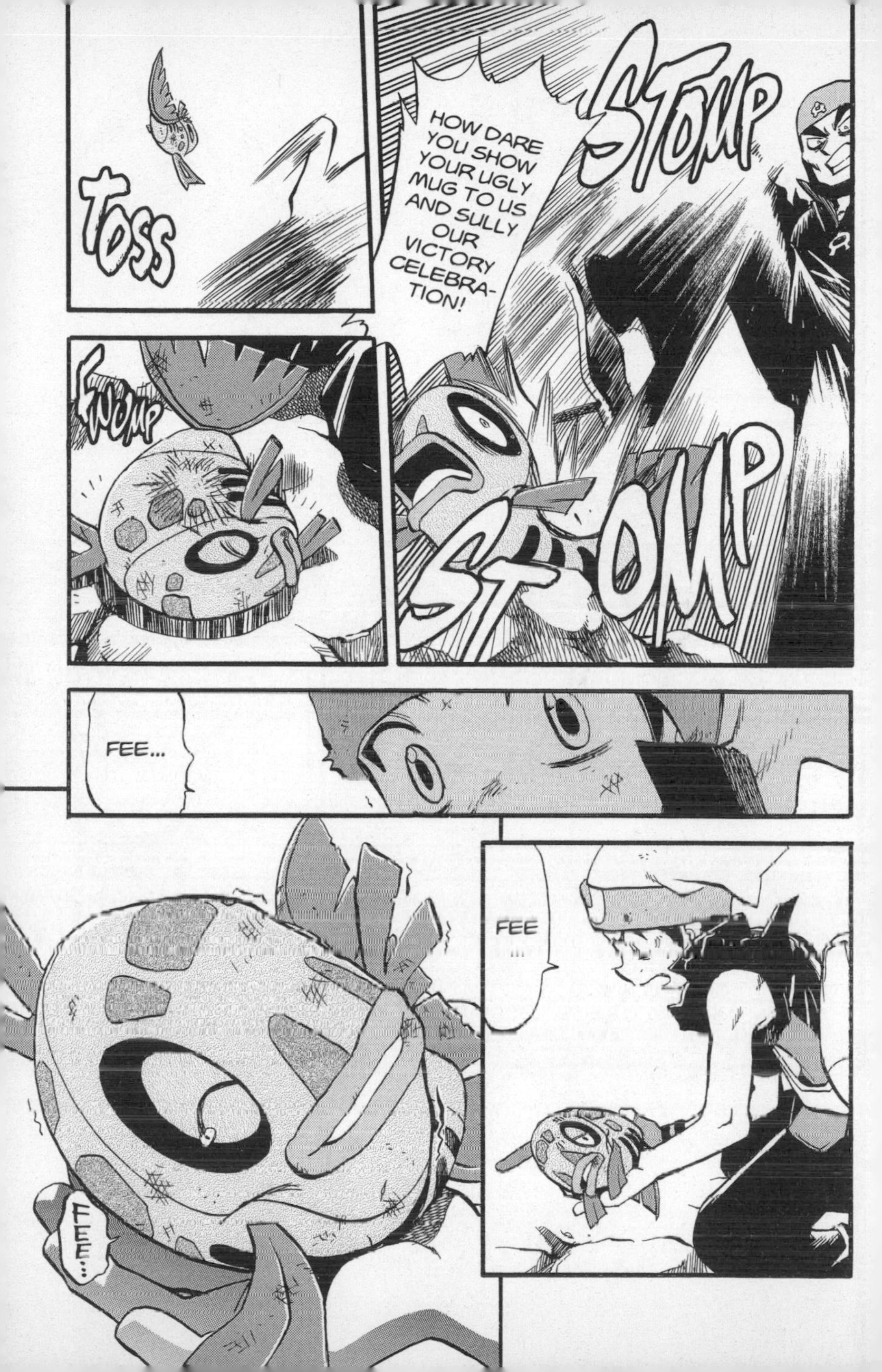
STOMP
HOW DARE YOU SHOW YOUR UGLY MUG TO US AND SULLY OUR VICTORY CELEBRATION!
TOSS
STOMP
FWOMP
FEE...
FEE ...
FEE...

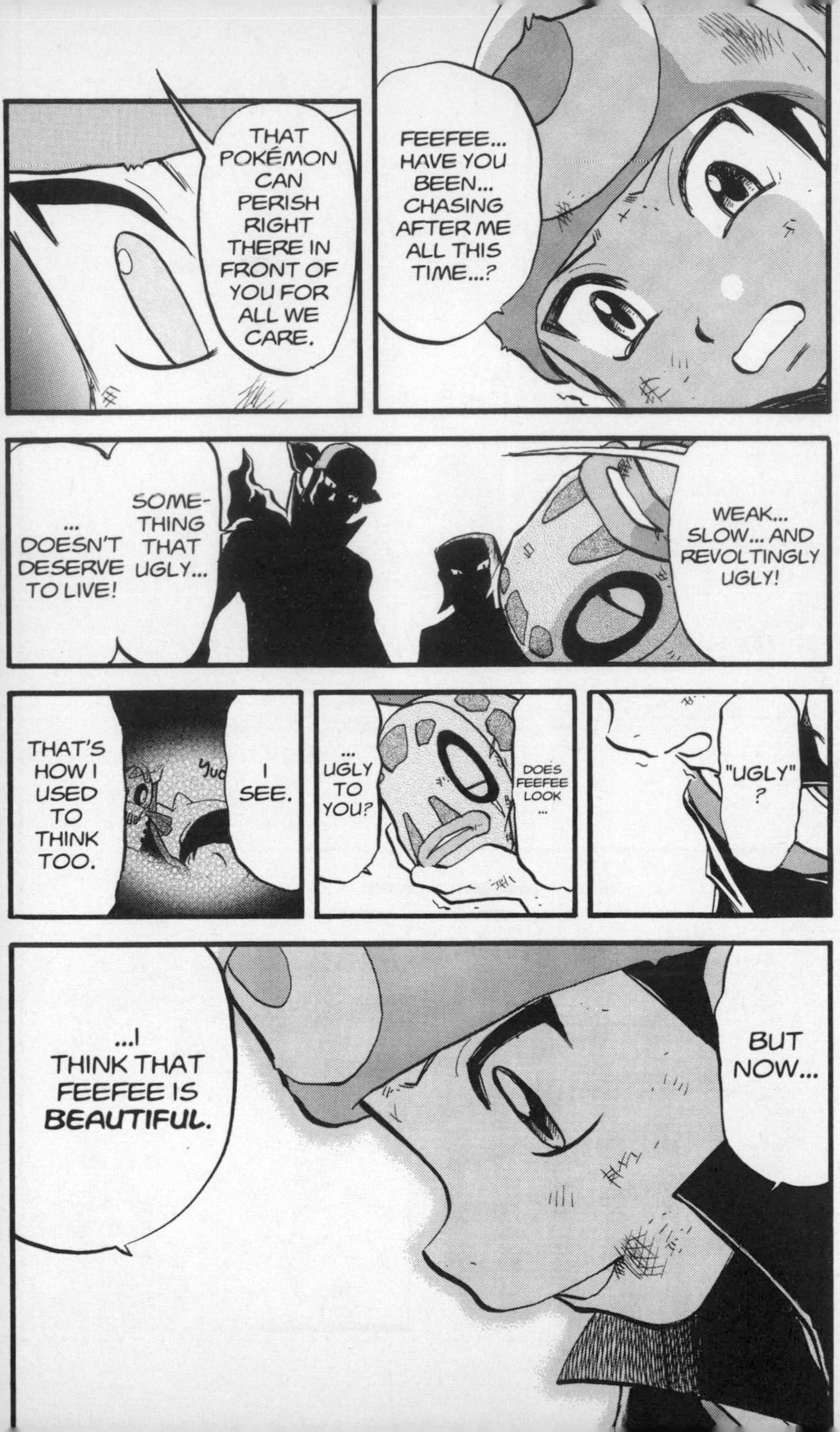
FEEFEE... HAVE YOU BEEN... CHASING AFTER ME ALL THIS TIME...?
THAT POKÉMON CAN PERISH RIGHT THERE IN FRONT OF YOU FOR ALL WE CARE.
WEAK... SLOW... AND REVOLTINGLY UGLY!
SOME-THING THAT UGLY...
... DOESN'T DESERVE TO LIVE!
"UGLY"?
DOES FEEFEE LOOK...
...UGLY TO YOU?
I SEE.
THAT'S HOW I USED TO THINK TOO.
BUT NOW...
...I THINK THAT FEEFEE IS **BEAUTIFUL.**

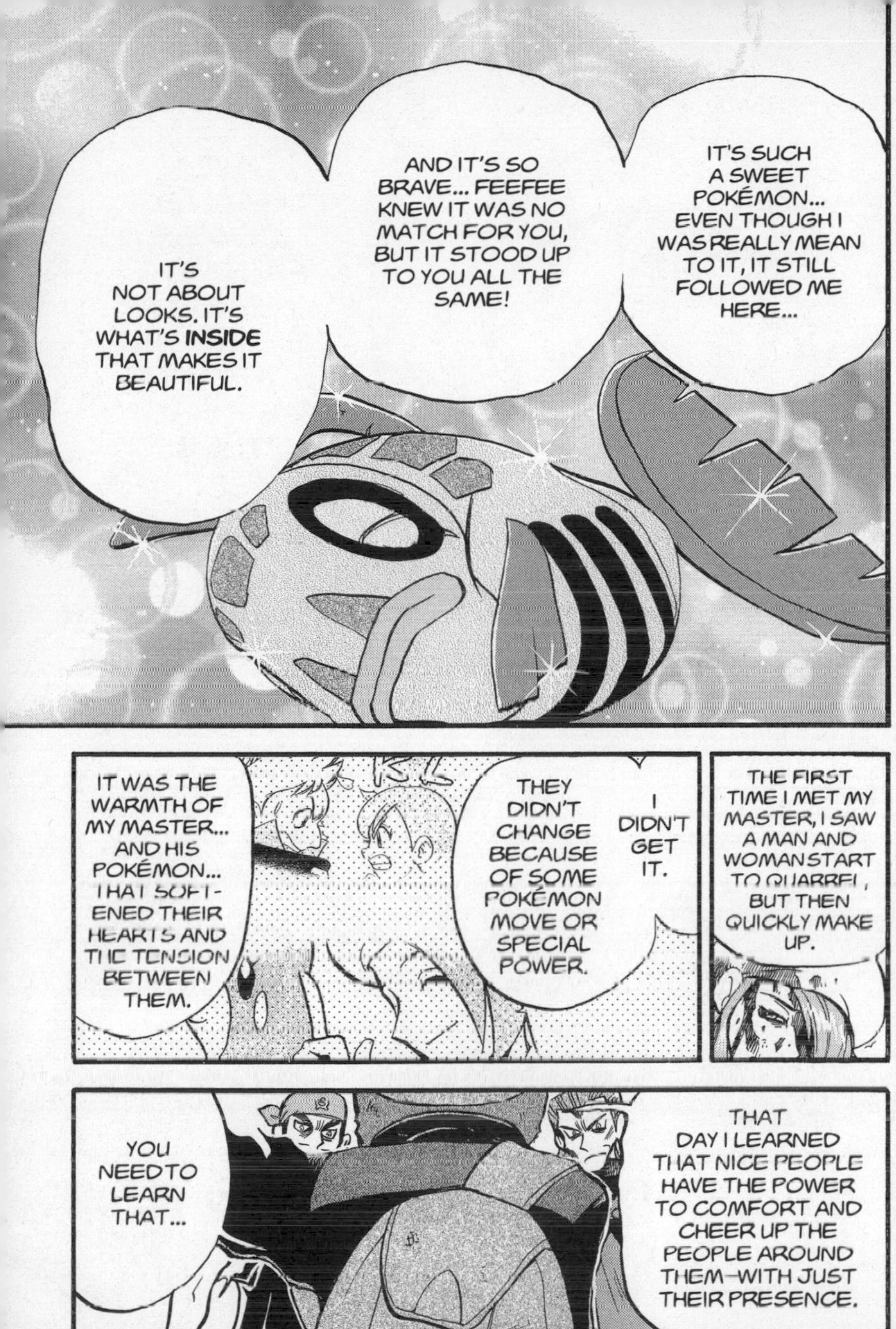
IT'S SUCH A SWEET POKÉMON... EVEN THOUGH I WAS REALLY MEAN TO IT, IT STILL FOLLOWED ME HERE...
AND IT'S SO BRAVE... FEEFEE KNEW IT WAS NO MATCH FOR YOU, BUT IT STOOD UP TO YOU ALL THE SAME!
IT'S NOT ABOUT LOOKS. IT'S WHAT'S **INSIDE** THAT MAKES IT BEAUTIFUL.
THE FIRST TIME I MET MY MASTER, I SAW A MAN AND WOMAN START TO QUARREL, BUT THEN QUICKLY MAKE UP.
I DIDN'T GET IT.
THEY DIDN'T CHANGE BECAUSE OF SOME POKÉMON MOVE OR SPECIAL POWER.
IT WAS THE WARMTH OF MY MASTER... AND HIS POKÉMON... THAT SOFT-ENED THEIR HEARTS AND THE TENSION BETWEEN THEM.
THAT DAY I LEARNED THAT NICE PEOPLE HAVE THE POWER TO COMFORT AND CHEER UP THE PEOPLE AROUND THEM—WITH JUST THEIR PRESENCE.
YOU NEED TO LEARN THAT...

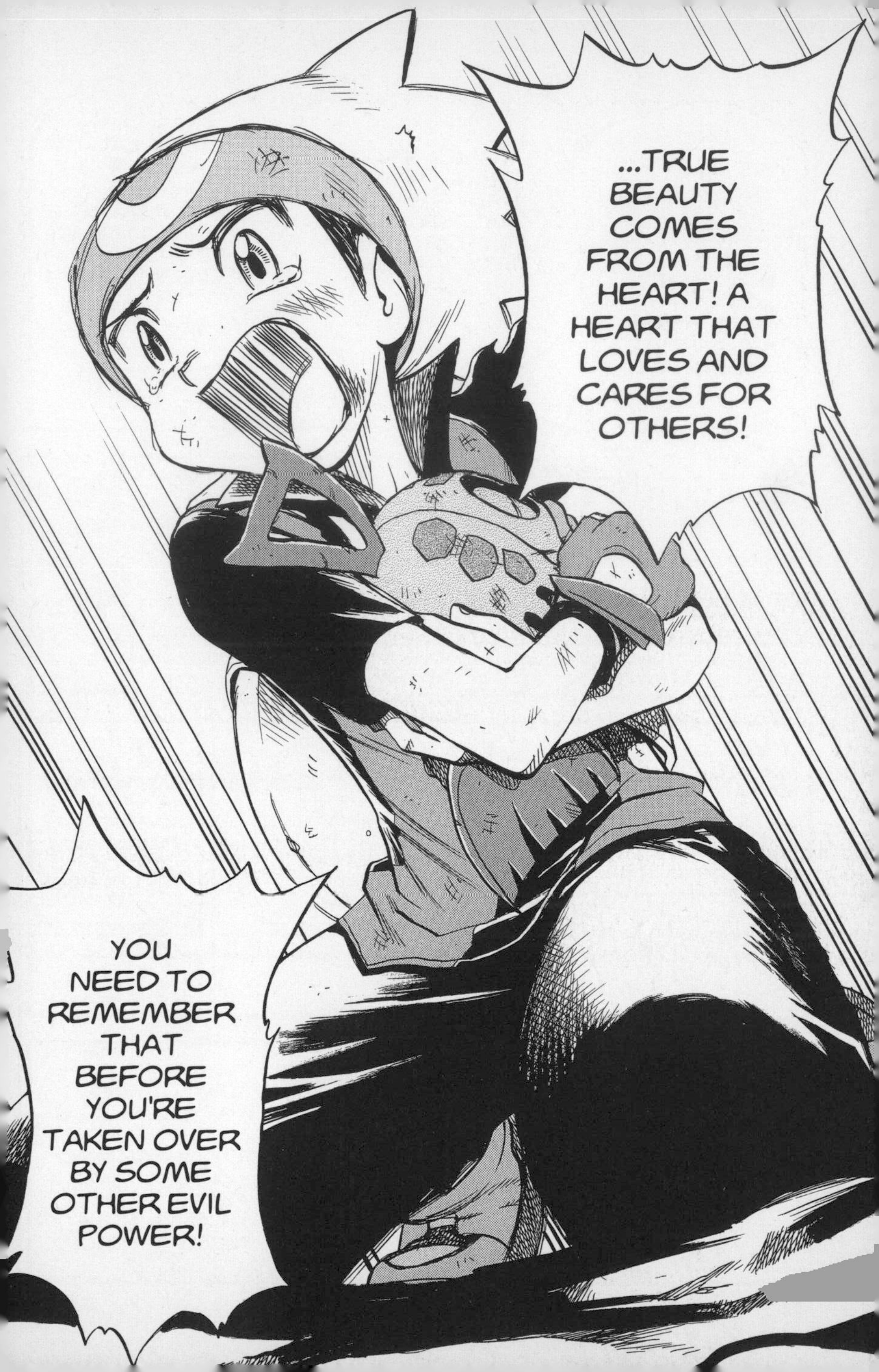
...TRUE BEAUTY COMES FROM THE HEART! A HEART THAT LOVES AND CARES FOR OTHERS!
YOU NEED TO REMEMBER THAT BEFORE YOU'RE TAKEN OVER BY SOME OTHER EVIL POWER!

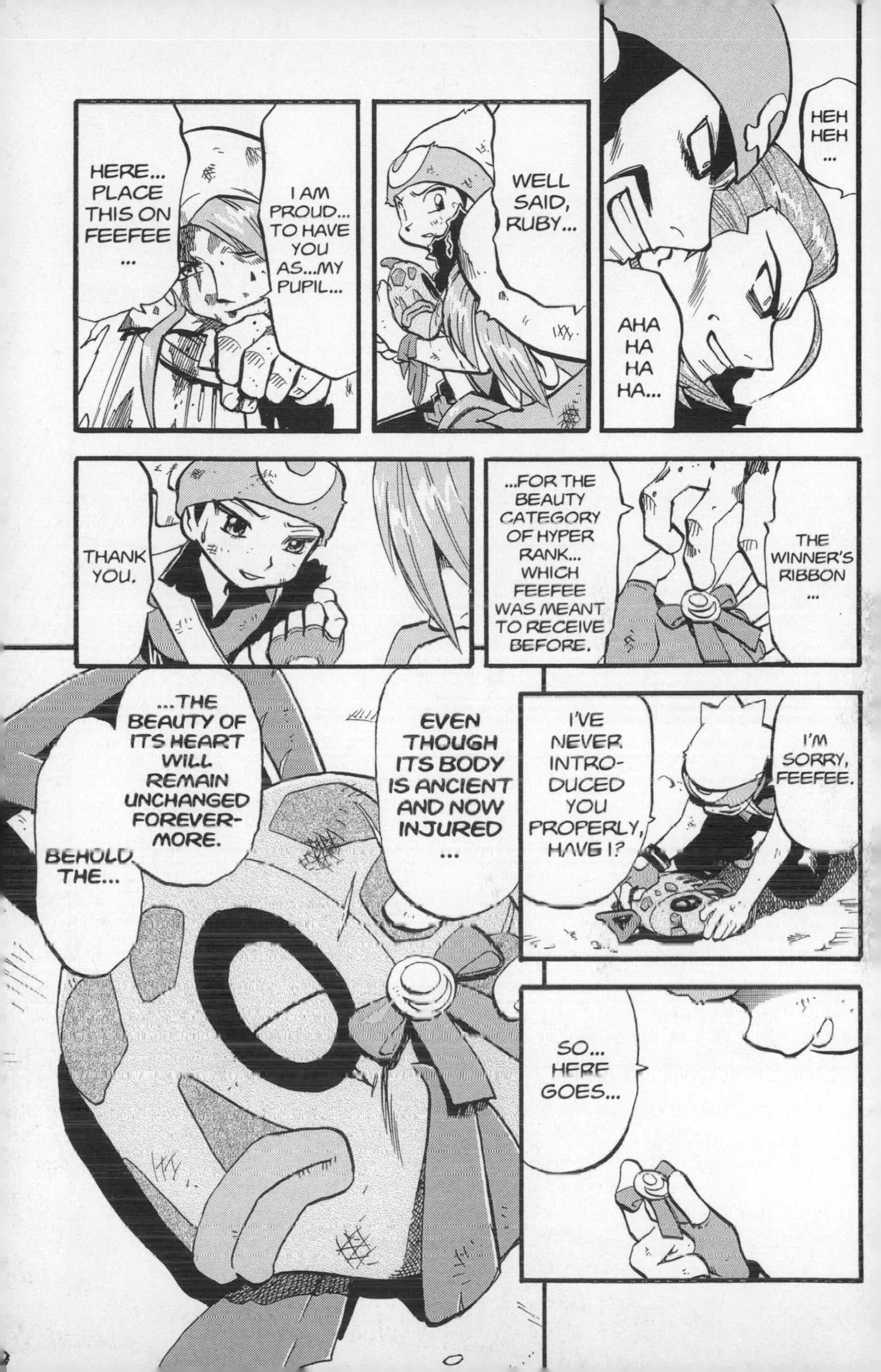
HEH HEH ...
AHA HA HA HA...
WELL SAID, RUBY...
I AM PROUD... TO HAVE YOU AS...MY PUPIL...
HERE... PLACE THIS ON FEEFEE ...
THE WINNER'S RIBBON ...
...FOR THE BEAUTY CATEGORY OF HYPER RANK... WHICH FEEFEE WAS MEANT TO RECEIVE BEFORE.
THANK YOU.
I'M SORRY, FEEFEE.
I'VE NEVER INTRODUCED YOU PROPERLY, HAVE I?
SO... HERE GOES...
EVEN THOUGH ITS BODY IS ANCIENT AND NOW INJURED ...
BEHOLD THE...
...THE BEAUTY OF ITS HEART WILL REMAIN UNCHANGED FOREVERMORE.

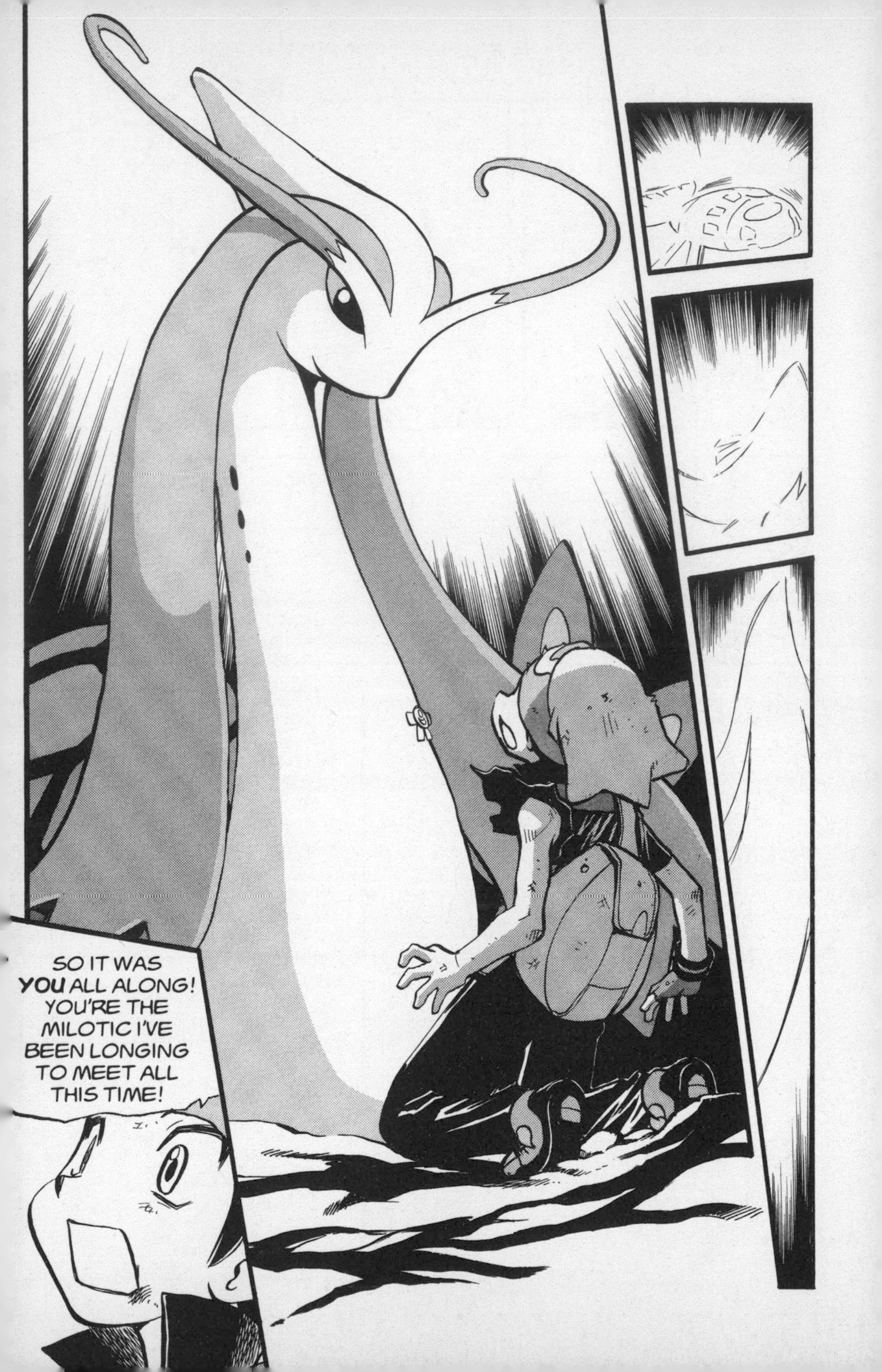
SO IT WAS **YOU** ALL ALONG! YOU'RE THE MILOTIC I'VE BEEN LONGING TO MEET ALL THIS TIME!

ADVENTURE MAP

SAPPHIRE

● Sootopolis City ●

RUBY

CHIC
Blaziken ♀
Lv59

RONO
Aggron ♂
Lv54

PHADO
Donphan ♂
Lv58

TROPPY
Tropius ♂
Lv56

MINUN
Minun ♀
Lv53

PLUSLE
Plusle ♂
Lv53

MUMU
Swampert ♂

NANA
Mightyena ♀

KIKI
Delcatty ♀

FOFO
Castform ♀

FEEFEE
Milotic ♀

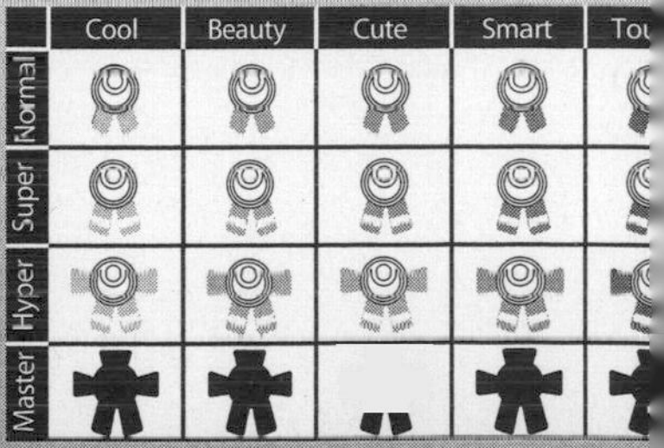

Stone Badge	Knuckle Badge	Dynamo Badge	Heat Badge
Balance Badge	Feather Badge	Mind Badge	Rain Badge

	Cool	Beauty	Cute	Smart	Tou
Normal					
Super					
Hyper					
Master					

● Chapter 267 ●

It All Ends Now VIII

Pokémon Adventures Ruby & Sapphire

The Fourth Chapter

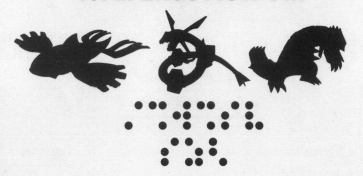

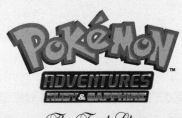

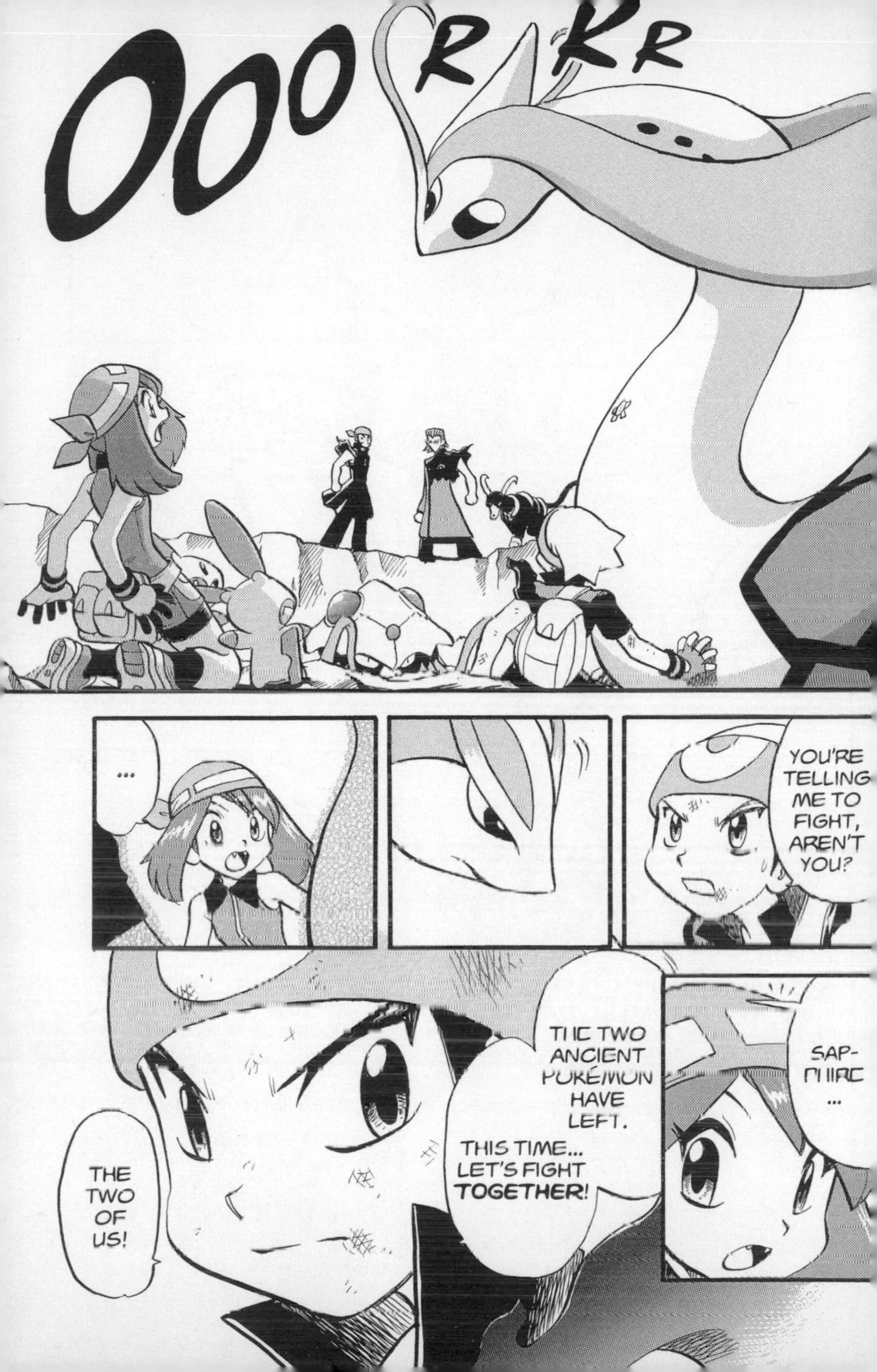
OOORKR
YOU'RE TELLING ME TO FIGHT, AREN'T YOU?
...
SAP-PHIRE ...
THE TWO ANCIENT POKÉMON HAVE LEFT.
THIS TIME... LET'S FIGHT TOGETHER!
THE TWO OF US!

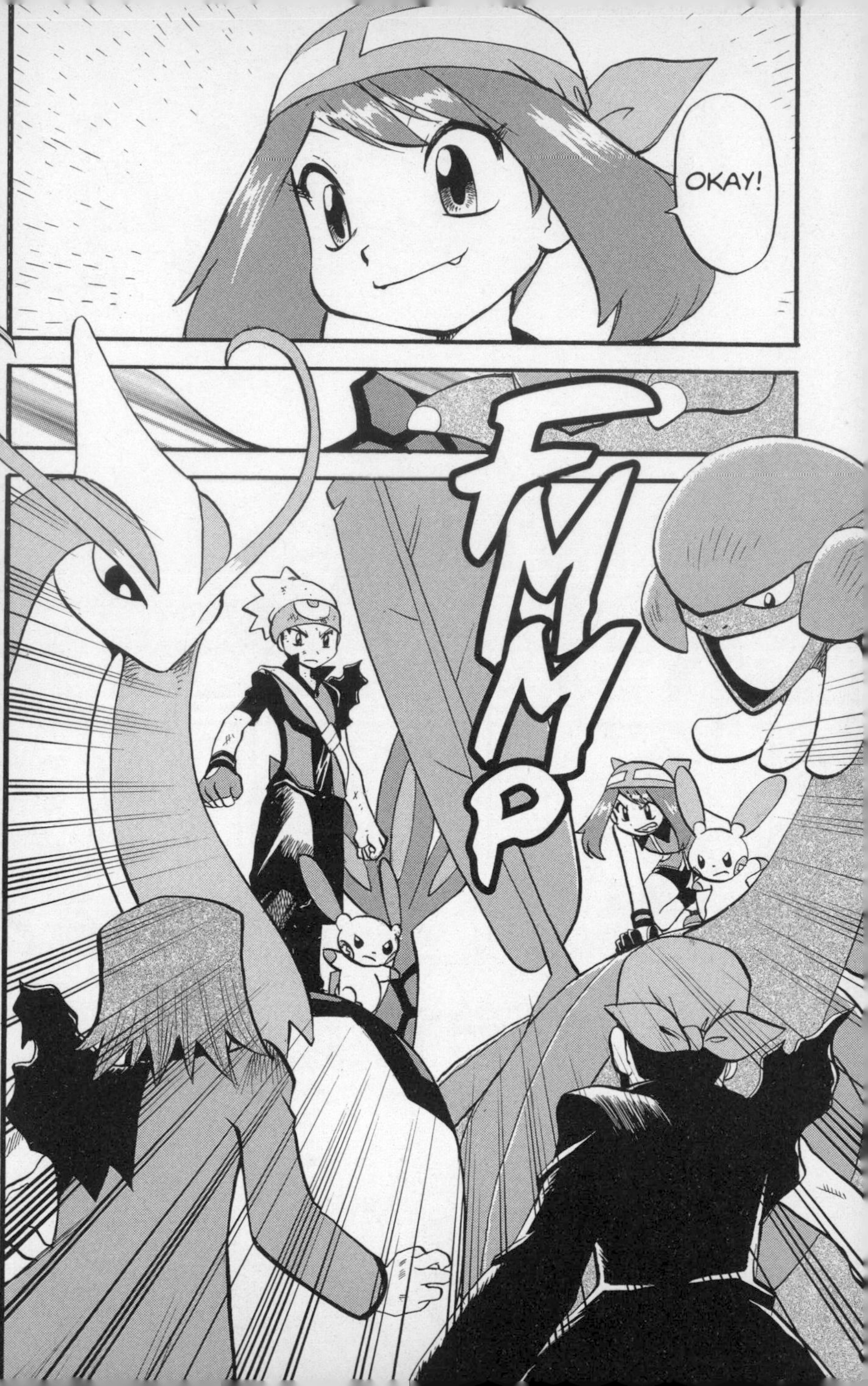
OKAY!
FMMP

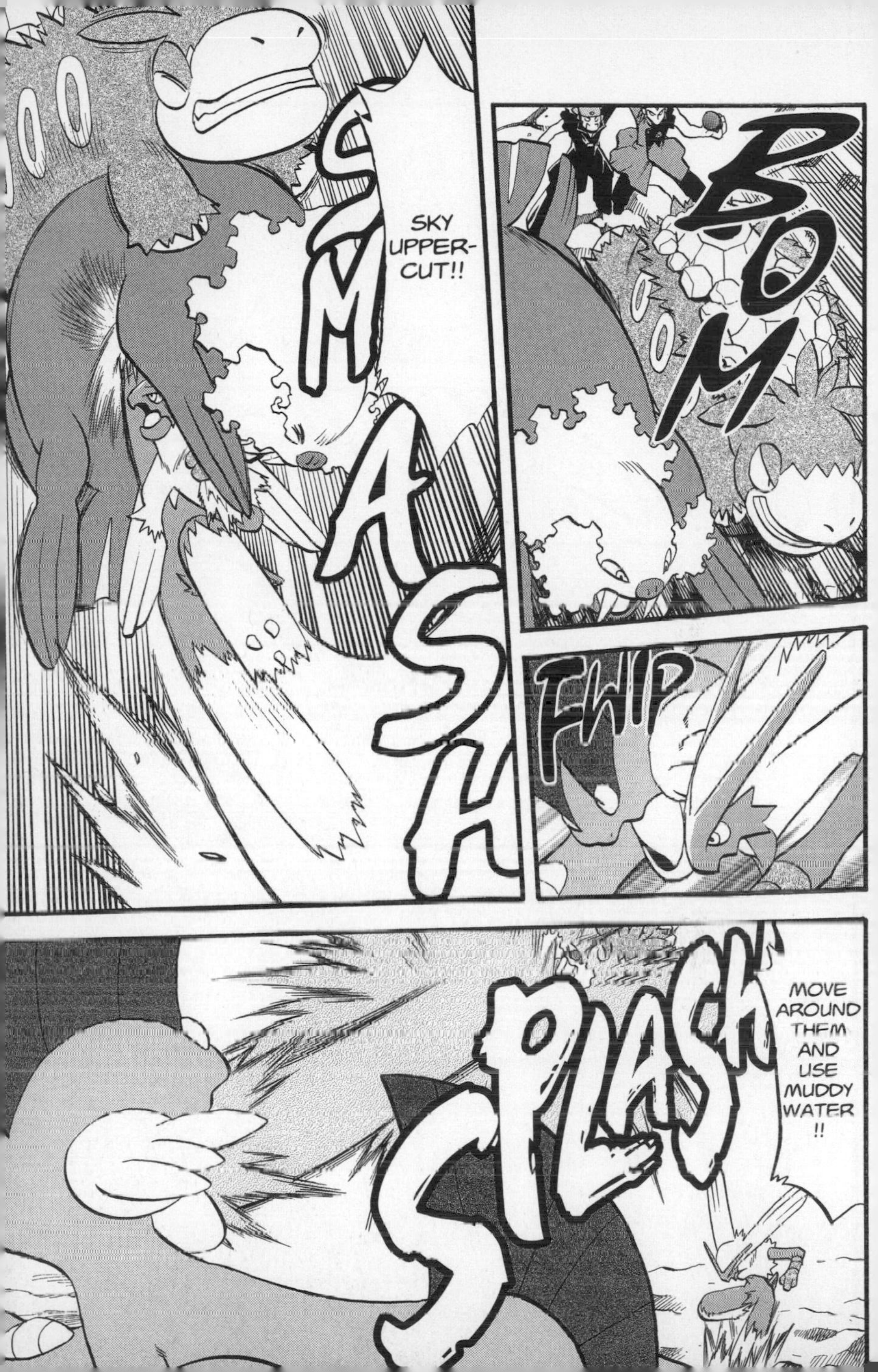
BOOM
FWIP
SKY UPPER-CUT!!
SMASH
MOVE AROUND THEM AND USE MUDDY WATER!!
SPLASH

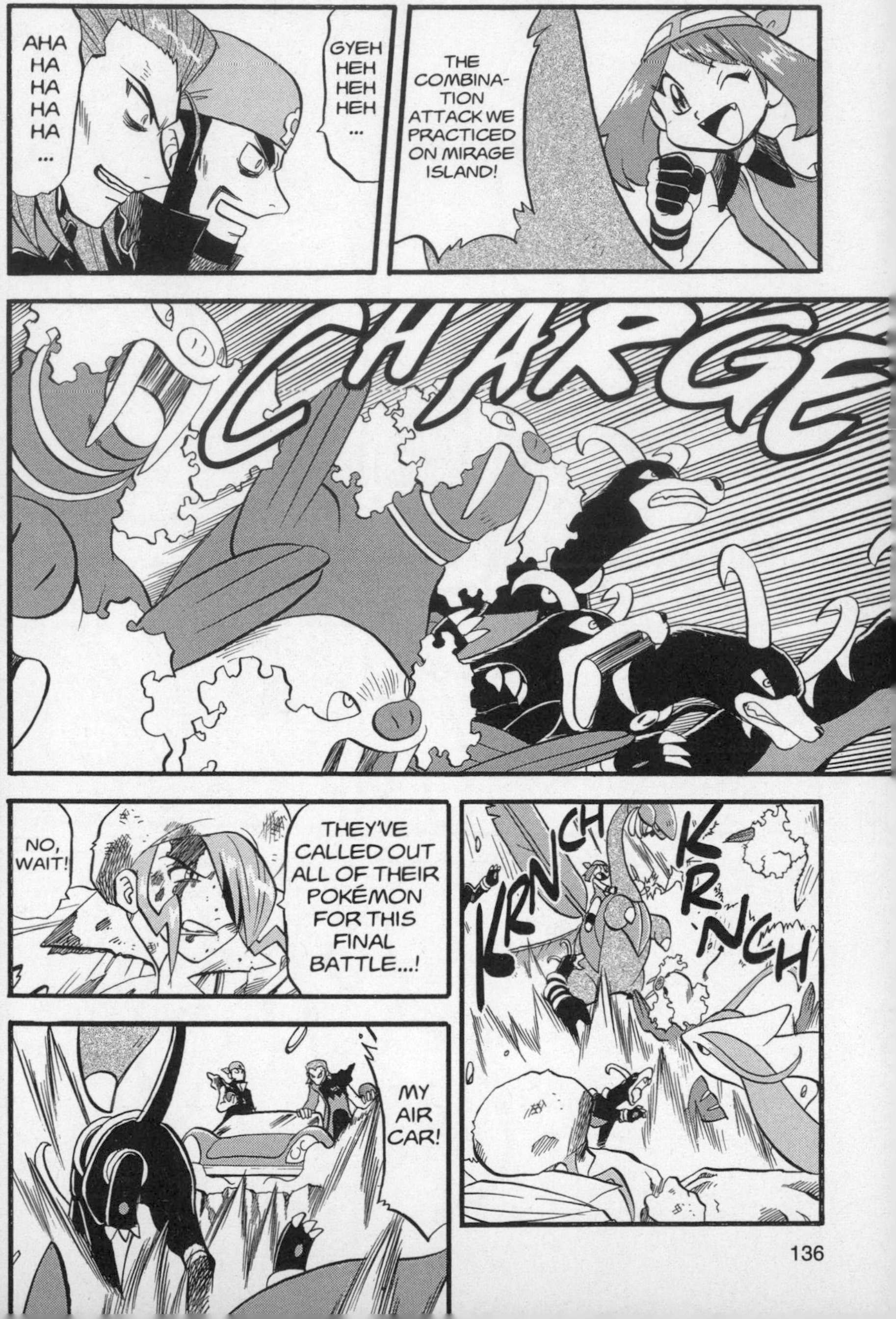
THE COMBINATION ATTACK WE PRACTICED ON MIRAGE ISLAND!
GYEH HEH HEH HEH ...
AHA HA HA HA HA ...
CHARGE
KRNCH
KRNCH
THEY'VE CALLED OUT ALL OF THEIR POKÉMON FOR THIS FINAL BATTLE...!
NO, WAIT!
MY AIR CAR!

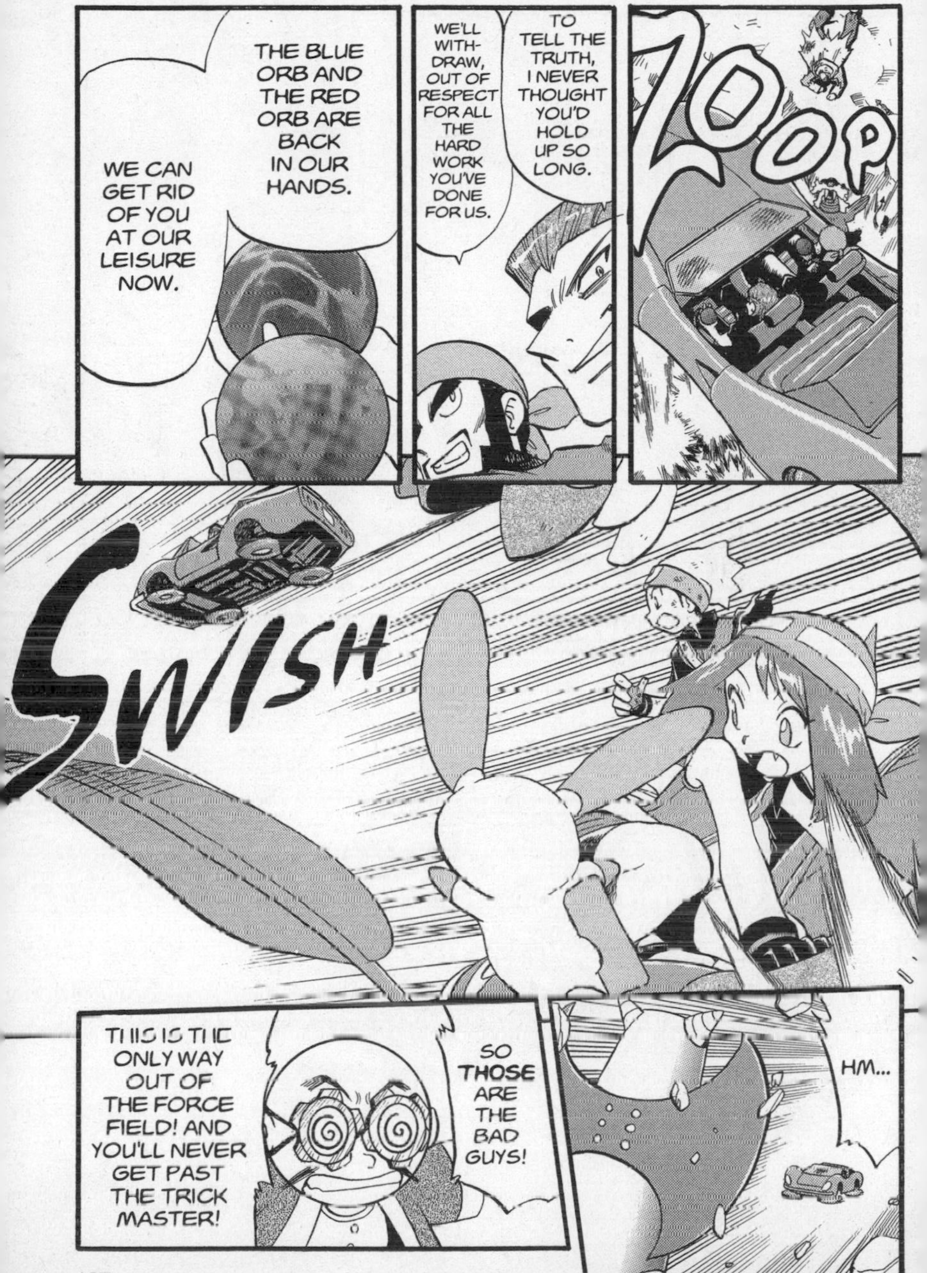
ZOOP
TO TELL THE TRUTH, I NEVER THOUGHT YOU'D HOLD UP SO LONG.
WE'LL WITH-DRAW, OUT OF RESPECT FOR ALL THE HARD WORK YOU'VE DONE FOR US.
THE BLUE ORB AND THE RED ORB ARE BACK IN OUR HANDS.
WE CAN GET RID OF YOU AT OUR LEISURE NOW.
SWISH
HM...
SO THOSE ARE THE BAD GUYS!
THIS IS THE ONLY WAY OUT OF THE FORCE FIELD! AND YOU'LL NEVER GET PAST THE TRICK MASTER!

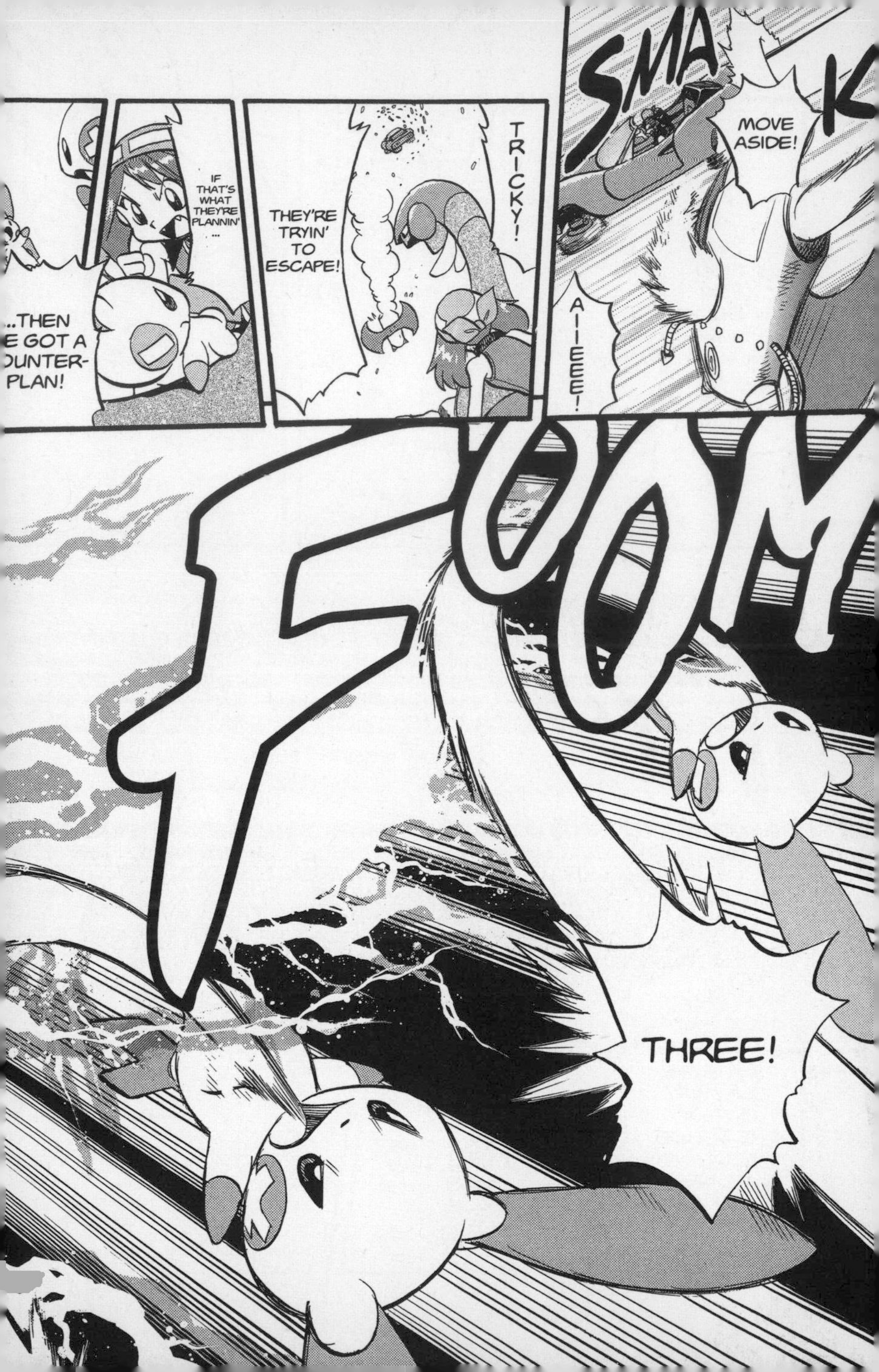
MOVE ASIDE!
SMA K
AIIEEE!
TRICKY!
THEY'RE TRYIN' TO ESCAPE!
IF THAT'S WHAT THEY'RE PLANNIN' ...
...THEN E GOT A DUNTER-PLAN!
FOOM
THREE!

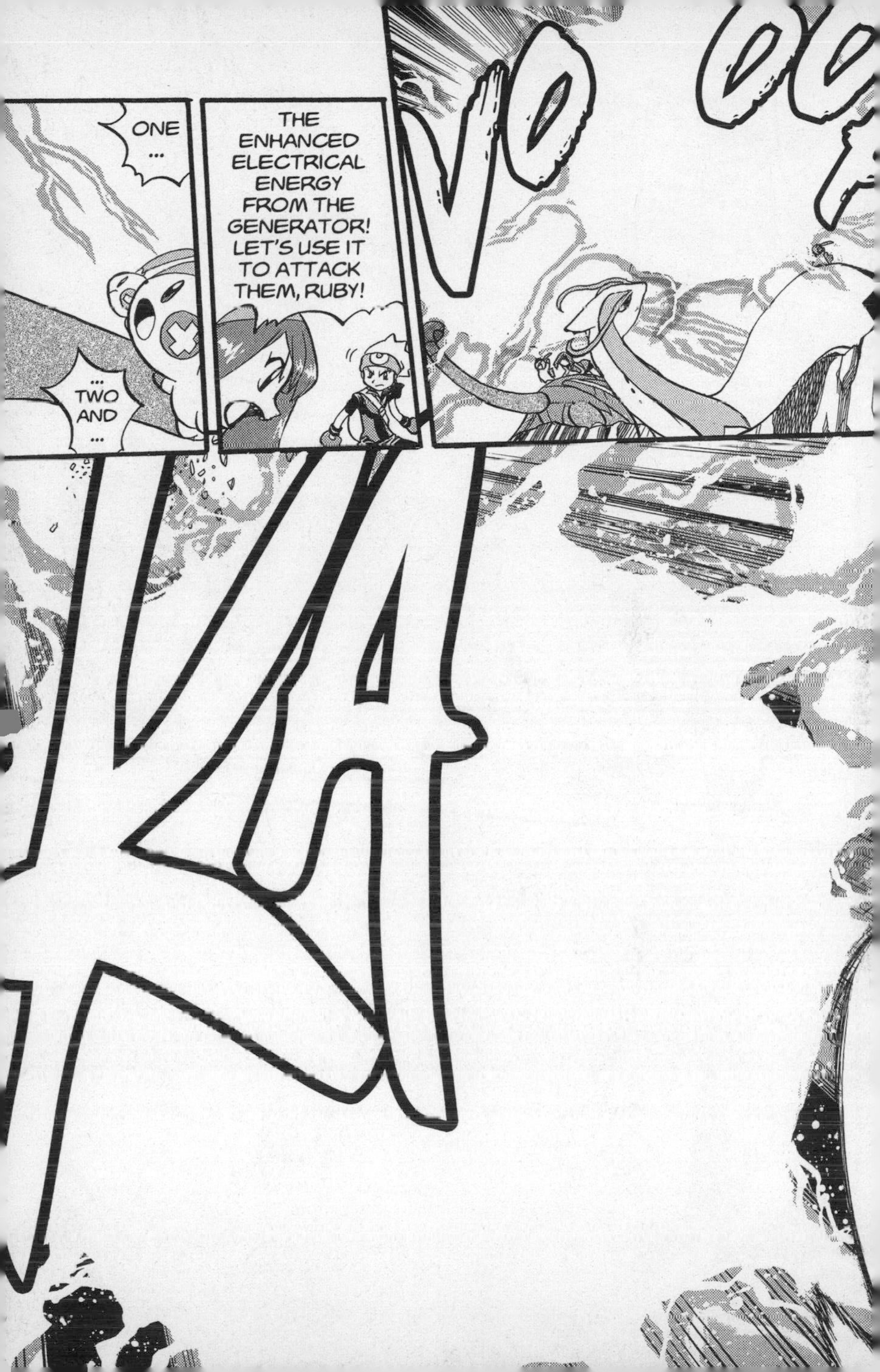
THE ENHANCED ELECTRICAL ENERGY FROM THE GENERATOR! LET'S USE IT TO ATTACK THEM, RUBY!
ONE ...
... TWO AND ...
KA

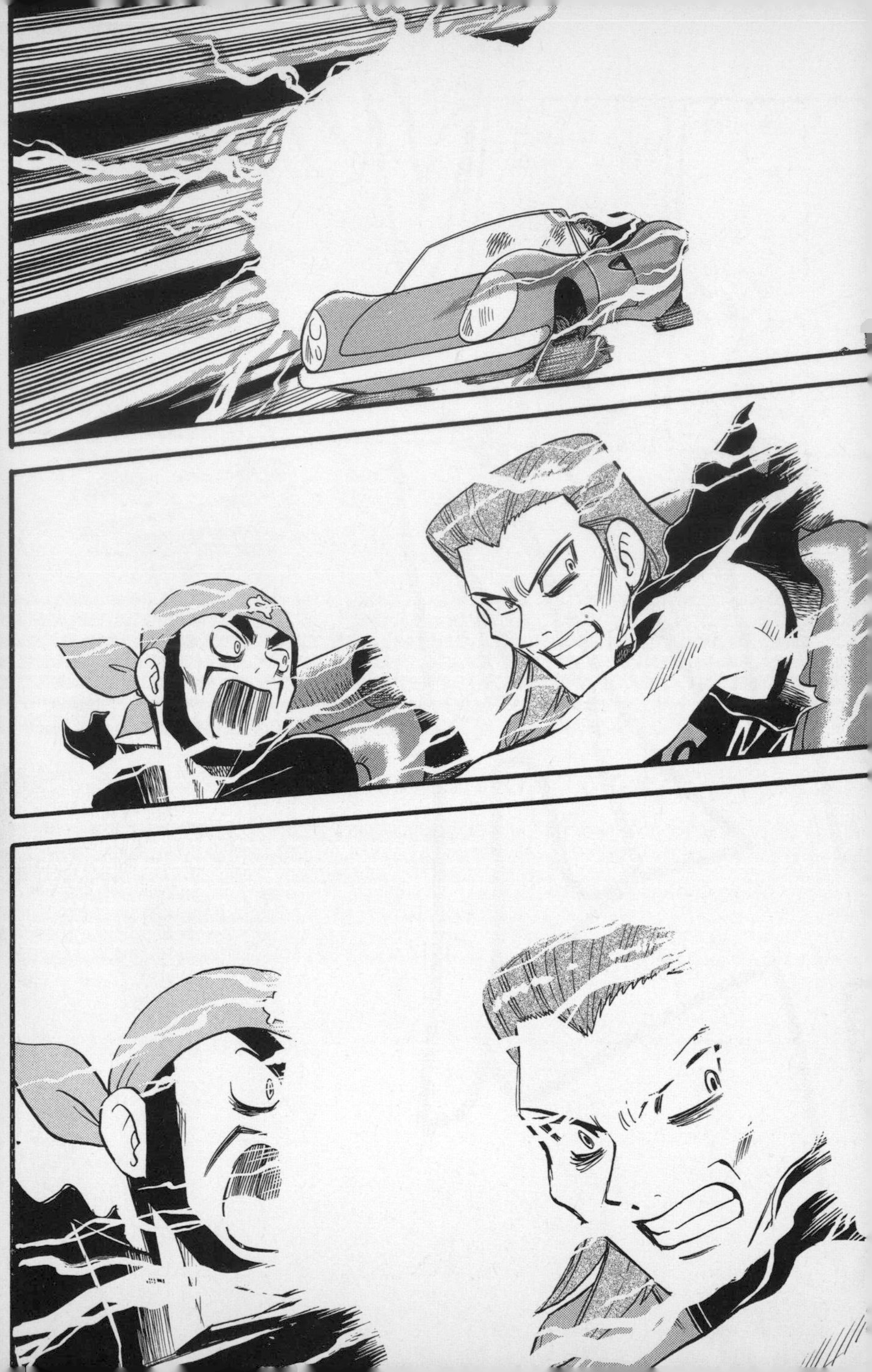

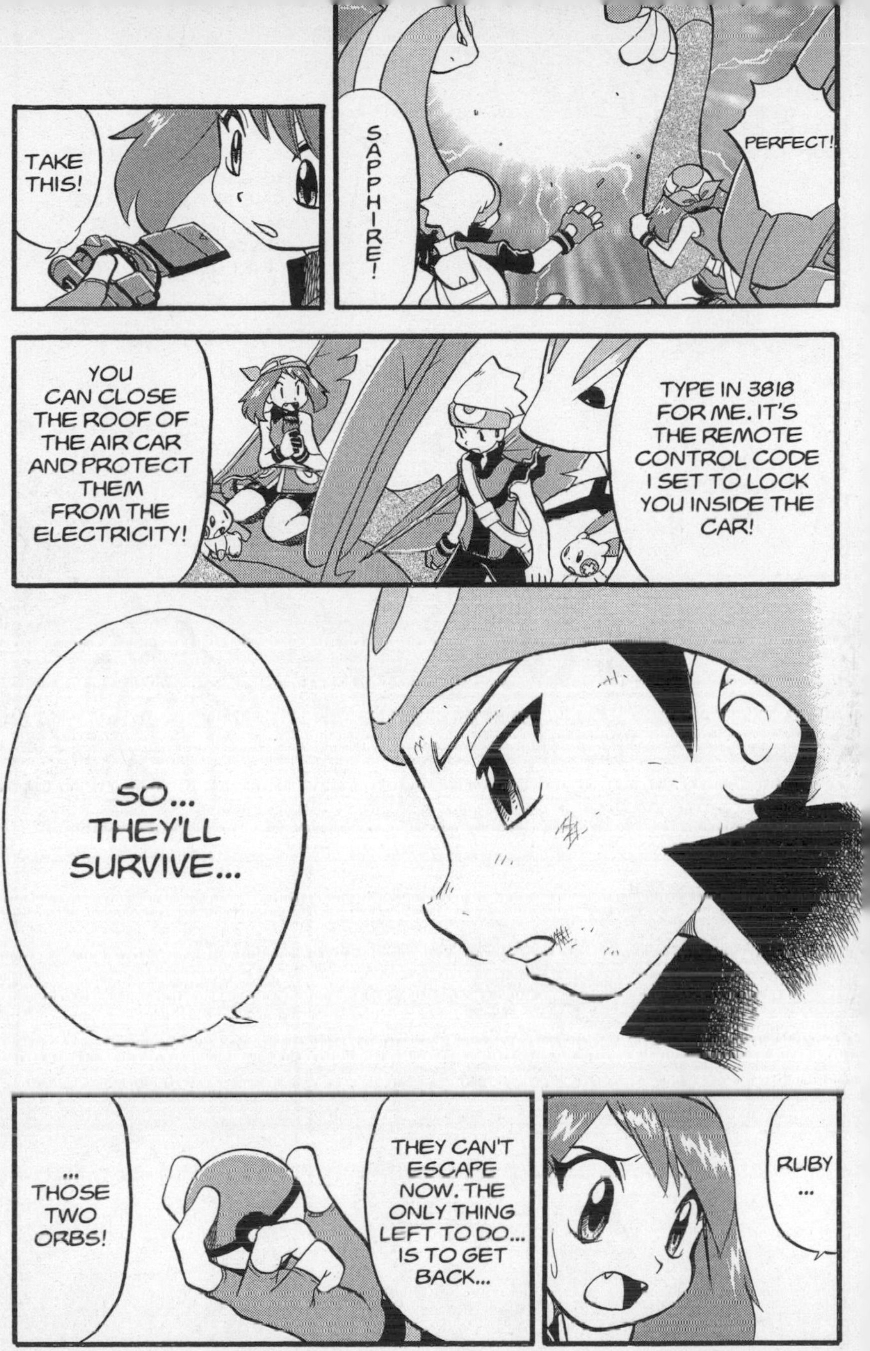
PERFECT!
SAPPHIRE!
TAKE THIS!
TYPE IN 3818 FOR ME. IT'S THE REMOTE CONTROL CODE I SET TO LOCK YOU INSIDE THE CAR!
YOU CAN CLOSE THE ROOF OF THE AIR CAR AND PROTECT THEM FROM THE ELECTRICITY!
SO... THEY'LL SURVIVE...
RUBY ...
THEY CAN'T ESCAPE NOW. THE ONLY THING LEFT TO DO... IS TO GET BACK...
... THOSE TWO ORBS!

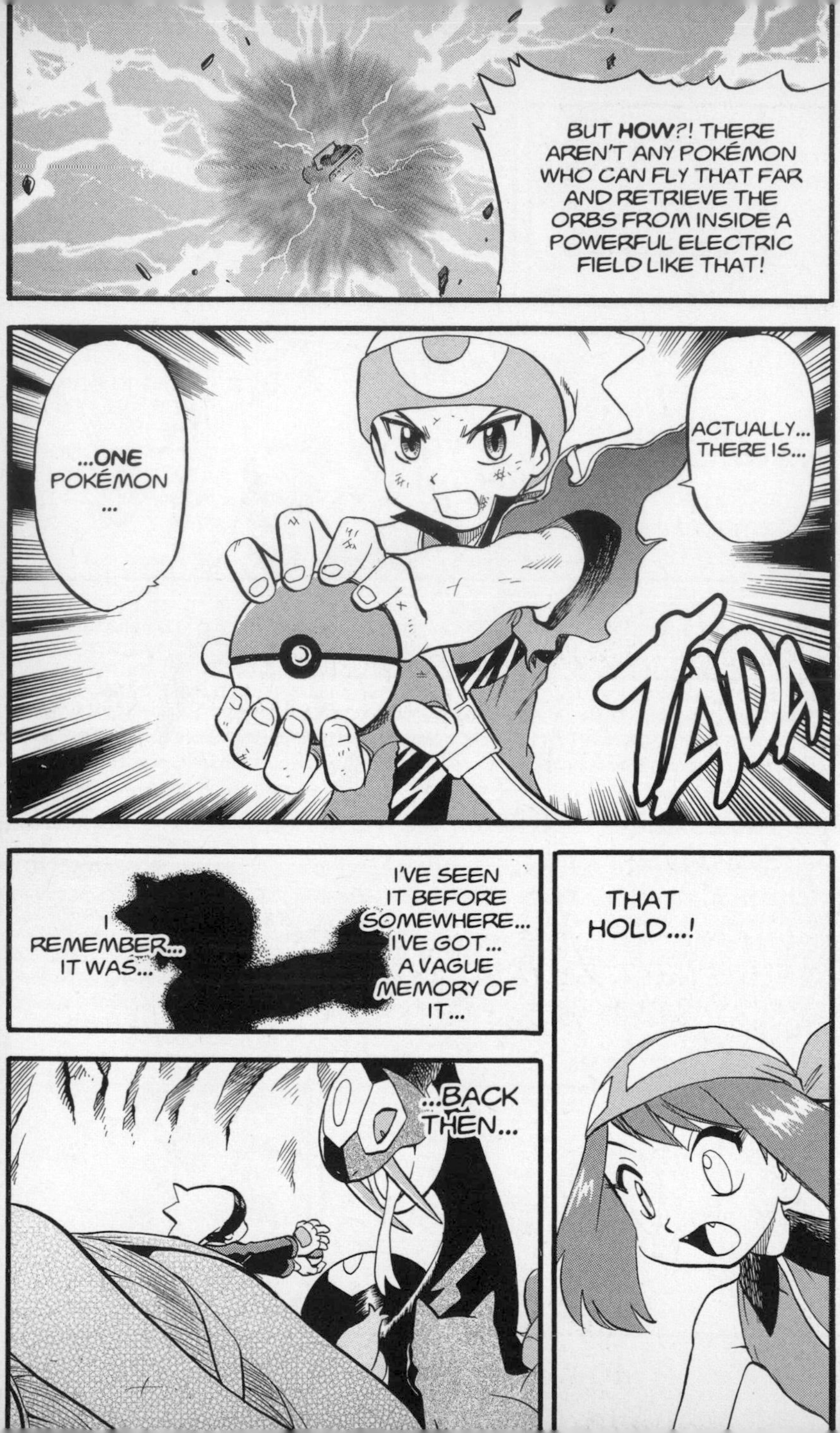
BUT HOW?! THERE AREN'T ANY POKÉMON WHO CAN FLY THAT FAR AND RETRIEVE THE ORBS FROM INSIDE A POWERFUL ELECTRIC FIELD LIKE THAT!
ACTUALLY... THERE IS...
TADA
...ONE POKÉMON ...
THAT HOLD...!
I'VE SEEN IT BEFORE SOMEWHERE... I'VE GOT... A VAGUE MEMORY OF IT...
I REMEMBER... IT WAS...
...BACK THEN...

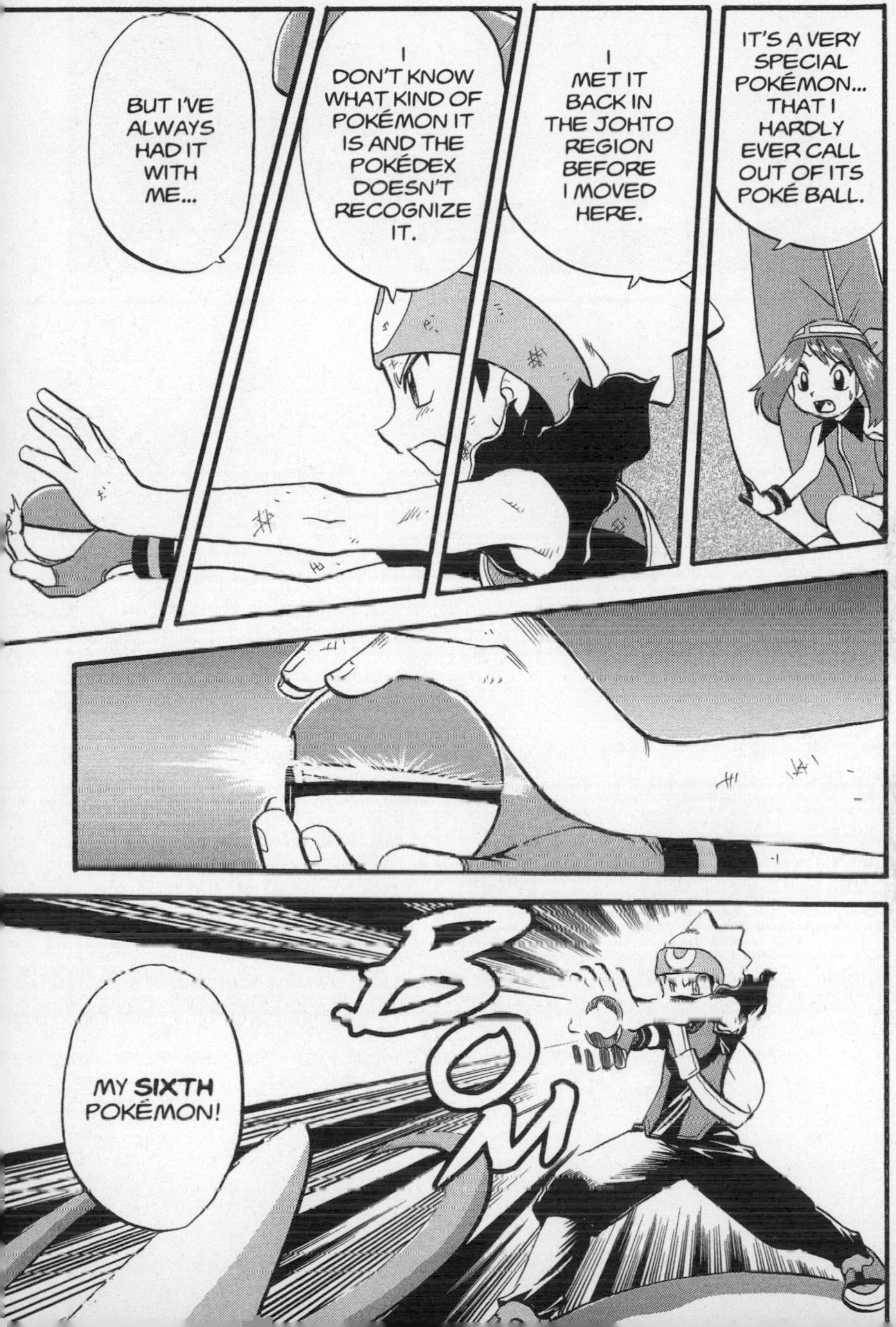
IT'S A VERY SPECIAL POKÉMON... THAT I HARDLY EVER CALL OUT OF ITS POKÉ BALL.
I MET IT BACK IN THE JOHTO REGION BEFORE I MOVED HERE.
I DON'T KNOW WHAT KIND OF POKÉMON IT IS AND THE POKÉDEX DOESN'T RECOGNIZE IT.
BUT I'VE ALWAYS HAD IT WITH ME...
BOM
MY **SIXTH** POKÉMON!

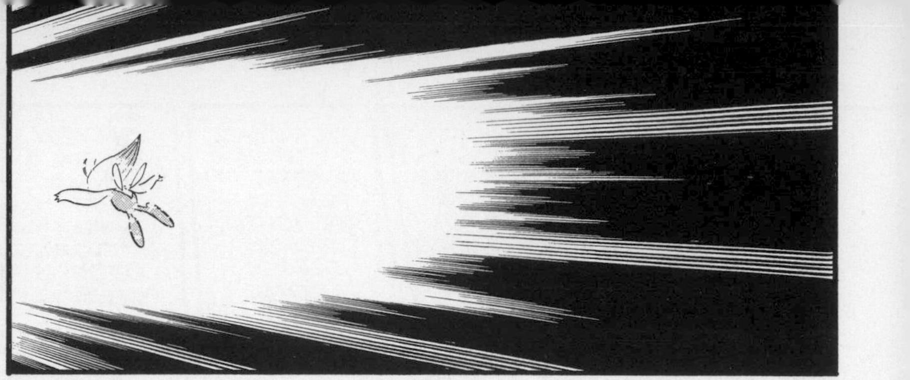
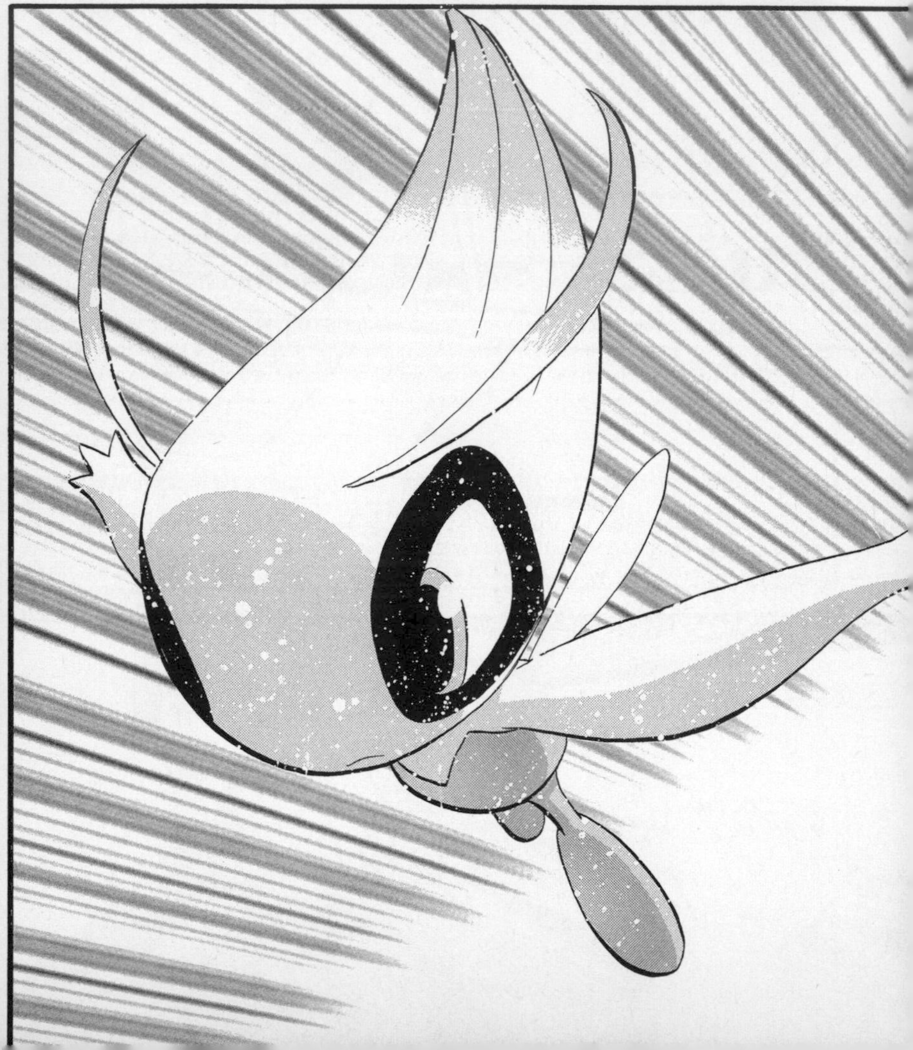

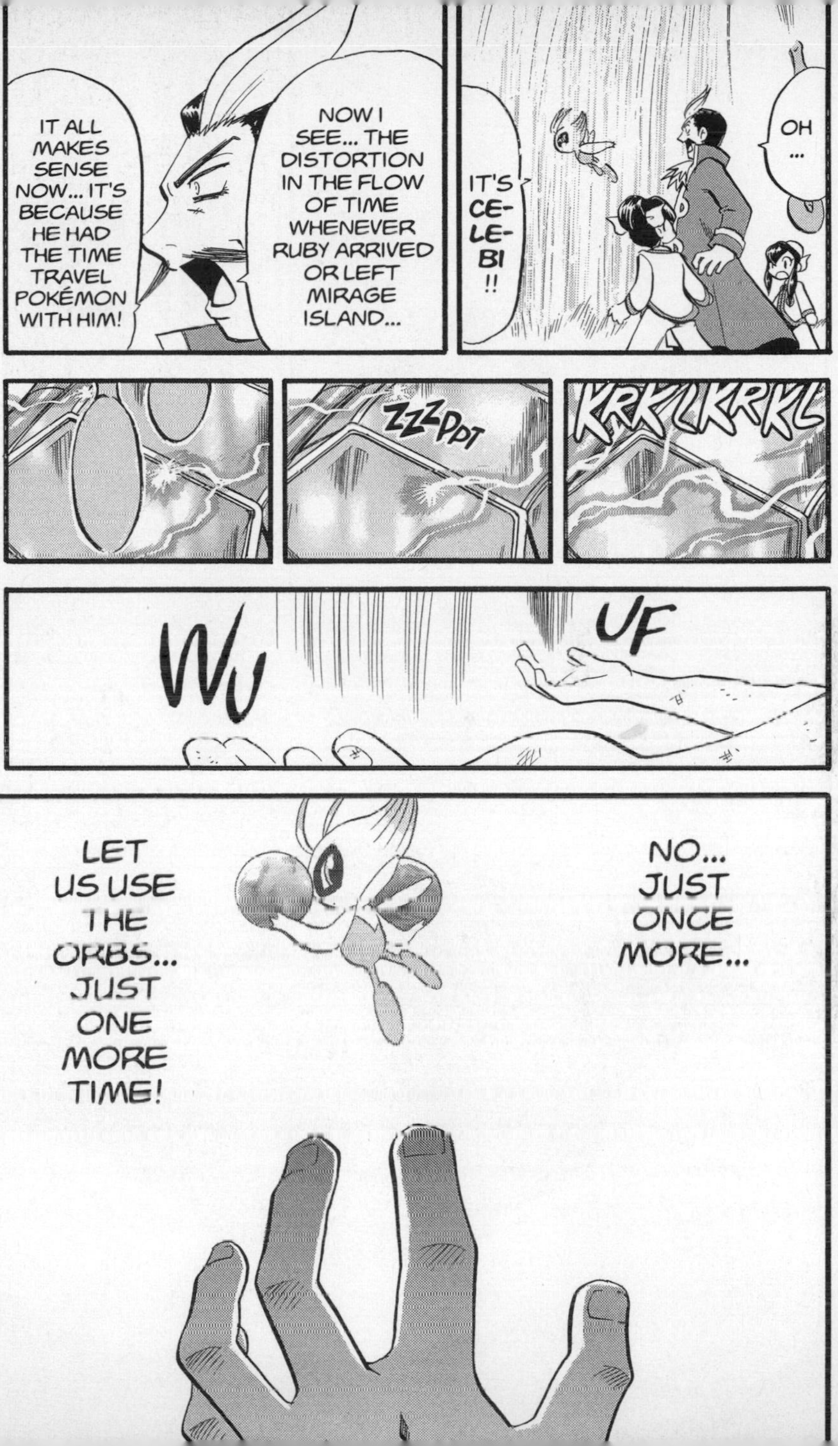
OH ...
IT'S CE-LE-BI !!
NOW I SEE... THE DISTORTION IN THE FLOW OF TIME WHENEVER RUBY ARRIVED OR LEFT MIRAGE ISLAND...
IT ALL MAKES SENSE NOW... IT'S BECAUSE HE HAD THE TIME TRAVEL POKÉMON WITH HIM!
KRKLKRKL
ZZZPPT
WU UF
NO... JUST ONCE MORE...
LET US USE THE ORBS... JUST ONE MORE TIME!

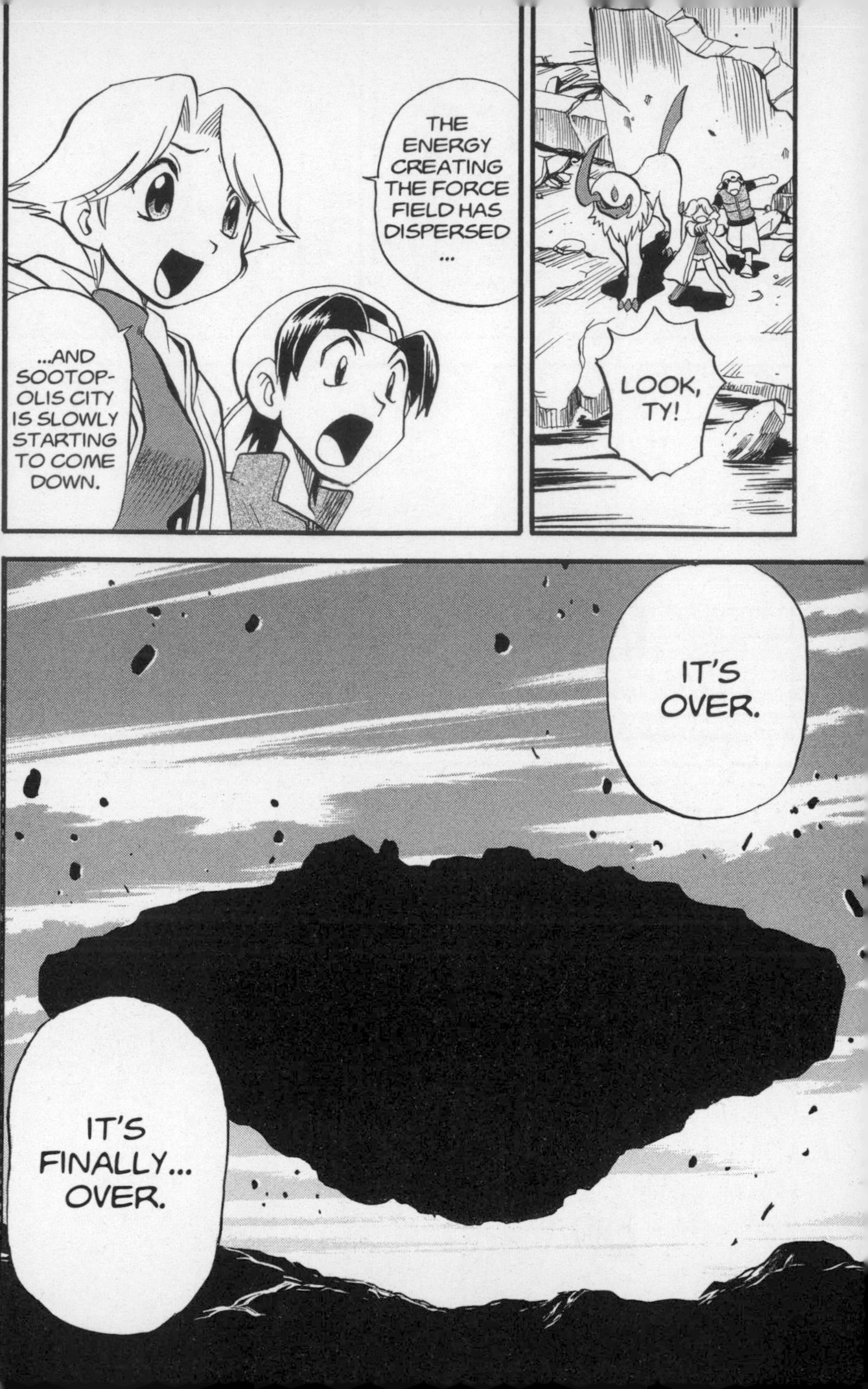
LOOK, TY!
THE ENERGY CREATING THE FORCE FIELD HAS DISPERSED...
...AND SOOTOP-OLIS CITY IS SLOWLY STARTING TO COME DOWN.
IT'S OVER.
IT'S FINALLY... OVER.

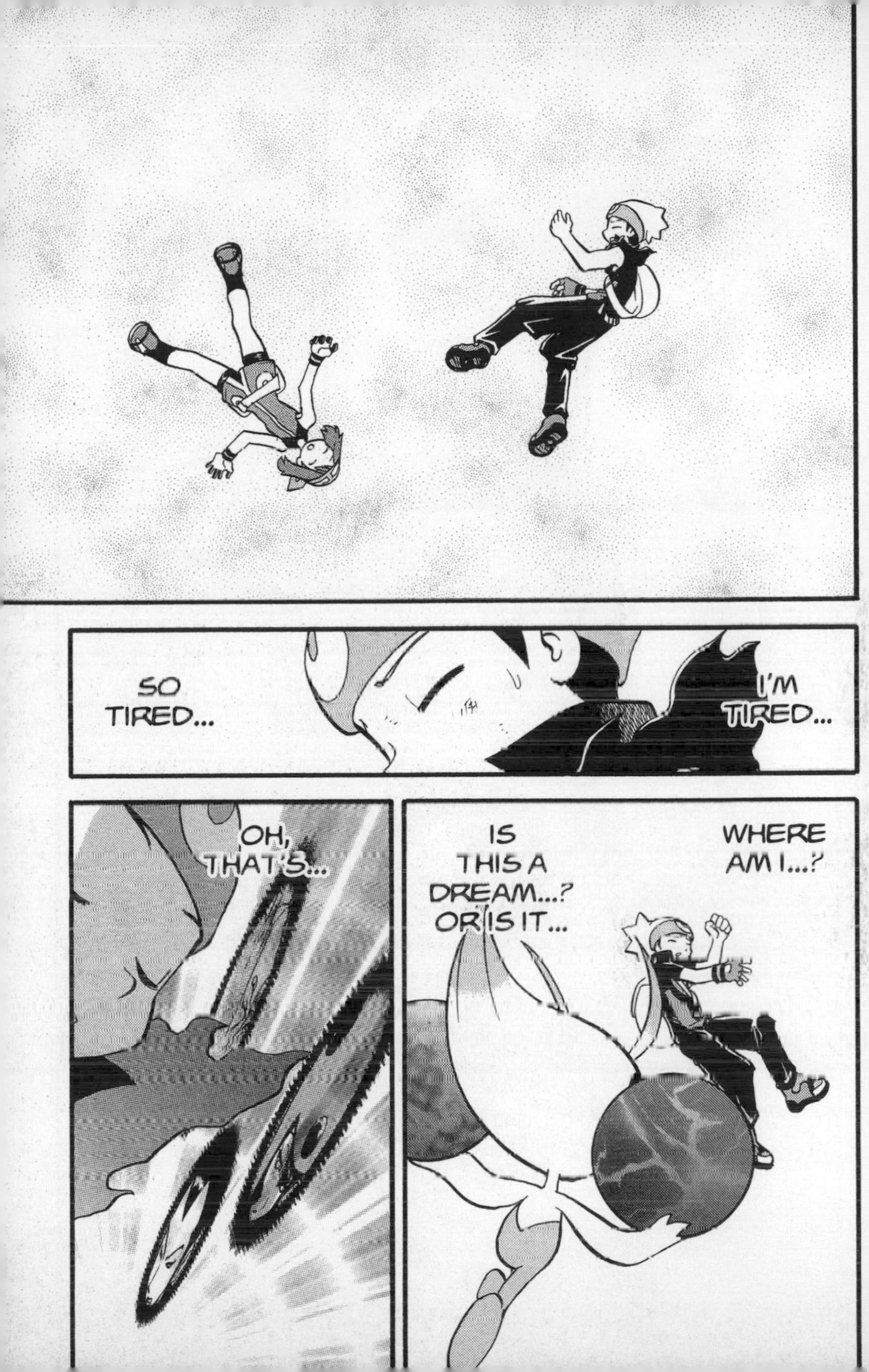
I'M TIRED...
SO TIRED...
WHERE AM I...?
IS THIS A DREAM...? OR IS IT...
OH, THAT'S...

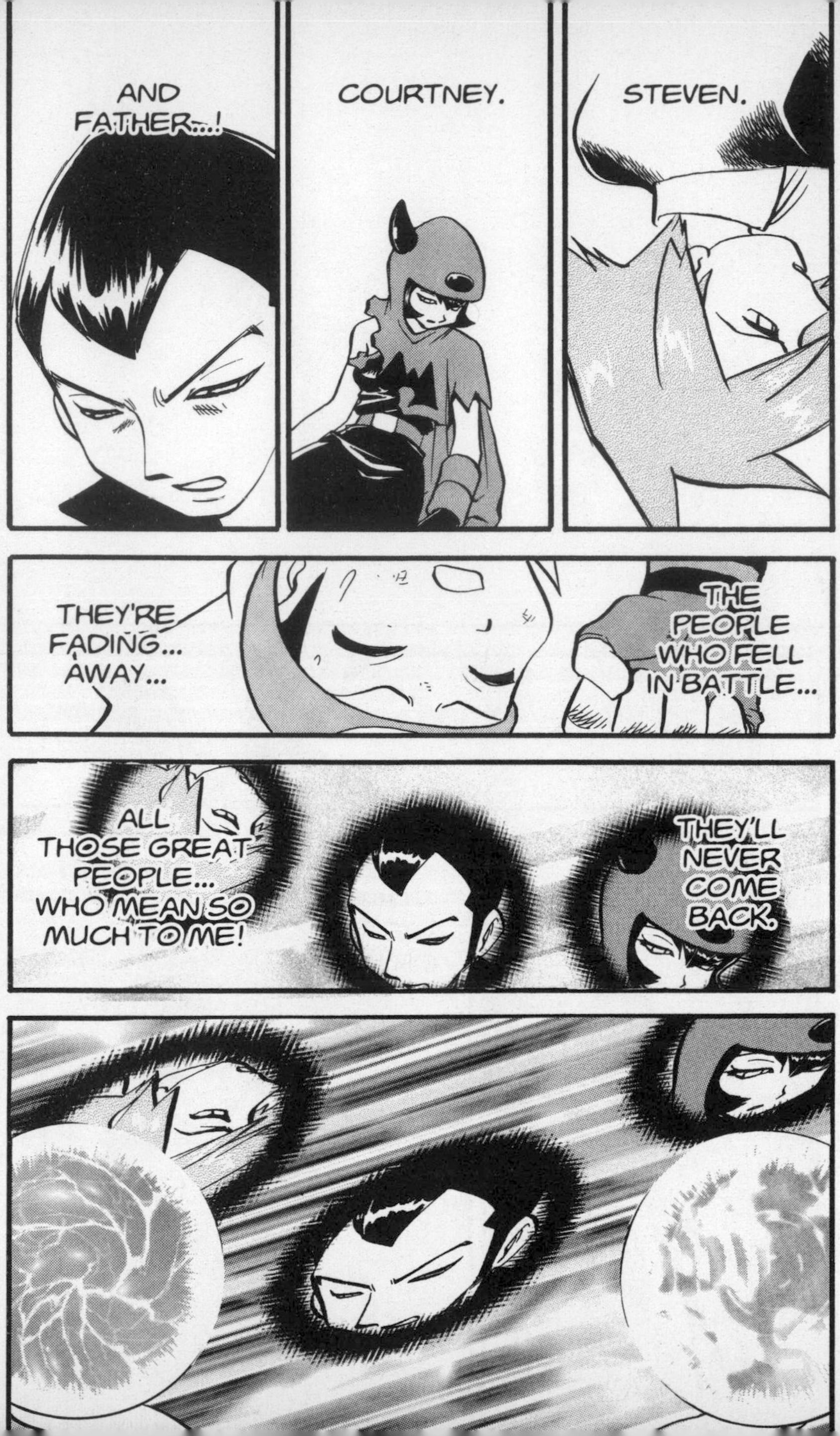
STEVEN.
COURTNEY.
AND FATHER...!
THE PEOPLE WHO FELL IN BATTLE...
THEY'RE FADING... AWAY...
THEY'LL NEVER COME BACK.
ALL THOSE GREAT PEOPLE... WHO MEAN SO MUCH TO ME!

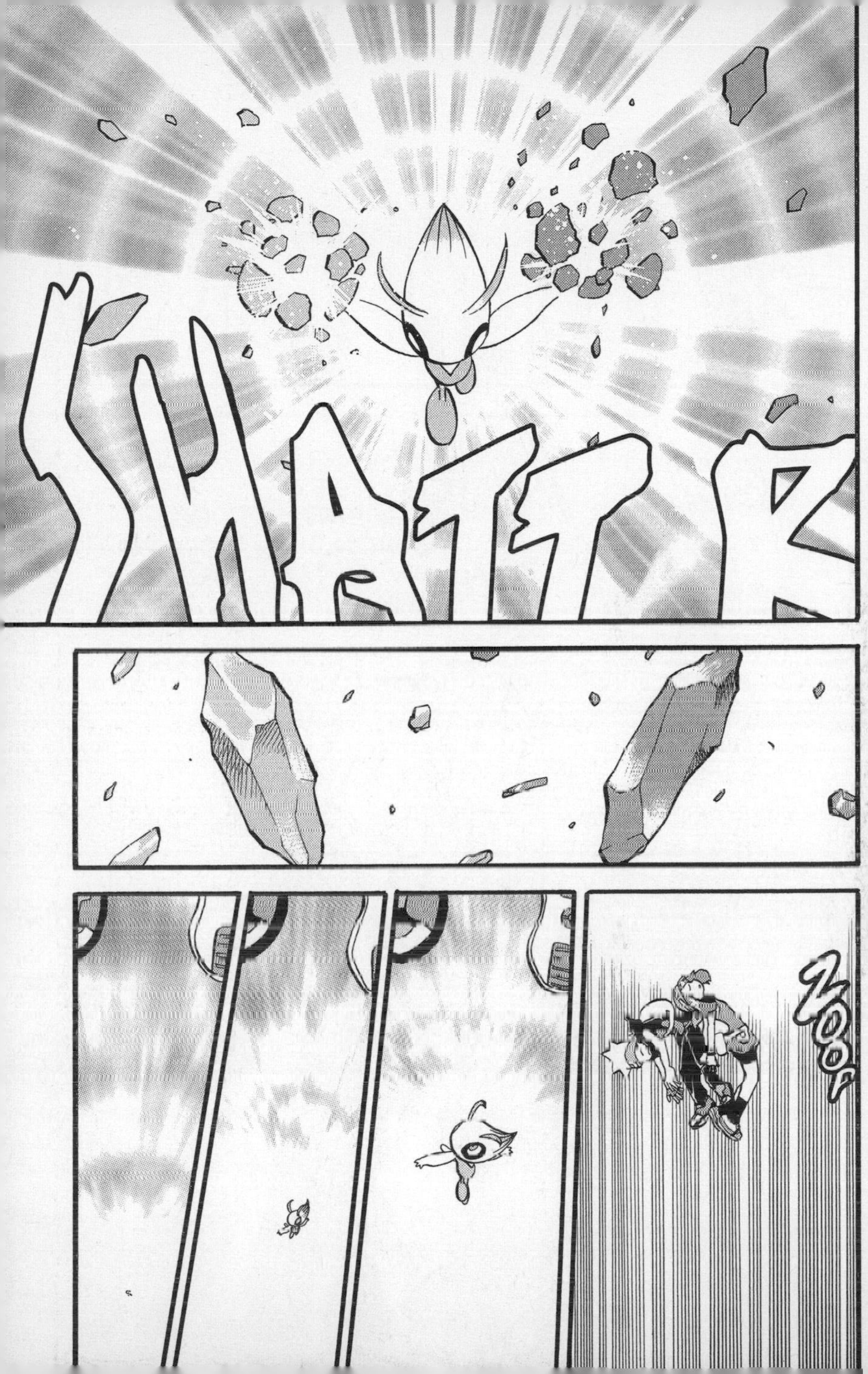
SHATTR
ZOOM

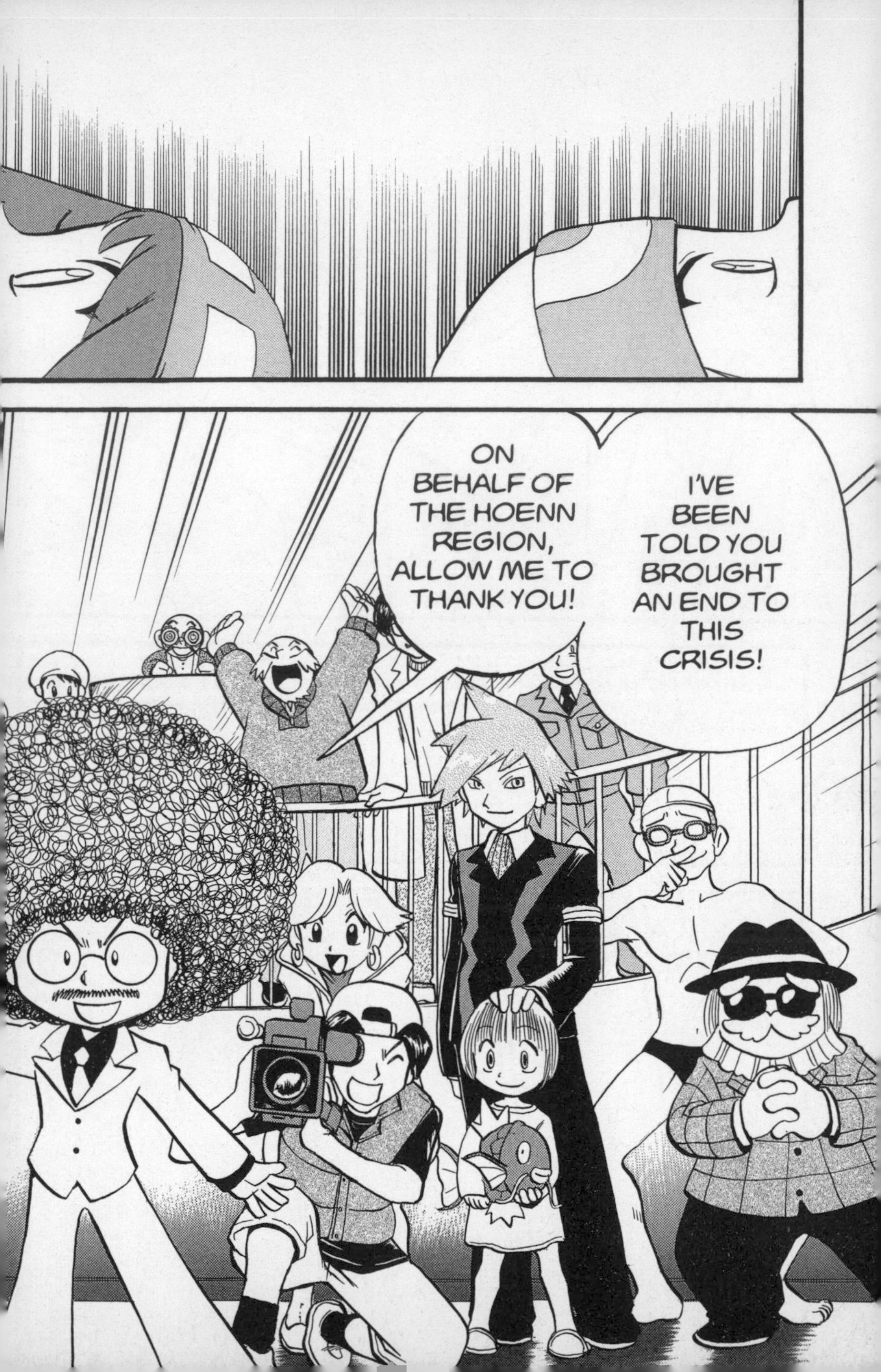
ON BEHALF OF THE HOENN REGION, ALLOW ME TO THANK YOU!
I'VE BEEN TOLD YOU BROUGHT AN END TO THIS CRISIS!

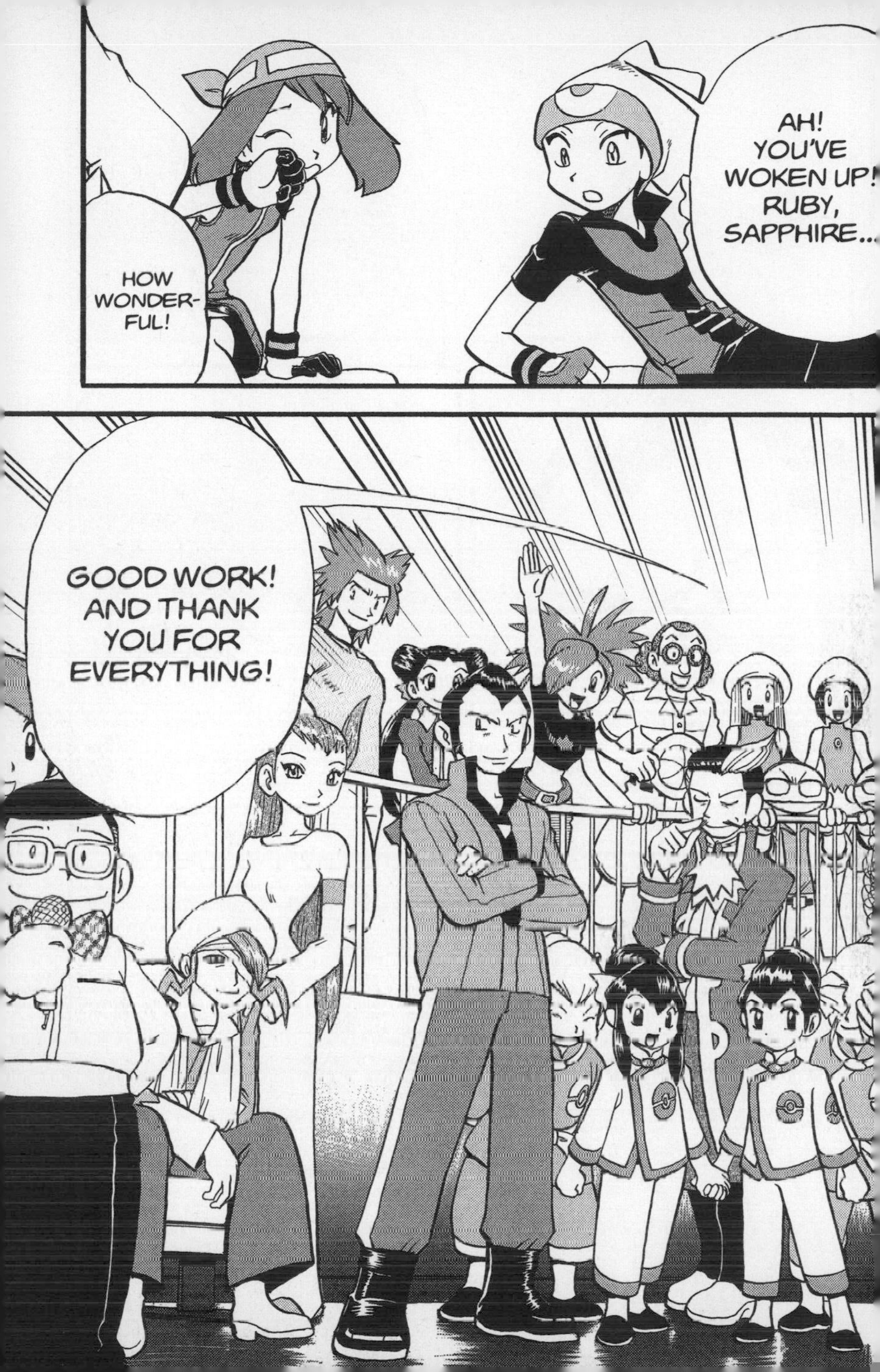
AH! YOU'VE WOKEN UP! RUBY, SAPPHIRE...
HOW WONDER-FUL!
GOOD WORK! AND THANK YOU FOR EVERYTHING!

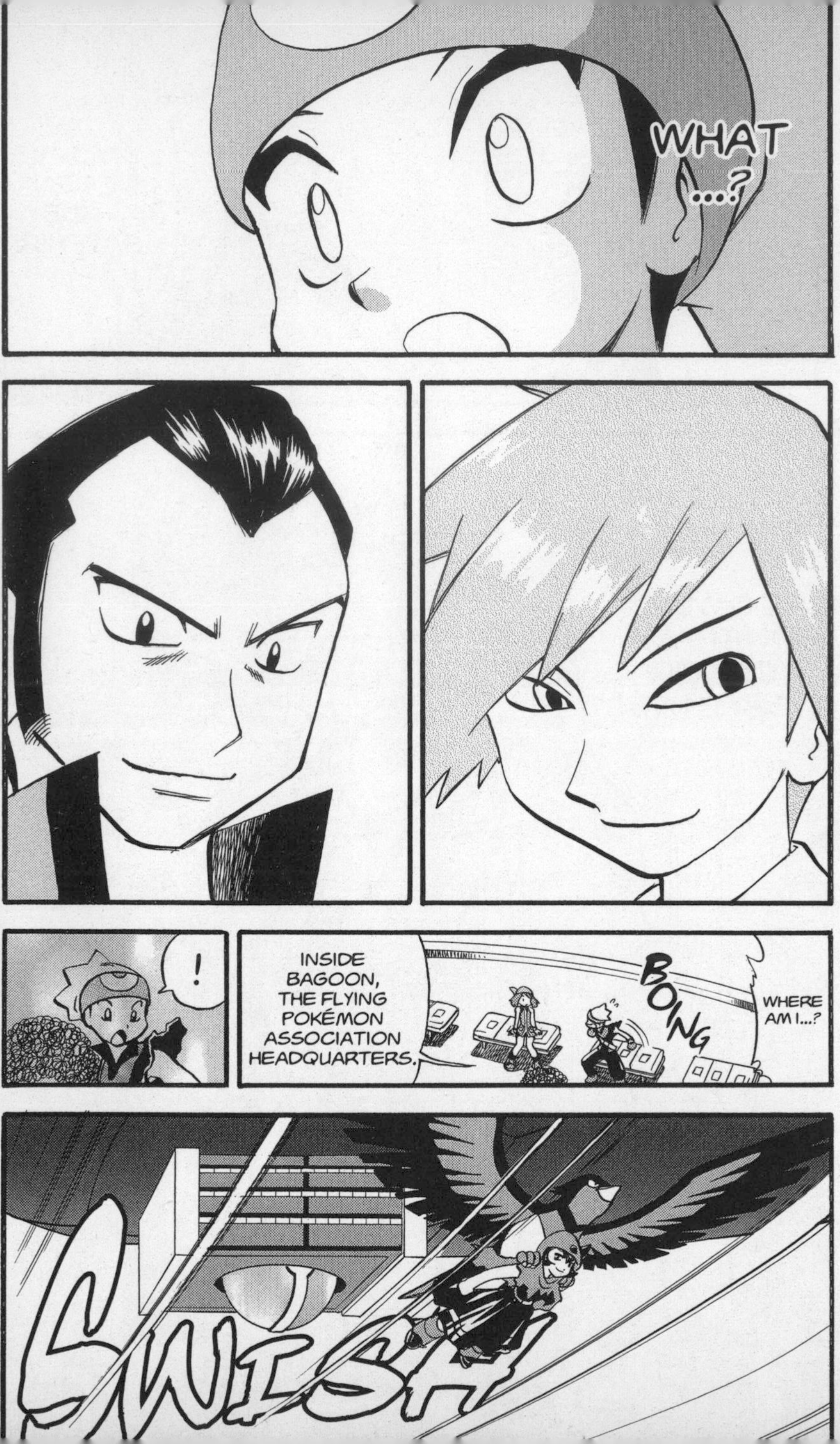
WHAT ...?
WHERE AM I...?
BOING
INSIDE BAGOON, THE FLYING POKÉMON ASSOCIATION HEADQUARTERS.
!
SWISH

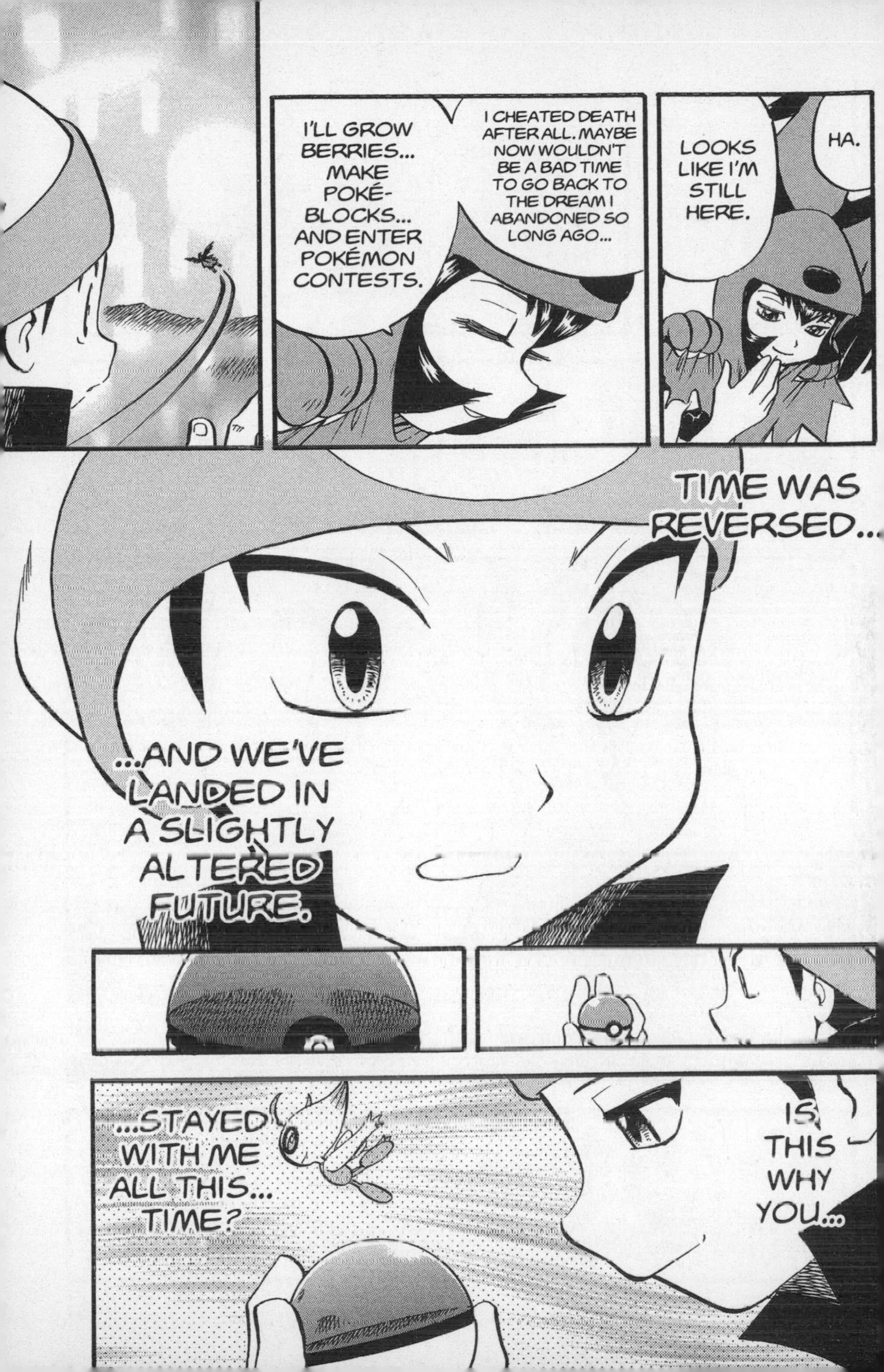
HA.
LOOKS LIKE I'M STILL HERE.
I CHEATED DEATH AFTER ALL. MAYBE NOW WOULDN'T BE A BAD TIME TO GO BACK TO THE DREAM I ABANDONED SO LONG AGO...
I'LL GROW BERRIES... MAKE POKÉ-BLOCKS... AND ENTER POKÉMON CONTESTS.
TIME WAS REVERSED...
...AND WE'VE LANDED IN A SLIGHTLY ALTERED FUTURE.
IS THIS WHY YOU...
...STAYED WITH ME ALL THIS... TIME?

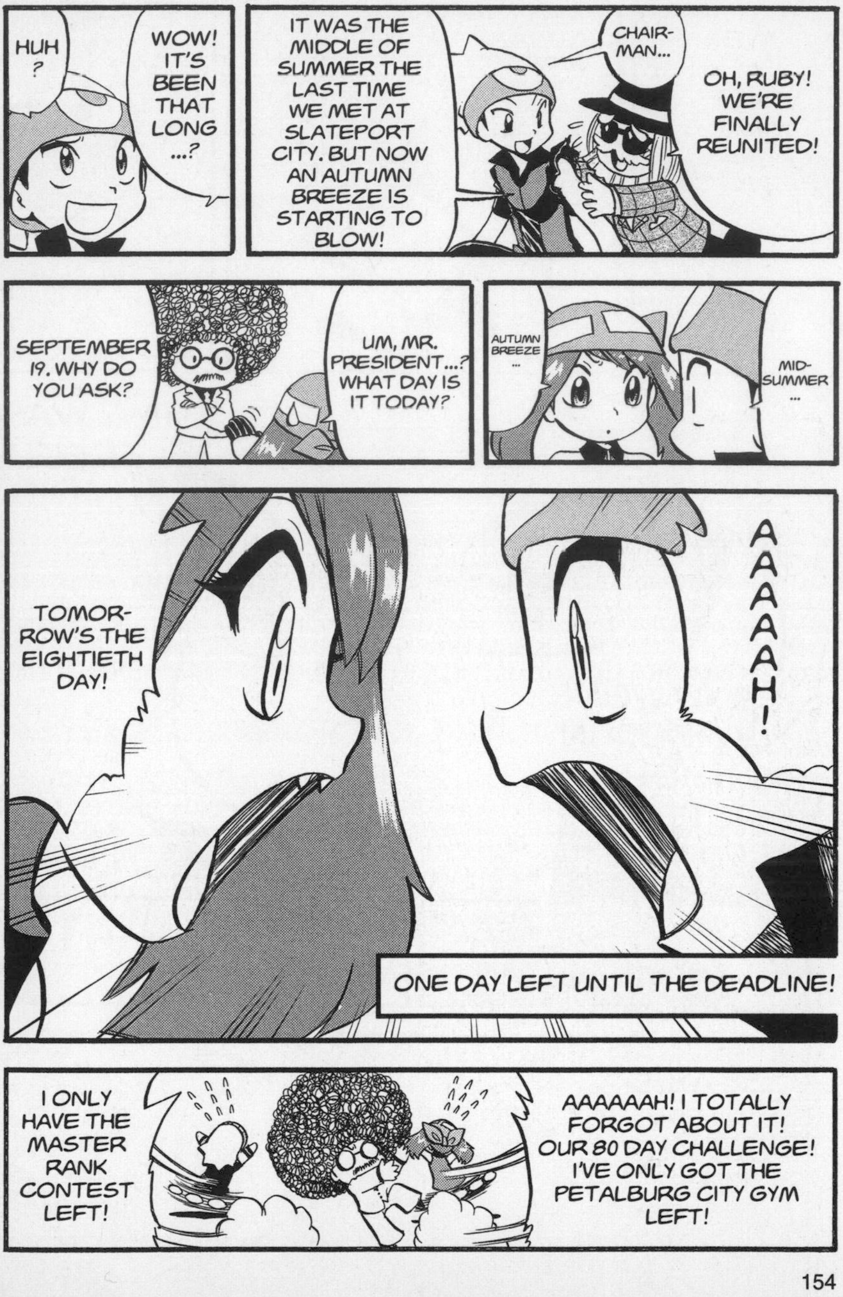
OH, RUBY! WE'RE FINALLY REUNITED!
CHAIR-MAN...
IT WAS THE MIDDLE OF SUMMER THE LAST TIME WE MET AT SLATEPORT CITY. BUT NOW AN AUTUMN BREEZE IS STARTING TO BLOW!
WOW! IT'S BEEN THAT LONG ...?
HUH ?
MID-SUMMER ...
AUTUMN BREEZE ...
UM, MR. PRESIDENT...? WHAT DAY IS IT TODAY?
SEPTEMBER 19. WHY DO YOU ASK?
AAAAAH!
TOMOR-ROW'S THE EIGHTIETH DAY!
ONE DAY LEFT UNTIL THE DEADLINE!
AAAAAAH! I TOTALLY FORGOT ABOUT IT! OUR 80 DAY CHALLENGE! I'VE ONLY GOT THE PETALBURG CITY GYM LEFT!
I ONLY HAVE THE MASTER RANK CONTEST LEFT!

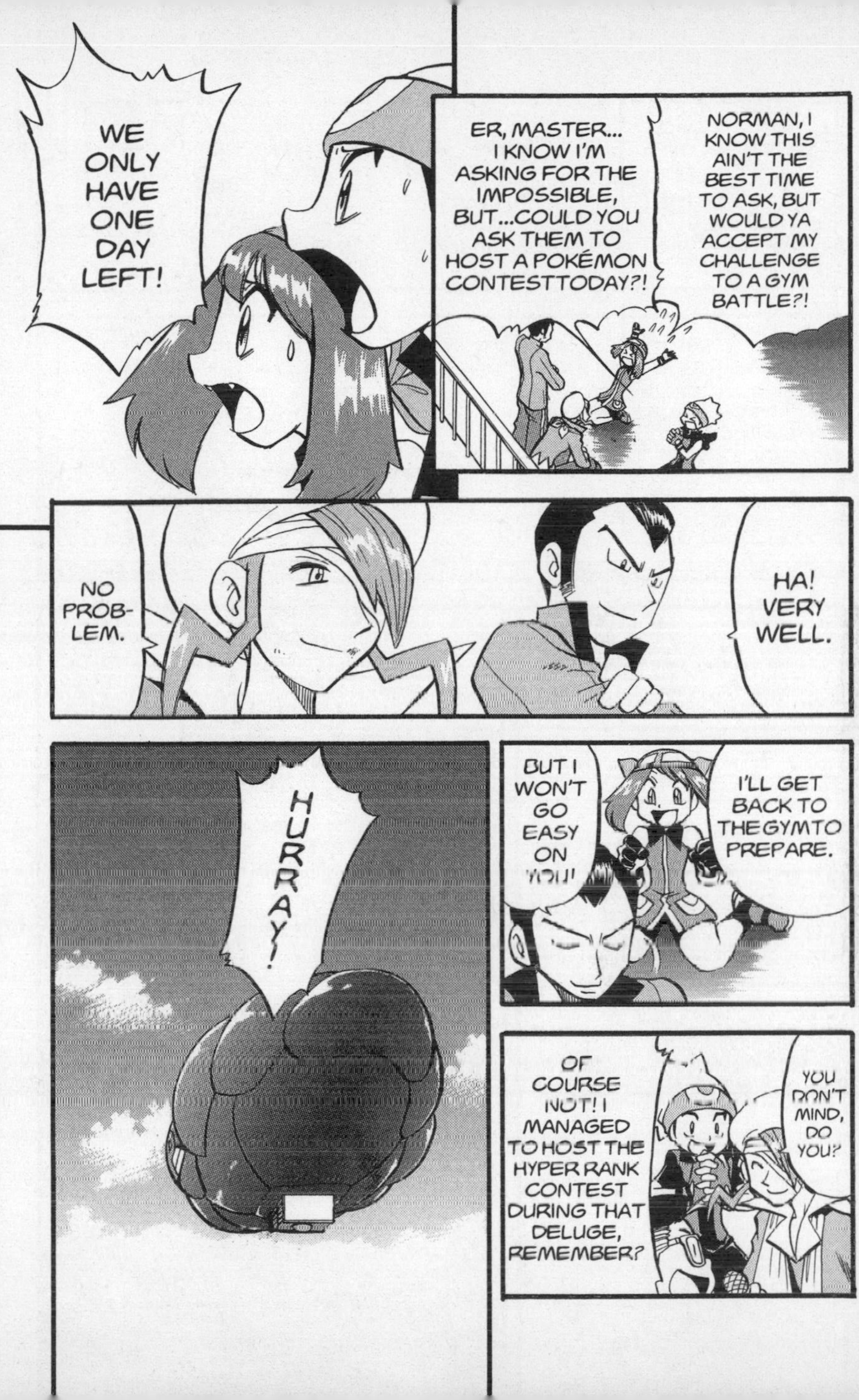
NORMAN, I KNOW THIS AIN'T THE BEST TIME TO ASK, BUT WOULD YA ACCEPT MY CHALLENGE TO A GYM BATTLE?!
ER, MASTER... I KNOW I'M ASKING FOR THE IMPOSSIBLE, BUT...COULD YOU ASK THEM TO HOST A POKÉMON CONTEST TODAY?!
WE ONLY HAVE ONE DAY LEFT!
HA! VERY WELL.
NO PROB-LEM.
I'LL GET BACK TO THE GYM TO PREPARE.
BUT I WON'T GO EASY ON YOU!
YOU DON'T MIND, DO YOU?
OF COURSE NOT! I MANAGED TO HOST THE HYPER RANK CONTEST DURING THAT DELUGE, REMEMBER?
HURRAY!

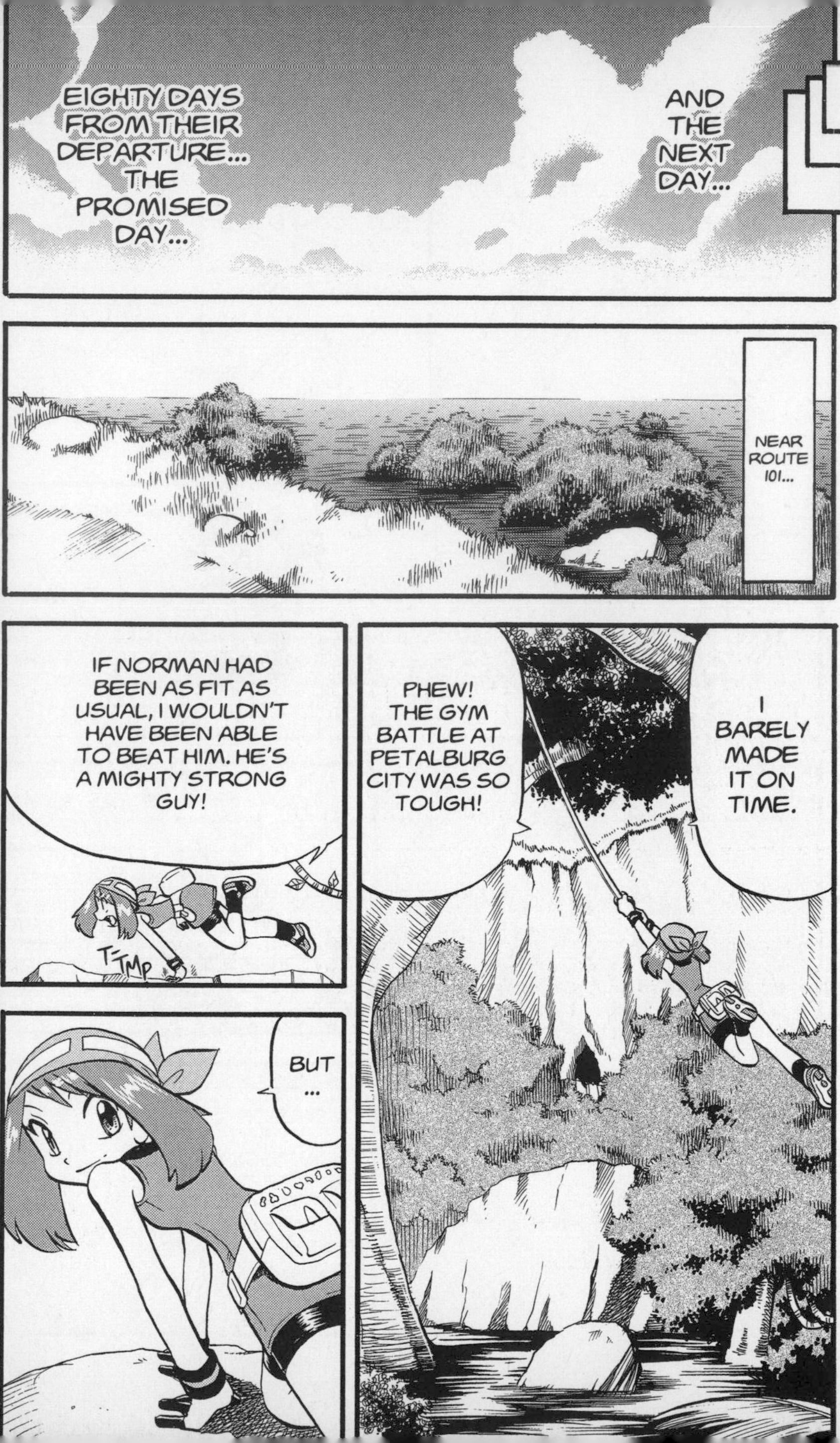
EIGHTY DAYS FROM THEIR DEPARTURE... THE PROMISED DAY...
AND THE NEXT DAY...
NEAR ROUTE 101...
I BARELY MADE IT ON TIME.
PHEW! THE GYM BATTLE AT PETALBURG CITY WAS SO TOUGH!
IF NORMAN HAD BEEN AS FIT AS USUAL, I WOULDN'T HAVE BEEN ABLE TO BEAT HIM. HE'S A MIGHTY STRONG GUY!
T-TMP
BUT ...

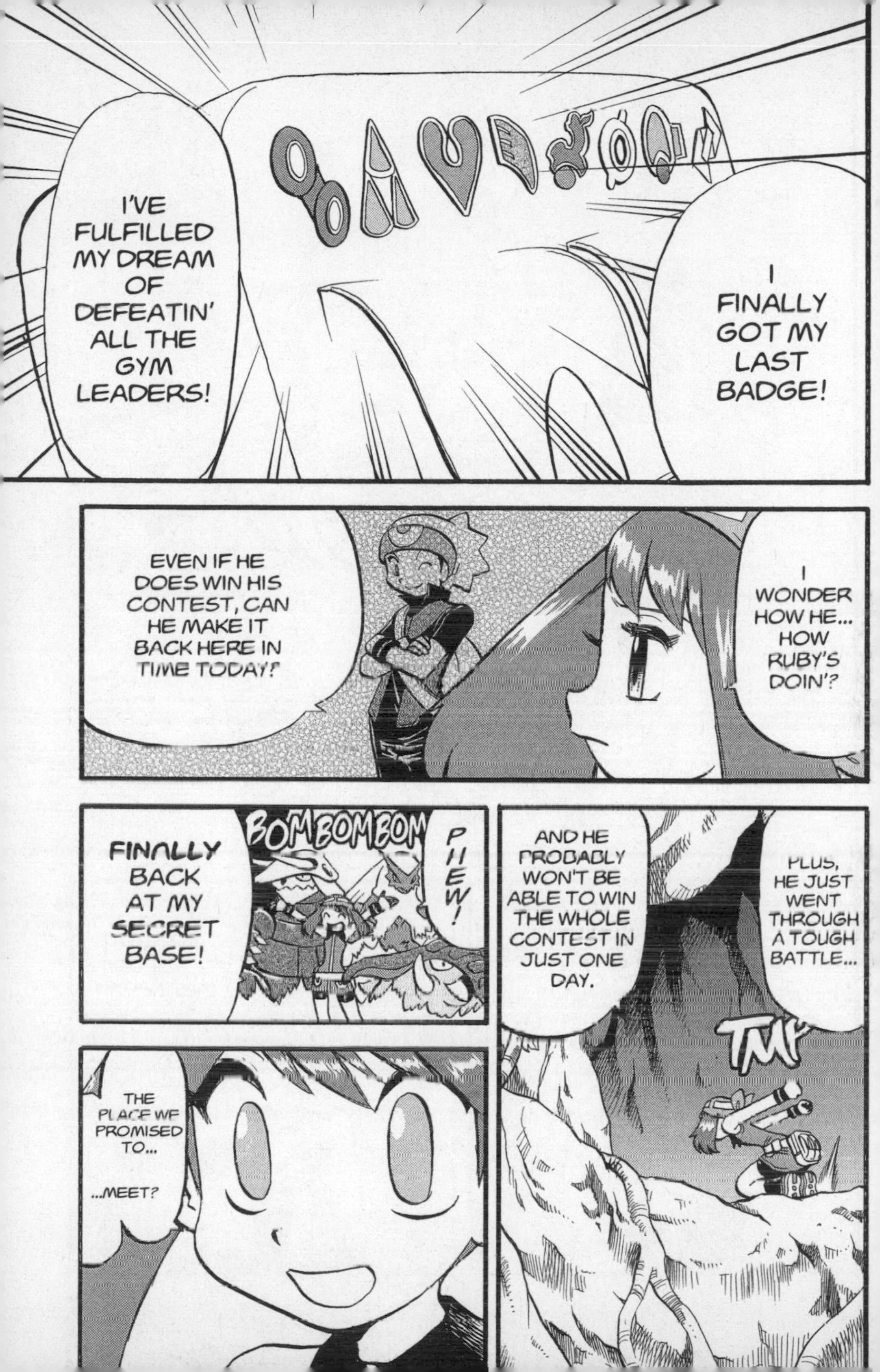
I FINALLY GOT MY LAST BADGE!
I'VE FULFILLED MY DREAM OF DEFEATIN' ALL THE GYM LEADERS!
I WONDER HOW HE... HOW RUBY'S DOIN'?
EVEN IF HE DOES WIN HIS CONTEST, CAN HE MAKE IT BACK HERE IN TIME TODAY?
PLUS, HE JUST WENT THROUGH A TOUGH BATTLE...
AND HE PROBABLY WON'T BE ABLE TO WIN THE WHOLE CONTEST IN JUST ONE DAY.
TMP
PHEW!
BOMBOMBOM
FINALLY BACK AT MY SECRET BASE!
THE PLACE WE PROMISED TO...
...MEET?

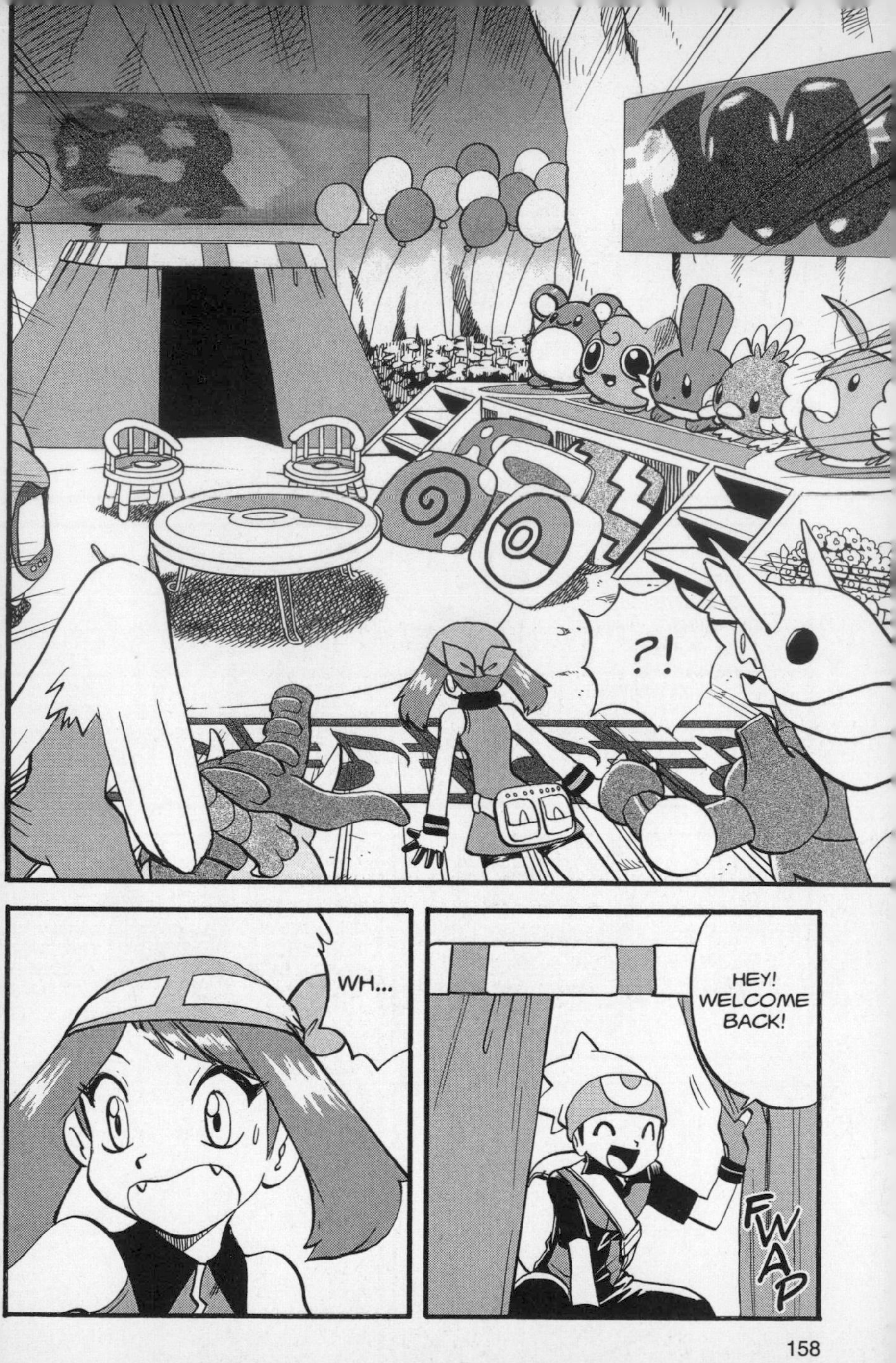
?!
HEY! WELCOME BACK!
FWAP
WH...

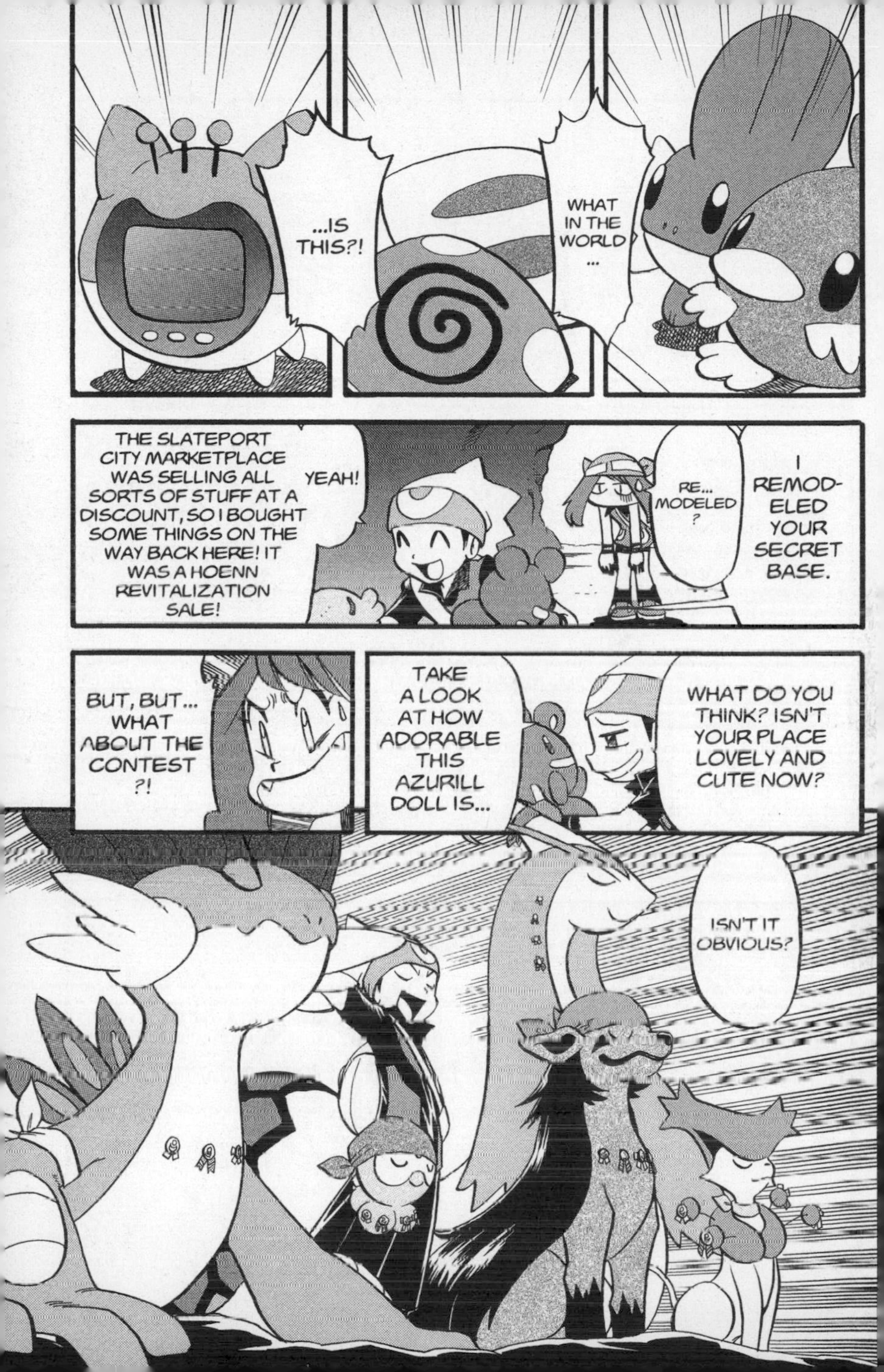
WHAT IN THE WORLD ...
...IS THIS?!
I REMODELED YOUR SECRET BASE.
RE... MODELED?
YEAH!
THE SLATEPORT CITY MARKETPLACE WAS SELLING ALL SORTS OF STUFF AT A DISCOUNT, SO I BOUGHT SOME THINGS ON THE WAY BACK HERE! IT WAS A HOENN REVITALIZATION SALE!
WHAT DO YOU THINK? ISN'T YOUR PLACE LOVELY AND CUTE NOW?
TAKE A LOOK AT HOW ADORABLE THIS AZURILL DOLL IS...
BUT, BUT... WHAT ABOUT THE CONTEST?!
ISN'T IT OBVIOUS?

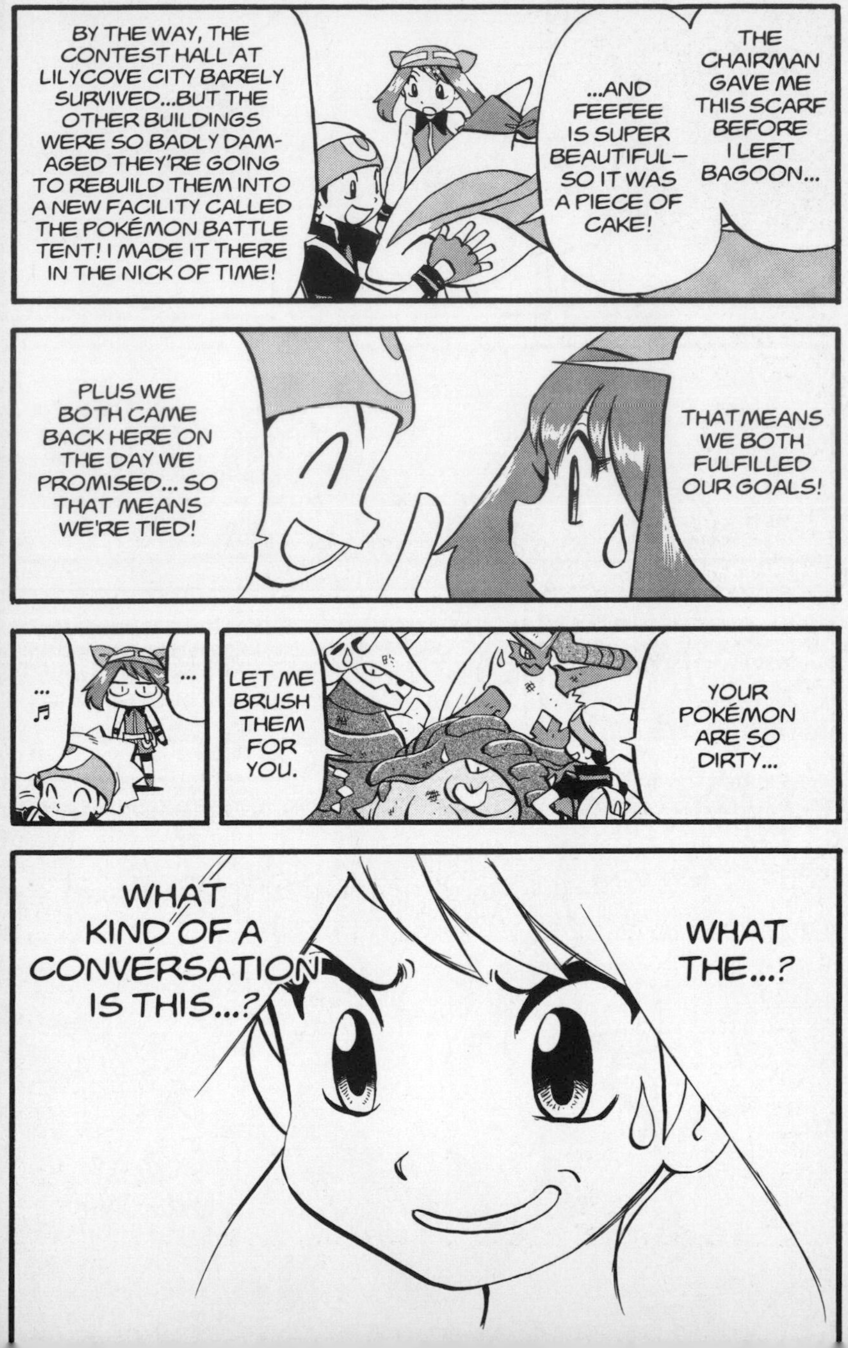
THE CHAIRMAN GAVE ME THIS SCARF BEFORE I LEFT BAGOON...
...AND FEEFEE IS SUPER BEAUTIFUL–SO IT WAS A PIECE OF CAKE!
BY THE WAY, THE CONTEST HALL AT LILYCOVE CITY BARELY SURVIVED...BUT THE OTHER BUILDINGS WERE SO BADLY DAMAGED THEY'RE GOING TO REBUILD THEM INTO A NEW FACILITY CALLED THE POKÉMON BATTLE TENT! I MADE IT THERE IN THE NICK OF TIME!
THAT MEANS WE BOTH FULFILLED OUR GOALS!
PLUS WE BOTH CAME BACK HERE ON THE DAY WE PROMISED... SO THAT MEANS WE'RE TIED!
YOUR POKÉMON ARE SO DIRTY...
LET ME BRUSH THEM FOR YOU.
...
... ♬
WHAT THE...?
WHAT KIND OF A CONVERSATION IS THIS...?

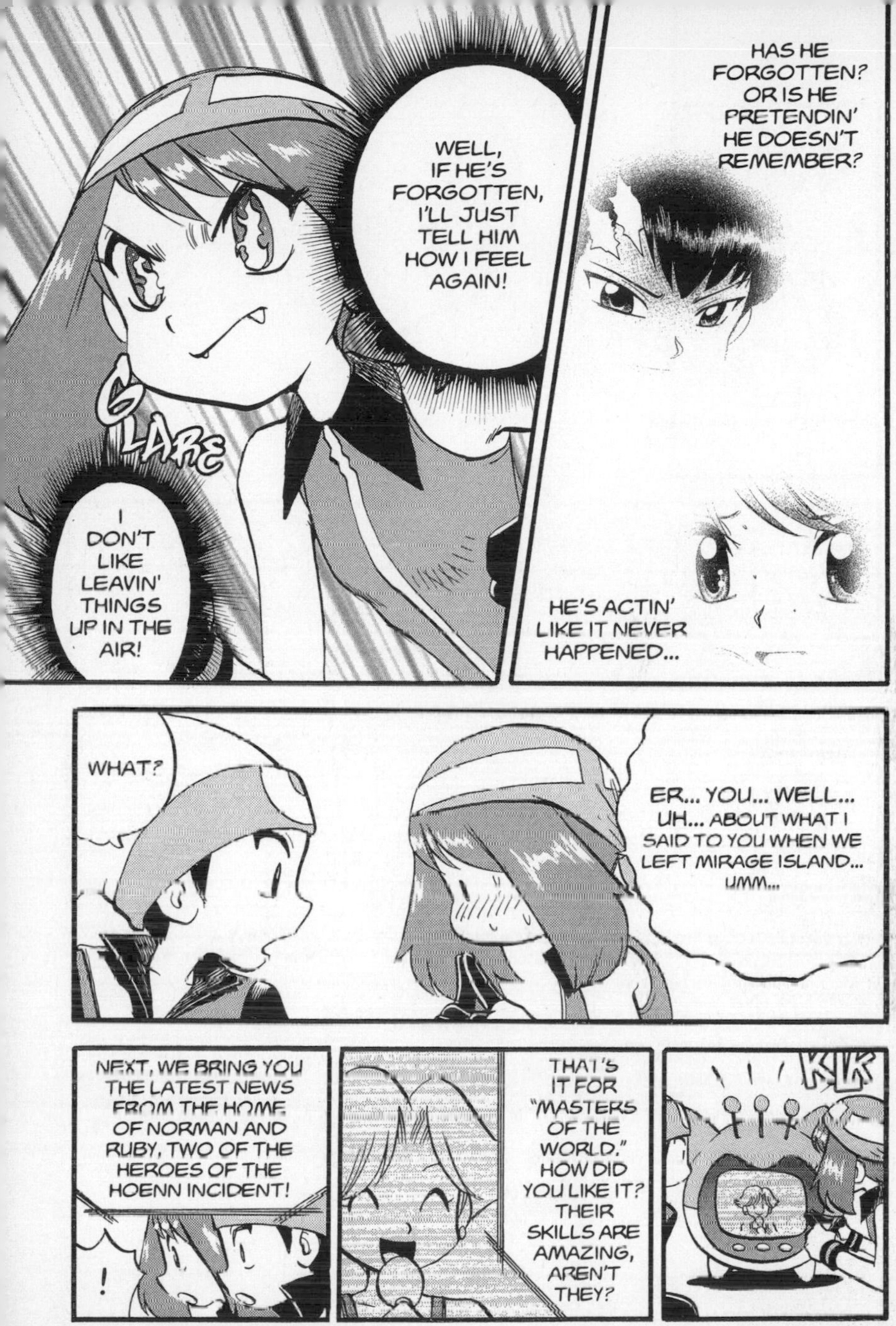
HAS HE FORGOTTEN? OR IS HE PRETENDIN' HE DOESN'T REMEMBER?
HE'S ACTIN' LIKE IT NEVER HAPPENED...
WELL, IF HE'S FORGOTTEN, I'LL JUST TELL HIM HOW I FEEL AGAIN!
GLARE
I DON'T LIKE LEAVIN' THINGS UP IN THE AIR!
ER... YOU... WELL... UH... ABOUT WHAT I SAID TO YOU WHEN WE LEFT MIRAGE ISLAND... UMM...
WHAT?
KLIK
THAT'S IT FOR "MASTERS OF THE WORLD." HOW DID YOU LIKE IT? THEIR SKILLS ARE AMAZING, AREN'T THEY?
NEXT, WE BRING YOU THE LATEST NEWS FROM THE HOME OF NORMAN AND RUBY, TWO OF THE HEROES OF THE HOENN INCIDENT!
!

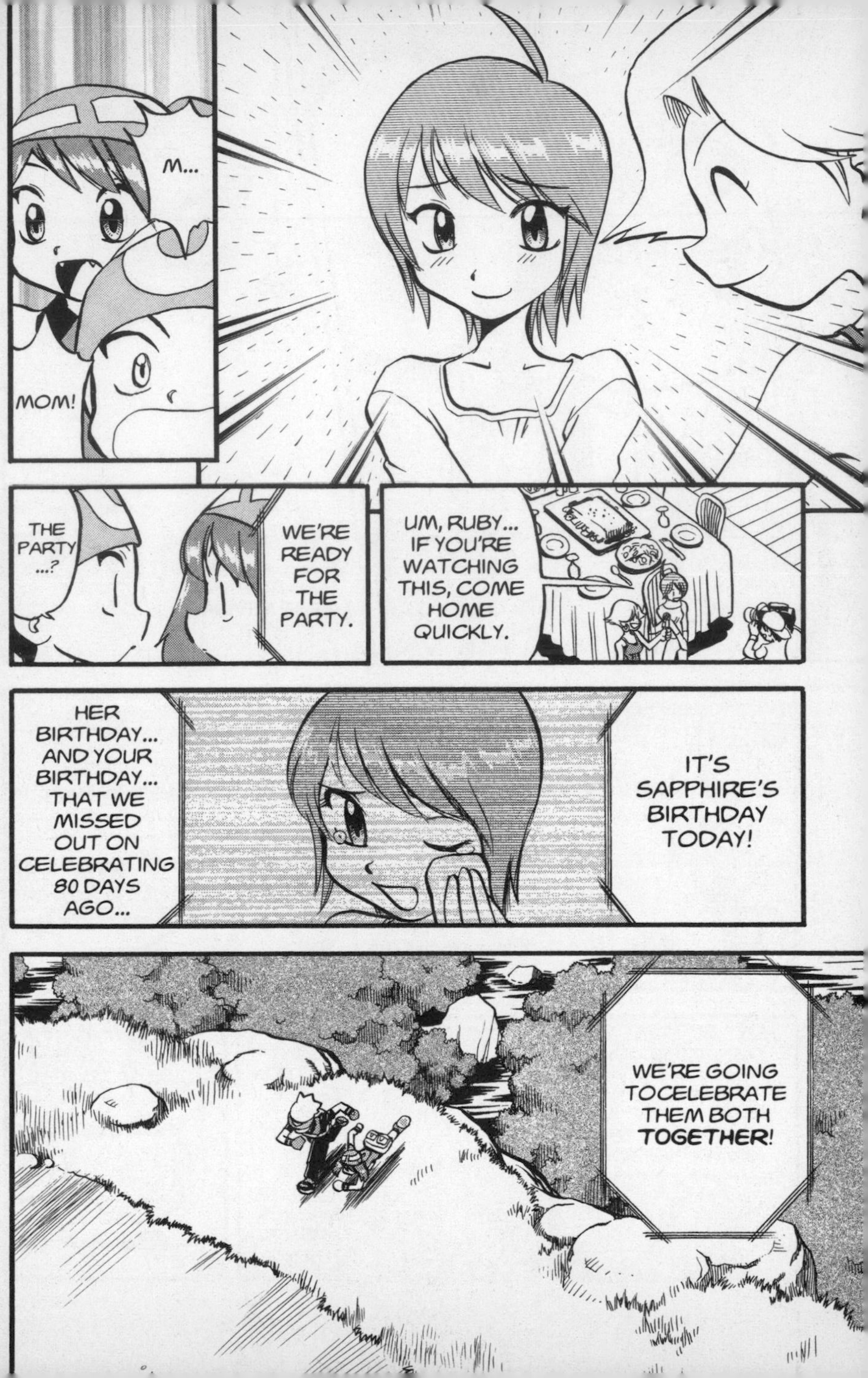
M...
MOM!
UM, RUBY... IF YOU'RE WATCHING THIS, COME HOME QUICKLY.
WE'RE READY FOR THE PARTY.
THE PARTY ...?
IT'S SAPPHIRE'S BIRTHDAY TODAY!
HER BIRTHDAY... AND YOUR BIRTHDAY... THAT WE MISSED OUT ON CELEBRATING 80 DAYS AGO...
WE'RE GOING TOCELEBRATE THEM BOTH **TOGETHER**!

S.S. TIDAL

Dear Ruby,
Thank you for
everything. I'm
returning Rara
to you.
Thanks to you, I've
[...] a great

Dear Professor Birch,
I found this Pokédex.
Please return it to
its rightful owner.

GRAND REOPENING!
THE LAVARIDGE TOWN
HOT SPRINGS HAVE
REOPENED!

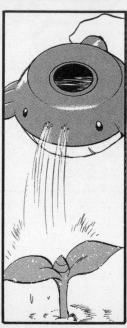

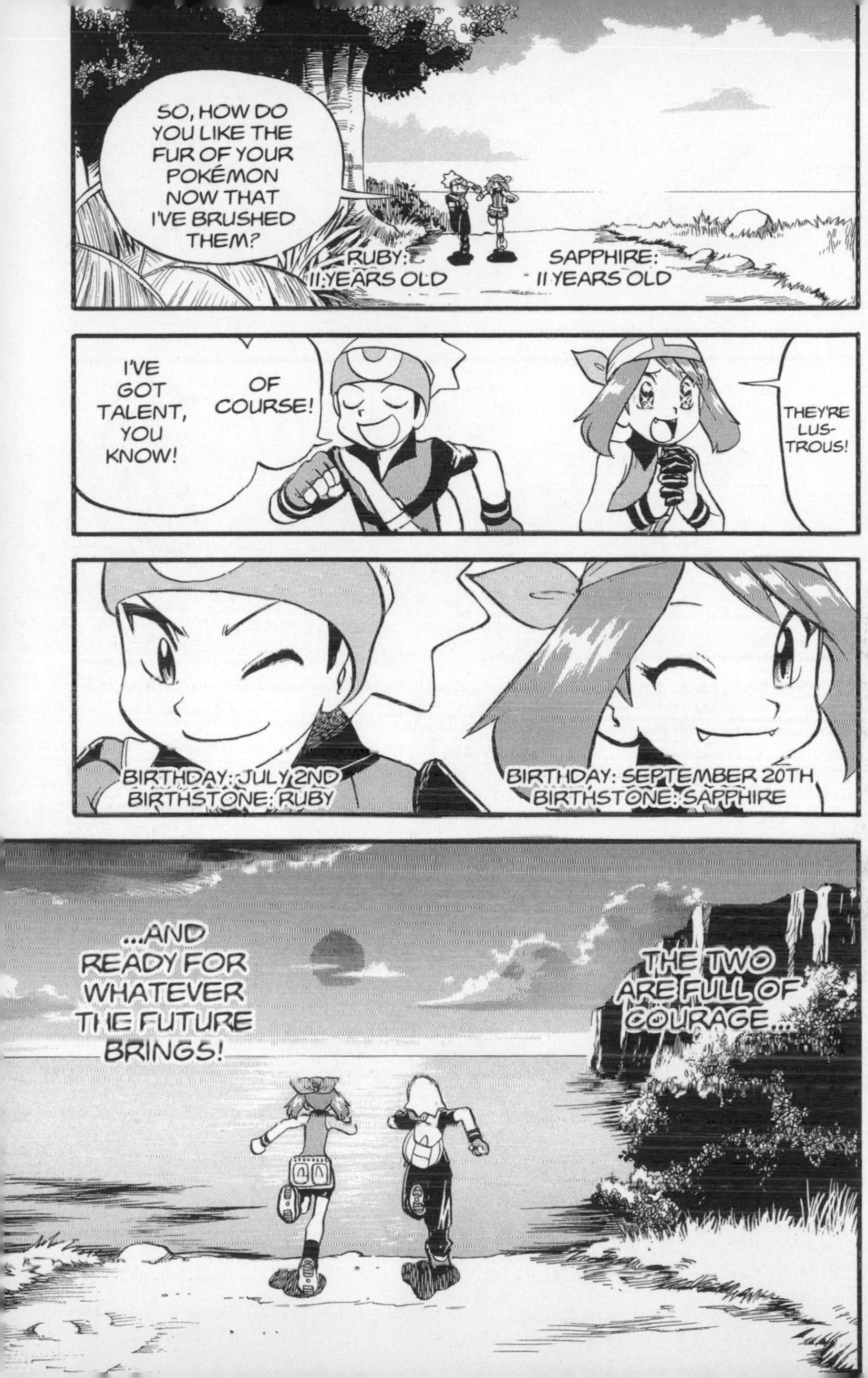
SO, HOW DO YOU LIKE THE FUR OF YOUR POKÉMON NOW THAT I'VE BRUSHED THEM?
SAPPHIRE: 11 YEARS OLD
RUBY: 11 YEARS OLD
THEY'RE LUS-TROUS!
OF COURSE!
I'VE GOT TALENT, YOU KNOW!
BIRTHDAY: SEPTEMBER 20TH BIRTHSTONE: SAPPHIRE
BIRTHDAY: JULY 2ND BIRTHSTONE: RUBY
THE TWO ARE FULL OF COURAGE...
...AND READY FOR WHATEVER THE FUTURE BRINGS!

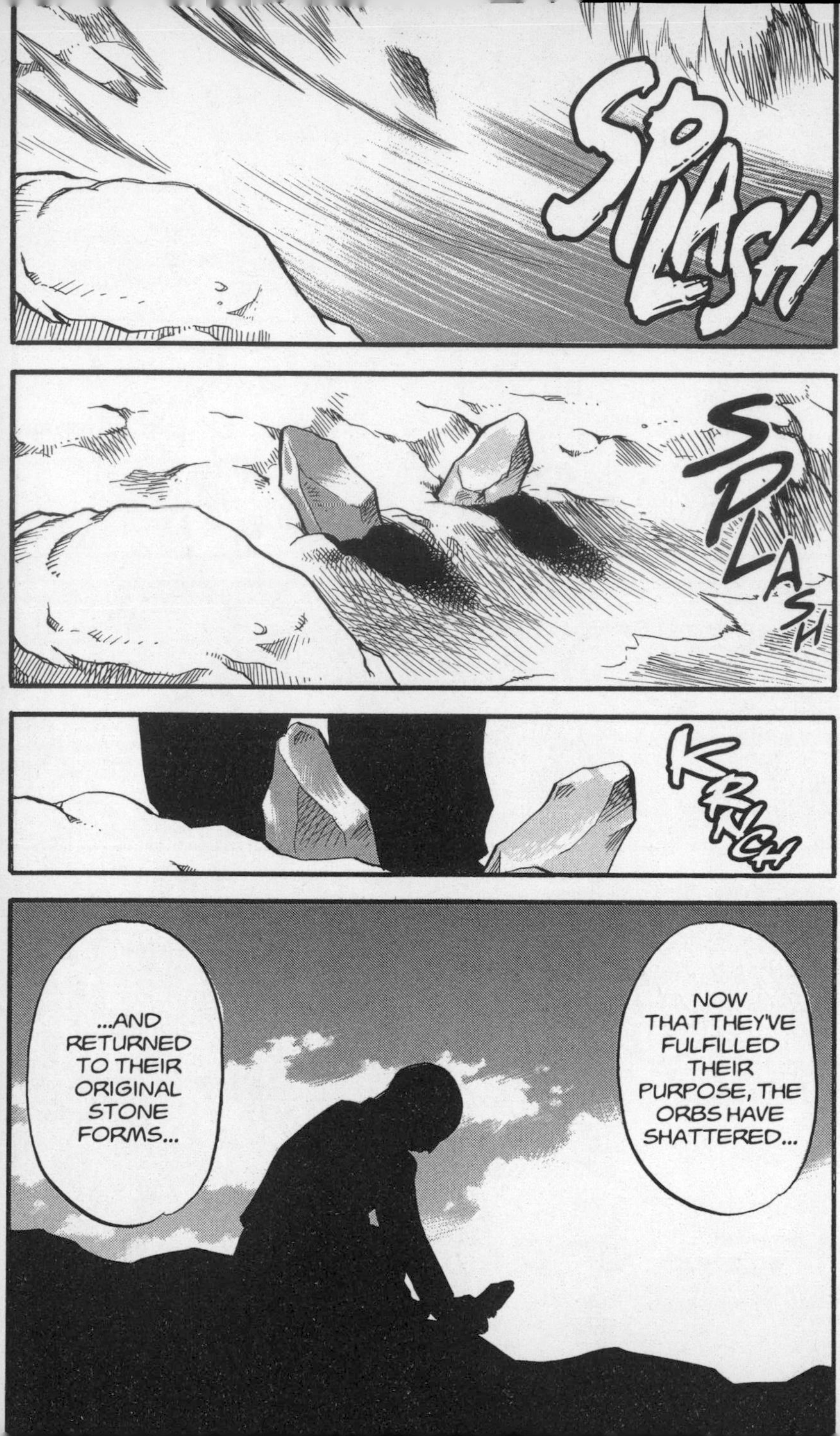
SPLASH
SPLASH
KRRCH
NOW THAT THEY'VE FULFILLED THEIR PURPOSE, THE ORBS HAVE SHATTERED...
...AND RETURNED TO THEIR ORIGINAL STONE FORMS...

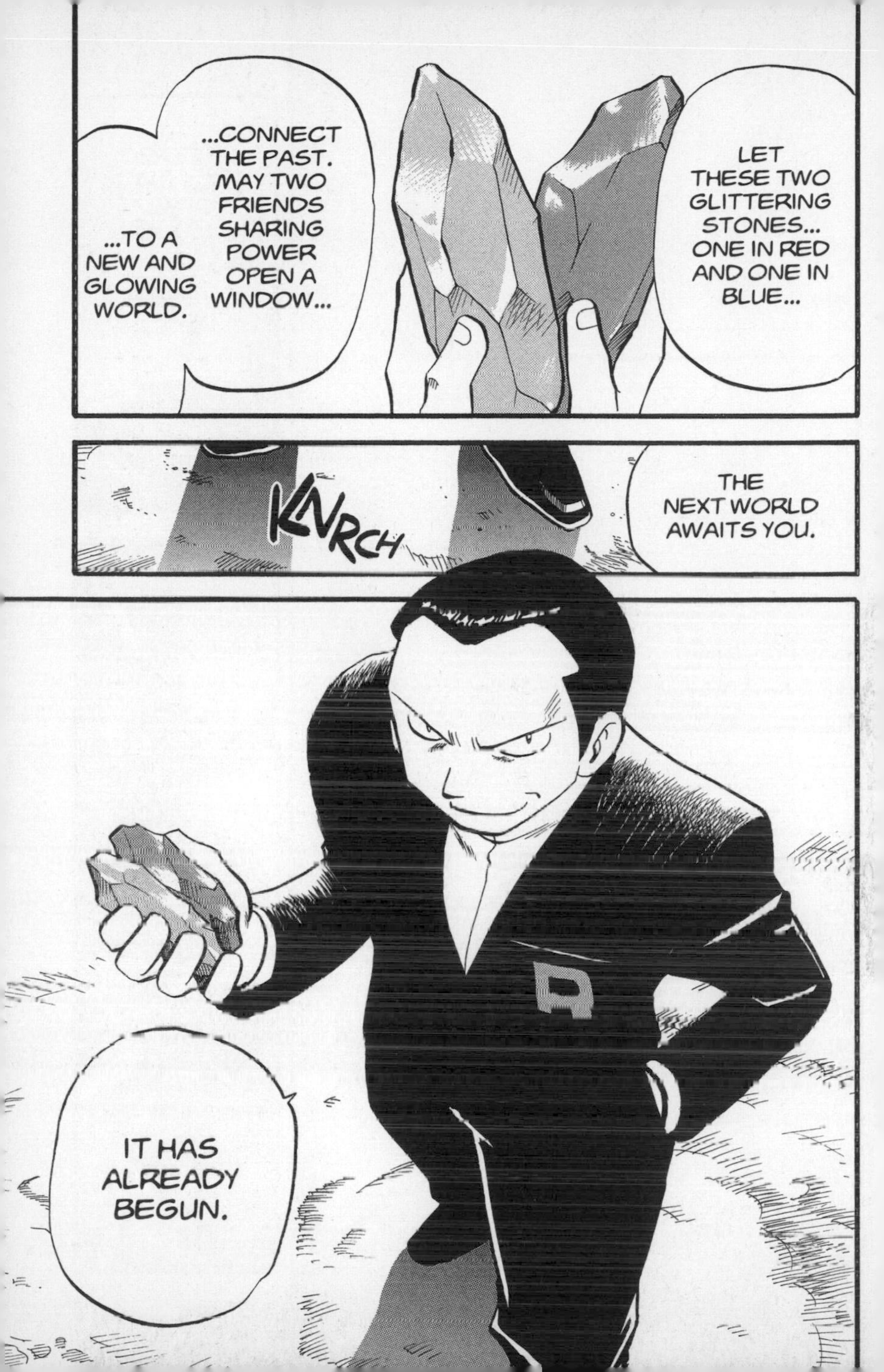
LET THESE TWO GLITTERING STONES... ONE IN RED AND ONE IN BLUE...
...CONNECT THE PAST. MAY TWO FRIENDS SHARING POWER OPEN A WINDOW...
...TO A NEW AND GLOWING WORLD.
THE NEXT WORLD AWAITS YOU.
KNRCH
IT HAS ALREADY BEGUN.

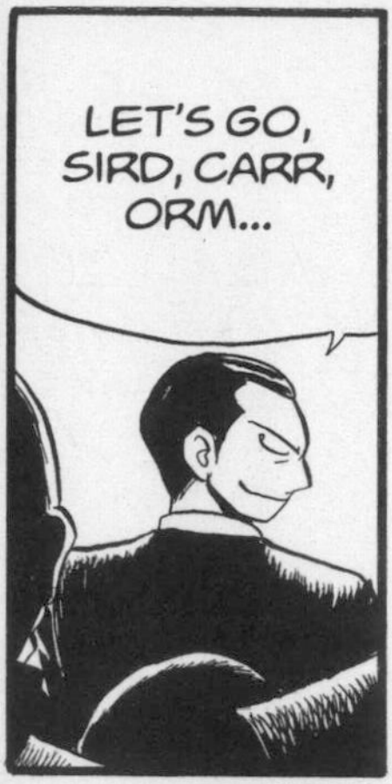
LET'S GO, SIRD, CARR, ORM...
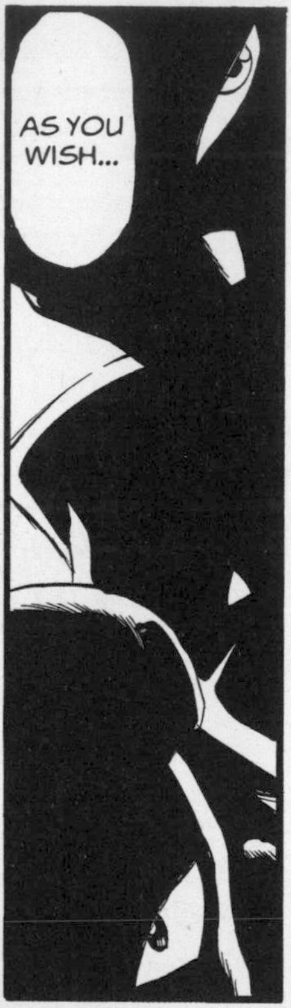
AS YOU WISH...
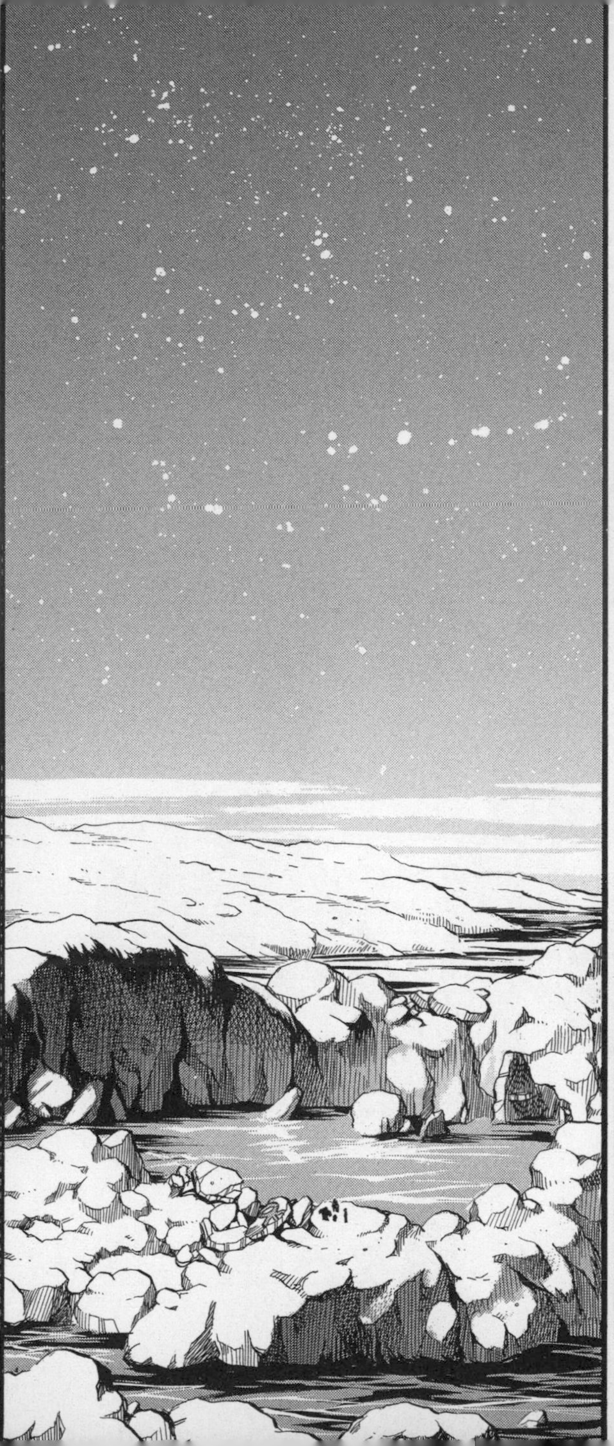

Fin *The Fourth Chapter*

Ruby & Sapphire: The Route of their 80 Day Challenge

Date	Remaining Days	Location of Ruby	Ruby's Progress	Location of Sapphire	Sapphire's Progress
JULY 2ND	80	LITTLEROOT TOWN	BIRTHDAY, RUNS AWAY FROM HOME IN ORDER TO COMPETE IN ALL THE POKÉMON CONTESTS	LITTLEROOT TOWN	MEETS RUBY AND CHALLENGES HIM TO AN 80 DAY BET
JULY 3RD	79	OLDALE TOWN	ARRIVES AT OLDALE, NAMES HIS POKÉMON	LITTLEROOT TOWN	DEPARTS IN HOPES OF VISITING ALL THE POKÉMON GYMS
JULY 4TH	78	PETALBURG CITY	MEETS WALLY, ALMOST BUMPS INTO HIS FATHER, NORMAN	TRAVELLING...	◀
JULY 5TH	77	PETALBURG CITY	CAPTURES POKÉMON WITH WALLY, FALLS INTO RIVER AND IS WASHED AWAY	PETALBURG WOODS	BATTLE AGAINST TEAM AQUA, PRESIDENT STONE ENTRUSTS HER WITH A LETTER TO STEVEN
JULY 6TH	76	ROUTE 106	UNCONSCIOUS, SAVED BY BRINEY AND BROUGHT ABOARD HIS SHIP	RUSTBORO CITY	BATTLE AGAINST ROXANNE, RECEIVES STONE BADGE
JULY 7TH	75	ROUTE 106	WAKES UP, BATTLES AGAINST CRAWDAUNT ON THE SHIP	OUT AT SEA	TRAVELLING VIA WAILORD
JULY 8TH	74	ROUTE 106	HEADS FOR DEWFORD TOWN	OUT AT SEA	◀
JULY 9TH	73	ROUTE 106	◀	OUT AT SEA	◀
JULY 10TH	72	ROUTE 106	◀	OUT AT SEA	◀
JULY 11TH	71	ROUTE 106	◀	OUT AT SEA	◀
JULY 12TH	70	DEWFORD TOWN	RUNS INTO SAPPHIRE, FIGHTS TOGETHER WITH STEVEN	DEWFORD TOWN	BATTLE AGAINST BRAWLY, RECEIVES KNUCKLE BADGE
JULY 13TH	69	ROUTE 108	TRAVELLING VIA SAPPHIRE'S WAILORD	ROUTE 108	TRAVELLING WITH RUBY VIA WAILORD
JULY 14TH	68	ABANDONED SHIP	BATTLE AGAINST TEAM MAGMA WITH PLUSLE AND MINUN	ABANDONED SHIP	BATTLE AGAINST TEAM MAGMA WITH PLUSLE AND MINUN
JULY 15TH	67	ROUTE 109	TRAVELLING VIA SAPPHIRE'S WAILORD	ROUTE 109	TRAVELLING WITH RUBY VIA WAILORD
JULY 16TH	66	ROUTE 109	◀	ROUTE 109	◀
JULY 17TH	65	ROUTE 109	◀	ROUTE 109	◀
JULY 18TH	64	ROUTE 109	◀	ROUTE 109	◀
JULY 19TH	63	ROUTE 109	◀	ROUTE 109	◀
JULY 20TH	62	ROUTE 109	◀	ROUTE 109	◀

Date	Day	Track 1 Location	Track 1 Event	Track 2 Location	Track 2 Event
JULY 21st	61	ROUTE 109		ROUTE 109	PARTS WAYS WITH RUBY, TRYING TO DELIVER THE LETTER TO STEVEN
JULY 22nd	60	SLATEPORT CITY	CAPTURED BY BLAISE, BUT ESCAPES FROM THE SUBMARINE IN AN ESCAPE POD	ROUTE 110	
JULY 23rd	59	ADRIFT		ROUTE 110	
JULY 24th	58	ADRIFT		ROUTE 110	
JULY 25th	57	ADRIFT	FISHES AND CATCHES FEEBAS.	MAUVILLE CITY	RECEIVES DYNAMO BADGE FROM WATTSON
JULY 26th	56	ROUTE 118		ROUTE 111	
JULY 27th	55	WEATHER INSTITUTE	BATTLES HIS FATHER, NORMAN. TRAVELS IN THE TV STATION'S VAN AFTER FIGHTING WITH NORMAN ALL NIGHT	ROUTE 111	HEADS TO MT. CHIMNEY
JULY 28th	54	TRAVELLING.		MT. CHIMNEY	
JULY 29th	53	TRAVELLING.		MT. CHIMNEY	
JULY 30th	52	TRAVELLING.		MT. CHIMNEY	
JULY 31st	51	TRAVELLING.		MT. CHIMNEY	
AUGUST 1st	50	TRAVELLING.		MT. CHIMNEY	
AUGUST 2nd	49	TRAVELLING.		MT. CHIMNEY	FIGHTS A FIERCE BATTLE AGAINST TEAM AQUA. RECEIVES HEAT BADGE FROM FLANNERY
AUGUST 3rd	48	TRAVELLING.		TRAVELLING.	HEADING FOR FORTREE CITY FROM JAGGED PASS
AUGUST 4th	47	TRAVELLING.		TRAVELLING.	
AUGUST 5th	46	TRAVELLING.		TRAVELLING.	
AUGUST 6th	45	TRAVELLING.		TRAVELLING.	
AUGUST 7th	44	TRAVELLING.		TRAVELLING.	
AUGUST 8th	43	TRAVELLING.		TRAVELLING.	
AUGUST 9th	42	TRAVELLING.		TRAVELLING.	
AUGUST 10th	41	TRAVELLING.		TRAVELLING.	

Ruby & Sapphire: The Route of their 80 Day Challenge

Date	Remaining Days	Location of Ruby	Ruby's Progress	Location of Sapphire	Sapphire's Progress
AUGUST 11th	40	TRAVELLING.	▲	TRAVELLING.	▲
AUGUST 12th	39	VERDANTURF TOWN	ARRIVES AT VERDANTURF TOWN.	TRAVELLING.	▲
AUGUST 13th	38	VERDANTURF TOWN	ENTERS THE NORMAL RANK POKÉMON CONTEST. FIGHTS COURTNEY AND ESCAPES.	TRAVELLING.	▲
AUGUST 14th	37	TRAVELLING.	HEADS FOR FALLARBOR TOWN VIA THE TV STATION'S VAN.	TRAVELLING.	▲
AUGUST 15th	36	TRAVELLING.	▲	TRAVELLING.	▲
AUGUST 16th	35	TRAVELLING.	▲	TRAVELLING.	▲
AUGUST 17th	34	TRAVELLING.	▲	TRAVELLING.	▲
AUGUST 18th	33	TRAVELLING.	▲	TRAVELLING.	▲
AUGUST 19th	32	TRAVELLING.	▲	TRAVELLING.	▲
AUGUST 20th	31	FALLARBOR TOWN	ENTERS THE SUPER RANK POKÉMON CONTEST. BECOMES WALLACE'S PUPIL.	TRAVELLING.	▲
AUGUST 21st	30	FORTREE CITY	REJECTS SAPPHIRE'S OFFER TO FIGHT TOGETHER WITH THE GYM LEADERS.	FORTREE CITY	MEETS THE GYM LEADERS AND ANGERS THEM.
AUGUST 22nd	29	FORTREE CITY	RUNS AWAY TO SLATEPORT CITY.	FORTREE CITY	GYM BATTLE AGAINST WINONA. RECEIVES THE FEATHER BADGE.
AUGUST 23rd	28	SLATEPORT CITY	ENTERS THE HYPER RANK POKÉMON CONTEST. LOSES FEEFEE.	FORTREE CITY	ENCOUNTERS KYOGRE AND GROUDON.
AUGUST 24th	27	SEAFLOOR CAVERN	DECIDES TO COOPERATE WITH SAPPHIRE AND THE OTHERS.	SEAFLOOR CAVERN	HEADS DOWN TO THE SEAFLOOR CAVERN WITH RUBY.
AUGUST 25th	26	SEAFLOOR CAVERN	BATTLES AGAINST MAXIE AND ARCHIE. KYOGRE AND GROUDON DRAG THEM TO SOOTOPOLIS CITY.	SEAFLOOR CAVERN	BATTLES AGAINST MAXIE AND ARCHIE. KYOGRE AND GROUDON DRAG THEM TO SOOTOPOLIS CITY.
AUGUST 26th	25	SOOTOPOLIS CITY	ATTACKS USING A PIECE OF THE METEORITE. DRAGGED INTO THE EXPLOSION.	SOOTOPOLIS CITY	ATTACKS USING A PIECE OF THE METEORITE. DRAGGED INTO THE EXPLOSION.
AUGUST 27th	24	MIRAGE ISLAND	UNCONSCIOUS. (THE FLOW OF TIME ON MIRAGE ISLAND IS UNSTABLE AND IS DIFFERENT FROM THE OUTSIDE WORLD.)	MIRAGE ISLAND	UNCONSCIOUS. (THE FLOW OF TIME ON MIRAGE ISLAND IS UNSTABLE AND IS DIFFERENT FROM THE OUTSIDE WORLD.)
AUGUST 28th	23	MIRAGE ISLAND	◁	MIRAGE ISLAND	◁
AUGUST 29th	22	MIRAGE ISLAND	◁	MIRAGE ISLAND	◁
AUGUST 30th	21	MIRAGE ISLAND	◁	MIRAGE ISLAND	◁

Date	Day	Location (Ruby)	Event (Ruby)	Location (Sapphire)	Event (Sapphire)
AUGUST 31ST	20	MIRAGE ISLAND	◁	MIRAGE ISLAND	◁
SEPTEMBER 1ST	19	MIRAGE ISLAND	◁	MIRAGE ISLAND	◁
SEPTEMBER 2ND	18	MIRAGE ISLAND	◁	MIRAGE ISLAND	◁
SEPTEMBER 3RD	17	MIRAGE ISLAND	◁	MIRAGE ISLAND	◁
SEPTEMBER 4TH	16	MIRAGE ISLAND	◁	MIRAGE ISLAND	◁
SEPTEMBER 5TH	15	MIRAGE ISLAND	◁	MIRAGE ISLAND	◁
SEPTEMBER 6TH	14	MIRAGE ISLAND	◁	MIRAGE ISLAND	◁
SEPTEMBER 7TH	13	MIRAGE ISLAND	◁	MIRAGE ISLAND	◁
SEPTEMBER 8TH	12	MIRAGE ISLAND	◁	MIRAGE ISLAND	◁
SEPTEMBER 9TH	11	MIRAGE ISLAND	◁	MIRAGE ISLAND	◁
SEPTEMBER 10TH	10	MIRAGE ISLAND	◁	MIRAGE ISLAND	◁
SEPTEMBER 11TH	9	MIRAGE ISLAND	◁	MIRAGE ISLAND	◁
SEPTEMBER 12TH	8	MIRAGE ISLAND	◁	MIRAGE ISLAND	◁
SEPTEMBER 13TH	7	MIRAGE ISLAND	◁	MIRAGE ISLAND	◁
SEPTEMBER 14TH	6	MIRAGE ISLAND	◁	MIRAGE ISLAND	◁
SEPTEMBER 15TH	5	MIRAGE ISLAND	◁	MIRAGE ISLAND	RECEIVES THE RAIN BADGE AND THE MIND BADGE AFTER TRAINING ◁
SEPTEMBER 16TH	4	MIRAGE ISLAND	AWAKENS, TRAINS WITH JUAN, TATE AND LIZA	MIRAGE ISLAND	◁
SEPTEMBER 17TH	3	SOOTOPOLIS CITY	FINAL BATTLE	SOOTOPOLIS CITY	CHASES AFTER RUBY VIA WALLACE'S AIR CAR
SEPTEMBER 18TH	2	SOOTOPOLIS CITY		SOOTOPOLIS CITY	FINAL BATTLE
SEPTEMBER 19TH	1	BA-GOON	ONLY ONE MORE CONTEST HALL LEFT TO COMPLETE (MASTER RANK)	BA-GOON	ONLY ONE MORE GYM BADGE LEFT TO COMPLETE (BALANCE BADGE)
SEPTEMBER 20TH	0	THE MEETING PLACE	WON ALL THE CONTEST RIBBONS	THE MEETING PLACE	BIRTHDAY, WON ALL THE GYM BADGES

The Fourth Chapter 4

Volume 15

Adventure 181: Creeping Past Cacnea
Adventure 182: Making Mirth with Mightyena
Adventure 183: Trying to Trounce Torchic
Adventure 184: Distracting Dustox
Adventure 185: Nixing Nuzleaf
Adventure 186: Brushing Past Breloom
Adventure 187: Tongue-Tied Kecleon
Adventure 188: Lombre Larceny
Adventure 189: Mowing Down Ludicolo
Adventure 190: Blowing Past Nosepass I

From Dewford Town to Slateport City

Continued into Volume 16...

Volume 16

Adventure 191: Blowing Past Nosepass II
Adventure 192: Stick This in Your Craw, Crawdaunt! I
Adventure 193: Stick This in Your Craw, Crawdaunt! II
Adventure 194: Guile from Mawile
Adventure 195: Mashing Makuhita
Adventure 196: Ring Ring Goes Beldum
Adventure 197: Heavy Hitting Hariyama
Adventure 198: Adding It Up with Plusle & Minun I
Adventure 199: Adding It Up with Plusle & Minun II
Adventure 200: Tripped Up by Torkoal
Adventure 201: Slugging it Out with Slugma

Battle Between Father and Son

Continued into Volume 17...

Volume 17

Adventure 202: Slugging It Out with Slugma II
Adventure 203: I'm Your Biggest Fan, Donphan
Adventure 204: Plugging Past Electrike I
Adventure 205: Plugging Past Electrike II
Adventure 206: Not So Fetching Feebas
Adventure 207: On the Loose and Hyper with Zangoose and Seviper I
Adventure 208: On the Loose and Hyper with Zangoose and Seviper II
Adventure 209: Hanging Around with Slaking I
Adventure 210: Hanging Around with Slaking II
Adventure 211: Hanging Around with Slaking III
Adventure 212: Bubble Bubble Toil and Azumarill I
Adventure 213: Bubble Bubble Toil and Azumarill II
Adventure 214: Assaulted by Pelipper I

Trainers Assemble

Continued into Volume 18...

Volume 18

Adventure 215: Assaulted by Pelipper II
Adventure 216: Mixing It Up with Magcargo
Adventure 217: Mind-Boggling with Medicham
Adventure 218: It's Absol-lutely a Bad Omen
Adventure 219: What Would You Do for a Whismur?
Adventure 220: Going to Eleven with Loudred and Exploud I
Adventure 221: Going to Eleven with Loudred and Exploud II
Adventure 222: Short Shrift for Shiftry
Adventure 223: I More Than Like You, Luvdisc I
Adventure 224: I More Than Like You, Luvdisc II
Adventure 225: Tanks, but No Tanks, Anorith and Lileep
Adventure 226: I Dare Ya, Altaria... Knock Chic off My Shoulder

Battle Against Evil

Continued into Volume 19...

The Fourth Chapter

Sub Titles List

Volume 19

Adventure 227: I'm Always Grumpig First Thing in the Morning I
Adventure 228: I'm Always Grumpig First Thing in the Morning II
Adventure 229: You Can Fight Day or Night with Lunatone & Solrock
Adventure 230: Walrein and Camerupt
Adventure 231:Master Class with Masquerain
Adventure 232: Always Keep Whiscash on You for Emergencies
Adventure 233: The Beginning of the End with Kyogre & Groudon I
Adventure 234: The Beginning of the End with Kyogre & Groudon II
Adventure 235: The Beginning of the End with Kyogre & Groudon III
Adventure 236: The Beginning of the End with Kyogre & Groudon IV
Adventure 237: The Beginning of the End with Kyogre & Groudon V
Adventure 238: The Beginning of the End with Kyogre & Groudon VI

Departing for the Third Time

Continued into Volume 20...

Volume 20

Adventure 239: The Beginning of the End with Kyogre & Groudon VI
Adventure 240: Talk About Timing, Treecko
Adventure 241: Dreadful Dealing with Dusclops
Adventure 242: Very Vexing Volbeat
Adventure 243: No Armaldo Is an Island
Adventure 244: The Beginning of the End with Kyogre & Groudon VI
Adventure 245: Bravo, Vibrava
Adventure 246: Can I Ninjask You a Question?
Adventure 247: The Beginning of the End with Kyogre & Groudon I
Adventure 248: The Beginning of the End with Kyogre & Groudon X
Adventure 249: The Beginning of the End with Kyogre & Groudon X

The Confession of One's Feelings

Continued into Volume 21...

Volume 21

Adventure 250: The Beginning of the End with Kyogre & Groudon XII
Adventure 251: The Beginning of the End with Kyogre & Groudon XIII
Adventure 252: The Beginning of the End with Kyogre & Groudon XIV
Adventure 253: A Royal Rumble with Regirock, Regice and Registeel I
Adventure 254: A Royal Rumble with Regirock, Regice and Registeel II
Adventure 255: With a Spoink in Your Step I
Adventure 256: With a Spoink in Your Step II
Adventure 257: The Beginning of the End with Kyogre & Groudon XV
Adventure 258: Rayquaza Redemption I
Adventure 259: Rayquaza Redemption II

The Land, the Sea, and the Sky

Continued into Volume 22...

Volume 22

Adventure 260: It All Ends Now I
Adventure 261: It All Ends Now II
Adventure 262: It All Ends Now III
Adventure 263: It All Ends Now IV
Adventure 264: It All Ends Now V
Adventure 265: It All Ends Now VI
Adventure 266: It All Ends Now VII
Adventure 267: It All Ends Now VIII

Message from
Hidenori Kusaka

I am very happy to hear that the Ruby/Sapphire story arc is being translated and published in English-speaking countries. I just read over the volumes again with the fresh perspective that the passage of time provides. The Hoenn region is a very appealing place, isn't it? The secret bases, fields of berries, dramatic weather conditions...they all bring back great memories, even after ten years. The fourth *Pokémon Adventures* story arc ends here, but the Hoenn Region will reappear in other major stories in the future. I hope those stories reach you as well!

Message from
Satoshi Yamamoto

"They've finally come back!" That is the single phrase to explain this volume, I think! In this volume you see the "return" of many people. When you talk about "return," you imagine the end of a journey or adventure, but there are "stories that unfold with the return of that person"! I hereby bring to you...the conclusion of the Ruby/Sapphire Arc!

More Adventures Coming Soon...

The Fifth Chapter of Pokémon Adventures, FireRed and LeafGreen begins!

Just as Green is about to meet her long lost parents, they are sucked into a vortex created by a mysterious Pokémon! Red and Blue want to help, but first they must improve their battle skills. Then, the Three Beasts of Team Rocket are up to their old tricks again!

Which former enemy will unexpectedly come to our friends' aid...?

AVAILABLE JULY 2014!

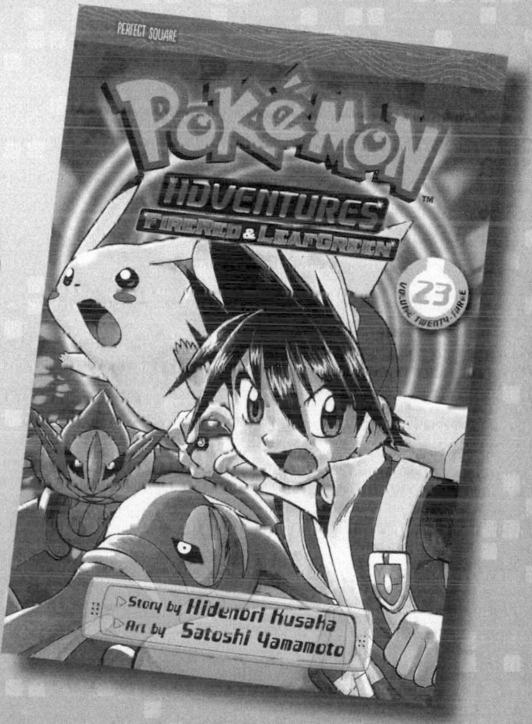
PERFECT SQUARE
POKÉMON
ADVENTURES
FIRERED & LEAFGREEN
23
Story by Hidenori Kusaka
Art by Satoshi Yamamoto

Pokémon
BLACK AND WHITE

MEET POKÉMON TRAINERS
BLACK AND WHITE

THE WAIT IS FINALLY OVER! Meet Pokémon Trainer Black! His entire life, Black has dreamed of winning the Pokémon League... Now Black embarks on a journey to explore the Unova region and fill a Pokédex for Professor Juniper. Time for Black's first Pokémon Trainer Battle ever!

Who will Black choose as his next Pokémon? Who would *you* choose?

Plus, meet Pokémon Snivy, Tepig, Oshawott and many more new Pokémon of the unexplored Unova region!

Story by HIDENORI KUSAKA

Art by SATOSHI YAMAMOTO

Inspired by the hit video games
Pokémon Black Version and *Pokémon White Version!*

$4.99 USA | $6.99 CAN

Available Now
at your local bookstore or comic store

vizkids

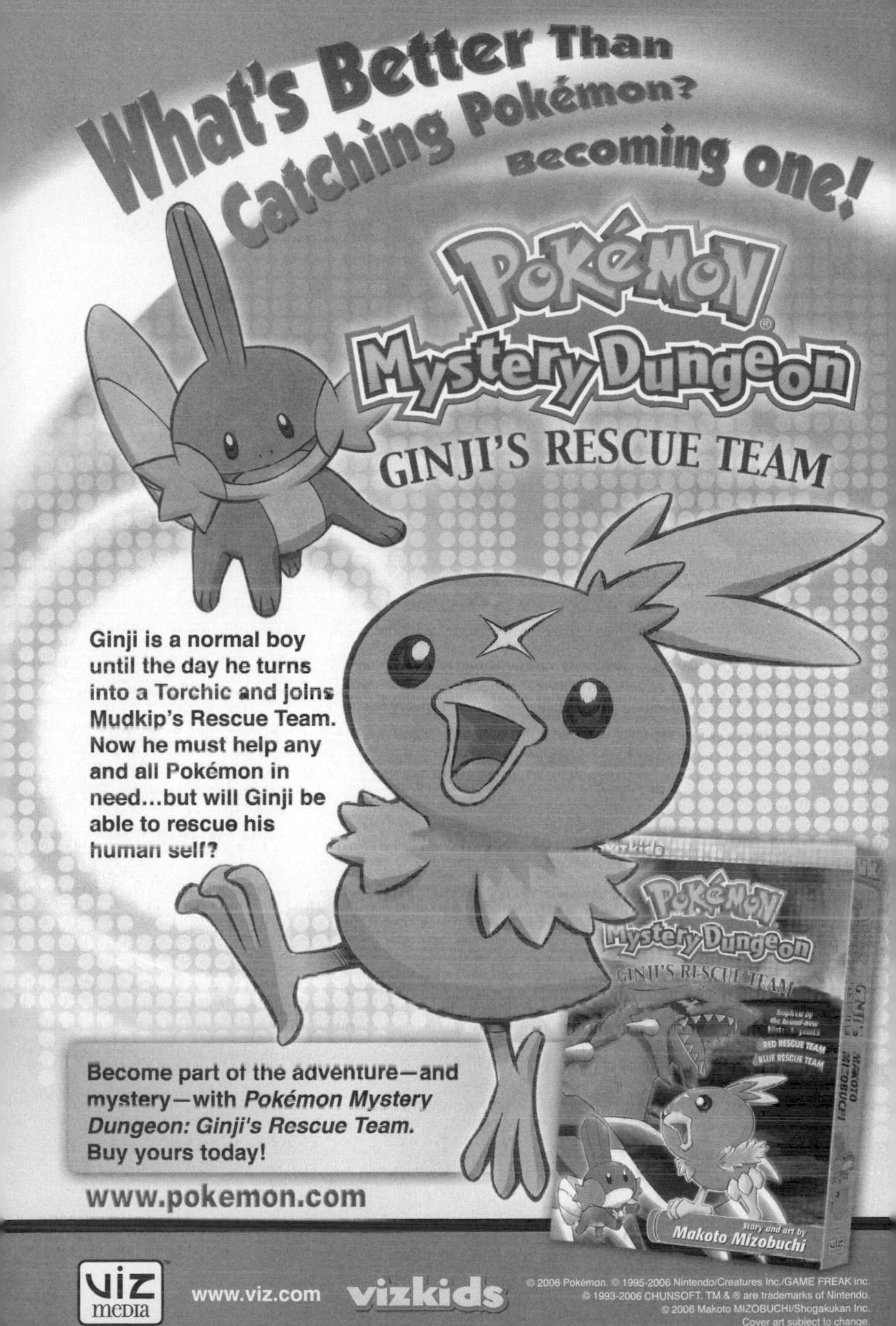
What's Better Than Catching Pokémon?
Becoming one!
POKÉMON Mystery Dungeon
GINJI'S RESCUE TEAM
Ginji is a normal boy until the day he turns into a Torchic and joins Mudkip's Rescue Team. Now he must help any and all Pokémon in need...but will Ginji be able to rescue his human self?
Become part of the adventure—and mystery—with Pokémon Mystery Dungeon: Ginji's Rescue Team. Buy yours today!
www.pokemon.com
POKÉMON Mystery Dungeon
GINJI'S RESCUE TEAM
RED RESCUE TEAM
BLUE RESCUE TEAM
Story and art by
Makoto Mizobuchi
viz media
www.viz.com
vizkids
© 2006 Pokémon. © 1995-2006 Nintendo/Creatures Inc./GAME FREAK inc.
© 1993-2006 CHUNSOFT. TM & ® are trademarks of Nintendo.
© 2006 Makoto MIZOBUCHI/Shogakukan Inc.
Cover art subject to change.

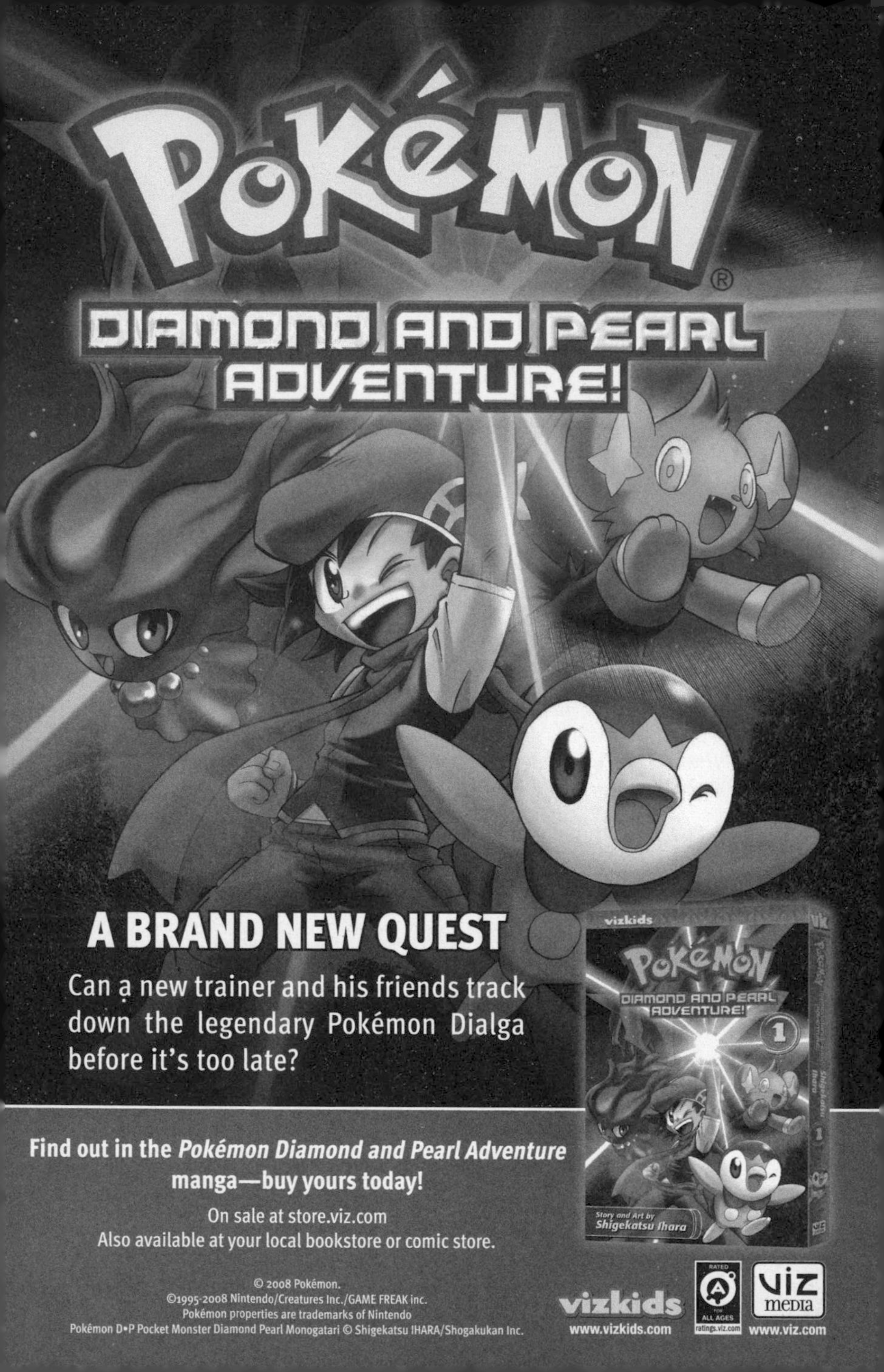

POKÉMON®
DIAMOND AND PEARL ADVENTURE!
A BRAND NEW QUEST
Can a new trainer and his friends track down the legendary Pokémon Dialga before it's too late?
vizkids
POKÉMON
DIAMOND AND PEARL ADVENTURE!
1
Story and Art by Shigekatsu Ihara
Find out in the *Pokémon Diamond and Pearl Adventure* manga—buy yours today!
On sale at store.viz.com
Also available at your local bookstore or comic store.
© 2008 Pokémon.
©1995-2008 Nintendo/Creatures Inc./GAME FREAK inc.
Pokémon properties are trademarks of Nintendo
Pokémon D•P Pocket Monster Diamond Pearl Monogatari © Shigekatsu IHARA/Shogakukan Inc.
vizkids
www.vizkids.com
RATED A FOR ALL AGES
ratings.viz.com
VIZ MEDIA
www.viz.com

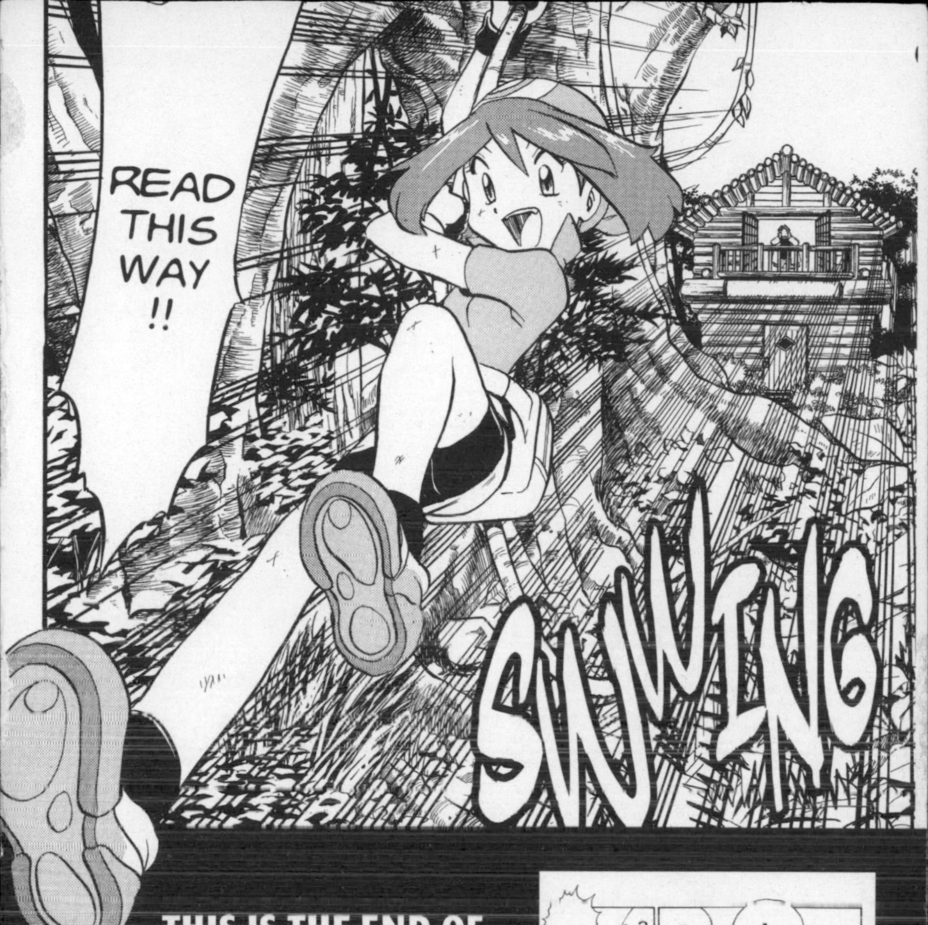
READ THIS WAY !!
SWWING

THIS IS THE END OF THIS GRAPHIC NOVEL!

To properly enjoy this VIZ Media graphic novel, please turn it around and begin reading from right to left.

This book has been printed in the original Japanese format in order to preserve the orientation of the original artwork.

Have fun with it!

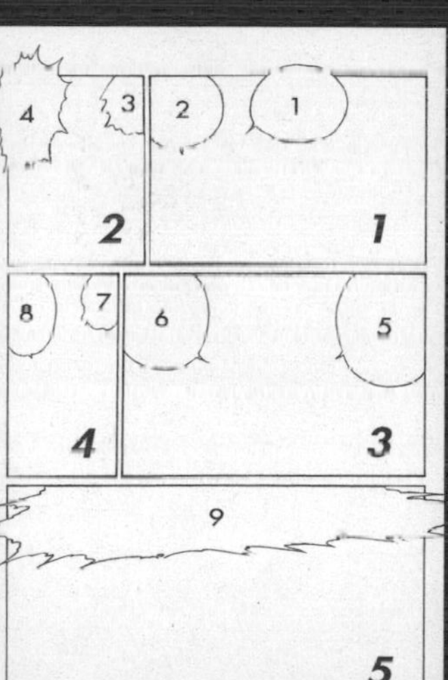
FOLLOW THE ACTION THIS WAY.

FUNKY FASHIONISTAS

Meet best friends Choco and Mimi. They get along great, and they're both super-cute and ultra-stylish. But is their friendship ready for the insanity that is eighth grade?

Find out in the ChocoMimi manga—buy yours today!